PRAISE FOR [illegible] NOVELS

"Fast paced and thr[illegible] ine. Sirantha Jax is an unforg[illegible] it to find out what happens to her next. The world Ann Aguirre has created is a roller-coaster ride to remember."

—Christine Feehan, #1 *New York Times* bestselling author of *Dark Slayer*

"The details of communication, travel, politics, and power in a greedy, lively universe have been devised to the last degree but are presented effortlessly. Aguirre has the mastery and vision which come from critical expertise: She is unmistakably a true science fiction fan, writing in the genre she loves." —*The Independent* (London)

"Once in a while you come across certain characters that just remain with you long after you've finished a book. For me, I found those characters in the cast of *Grimspace* and *Wanderlust*." —*Dear Author*

"Emotions run high in *Wanderlust*, and the many twists and turns will leave readers hungry for more." —*Darque Reviews*

"Vivid world-building accented with gut-wrenching action ensures that following Sirantha Jax through her first-person adventures will leave you breathless." —*Romantic Times*

continued . . .

GRIMSPACE

"A terrific first novel full of page-turning action, delightful characters, and a wry twist of humor. Romance may be in the air. Bullets, ugly beasties, and really nasty bad guys definitely are." —Mike Shepherd, national bestselling author of the Kris Longknife series

"An irresistible blend of action and attitude. Sirantha Jax doesn't just leap off the page—she storms out, kicking, cursing, and mouthing off. No wonder her pilot falls in love with her; readers will, too."

—Sharon Shinn, national bestselling author of *Quatrain*

"A tightly written, edge-of-your-seat read."

—Linnea Sinclair, RITA Award–winning author of *Hope's Folly*

"An unflinching tale of survival, redemption, and serious ass kicking. Jax's brutal eloquence will twist your heart when you least expect it."

—Jeri Smith-Ready, award-winning author of *Bad to the Bone*

"An exciting, evocative, and suspenseful science fiction romance, reminding me of *Firefly* and *Serenity*. Characters and a world you'll think about long after the book is done. Fascinating!"

—Robin D. Owens, RITA Award–winning author of *Heart Fate*

Also by Ann Aguirre

Sirantha Jax Series

GRIMSPACE
WANDERLUST
DOUBLEBLIND

Corine Solomon Series

BLUE DIABLO

DOUBLEBLIND

ANN AGUIRRE

THE BERKLEY PUBLISHING GROUP
Published by the Penguin Group
Penguin Group (USA) Inc.
375 Hudson Street, New York, New York 10014, USA
Penguin Group (Canada), 90 Eglinton Avenue East, Suite 700, Toronto, Ontario M4P 2Y3, Canada
(a division of Pearson Penguin Canada Inc.)
Penguin Books Ltd., 80 Strand, London WC2R 0RL, England
Penguin Group Ireland, 25 St. Stephen's Green, Dublin 2, Ireland (a division of Penguin Books Ltd.)
Penguin Group (Australia), 250 Camberwell Road, Camberwell, Victoria 3124, Australia
(a division of Pearson Australia Group Pty. Ltd.)
Penguin Books India Pvt. Ltd., 11 Community Centre, Panchsheel Park, New Delhi—110 017, India
Penguin Group (NZ), 67 Apollo Drive, Rosedale, North Shore 0632, New Zealand
(a division of Pearson New Zealand Ltd.)
Penguin Books (South Africa) (Pty.) Ltd., 24 Sturdee Avenue, Rosebank, Johannesburg 2196,
South Africa

Penguin Books Ltd., Registered Offices: 80 Strand, London WC2R 0RL, England

DOUBLEBLIND

An Ace Book / published by arrangement with the author

PRINTING HISTORY
Ace mass-market edition / October 2009

Cover art by Scott M. Fischer.
Cover design by Lesley Worrell.

For information, address: The Berkley Publishing Group,
a division of Penguin Group (USA) Inc.,
375 Hudson Street, New York, New York 10014.

ISBN: 978-0-441-01781-2

ACE
Ace Books are published by The Berkley Publishing Group,
a division of Penguin Group (USA) Inc.,
375 Hudson Street, New York, New York 10014.
ACE and the "A" design are trademarks of Penguin Group (USA) Inc.

PRINTED IN THE UNITED STATES OF AMERICA

10 9 8 7 6 5 4 3 2 1

For Carrie, to whom I have only one thing to say:
Turk.

ACKNOWLEDGMENTS

I love my agent so much that I'd totally drink a margarita and sing Barry Manilow's "Mandy" to her at a karaoke bar, except her name is Laura, and that might be slightly unprofessional. So maybe not, but it's the thought that counts. Moving on!

Working with Anne Sowards is the culmination of all my lifelong dreams, and to be honest, anytime I get an e-mail from her, I still get that "OMG, the quarterback noticed *me*" feeling. She's a brilliant editor and she always rocks me with her fabulous insights. *Doubleblind* is a much better book because of her suggestions. Meanwhile, her assistant, Cam, works behind the scenes with such efficiency and expertise that I suspect she outsources to Santa's elves. Thanks, Cam! Everyone at Penguin has been beyond wonderful, so they deserve a big "woot" as well. You can't hear it, but I just wooted. The noise agitated the dog.

Next, my family deserves a special mention for never complaining if I'm distracted or if we eat rice and beans three nights a week while I'm working on a first draft. Finally, but never least important, I thank my readers. Your e-mails mean the world to me, so keep them coming. That's ann.aguirre@gmail.com.

CHAPTER 1

The ship cuts through the atmosphere, taking us down.

Below, the spaceport waits, white as bone beneath the pallid sun. From its quiet appearance and weathered exterior, I can tell this is a relic of ancient times. Though the Ithtorians once explored the stars, they do so no longer. They retreated many turns ago and cut off all trade.

It's my job to change all that.

The structure is shaped like a dome, which opens to admit us. I find that disconcerting, as if we're being ingested. Our pilot has steady hands, but he's not an artist like March. Nonetheless, we put down sooner than I'd like.

I'm not ready.

That doesn't stop me from heading to the exit ramp. My personal crew will meet me there. The rest line up and salute as we pass. They're mostly clansmen, with a few ex–freighter crew who got stuck on Lachion before the war. I don't know all their names and faces yet; I didn't spend long enough on board.

We won't be taking everyone from the *Triumph* on world. The Bugs would doubtless panic and think they were being invaded. It's significant that they let us dock here at all. Baby steps before we take a giant leap for mankind.

I find Jael, Hit, Dina, March, and Vel waiting when I arrive. Jael is my bodyguard, and he frankly looks too pretty for the job unless you stare him in the eyes. That's when you realize there's more to this merc than the surface suggests. We all have our secrets, but Jael's may be the most dangerous. I can think of a dozen different consortiums that would love to get their hands on him and see if they can replicate him.

You see, he's Bred, a surviving specimen of the Ideal Genome Project. Most of them went mad or died in utero. Damn few survived to adulthood, but Jael has managed to surmount unspeakable odds. And because Tarn—the Conglomerate official who calls the shots on this mission—pays him, he's committed to my safety.

So is Constance. Long ago, she was just a little silver sphere, owned by Mair Dahlgren. Now she's so much more than an artificially intelligent Personal Assistant, and though I wouldn't admit this to anyone else, she seems to be evolving. With each incarnation, she learns more, extrapolates more, and changes her primary function. Now that she's embedded in an ambulatory frame, she's determined to be the perfect assistant.

At length, Constance finishes her inspection of me, and says, "You look most appropriate, Sirantha Jax."

Hit smothers a grin. She's a pilot we picked up on Lachion during the last clan war, before they all swore fealty to Gunnar-Dahlgren. She's tall, slim as a knife, with dusky skin and a pouf of dark, tight curls. She has eyes that shine like a night-hunting cat, and she's so lethal she can kill somebody with just her pinky.

I'm not kidding about that.

During our last mission, I found out she has a poison hypo in her littlest finger. Hit isn't someone I want to cross. At one point, she worked for Madame Kang on Gehenna; but when her house fell, her remaining girls scattered, not wanting to die in the coup. She wound up running freight with a merchantman and had the bad luck to be stranded on Lachion when things reached critical mass. Luckily, she's taken a liking to Dina, and seems committed to our side.

Dina is our ship's mechanic and gunnery specialist. With those skills, you expect her to be tough as nails, but she's pretty, too, with her heart-shaped face and green eyes. Just by looking at her, you'd never know she's a princess in exile. She can never return to Tarnus. Her family is long gone; she's the last of the royal line.

We didn't get along at first. She blamed me for the loss of her previous lover, Edaine. It wasn't really my fault, but they didn't have too many options when they came to break me out of the prison on Perlas Station. Edaine made her last jump saving me, and that's a navigator's lot.

Unless you're like me. I've made so many jumps at this point that I'm not sure I believe burnout is inevitable for me anymore. Something always drags me back from the brink.

Or *someone*, like March.

I gaze at him for a few seconds. He doesn't respond or glance my way. Ice blazes in his eyes like bits of amber. We're all standing too close to him for our own good. As well as my pilot, he used to be my lover, and maybe he will be again. I have to hold on to that, or everything else seems meaningless.

Well, almost everything. If I lose March over what he did on Lachion, I'll still have Vel. The Ithtorian bounty hunter once tracked me across the galaxy; now I couldn't ask for a better friend. In this mission, he's our not-so-secret weapon. Unlike any delegation before us, we have an Ithtorian to guide us and prevent us from making catastrophic mistakes. If we succeed here, it will be because of Vel.

As I've been studying them, they've been checking me out. A few of them smirk at the sight of me in the ceremonial robe I swore I'd never wear. My jaw clenches.

Dina clears her throat. "We good to go?"

Tapping the exit panel, I answer, "Let's do it."

There's a Bug escort waiting for us at the bottom of the ramp. They look militant, but not hostile. Vel deals with them and confirms they're supposed to convey us to the formal reception. The wait gives me ample time to fret.

I'd say I have butterflies in my stomach, but with my luck, the Ithtorian delegate would overhear, and it would be mistranslated to mean I've eaten some sacred planetary flora. And then I'll ruin everything before it's begun.

Actually, that's not fair. Since Vel functions as my translator, he'd never make such a mistake. That thought is just a manifestation of my fear something will go wrong.

I surreptitiously swipe my palms against the sides of the stupid gold robe. So far, so good, but I'd be lying if I claimed not to be nervous as hell. Never has so much weight rested on my shoulders.

Dina, Hit, Jael, and March stand at my back, a silent honor guard. Doc stayed aboard the ship with Rose to work on some data he received from Keri on Lachion. Vel stands on one side of me, ready to interpret. On my left I have Constance, who looks almost prim in her black suit. I hope I don't make any terrible mistakes here.

The chamber where the Ithtorian council has received us defies my expectations regarding alien aesthetic sensibilities. Instead of inert furnishings or fabric on the floors, everything appears to be . . . *alive*. Chairs are dense, cultivated shrubberies with petal-soft leaves; I run my fingers along the "arm" and enjoy a purely sensual shiver.

I've never stood inside a room that felt like a living entity, but I'm conscious of a gentle pulse all around us, almost like a heartbeat. So much greenery, splashed with crimson, cream, apricot, azure. It's intoxicating.

With some effort, I pull my attention back to the Ithtorian councilman. His markings are different from Vel's, brighter and more varied. Slashes of yellow and orange cross his thorax, but I'm not sure what they mean, whether they're a natural display or an artificial one that bespeaks status. I make a mental note to ask Vel.

Though I can't yet tell by physical appearance, Sharis is male. Vel explained Ithtorian naming conventions to me, so I understand that the prefix "Il" means "son of" whereas "Ib" means "daughter of." They trace their lineage through the maternal, so whoever laid their egg provides the family name. Thus, Vel is the son of a politician named Nok.

Sharis Il-Wan is speaking now, his gestures strange and measured. I watch his mandible, but I can't read him as I do Vel. The bounty hunter who first stalked me, then saved my life more times than I can count at this point, considers for a moment before he begins the translation.

"Sharis bids you welcome to Ithiss-Tor," Vel says. "And hopes you are cognizant of the honor, for they have not permitted an outworld ship to dock in two hundred turns."

Though I've practiced for this occasion, I feel my hands trembling as I construct a proper response. "The Conglomerate *is* honored by your hospitality and looks forward to shaping a new accord between our people."

As Vel relays my words, I fret over them. *Is what I said enough? Too much?* Doubt ferments inside me like tainted wine. Fortunately, I don't have to wait long for Il-Wan's response.

"Well-spoken," Sharis says, via Vel's translation. "It would gratify me if you would consent to accompany me to the banquet hall. We have researched your preferences and are confident you will find a number of palatable dishes."

I'm not sure whether he means me specifically or humanity in general. Nevertheless, I nod. "It would be my pleasure."

Sharis leads the way along a bioengineered hallway. As best I can tell, the entire building is alive, and it's been sculpted to its current dimensions. Movement catches my eye, and I just catch a tiny creature scuttling back into the wall. I pause long enough to take stock, realizing that the structure is hollow, more like a honeycomb than any building I've ever seen.

"It's taking care of maintenance," Vel reminds me.

I remember then: He told me about them during our long cram sessions aboard the Lachion ship. The Ithtorians have developed a part-organic, part-machine intelligence that's constantly improving and renovating their surroundings behind the scenes. I'd be a little suspicious of such a convenience, waiting for the little bugs to turn on the big ones, but then I'm always looking out for a knife in the back.

Behind us, my entourage follows in neat pairs: Vel and Constance, Dina and Hit, Jael and March. My lover worries me. He's not the man I fell in love with anymore; there's darkness and a coldness in him that burns like ice pressed too long against naked skin. I can't touch him without sparking some brutal retaliation . . . it's like his nerves are wound too tight.

There's precious little gentleness left in him. All that remains is the cold, competent killer. Perhaps I should be grateful he came back to me at all. He could have walked away, taken up his old life as a merc without ever looking back. Earlier, he said he remembered loving me, but he couldn't feel it anymore.

That hurts in ways I can't allow myself to think about. Once I get past this initial contact, I'll let myself consider the problem. Try to find a solution. But I can't fret about personal matters right now. I was serious when I said I meant to give this ambassador thing my all, no matter how much the Syndicate—and my mother—want me to fail.

I still have a hard time crediting the truth. My mother runs the Syndicate, the single largest organized-crime collective in the galaxy: bookmaking and gambling, loansharking, prostitution, chem, weapons, murder for hire, extortion, protection rackets, smuggling of goods and slaves—nothing is too dirty for her, as long as it promises to make a buck. Worse, she's not above fomenting an interstellar conflict to improve her bottom line.

Vel and Constance give me courage with their proximity. The Ithtorian councilman looks neither left nor right as we pass through a series of latticed archways, then into a wide, almost cavernous chamber filled with Bugs. It's insulting; I shouldn't think of them that way, but I can't help it. As long as I don't speak the designation out loud, we should be golden.

At first, they all look alike to me, but as Sharis speaks and Vel listens, preparing to translate, I notice differences in eye placement and width of mandible. Some have colors on the tips of their claws, and others wear stripes on their thoraxes. Constance leans forward and begins imparting information about their social status, based on the placement and hue of their markings.

With Constance's help, I locate the female Ithtorian who's in charge of . . . well, pretty much everything. She's tall and lean, even for an Ithtorian, and her claws are tipped with red. She also wears six xanthric stripes in a diagonal across her thorax. There's nobody else on planet with those stripes; they're akin to a general's bars, except the Ithtorian's uniform has been permanently integrated into her chitin.

Vel tells me her title translates best as Grand Administrator, but I get the feeling that designation doesn't encompass the nuances of her real power. She's surrounded by an entourage of lower-ranking Ithtorians; they ring her in a half circle, either for protection or sycophantic purposes. Possibly some enterprising males combine the two. In human terms, she's along the lines of a chancellor, but she couldn't veto the council's decision after they voted to hear us out. That has to rankle.

From across the room, Grand Administrator Otlili Ib-Ekei returns my regard. I wouldn't call her look warm either. By the cant of her mandible, she belongs to—or sympathizes with—the opposition party. Vel warned me about our enemies on the ship. The Opposition Party—OP—would like nothing more than to enslave the whole delegation and send us to work in a barbaric prison facility reserved for violent criminals and the incurably insane. Based on past interactions, Ithtorians reckon humanity as both the former and the latter.

Well, it doesn't matter what they think. If I fail here, the Morgut will grow in strength and audacity. A shiver rolls through me, remembering the carnage on Emry Station. That little girl spent countless hours, entombed in their webs. If the eggs had hatched, they would have sucked all the nutrients from her living body and left her a withered husk. The worst part? Mature Morgut are worse.

A touch on my shoulder draws my gaze, pulling me out of reverie. "Vel is ready to begin," Constance tells me.

The bounty hunter confirms with an abbreviated nod, another human gesture that sits oddly on him in his natural form. "Sharis bids you welcome to the feast convened in your honor. The most important members of the Ithtorian government have been invited to share this auspicious occasion, which marks a new chapter in Ithtorian-human diplomacy. We are confident you will be pleased with both the menu and entertainment, as our human preferences committee has devoted many hours to the planning."

Boiled down? *Hi, welcome to our world. Enjoy the food and the show.*

When they wheel out a table that has to be six meters long if it's a centimeter, full of strange, scary dishes—the contents of several appear to be writhing—I decide that might be easier said than done.

CHAPTER 2

There are no plates. There's also nowhere to sit down.

That doesn't surprise me, however. I've been fully briefed on Ithtorian culture and customs. It's good manners to reach into the communal dish and pluck out a single morsel without touching the other food, then eat. Ithtorian claws aid greatly in the neat execution of this maneuver.

"It reduces waste," Vel tells me quietly. "People eat only what they take, no extra servings ladled into bowls and discarded." He sounds vaguely disapproving of the idea that someone's eyes would be bigger than his stomach.

I acknowledge that with a nod and select the least offensive-looking entrée. Trying to seem deft, I snag something in sauce that resembles seafood. The flavor is sweet and peppery; the morsel dissolves on my tongue. Sharis moves his mandible in what I take to be approval. I can't understand the subsequent clicks and chitters until Vel interprets, but I receive the impression I'm doing well.

"That is candied kir," Vel says after a moment. "You show high discernment in trying raw . . ." He pauses, as if his vocalizer doesn't know what word to substitute. "Flesh," he finishes.

Raw . . . flesh? I better not think about that too long. My stomach gives a lurch, but I manage a smile. "It was delicious."

It was, too. I'm sure kir is some type of animal. I hope. My palms start to sweat as I realize I'm expected to eat as long as everyone else does. First impressions can be crucial, so I better not offend anyone.

If nothing else, I look the part. Vel has me garbed in a golden robe, half a step down from the royal yellow stripes on the Grand Administrator's thorax. The garment proclaims my importance in my delegation. That's why everyone else is wearing black, although with March it's more of a mood than fashion.

Vel guides me discreetly, indicating which dishes I should try and which I should leave for the Ithtorians. The bounty hunter is good at his job, facilitating my communication with Sharis so smoothly that I eventually stop noticing his translations. When we've finished eating, low-ranking workers bring us damp cloths for our fingertips. I wipe my hands clean with all due ceremony and return the cloth to the server.

Then it's time to mingle.

The Ithtorian representative leads me to the rest of the council members, including the Grand Administrator. Even I can tell how much power she wields, how the rest of her council holds her in awe. It's apparent in their stance and posture, the way they stand a respectful meter from her, revering her as the nucleus of their group. Other Ithtorians who hold a high enough rank have been invited to attend the feast, but they don't merit my attention, apparently. At least not right now.

There are six members on the council, of which Otlili Ib-Ekei is the titular head. As I understand it, she doesn't actually vote, however. She shapes the creation of policy and administers other aspects of the government on her own. For instance, the judiciary and prison systems fall entirely within her sphere of control.

Each member represents his or her home constituency, voted in by popular accord. However, there is no time limit imposed upon terms of service. So long as the populace is satisfied, a councilor may remain active for life. However, the leaders of the three major political parties may call for an inquiry, then a vote for dismissal if there is evidence of corruption and/or incompetence. Ithtorians frown more on the latter than the former. That also includes physical infirmity. Only a powerful council member can suffer anything other than minor illness and expect to keep to keep his or her job. They don't look well on weakness.

Bribery—or a complex system of favors and boons—seems to be a way of life here. We might be able to use that. I just don't know if they would take kindly to incentives or gifts, as presented by outworlders. I'll ask Vel once we manage to get through this first state occasion.

For now, I'm afraid it will be hard for me to match names and faces later, so I whisper to Constance, "Log this for me, please. And help me remember who is who?"

"Acknowledged," she replies quietly.

Reassured, I devote myself to the minute courtesies expected of me. Sharis executes what looks like a half bow as he presents me to the assembled august company. Recognizing my cue, I tuck both hands beneath my arms, tight against my chest, and return the honorific. Vel touches me lightly on the spine, unseen, and I remember to lower my eyes for a count of five. This posture represents peaceful intent and high reverence for my hosts.

"Well done," Sharis says, by way of Vel.

I acknowledge that with a smile, not showing my teeth because that could be construed as aggression. With some effort, I commit their names to memory: Devri Il-Waren, Mako Ib-Mithiss, Karom Il-Fex, Sartha Ib-Ulik, and, of course, Sharis and Otlili.

Devri is the tallest, so I won't have a problem picking him out. His chitin shines with a coppery sheen, marked with pale green striations. If I had to choose, I'd name him the handsome one.

Mako is small, almost delicate in build, and her side-set eyes glimmer like onyx. Her thorax is dark amber, touched with darker green. Her stripes denote a lesser status, so it's impressive she has risen so far. I notice she wears the same pattern as the workers who brought us the damp towels.

The third councilman, Karom, would be considered portly by Ithtorian standards. He stands the same height as Vel, but he's easily half again as wide. His shell gleams dark blue, indigo, really. Matching the polished amber of his eyes, his stripes show tawny, signifying high status—not quite royal yellow, but he's an important member of the council. Unfortunately, by the way he holds his mandible he's not a fan of the human delegation. Mentally, I cross him off our list of potential allies.

That leaves Sartha, who resembles Vel in terms of size and coloring. They're both a dark green, bordering on olive, but like the other council members, she bears a pattern tied to her personal status. Vel looks more naked by comparison, and for the first time, I start to understand just how much censure he incurred by forsaking his homeworld.

By their standards, he has achieved nothing. The stories of his accomplishments should be etched on his thorax for all to see. Instead, he travels with human beings and even translates for them, which puts him in a subservient position. I wish I could change their minds about his worth, but I probably won't be able to. I just hope being here doesn't hurt him in some way I can't fathom.

I'm surprised when Sartha acknowledges him. It's a personal greeting, subtle and silent. I would have missed it if not for my recent crash course in Ithtorian body language. But I do notice the way she angles her head, letting her eyes meet his briefly.

Now I understand why Vel advised me to leave my arms bare. Here, my scars are fortuitous, signifying high social status. A totally unmarked person would be adjudged to have lived a singularly uneventful—and unimportant—life. The Ithtorians would reckon the appointment of such an undistinguished individual a mortal insult.

Through Vel, the council members say:

"I am honored to meet you." This comes from Sartha.

Mako adds, "Welcome to Ithiss-Tor. May our association be long and profitable."

"You do my house great honor with your fine *wa*." Yes, I was right to call Devri the handsome one.

My what? Another question I need to ask Vel. After hearing his words, I decide he's charming as well. If my ability to read Vel's expressions translates at all, I'd say Devri is very curious about us. His gaze roams between Constance, Dina, Hit, Jael, Vel, March, then back to me. I wonder if they've studied up on humanity.

Karom looks as though it hurts him to be polite. "We are pleased to receive you."

Yeah, right. I don't buy that for a minute. He doesn't want us here any more than Otlili does, which leads me to believe our support comes from lower-ranking Ithtorians. That makes sense, too. People who are satisfied with the status quo, enjoying their current level of perks and advantages, never want to see the natural order overturned.

Sharis has already greeted us, which leaves only Otlili, the Grand Administrator. She still hasn't spoken, studying us with wide, glittering eyes. There's an immense sense of leashed power about her, as if she could click her claws and have us all beheaded. Sadly, it's probably pretty close to the truth. She doesn't need a vote on the council to make her influence felt.

The ambient chittering from the assembled Ithtorians quiets as if in anticipation of her speech. I can just about hear March breathing behind me; the room is that quiet. When she finally speaks, I wish I could interpret the sounds on my own, but I have to wait for Vel to listen, process, then employ his vocalizer. By the response her words receive from the gathered company, I suspect it must be rousing, patriotic, and possibly inflammatory.

"Honored guests," he begins, "esteemed countrymen, we are gathered on the cusp of greatness. The time has come for Ithiss-Tor to set aside its separatist ways and take our place among the stars. There is no reason we should not seek our fortunes and make our voices heard in the wider galaxy. Of a surety, do we not possess wisdom and technology superior to those who squabble for the right to govern?"

I don't like the sound of that. To my mind, it hints that Otlili would like to subjugate humanity in exchange for protection against the Morgut. The Conglomerate won't be interested in accord on those terms, even if it would be cosmic justice on some levels, considering what humanity did to the La'hengrin.

As a result of first contact, which resulted in armed conflict, humanity seeded their atmosphere with a pacifying chem. It was supposed to make them amenable to trading with us. We didn't take into account their adaptive physiology; our interference left their species unable to fight, even to save their own lives. With our ignorance and hubris, we created a slave race. The knowledge makes me sick, and I worry that the Ithtorians might balance our karmic scale. The Grand Administrator certainly looks forbidding enough.

Once she speaks, Otlili dismisses us, and Sharis says, "Enjoy the party."

The entertainment arrives then. I'm hard-pressed to identify what the Bugs are doing. Sometimes it resembles a dance; other times it looks like enthusiastic acrobatics. I glance at Vel for clarification.

"It is a display of the most popular fighting forms."

Oh. Now that he's pointed it out, I can see the martial applications. After the show, I make the rounds, meeting and greeting everyone who shows an interest in our delegation. I don't have to worry about names and faces because Constance is logging them for me, but I must admit I'm relieved by the time we're escorted to our quarters. I can use some time to talk to my team and think things over.

The hard part lies ahead of us, no question.

CHAPTER 3

My suite is palatial, if alien.

It's decorated in shades of gold, making me feel as though I've stumbled into a jeweler's shop by mistake. I wouldn't call it restful, but the opulence leaves me no doubt the Ithtorians care about making a good first impression. The furniture isn't quite right—for instance, the chair seats slope slightly downward—but I can tell they tried.

They've filled the room with genuine human artifacts, such as a hand-built console suitable for a human interface. I particularly like the standing lamp. I haven't seen anything like it outside a museum. Idly, I wonder how old the schematics were that they downloaded from the satellite, or perhaps they're working off the data they received from the first human landing party over two hundred turns ago.

Based on the way this terminal looks, that makes sense. It has no voice-command system; you have to key everything and manually bring up the software to send a message. Thankfully, they did include a video program.

But there are no windows in here, which worries me. I can't decide if I've been imprisoned or if I'm being protected for my own safety. Neither option strikes a note I want to hear. Both scenarios bode ill for the alliance.

First thing, I fire up the terminal and bounce a message to Chancellor Tarn. I want to assure him I'm serious about doing this right, and I can do that best by keeping him in the loop. My first report is by necessity brief, but I'm pleased to tell him the initial meeting concluded without a hitch. I don't think anyone could have done better.

Vel has quarters in this same wing. He took Constance

with him to improve her database on Ithtorian customs. I expect them to come by later. Jael has a room next door; he claims he's ever vigilant with regard to my safety, but I stand by my initial assessment. He's the worst bodyguard ever. By now, he's probably back on the ship, running a gambling racket on clansmen who've never been off Lachion before.

March settles quietly on one of the sloping chairs, regarding me with a detachment that makes me nervous. It had to be tough for him to stand in a room surrounded by aliens without reacting to what feels like a threat. Outwardly, he bore the strain well, but he's showing signs now. His eyes look darker than usual, his face sharp and haggard.

"That went well," he says. "You impressed them."

I settle into a nearby chair with a heartfelt sigh. "I hope so. I feel like I'm picking my way through a minefield."

If things were different, I'd curl up in his arms. But March can't stand being touched now; human contact triggers swift, sure violence, not warmth. I think there's something askew in his head that makes him register any contact, however gentle, as a threat. While he remembers what he felt for me, he can't access it anymore. He's cool and remote as a sunrise on Ielos, full of the same stark, dangerous beauty.

I want him so much I ache with it, but I don't know if I'll ever be able to replicate what Mair did when she fixed him. He doesn't talk about it, so I have no way of knowing how she went about it. Making matters worse, she had training and advantages that I lack, but it won't stop me from trying . . . once I have some idea what I need to do. Impotent gratitude weighs on him. He wanted to repay Mair for her kindness, which he tried to do by acting as a general on Lachion. That cost him dearly.

For now, I haven't entirely processed the idea that he survived the carnage on Lachion—or that he came back to me, as promised. He could have left, gone back to the life he had before. But he wants more than endless war for himself, or he did, at least. I'm not sure what this March wants. I don't recognize him.

"Yes, the situation is precarious. And I'm going to prove a detriment," he says quietly. "I was hoping I could control it, but I can't see those Bugs as anything but a threat. Sooner or later, I'll snap. I wish I'd stayed on the ship."

Is this where I make a hard decision? Do I go with his self-assessment and send him back to the ship for the duration of our stay on Ithiss-Tor? I don't know if March can be impartial. He seems to believe himself some kind of monster. And maybe he's right; I didn't see what he did on Lachion. I know he has nightmares.

I exhale slowly. "If you really believe that, we should have Doc check you out. He can probably prescribe something to keep you calm."

I'd like to see if he could fit me with a translator, too. Waiting for Vel is getting old, and we were only in there for an hour. I don't mention that to March, however.

March studies me for a long moment, jaw taut. I know him well enough to realize he loathes the idea of behavior-altering drugs, but he eventually comes to his feet without protest. "Let's go see Doc," he agrees.

First I change out of the ornate, cumbersome robe and don my usual trousers. I don't want to draw more attention than we must. They asked us to stay in our quarters until morning while they make arrangements for the first session, wherein I will have an opportunity to plead the Conglomerate's case, and the council members will be allowed to voice their concerns about the alleged benefits of an alliance.

I do wonder why they don't want us wandering around unsupervised, however. Is it for our own safety, or is it because they have secrets they need to safeguard? I'd call for an escort, but I think it's ill-advised to reveal that my lover may have a psychotic episode if he's not medicated.

If Jael paid more attention to his job, he'd notice me slipping out, but there's no sign of him as we pass from our room into the corridor. We're housed well away from the Ithtorian dignitaries, and I don't know if I should be alarmed or honored by that. But, then, we already know this will be an uphill battle.

All the hallways look more or less the same to me, and there's no map, even assuming we could read one. I look left and right, admiring the lovely biosculpture of the walls. The densely woven leaves gleam nearly aquamarine in the filtered light, but the exotic beauty doesn't help me navigate.

"Which way?"

"Right," he says without hesitation.

"You're sure that goes back to the ship?"

"Relatively." For a moment, I see a glimmer of the old March in his eyes, just a ghost of humor that reminds me of how he used to smile.

"Then let's go." Trusting him, I make the turn.

Along the way, we pass a couple of Ithtorian workers, who gaze after us with apparent puzzlement and distrust. They don't try to interfere with us, however. It wouldn't do them any good if they did—we don't have our interpreter with us. I'm not sure how we're going to get back to the docks, assuming we can find our way out of the warren where we've been quartered.

"I'm sorry."

If I turn, I'll see no sign of what he means on his face anyway, so I don't look back. I think I remember making a left here. "What for?"

"Letting you down."

A fierce wave of love washes through me. I wish so hard I could comfort him, but he has wounds in places I can't reach. Tears burn behind my eyes. "You didn't. You're here, aren't you? You could have walked. But you didn't. So that tells me deep down that you hope I'll be able to fix you."

His voice sounds gravel-rough. "I *don't* hope for that. I dream of killing, Jax. I wake up twitchy with the need for it. The least things make me angry—that's about all I feel these days—and I want to lash out. I haven't felt like this since I punched Hon in the face, stole his ship, and fled Nicuan."

Somehow I manage not to say "I told you so." I saw the darkness swallowing him up, even before I left Lachion, but he would have stayed, no matter what. He felt like he owed it to Mair's memory to assist her granddaughter, Keri, who has been struggling to hold on to the reins of Gunnar-Dahlgren ever since her grandmother's demise.

The clans are full of outlaw types, who glory in frontier life, but it also comes with its share of risk. Sure, nobody else wants to try to settle on Lachion, which means the clans remain free to govern themselves, but the conflicts can be brutal and devastating . . . to say nothing of the risk of native planetary wildlife. It's not my favorite place in the galaxy, but March has ties there.

We make a right turn. I'm going by instinct, but the low hum of the building's walls, which seems oddly like a pulse, seems to drive us this way. I hope it's toward the front of the building and not some alien security measure that will wind up with us facing some awkward interrogation about our intentions. As I walk, I try to think of what to say to him.

"Do you remember what you said to me when I was screaming my head off over things other people couldn't see?" I ask at last.

He's a few paces behind me and to the left. I can't see his face, but I know the silence means he's thinking. "I'll always come for you, Jax."

I smile. "Yeah. And here you are. You know what that says to me?"

"I have no idea."

"That you keep your promises." It takes a lot for me to articulate the feeling. "That I can rely on you, no matter what." I bite my lip, fighting for the strength to continue. I don't like talking about stuff like this; it makes me feel weak, vulnerable, and naked. "It tells me you're rock solid, and you're here for me. I'm sorry you're going through this for the second time, March, but you're not alone. I won't let you be."

The hallway ends in a spacious, glastique foyer. To the left, I can see the tunnel that leads to the underground. We can take the tube to the spaceport. Since they don't travel on the surface, everything is pristine, nothing like New Terra. Idly, I wonder what the Ithtorians would make of Wickville, with its vice and easy violence. Doubtless they'd take it as justification for their wariness of humanity.

With the lights behind and the crystal before us, I catch March's blurred reflection; he looks strange and stricken. By the time I spin to see him straight on, he's mastered his expression, eyes dark as a starless sky. I don't know what to do with him, but I won't let him go either.

"Thanks," he manages to say finally. "Right now, if I could be, I think I'd be glad of how stubborn you are."

"Damn right."

The doors slide open at our approach, allowing us to pass into the sloping corridor. More of those glossy aquamarine leaves surround us, pretty and functional. I have some idea that they aid with ventilation and air purification, as well as emitting faint warmth. I'm interested in their technology, but first things first.

CHAPTER 4

Glastique limns the tunnel to the underground, allowing our first private glimpse at the planet from the ground. I stand for a moment, admiring the view. The outside of the buildings seems vastly at odds with the almost tropical appearance of the interiors. It's as though they've created an exoskeleton of iron and titanium, polished to an unearthly sheen, then filled the heart of their world with the sweetness of living things.

Ithiss-Tor is an icy planet. As I understand it, the surface was once covered in a tropical jungle, but as a result of their constant warring and the use of dangerous, high-tech weapons, the climate changed permanently. The Bugs adapted to the cold. In terms of physiology, Ithtorians are not so different from us. The climate, along with their predatory past, dictated the development of the excretory glands that allow them to cover their exoskeletons with insulation. They, too, need an oxygen-rich environment, although they like it spiked with a little nitrogen, which makes us silly in larger concentrations.

The sky is gray as nebulous morality, clouds fusing with whatever colors might swirl up there naturally. I've been studying the culture, not atmospheric conditions. March stands beside me, close enough to defend me but not making contact.

"We should be able to take the tube to the spaceport," I offer hopefully.

He nods. We pass downward, away from the windows. I hear the smooth rush of cars leaving the station. The underground operates on a magnetic system, I think. If we can't figure it out, I don't know how we'll get back to the ship without alerting Sharis to our intentions.

The station at the governmental hub is nearly deserted. I wonder if that's common for this time of day as we join the four Ithtorians waiting for the next tram. They recoil when they catch sight of us, sidling away with clicks and hisses that sound almost hostile, though I can't make out what they're saying. Their reaction doesn't bode well for the proposed alliance.

Their faceted gazes touch on us and slide away. Not being able to understand them frustrates me. I need that implant sooner rather than later. Beside me, March tenses, anticipating trouble. Given our history, that's not entirely paranoid. I'm starting to wish we hadn't ventured out alone. I was just thinking about protecting March.

To my relief, the Ithtorians decide to ignore us. Their conversation subsides as the next train arrives. The doors slide open with a hiss, and we board. Calling on my crash course in Ithtorian symbology, I'm almost positive I've identified the one that represents the spaceport. Not surprisingly, it's the last stop, and the Bugs disembark before us.

"This must be the place," March says, as we get off.

"I hope." Since I'm worried about him, my smile doesn't come off as sincere as I'd like. I hate playing politics with my lover. He could detect my falseness if he wanted to, but he doesn't anymore. I miss him.

This station is a stark and sterile gray, with seamless walls that provide a dizzying sense of distance. I don't recognize the place, but perhaps we took a different line earlier. Maybe we're not lost.

My throat tightens as we climb an upward-sloping ramp. It's hard telling where we'll come out. I hope I made the right call, and that we're about to enter the spaceport via some connecting tunnel.

A cold wind seems to deny that possibility.

"Shit," I mutter.

"What do you think?" March asks. "Do we see where this leads or go back the way we came?"

I don't know why, but the question strikes me as symbolic,

like if we go back, I'm expressing some subtle regret. Maybe I'm reading too much between the lines, but he has to know I'm not sorry for anything that has passed between us. I only wish he was with me all the way, as I remember him.

"Let's go forward."

March's look is inscrutable, but he merely lifts his shoulders in a shrug. For now I'm in charge . . . because he doesn't trust his own judgment anymore. Talk about an ironic juxtaposition—I'm not exactly a sterling candidate for mental stability.

We emerge into an open plaza underground. The floor has been laid with some unknown stone-metal hybrid swirled with strange patterns. This dark gray material shines as though glazed with glastique, but as I take two or three steps, it seems as though the colors shift beneath my feet, giving glimmers of violet and aquamarine. A sculpture stands in the middle of the square; if it were a human piece, I would say it looks incomplete, nothing more than a skeletal frame with an enormous head. Since it's designed by Bugs, I'm not even sure it's meant to be art.

Around us, the area is filled with scurrying Bugs. Tunnels slope down from four corners here, leading Mary only knows where. This appears to be something like a public park. It's a little cooler here than in other parts of the city. That seems to lend itself to more strenuous activity, and there are a few Bugs doing something that I'd call exercise in a human.

Apart from the athletes, there's another subsection of the crowd that isn't hurrying to some other destination. They're assembled in a semicircle with one Ithtorian as the focus of the others' attention. By its gestures, which are fierce and sweeping, it's giving a speech. Now and then it pauses to let the audience respond with high-pitched sounds that hurt my ears. I remember from my studies, that noise qualifies as applause.

As we hesitate at the top of the ramp, we draw the notice of some Bugs at the back of the crowd. They alert the others quickly, and before we can react, they surround us. We could turn and go the way we came, but I'm not sure we should make any sudden moves. Hostility bleeds from their claws, echoed by their clicking and hissing. They have to be wondering what the hell we're doing here, if they're being invaded, although March and I don't quite qualify as a dangerous force.

Well, maybe March does.

I'm still a little weak from the debilitating bone condition; my ability to repair grimspace damage via a freak mutation did a number on my skeletal system, but the daily injections have helped. More to the point, I'm completely unarmed. I don't know what they're saying, but a Bug with yellow stripes on his carapace steps forward. Those markings mean he enjoys high status, so maybe he realizes we're with the human delegation. I think that right up until he curls his claws up against my abdomen.

I freeze. If I shift a millimeter, those talons will pierce my gut. This isn't how the mission is supposed to end. Beside me, March tenses, one heartbeat away from going into kill mode. In fact, I'd guess the only reason he's restraining himself now is because I'm being threatened, not him. He lacks any emotional attachment to me at the moment.

All told, that's probably a good thing, even if it breaks my heart.

My knees go soft when I recognize Vel pushing through the crowd. He speaks to my captor in the native tongue. For obvious reasons, he doesn't translate for me, but whatever he says, the other lets go. I stumble back, rubbing my stomach.

"How'd you find us?" I whisper.

His vocalizer takes a second to kick in. "While we were on the ship, I isolated the isotope the Syndicate utilized to track you and input the signal into my handheld. Somehow I did not think you would remain in your quarters, as instructed."

I feel a hot blush steal over my cheeks. He knows me too damn well. Either that, or I'm predictable in my propensity for doing other than what I'm told. I could take offense, but Vel's caution has prevented us from landing in worse trouble, so I decide to be grateful he's able to calculate my behavior based on past experience. That ability is probably part of what made him such a great bounty hunter.

"Thank Mary for that," I mutter.

The ring around us doesn't look inclined to disperse. March hasn't given up the stance that says he'd like to fight; in fact, according to his body language, he's aching for it. And the Bugs don't look like they're ready to let us walk either.

Vel speaks without moving. "Why did you come here, Sirantha? What did you hope to gain?"

I hunch my shoulders against the wind. "I didn't mean to. I thought I recognized the symbol for the spaceport. Doc needs to take a look at March."

And me, I add silently. Getting a translator chip implanted has just moved up to the top of my to-do list.

"The symbols might look similar," Vel murmurs. "If you're not a native speaker. The spaceport sign has a bend to the right on the top of the character, not left. It also has a tiny dot on top."

That doesn't help a whole lot right now. The Bugs who have penned us in grow impatient with our conversation, and the one who threatened to disembowel me confronts Vel, belligerence in every click of his mandible. I can tell by his posture that he's the highest-ranking Ithtorian on scene. The others will follow his lead.

"Can you do some fancy talking?" I whisper. "Get us out of this?"

"Unlikely," he returns, when his dialogue with the leader comes to an ominous conclusion. "You have stumbled into a demonstration."

Uh-oh. "Against what?"

"By the way they're looking at us," March says, "I'm going to guess . . . humans."

CHAPTER 5

I so don't want this to turn into a fight.

The Ithtorians seem as if they'd be happy to execute us without a trial, though on what charges I can't even guess. I'm doing my level best not to make the situation worse, other than the stupidity that landed us here. Vel does all the talking for obvious reasons.

I stand with my hands in plain view. *See, I'm not moving at all. Not a threat. Just a cute little cuddly human.* Inexplicably, I want to giggle. It's the higher nitrous content in the air, I know, but it's starting to affect me.

It seems like my silly, not-hostile stance might be working.

Until the missile hits me in the face. I don't see which Bug threw it—or what hit me—but it hurts. The hot trickle down my cheek makes me think I've been injured.

Seeming not to care if he lives or dies, March throws himself at the five Ithtorians closest to him. I don't know why he snapped, but with his bare hands, he's more lethal than most would be using a weapon. In two brisk moves, he puts a couple of them on the ground by slamming their heads together. He's quick and angry, but the Bugs fight back without hesitation. Soon we're lost in a brutal melee, and March stands at the center of it.

I don't know what the hell would have happened if a siren hadn't sounded. Everyone stills, turning to face the authorities. Vel speaks to them quickly, and before I can hardly process what's happened, we're loaded into a small private vehicle. The pair of Bugs who extricated us gets in the front, leaving us in a cargo area in back.

"What's going on?" I ask Vel as heat washes over me. "Are we being arrested?"

I'm more than a little concerned about March—and the fate of our mission. Wouldn't my mother laugh to learn I've already screwed this up, despite my best intentions? *That's my girl,* she'd say with a delighted smile. Thanks to my good offices, the Morgut will eat their way through human settlements while she gets rich off the terrified survivors.

"Your party has diplomatic immunity," Vel explains. "The cut on your cheek, plus the footage from public-security surveillance proves you did not offer aggression first. It can be argued that March acted in defense, fearing for your life. It would have brought great shame to our people if anyone in your delegation suffered irrevocable harm after offering safe passage."

I'm pretty sure the only thing on March's mind was squashing Bugs. His expression makes me doubt he wanted anything more than to kill something. Even now, he looks savage and feral, unsatisfied by the brutality he inflicted. I shiver a little.

"So where are we headed?" March asks in a low growl.

"The spaceport," Vel answers. "We will use the maintenance tunnels that run parallel to the underground. I explained to the peace officers that you needed to retrieve equipment from your ship, but became disoriented in the underground."

Which made us sound stupid, but that story had the virtue of being true. We could work with it. They might ask why we didn't simply send a messenger for the item, or request an official escort. I'm starting to wish we had.

On the other hand, meeting that angry mob gives me a better idea how the average Ithtorian feels about the proposed alliance. It's not going to be all sunshine and roses, no matter what Chancellor Tarn hopes. The Grand Administrator doesn't favor the measure, and it sounds like the people echo her misgivings.

My bare arms sting from the abrupt switch from cold to heat. More than anything, I'd like a reassuring touch from March, even just his mind to mine, but there's nothing. He might as well be on a different continent, and, Mary, I want him back like he was. Like *we* were.

"Why did you not request my help?" Vel asks quietly. "Even if you had a surreptitious agenda, you must have known you could rely on me."

Even against your own people? Though I don't want to say it out loud, I realize now I subconsciously lumped him with "them," the nebulous collective against which I need to be on guard. I was afraid to tell Vel about March's instability, afraid it could somehow be used against us. And I was worried he might take it wrong, if he learned I wanted to have my own chip implanted.

"Do I?" I try to soften the implicit question.

March shifts in his seat, regarding us silently. I mentally will him to stay out of it, but I don't feel the telltale prickle that alerts me when he's reading me. No, in this moment, he's no more than a mute observer. My problems aren't his.

The bounty hunter turns his face away, choosing to look out instead of answering. The vehicle roars as the driver switches from ground to hover mode. We soar over titanium spires toward the delicate firefly flicker of the spaceport.

"These are not my people." The neutrality of the vocalizer makes his words more poignant for their lack of vehemence. "This is my race, but these are not my people." I don't know what to say to that, but he goes on, so I don't need to deal with my inadequacy. "I left here because I did not fit. I traveled, but never did I . . ." He pauses, as the translator seeks a word—or perhaps he is thinking. "Belong. In more turns than you can imagine, the closest I have ever come to a home is with you, Sirantha."

I still am not sure how to respond. Part of me wants to hug him, but he's told me Ithtorians don't form emotional bonds, and that a hug would be construed as an aggressive act. But hasn't he just said he's not like others of his kind?

"But surely with the Guild—" I begin.

"I made money for them," Vel tells me. "I am excellent at hunting fugitives. Even now, my record remains impeccable, but I did not feel entirely accepted. I was still alien, still other."

Sudden insight washes over me. "You were that here, too."

Vel inclines his head, a learned human gesture that reminds me how familiar he's become to me over the past months. Whether he would agree with the assessment or not, I consider him my friend—and the one person I can trust at my back, no questions asked. I see now that trust can extend even here on Ithiss-Tor. He would choose us over his own people. For that, they would doubtless call him traitor, or worse, and I can see how my decision must have slighted him, shaken his sense of belonging, even if he doesn't know emotional pain as we do.

"I'm sorry," I say quietly. "I won't cut you out of the chain of command again. You're a valuable team member, and I don't think I realized until this moment—"

Before I can finish my thought, the comm crackles to life. Clicks and chitters come across that make sense only to Vel, but I can interpret what I see out the window well enough. What would have taken March and me ages to sort out, Vel handled with a few words. We've come up one of the side tunnels and emerged behind the underground. From the station adjacent to the spaceport, we walk up the ramp into the docking authority proper. It's cold in here as well, with bizarre-looking droids darting around on six legs. What I presume to be a san-bot comes up to me and nudges my foot. *Pushy little bastard, aren't you?* I step aside and let it get the smudge.

With some relief, I recognize the Lachion ship, which is much different in design from Ithtorian vessels. The ones that are kept here look so ancient I can't imagine they would even fly without a significant amount of work. Theirs tend to be long and narrow, with a multiplicity of decks. Our ship is fat and broad, only two levels.

Vel pauses to converse with the peace officers, which I take to be something like policemen. I reflect how much I hate being left out of a conversation. Once we're on board, I'll tell Vel about my plan to get an implant. I owe him a tangible demonstration of the trust I damaged by not including him in the first place.

He and I have been through so much together, I feel stupid for thinking he might forget that just because we're on his homeworld. I know if I had the choice between helping Vel and a bunch of strange humans, Vel would win every time. I'll never be one to sacrifice the few for the many.

March and I wait while the Ithtorians wrap up their conversation. Then the bounty hunter turns to us. "They cannot keep news of the altercation from reaching the council, but they are not going to make the report themselves. I suspect they would merely like to avoid dealing with the paperwork. They're also very interested in visiting our vessel. With your permission, I could give them a tour."

That sounds like a fair reward for our relatively bloodless extrication from the square. I nod. "Sure, they can come along. Just keep them out of med bay for a while, will you?"

Vel agrees. "I will save that for last . . . and alert you on the comm before we come in. Does that sound feasible?"

"More than."

So now we're off to see Doc.

ACCESSING TRANSCRIPT . . .

Omni News Net: Special Report—the *Real* Syndicate

[A young brunette faces the vid, settling herself comfortably in her chair. Behind her, there is a wall of images reflecting the important guests she has interviewed over the years. Another woman joins her; dark-haired and impeccably coiffed, she is older but gives the impression of being ageless.]

Lili Lightman: If you've just joined us, welcome to *Lili Lightman Live*. I wrapped up my report on toxins in the water supply on Saleris, and now I'm privileged to have a guest on the program. She doesn't usually permit interviews, but she's made an exception today. Please welcome Ramona Jax.

Ramona Jax: Thank you, Lili. It's a pleasure to be here.

Lili: You initially refused the invitation when our producers contacted you. Is that right?

Ramona: It is.

Lili: May I ask why you changed your mind?

Ramona: [She offers a winning smile.] Certainly. It occurred to me that this could be an opportunity to shed some light on the truth about our organization.

Lili: And what would that truth be?

Ramona: The perception is, we're a band of bloodthirsty criminals. [She leans in toward the vid, encouraging the close-up.] And that simply isn't the case. We are businesspeople, nothing more, nothing less. We provide a wide variety of goods and services, but we force none of our goods and services on those who choose not to patronize us.

Lili: So you claim there's no criminal element?

Ramona: My dear, trade agreements vary so widely from planet to planet that it's become a gray area for nearly any large company. For instance, the sale of slaves is clearly prohibited on New Terra, but is lawful on Nicu Tertius. As long as we do not traffic in proscribed regions, in what way are we breaking the law, should we trade with the Nicuan Empire?

Lili: I think my viewers would argue there's a moral imperative at work that supersedes any planetary policy.

Ramona: But isn't morality an artificial value system imposed via the codification of cultural norms? On one world, they accept human sacrifice as part of their religion. On another, brothers and sisters marry. What right have we to condemn others for their beliefs? [She lofts a brow.] Do you feel qualified to sit as judge?

Lili: [She shifts, obviously uncomfortable.] Well, no. So you're saying there are no absolutes.

Ramona: Indeed. The Syndicate offers value to all, regardless of creed, culture, or species.

Lili: [She looks uncertain and confused.] That's very . . . egalitarian.

Ramona: Exactly. I'm quite proud of our organization, but concerned with the dissemination of deliberate misinformation. Too long has the public been misled by the pathetic tidbits let slip by the Farwan regime, and it seems as if the Conglomerate intends to continue that same fascist censorship policy. For instance, consider this proposed alliance with Ithiss-Tor. Has anyone examined the long-term ramifications of having the Ithtorians involved in interstellar affairs? They have a history every bit as violent as the aliens from whom we would ask them to protect us. What if the Ithtorians choose to side with the Morgut? Can we accurately predict their loyalties, based on our knowledge of them? I think not, and it troubles me that humanity decided not to ask its own for aid.

Lili: What do you mean?

Ramona: The Syndicate has an extensive fleet, Lili. Our services can be retained for a reasonable fee, which includes private security and military applications. If humanity needs a defender, surely we are the reasonable choice.

Lili: [She listens for a moment to an unheard voice.] I understand your daughter has been dispatched to Ithiss-Tor to broker this alliance. How do you feel about that?

Ramona: Naturally, I advised against it, but you know how mothers and daughters can be. She discounts my age-earned wisdom, so I can only tell you that I'm proud of her, regardless of how misguided her decisions may be. I only hope her work there doesn't cost us.

Lili: [Her eyes widen.] What are you implying?

Ramona: I'm sure it's already on everyone's minds—what a misstep could mean. [She lowers her voice, conspiratorial.] The Axis Wars.

Lili: [She looks troubled.] You've given us a great deal to think about today, Ramona. Thanks for appearing on *Lili Lightman Live*, and we appreciate you offering your insights on current events. [She gazes intensely into the vid.] If you have thoughts on the alliance or the Syndicate—or the lovely blue dress Ramona is wearing (design by Care-wear)—you can bounce your thoughts to me at satellite 11.23.044.3340. Thanks for watching, and as always, keep reaching for the stars.

CHAPTER 6

On the way to medical, Jael steps out of the lounge, intercepting us. "What're you two doing back here? I thought you were instructed to stay in your quarters. Are we making a run for it?"

I give him a sour smile. "None of your business."

"Where you're concerned, everything's my business, darling." He props himself up, obviously not intending to let us pass until his curiosity has been satisfied.

March tenses dangerously, still seething with unspent impulses. The fight with the Ithtorians was broken up too soon for him to feel satisfied. Mary, I hope Jael doesn't provoke him.

"It doesn't impact your assignment," I tell Jael firmly.

"I'll decide that."

When March moves to push past him, Jael puts a hand on his shoulder, and that's the last straw. March lashes out with a blow that would fell anyone else. Jael's head snaps back, blood spurting from his nose, but an answering light kindles in his eyes. To these two, this is probably like foreplay.

If I had any sense, I'd run.

Instead, I skitter back a few paces as they slam into the wall. Jael's slight build indicates he should be an easy opponent for March, but he's stronger than he looks. Fists crash into jaws, fingers dig into each other. March lands an elbow in the sternum and follows with a kick that should've broken Jael's kneecap, but the other man leaps aside.

Jael retaliates with a flurry of blows, almost too fast to track. I wince as they land on March's chest. The merc is too smart to go for the head. He knows the body is where you do the most damage.

March doesn't seem to feel it. He grabs Jael and slams his head into the wall with such force I expect to see his skull shatter. This can't go on. I tap the comm.

"Doc, I need you down on deck two, section A-12. Bring a tranq."

They grapple, better than a constant exchange of punches. Jael breaks free and slams his head into March's chest, rocking him back. March replies with a strong right hook. If Jael had a glass jaw, he'd go down right there. The punch had all March's power behind it. Instead, he takes the hit and slams an elbow into March's gut. March in turn takes the blow and slams a roundhouse into Jael's left cheek, and I swear I hear the crunch of bone.

By the time Doc gets here, they've beaten each other bloody. Jael looks like he got the worst of it, but that's only because of the broken nose. Blood has spattered all over both of them, and they show no sign of calming down.

Doc assesses the situation in a single glance and tranqs them both. "You're back sooner than I expected." Only he could make such a moment conversational. "What brought this on?"

He's a short, stocky man with the heavy musculature of those from high-G worlds. I don't think he was born on Lachion, though he has certainly been adopted into the clans. Doc's real name is Saul Solaith, and he's more a geneticist than a practicing physician, but he takes care of the crew nonetheless.

A few clansmen help transport Jael and March to medical. I follow along behind, feeling sick. March has winked out completely, but Jael is fighting the meds; he'll shake them off soon.

"March is having trouble being surrounded by all those Ithtorians," I explain. "It rouses his 'fight' instinct. We came in to have him checked out, and Jael decided he needed to interfere."

The merc glances up, groggy and squinting in the bright lights. "I thought he might be dangerous, Jax. What if he'd gone after you instead of me?"

I ignore that, addressing Doc. "What can you do?"

"Medicate him." Doc narrows his gaze on March. "I can synthesize a wide range of behavior-modification drugs, but I'll need to run some tests to confirm the dosage."

"We don't have to be anywhere before tomorrow," I add. "Can you do something for him that quickly?"

A little voice reminds me I could leave him on the ship. Maybe March wouldn't even care, but I would. I'd feel like I was abandoning him, unwilling to deal with the drawbacks associated with being with him. And yeah, right now it's hard as hell; I can't even touch him.

But I remember what we were like together, and I won't get that back without some effort. I've never been afraid to fight for what I want. Time to prove to him that I won't walk when the going gets tough.

Maybe he'll find that confusing and incomprehensible in his present state. Maybe he won't even appreciate it until after we fix him, but it's when, not if. I won't give up.

He thought I gave up on us when I was at my weakest, but I've only ever wanted to keep from hurting him. March is such a maddening bundle of contradictions, brutal strength wrapped around a vulnerable core. The way he used to need me scared me to death—and now I'm afraid he'll never need me again.

I'm just never satisfied, am I?

Doc has been tapping away at his terminal, trying to answer my question. Finally, he says, "Yes, if I get started right away, I should be able to pin down what he needs."

"What about me?" Jael asks, becoming more alert by the second. "Do I get anything recreational while I'm here? I've been a good boy."

Doc ignores him, but I'm finding it hard. "Could you piss off already? Go clean up. You don't need to be here."

Jael sighs and pushes himself upright. "That's the thanks I get for saving your ass? He could've really hurt you."

"You set him off." But the idea takes root, and I don't like the accompanying fear. It doesn't look like it would take much to make March think I'm a threat.

The merc sighs heavily and staggers toward the door. "I'm warning you, Jax. He's not stable, and I'm not saying that to be a pain in the ass."

After Jael leaves, I watch while Doc hooks March up to various lab gear. "Do you want me to stay?"

Saul shakes his head. "I'd rather you didn't." He pauses in his assessment of various readings. "But I think Jael's right. March is in trouble."

Mary, I hate hearing that from Doc. He wouldn't exaggerate the problem.

"Buzz me on the comm if you find anything interesting or unexpected?"

"Absolutely, Jax. Don't worry . . . I'll take good care of him."

I slip out, and afterward, I realize I didn't ask Doc about the implant. Well, I guess that will keep. March was my first priority anyway. If I'm going to thaw him out, I need to keep him nearby so I can work on him in my spare time.

That sounds terrible, as if he's some scrap Skimmer I hope to refurbish, when it's not like that at all. I'd say he's my reason for living, but that sounds melodramatic even in my own head. So I'll just say I owe him that.

My steps turn toward the quarters Dina shares with Hit. They returned to the ship right after the party. Neither of them wants to stay on Ithtorian soil.

Dina has recovered from the Teras attack better than anyone could have expected; she only moves with a slight limp now. When the door-bot announces me, they, too, seem surprised to see me back so soon.

Hit greets me with a smile. "Jax."

"Did you already frag things up?" Dina cracks, as I step inside.

I think about that. "Not irrevocably, I hope."

They offer me some hot choclaste, slightly bitter just the way I like it. My bones ache a little as I settle into a chair. As I sip, I sum up what's happened and why we're back on the ship.

That sobers Dina immediately. "Damn. I didn't realize war took such a toll on him. Is Doc going to be able to help him while he . . ." She hesitates. "Works through the nightmares or whatever?"

I'm sure she knows soldiers can get flashbacks if the

combat is intense enough, but she doesn't know the half of it—how bad it strikes March—and I can't tell her.

So I shrug. "I hope so. Otherwise . . ."

"He can't take part in the diplomatic process," Hit supplies. "Not when he's having trouble restraining violent urges. Sometimes it's pretty hard to come back to civilian life when all you know how to do is kill."

She sounds like she speaks from personal experience. I wonder if she knows anything that could help March. "Can you think of anything I should do—or not do—to help him recover?" Damn, I wish I could be more specific, but I can't.

Hit considers for a moment. "No sudden moves, no loud noises if you can avoid it. Sights, sounds, and smells can trigger an event. He may suddenly feel like he's under attack . . . and it can seem so real."

Put that way, I'm amazed March managed to control himself so well out in the square. It wasn't until they offered the first hostile action that he slipped his leash. He's stronger than I knew.

"Noted," I say aloud.

"He probably feels like he's losing his mind," Hit goes on.

I realize she's describing postwar trauma for a non-Psi veteran. In March's case, everything is probably multiplied by a factor of ten. That makes my job harder, but it's not impossible.

"Save him," Dina says quietly. "I don't know exactly what's wrong, but I do know he's not the same since he came back."

The urge to unburden myself is nearly overwhelming. To fight the impulse, I set the cup aside and get to my feet. "Thanks for the drink. I need to track Vel down and talk about the meeting tomorrow."

"Good luck," Hit says with a solemn expression—and I know she doesn't just mean in my diplomatic endeavors.

I acknowledge that with a nod before heading out. In the hall, I touch my comm. "Vel?"

His immediate response is reassuring. "Yes, Sirantha?"

"How's the tour coming?"

"The peace officers have departed," he tells me. "They were much impressed with our facilities, especially the wardrober. The idea of wearing anything other than color for personal adornment intrigues them. I believe they intend to discuss the possibility of sashes and belts as an additional sign of rank with their commanding officer."

"Where are you?"

"My quarters," he answers.

"I'm on the way. We need to talk."

And not on the comm, where anyone could be listening in, I add silently. Ithtorian technology is certainly capable of it; but if we did it to *them*, it would be construed as an aggressive act, spying as a prelude to war. So I don't know if they would take that risk this early in the game. I increase my pace so that I'm nearly running.

I'm almost there when he asks, "March is settled then?"

"Yes." With a click, I switch off my comm.

Slightly out of breath, I press the panel beside his door and wait for the door-bot to announce me. Vel answers the door himself, wearing—unless I misinterpret his expression—a look of mild concern. He steps back, ushering me into his quarters, then, as a precaution I appreciate, he seals the door behind us with a command to the bot:

"No interruptions, no exceptions."

Vel picks a seat before the terminal, where he was evidently working before I arrived. That seems like all he does; I realize I don't know of anything he does for fun.

I sit down across from him. "I'm bringing this to you because I don't want to leave you in the cold like I did before. And who knows, maybe you can even help me."

"'In the cold . . .'" Vel repeats. Sometimes I'm not sure how much universal he understands on his own and how much he relies on the translation provided by the chip attached to his vocalizer. "You mean because you did not share your plans?"

"Yeah, exactly. I want a chip that lets me understand Ithtorian. I've thought about it, and I don't need the complementary vocalizer installed right now. The surgery would take too long anyway . . . I wouldn't be able to use it tomorrow at the summit. I'd be incapacitated for a couple of days. But chips only take a matter of hours, right?"

"That is essentially correct," Vel says. "Might I ask *why* you want this, Sirantha?"

Here we go, testing that trust between us.

"Because your people will talk freely around me if you're not there to translate," I tell him. "That riot earlier opened my eyes to the fact that things may not be as straightforward as Sharis Il-Wan would have us believe. He wants this alliance, but the Grand Administrator doesn't. Nor does that group we ran into in the square."

"The Opposition Party." Vel identifies them for me, giving no hint as to his thoughts.

"What do they oppose?"

"It is hard to pin down," he says, "but in general terms . . . progress. They despise change. They see it as destructive to our cultural heritage, disrespectful of the past." Vel clicks his claws thoughtfully, clearly thinking of what I've said and not the politics of his homeworld. "My people would expect you to reveal the addition of such nanotech. Failure to do so would be considered bad form, borderline espionage."

"So they would never consider acting in a way that offered unfair advantage?" That doesn't seem to track with what I've learned of Ithtorian business practices.

Vel's mandible splays in a movement I recognize as amusement. "I did not say that, Sirantha. The key is to avoid getting caught. Many things take place that would not be acknowledged. The only shame is having one's schemes uncovered."

"Then you support the idea?" I ask in relief. "I'll talk to Doc before we leave."

"You do not need Doc for this," Vel tells me. "I keep a spare blank chip in my pack in case I must hunt on a world whose language is not included in my current configuration. That way I can download the data and implant it before I travel. As you point out, the chip bonds with the language center of the brain in a matter of hours."

"So you're saying you can handle the installation for me?"

In reply, he lofts a wicked set of pincers. While I watch, mildly alarmed, he works on his terminal, then clicks the chip into a memory spike. I presume he's downloading Ithtorian for me.

"Are there any other languages you would like while we are doing this?" he asks. "We will not be able to modify the chip once it is in your body."

I think about that for a moment. "Is there anything that would help me understand the Marakeq natives?"

Before the vocalizer kicks in, Vel shakes his head. "They are class P, so no translation programs have been written, and the only available research comes from Fugitive scientists."

"I suspected as much." I shake my head. "Never mind then. What about the Morgut?" It seems like it would be an advantage to understand my enemies.

He considers. "I can offer you a partial vocabulary, I think, but I do not know how it would interface with your brain stem. I can't offer any guarantee of complete comprehension. The Morgut language is alien, even to me."

"Give it a whirl."

CHAPTER 7

Before I can reconsider, Vel pounces.

He knows me so well. If he'd given me time to think, I would have tensed up, and it would have been much worse. Therefore, the pinch on the side of my neck surprises me with its mildness. "That's it?"

Vel inclines his head. "In six to eight hours, you will begin to be able to understand Ithtorian. Within twenty-four, all the necessary connections will be in place, and you should comprehend the language fully."

Interesting. He said "the," not "our."

"Will it leave a mark?"

"Not so anyone will notice."

"Realistically, how much trouble am I going to be in with the council for not obeying their directive to remain in my quarters?" I ask.

"You are not a prisoner, Sirantha. You are an honored guest, and it is their duty to protect you. They will be shamed that you took even a small injury during your stay on Ithiss-Tor."

"So this can be spun to our advantage?"

I don't want them to focus on my outlaw tendencies. If they knew what a long, messy history I have of doing the opposite of what I'm told, things could get ugly. I wish I knew why, but it's so deeply ingrained in me that it doesn't even feel like an impulse. I process what I'm supposed to be doing, then before I know it, I'm off doing something else entirely, usually for very good reasons, but my motivations don't change the outcome.

Deep down, I'm sure it has to do with my origins. I was

conceived in grimspace. Humanity discovered grimspace via technology seeded by the old ones; we pass through it like a fold in space, allowing us to travel great distances in a short time. I'm one of those gifted with the J-gene, which lets me navigate this primordial matter. At the heart of grimspace lies pure chaos, the maelstrom from which all life originally sprang, so it makes sense to reckon a thread of disorder runs through my very DNA.

"I think it can be," he says, after a moment's thought. "But do remember, I have not lived on Ithiss-Tor for many turns. My recollections and assessments may not be entirely accurate any longer."

"Noted." I start to apologize again for not asking him for help, but I guess he can read my body language now, because he holds up a hand.

"Shall we see about March?"

"Sounds good," I agree.

I lead the way from Vel's quarters back to medical. Along the way, we greet various crew members, who must have been briefed to expect Vel's natural appearance because they don't recoil or otherwise react. I can remember a time when March would have touched my mind half a dozen times while we were apart. Right now, I feel incredibly alone and in over my head, despite my significant volume of knowledge regarding Ithtorian culture and customs.

When we arrive, we find Doc wrapping up. Now awake, March looks more than a little edgy, his hands curled into fists on his upper thighs. Doc greets us with a wave, but he doesn't turn away from the terminal where he's working on test results.

"Good timing," Doc says. "Get him out of here, will you, Jax? I need some peace to get this done, and he glares too loud for me to concentrate."

"Can do," I say, stifling a snicker. "Come on, you."

I wish I could reach for him, lace my fingers through his. Instead, we step into the corridor, completely separate. If you'd told me I would one day come to miss having March in my head, I would have said you were crazy. But even more than his mind brushing mine, I miss his physical warmth.

Vel starts to follow, but Doc says, "Velith, if you could stay a minute, I have a couple of questions about the atmosphere on Ithiss-Tor."

"Certainly."

The door swishes shut, and I look at March hesitantly. "It'll just take an hour or two for Doc to synthesize something. We might as well wait until he's done."

That would leave plenty of time for me to get back to my quarters in the council building, and get some sleep before the summit in the morning. Wordless, he nods. I head for our quarters, leaving Doc and Vel to talk.

The vast sea of screens, all playing Jax, has gone back into the wall, leaving the room stark and bare. I remember how I found him watching old vids of me after I woke up from the accident. He didn't want to face me, didn't want to admit I was right, and he lost himself on Lachion. It was easier to look at electrical slivers that offered a facsimile.

Separate bunks on opposite sides seem to encapsulate the problems between us. I don't know how to bridge the gap, and in his current state, March doesn't even care if I try. He'd rather go back to Nicuan, return to the life that nearly killed him once before.

The old Jax might have written him off as too much trouble. I'm delighted that's no longer an option for me. Fixing March is my number one priority, apart from my ambassadorial duties.

"So," he says, sprawling into a chair, "you're going to drug me and keep me close as what . . . arm candy?"

I start to smile because, let's face it—March is *not* arm candy. He's big for one thing, bulky, not slim enough to wear clothes well. His black hair hasn't been trimmed in a while, so it spills nearly to his shoulders. He'd hate to hear it, but apart from his eyes, his hair is his best feature. It's silkier than it looks, and grown out, it has a touch of a curl.

He has a strong, rough-hewn face, more authoritative than attractive. His jaw says he's pugnacious; his nose says he's lost a few fights. But he has the most amazing eyes, fine sherry with gold and toffee flecks, fringed in glorious, ridiculous lashes that curl up on the ends. They're even longer than they look because the tips have been bleached gold by the same sun that left his skin a burnished brown.

But my smile fades because he's not joking. Does he see this as an imposition? Oh, Mary, would he *prefer* to leave? If it's just a promise that keeps him here—and not the hope we can one day be together the way we were—then I don't know if I can be the person who clings, insisting it's for his own good.

"No." My voice sounds soft, unsure.

For a few seconds, I can't say more. I'm not the mind reader in our duo, so I can't check to see if he's just trying to drive me away for my own good, as I did to him when I was sick. The irony of that doesn't escape me.

I learned one thing from Kai, one unshakeable truth. People stay together and stay true only as long as they both want to. And all the promises in the world don't change the length of time. Nothing comes with a guarantee. Maybe I'm just lucky I have a few months with March to remember.

With some effort, I go on, "It's just a temporary measure to help you cope. Unless . . . you want to go." These words stick in my throat as if they're spined. "If you do, then you can walk. Things have changed."

He gives a sharp nod. "It's not fair to you."

That's the last thing I expect to hear. Mary, we're so alike in some ways—it's frightening. But because I understand why he's thinking along those lines, I won't react as he did when I thought I might be terminal. I won't let fear and hurt dictate my response to him.

This is also reassuring. If the March I love were entirely annihilated, he wouldn't care whether it was fair or not. He wouldn't care about me in any capacity. His vague guilt tells me that some of his emotions must be connecting on some level. Guilt is probably the hardest to eradicate, being the most wretched thing a person can feel.

I'm not the nurturing sort, though. So I poke at him. "Oh, is that your issue? Then we may as well call it. Because Mary knows, I can't function without constant coddling. You'd better head for Nicuan, so I can latch onto the next poor sucker who will prop me up emotionally."

"You think this is funny?" he demands.

I shuffle my feet. "A little."

"It took Mair a turn to unscramble my brain," he tells me in a dead whisper. "I spent three months tied because she knew I'd try to kill her—and anyone else I could get my hands on—because they wanted to help me, transform me. Do you understand what I'm saying, Jax?"

My knees feel weak, so I sink down into a chair at last, eyes locked on his. "You didn't want to be fixed."

"Now you get it," he bites out. "And this . . . this is ten times worse."

"Why?" I lean forward, elbows on my knees.

His face seems strange and sharp, new hollows that I don't remember. It's almost as though he's turning into someone else physically as well. The longer hair adds to that impression. March was always neat, shaved, and shorn. His jaw bristles with black scruff this evening, two or three days' worth at least.

He terrifies me.

"Because I don't have voices driving me crazy anymore. I can block now. That makes me the perfect killer, no remorse, just the satisfaction of seeing the light leave somebody's eyes. And I'm good at it," he adds deliberately as if he wants to shock me.

"You've had practice," I answer quietly.

"There's no pain anymore. No fear. I don't care about anything but what I want. I don't have people hanging on me, asking me what they should do. Know what's more? The longer I stay like this, the more I like it. This is freedom . . . and I could make a fortune on Nicuan. Live like a king."

To hear March talking like this breaks my heart. Even if his body didn't die, the hero I first admired, then later adored, perished on Lachion. The irony is that the old Jax probably would've had a hell of a good time with him. She didn't care about consequences or promises; she didn't care about anything outside her tiny world. She just wanted to chart beacons and have a good time.

I'm not that woman anymore.

Outwardly, I make myself shrug. My indifference is pure

façade, a pretense he could dispel with a quick mental touch, but he doesn't. There's no telltale tingle on the nape of my neck, no chill that signifies his presence.

"The choice is yours. But if you're so bad now, why haven't you hurt me?"

His smile chills me. "Two reasons, baby. I haven't been paid to, and you haven't given a reason. Yet. If you were smart, you'd release me from that promise before I lose my patience. In the meantime, we can still have a physical relationship," he goes on. "What was it you said when I was so desperate for you? Mary, I was so fucking pathetic then. Oh yeah. I'd just be using you for sex."

CHAPTER 8

"No thanks," I say softly. "That's not what I'm looking for."

"That's all I can give you."

Right now. I don't say it out loud because March is growing accustomed to his new state. He's on the cusp of forgetting the value of who he used to be. In another month, he won't even want to change. I'll have to force it on him like Mair did. And that's assuming I can correct those severed neural pathways.

When I think about everything that could go wrong here, I feel slightly sick. Worst-case scenario? I frag up the alliance *and* lose March for good. But that's not going to happen; I won't let it.

For now, I just need to buy some time. "If you want to go to Nicuan, we'll take you after we finish here. I'd say you can go now, but no other ships will be landing."

His eyes seem shadowed and smoky, as he studies me. "Fair enough. With the help of Doc's mood-altering drugs, I'm sure I can keep quiet and stay out of your way long enough for you to do the job here." He hesitates. "Even I know this is important, Jax. I don't want to mess it up. Things will get ugly out there without this alliance."

By "out there," he means the deep, silent reaches of space. The Morgut are growing bolder, raiding human outposts just for the pleasure of our meat. We fought off a hunting party on Emry Station, purged the place, and only managed to save one little girl. I'll do better here. I have to.

I don't like to remember how bad it was there. Knowing there were monsters hiding up in the ducts, well, I can't articulate how scary that was. And these monsters don't just hide under the bed; they eat you. What we went through on Emry . . . that will be the fate of the whole galaxy unless we can convince the Ithtorians to side with us in the coming conflict.

So much depends on me. I can't help but wonder how it came to this. I shouldn't be in charge of something so important. But now that I am, I will give it my absolute best. I just hope I don't have to make any real sacrifices.

"Thanks," I say. "I hope it won't take too long. Shall we go see if Doc has your meds ready?"

It costs me more than he will ever know to wear a face of quiet indifference. Who knows, I might even make it look effortless, but it's never been easy for me to think about losing people I love. Not since I lost Kai—he taught me everything I know about devotion. And I still miss him.

In answer, March stands up. "Sure. Let's take a walk."

It's as if those terrifying moments never happened. He's pushed back the menace, reined it in. I can tell he's got himself on a tight leash, and I hope it will hold. Whether I like it or not, our mission here is more important than feelings.

I take one last look around our quarters. This has never been home for us. As we pass through the doors, I'm not sure I'll ever have a home with March. Sadness washes over me, endless waves crashing against a lonely shore.

I miss the way he used to touch me. I miss his smile. I miss the way he used to tease me, but now he's just a man who looks like the one I used to love, a doppelganger who wears his skin.

We step out into the hall. The lights have been dimmed, telling us that the hour grows late. The crews are on half watch now; most personnel are enjoying some leisure time. So we pass only a couple of people on the way back to med bay.

Doc doesn't look surprised to see us. "Just in time," he says. "Based on his test results, I've whipped up a fine concoction that should keep him mellow, even if he's surrounded by Ithtorians."

"Pill or injection?" March asks.

"Injection, of course. I've prepared thirty days of meds

for you. One shot a day should do it." Doc does the honors, giving March his first dose.

I wonder if we'll see an immediate difference. "Thanks, Doc. We should be getting back to council quarters."

Doc regards me with a faintly worried expression. "Good luck, Jax."

I have the feeling I need it.

Before heading back, we go looking for Vel. He's in his quarters, doing some research on his terminal. I don't think I read him wrong when I judge him pleased to see us. His mandible moves in a way that tells me he's pleased about *something* anyhow.

"Sirantha, March," he greets us. "Are you finished here?"

I answer, "I think so, you ready to go?"

It's only after I speak that I realize he didn't use his vocalizer. I understood his clicks and whistles thanks to the chip that's obviously already starting to work. I've always had a thing against implanted cybernetics. Hell, I hated the thought of the shunt they put in my wrist, and I need that to jack in. But I have to say that this translation device is going to prove very useful; I just hope I can remember not to answer in universal when I hear the Ithtorians speaking.

Though I know that the translator doesn't have anything to do with being able to interpret body language, I still feel better able to read Vel. No wonder he's pleased, the device's already working, and it hasn't been quite two hours. Does that mean the installation went well? I hope so.

"Congratulations. The operation was a success."

March glances between us, obviously realizing that we share a secret. I don't know if I want to tell him; I'm not sure if we can trust him, not in his current state. He makes the decision, though. Not me.

"I don't want to know," he says.

That wounds me because it symbolizes how he prefers distance when he used to crave closeness. I guess I should be careful what I wish for because I remember wanting him to leave me alone. That was a long time ago, but my wish has been granted.

Time to go. Time to stop thinking about things I can't

change right now. We leave Vel's quarters and head off the ship. The spaceport is quiet, no other ships in dock. Not surprising considering how xenophobic they are here. If they have any new vessels, they're hidden. They probably don't want us checking out their technology until we have hammered out this deal. And I don't blame them. It's also possible that these antiques on display are all they have.

Vel finds us a private car to take us back to council quarters. This time I pay more attention to the view out my window. The vehicle is closed, totally automated. We pass through the maintenance tunnels once more, and I gaze out the glastique panels on either side, admiring Ithiss-Tor at night. This place has a haunting loveliness. The constellations gleam bright as diamonds, and they're arranged in alien formations.

A light snow has begun to fall, dusting the world in white lace. Their buildings are tall, interconnected with a warren of tunnels and enclosed bridges. Nobody travels on the surface here. The architecture here reminds me of nothing so much as an insect hive. I've seen similar structures built by wasps and bees, but the Ithtorians construct their homes from titanium and steel instead of earth.

I remain intrigued by the apparent contradiction between their architecture and the way they design the interiors of their structures. Am I to assume that the Ithtorians present a hard carapace to the world but in truth they are softhearted? I don't think I can use Vel as my example in this case; he is no longer typical of his people, if he ever was. Since he chose to leave his home, I think that he was not.

Nobody speaks as the car purrs along, coming up from the tunnels into the station that adjoins the government center. It apparently knows it can take us no farther because it stops and offers a basic "thank you, have a nice day" sort of sound. Vel, March, and I climb up, heading up the ramp into the foyer.

With Vel to guide us, we pass much more quickly through the government warren into the housing annex. When we reach the council quarters, there is only a single guard on duty. To my vast pleasure, I understand what Vel says to him, but I keep my expression blank. It will completely devalue my advantage if they realize what I've done. Not to mention spoiling any possibility of an alliance.

"We needed to retrieve something from the ship," Vel explains.

The guard answers, "Was there any trouble in the square? The council was concerned about the ambassador."

"As you can see, she is well except for a minor scratch, but she, too, has concerns about the candor of the council. She will discuss them tomorrow at the summit. For now, we are all weary and would seek our rest."

March seems remarkably calm about not knowing what's going on. It must be the drugs. He just waits patiently for Vel to conclude his business. The guard waves us in.

To show that I know something of their culture, I fold my arms flat against my body, hands tucked beneath my forearms and execute a tight bow. A *wa*, one of the councilmen called it. I read astonishment in the clicking of the guard's mandible, but he returns the courtesy

Maybe I should talk to March, but I can't tonight. I need to get some sleep before the summit. His room adjoins mine, but he has his own entrance. So I part from him in the hallway, and we go our separate ways.

I hope it's not symbolic.

CHAPTER 9

Vel escorts me into my suite.

I don't know if he's concerned about my welfare or if he just wants to make sure I stay put this time. That idea makes me smile faintly.

"*Wa* is the bow made in greeting and parting?" I ask as we go into the living area.

"Correct," he tells me. "I will go over all the nuances at another time. For now, I will bid you good night, Sirantha. If you have need of me, you know how to reach me." That's a very mild rebuke, based on what could have happened if he hadn't turned up in such timely fashion. I acknowledge that with a nod. Vel executes a neat *wa* before he goes, and I practice mine as well.

Constance waits politely for us to finish our conversation. "There is a break in the surface of your face," she observes. "Do you require treatment?"

I shake my head. "I've already seen Doc. If he'd thought it needed attention, he would have done something about it."

She accepts this. "Have I displeased you in some fashion, Sirantha Jax? I understood I was to assist you under all circumstances."

Oh man. It's too late for me to want to reassure an android who, not too long ago, could be tucked into my pocket or snapped shut when I didn't want to deal with her. When Dina installed her in the Pretty Robotics frame, it enhanced the type of tasks my PA could perform, but it also makes her harder to ignore.

I say, "No, of course not. I didn't expect to be gone so long. Don't worry, you'll see plenty of work tomorrow."

"Very well."

That's the primary difference between her and a human being. She doesn't look for subtext; she doesn't second-guess me or wonder about my motives. While I get ready for bed, she jacks into the terminal to recharge. I'm glad my bed is in another room. I don't mind sharing space with her, but it might be a little weird trying to drift off with her sitting motionless in sleep mode.

Just before I retire, Jael stops by my quarters, so he must know the symbols well enough to have gotten back from the spaceport on his own. Constance lets him in while I'm changing, and I hear him making conversation with her. That softens me because he's about the only one besides me who treats her as more than a san-bot.

He already looks better. The bruises on his face could be several days old at this point. Ah, the advantage of being Bred. Given the way they persecute him, however, I don't think I'd want the ability if it comes at such a price.

"I just wanted to check on you before bed," he says by way of greeting.

"You mean make sure March hasn't beaten me to death? He's medicated."

"I know you trust him, but you shouldn't. I've seen this kind of thing before. As your bodyguard, I'd be remiss if I didn't advise you to move him out of those quarters."

I raise a brow. "And put you in there instead?"

He shrugs. "Since I'm in my right mind, I'd offer more protection if the Bugs get any inhospitable ideas."

"Thanks, but I'm fine."

"If you're sure." He pushes to his feet, subjecting me to a lingering look. "If you need *anything*, just let me know. I'll be here."

Though I'd once have sworn he wasn't interested in me that way, there's a certain warmth to his look. I tell him gently, "I won't."

"Fair enough. Good night, then."

As I get into bed, I tell myself he's just doing his job. There's nothing special in the way he treats me. If he were guarding Doc, he'd make the same recommendations.

In the morning, I wake in a gilded cage.

I cleanse myself according to Ithtorian customs, but I hope they will forgive me if I wash my hair as well. The Bugs don't have to worry about that aspect of personal grooming, but I'm pleased to report that my hair is finally growing back. It hangs in coarse black spirals down to my shoulders. When March hacked it off, hoping to hide me from bounty hunters on New Terra, I cried. I can finally look at my reflection without cringing, which is good, because a lot of Ithtorians will be watching me today.

The last step comes in donning the golden robe that leaves my arms bare. Constance watches me as I prepare for the summit, her face blank as only an android's can be. She's unplugged from the terminal and ready for the day, clad in her sober black suit.

"Your hair should be up," she tells me, surprisingly. "This is a state occasion. I can replicate the style other ambassadors favor. It also possesses the virtue of giving your head a shape more pleasing to the Ithtorian aesthetic. Would you like me to do so?"

"If it will make them take me seriously, go for it."

Without another word, she goes to work on my hair, wrapping it into a pair of neat twists on the back of my head. Her motions feel deft and sure as she affixes the sweep in place with jeweled pins. I touch it gingerly when she's done.

"There. We have seven minutes before we are expected at the summit."

"I didn't think I had enough hair for this yet. Thanks." My smile goes unanswered, and I wonder if she'll eventually assimilate human facial expressions. I'm not sure of the limits on what she can learn.

"I am here to serve."

I square my shoulders. "Let's do this."

The summit is being held in a meeting hall downstairs. It's an interesting place, I decide, as Constance and I enter. The walls are smooth black metal, overlaid with a lattice of complex stonework that seems curiously light, almost hollow in fact. It gives the impression, as does the rest of this city, of a hive. A soft, rich compost material covers the floor in lieu of carpet or tile; the chamber smells oddly of jasmine, but that might be the greenery that aids in climate control and ventilation.

The chairs, if you could call them that, are oddly shaped, a distorted L, and by watching the councilmen who filter past us, I can see they sit backward as we think of it, with their carapaces resting against the spine of the "L." There's a circular viewing chamber through which other high-ranking Ithtorians can watch the proceedings if they so desire. Just thinking of it makes me sweat.

I recognize Sharis first. In case I failed to do so, Constance whispers, "That is Sharis Il-Wan heading toward us."

So I greet him with a respectful *wa*, not as low as the one I will offer the Grand Administrator when she deigns to arrive. Somehow I imagine she will be fashionably late, a subtle way to convey her disdain. He returns the courtesy with a pleased click of his mandible. I notice he did indeed hide all of his claws, which means he's not offering me false civility.

The Ithtorians have so many sly ways to convey an insult; I need to be wary I don't inadvertently cause offense. So far, so good.

He doesn't try to talk to me because Vel hasn't arrived yet. Instead, he hurries to intercept another council member. I recognize Devri at once. His tall, slender figure towers over the rest. This morning, his coppery chitin has been burnished to a sartorial gleam. Yes, he's the handsome one.

I try to look bored as Sharis says, "Things are not off to a good start. The Grand Administrator has already heard of the riot in the plaza." The translation offers no sense of his mood, just interprets the sounds in a way my brain can process them. I attribute the emotional response all on my own.

Devri glances over at me. "Her actions seem impulsive. She does not listen well, even if she is not as homely as some of her compatriots." His faceted eyes slide along my scars. "Perhaps they erred in sending us a well-adorned human. As important as this is for both our peoples, they should have sent a smart one."

Hey, I resent that. Maybe.

"Velith Il-Nok thinks well of her," Sharis protests. "And

given his family connections, he might have been a council member himself by now if he had not fled prior to the election. So perhaps she is not entirely lacking in value. We will simply have to wait and see. For now, I am more concerned with how we present the recent unpleasantness to the council. Further proof that the OP will vehemently oppose this alliance can only hurt us when it comes to a vote."

"By vehemently, you mean violently," Devri says.

Sharis clicks his claws scornfully. "They know no other way. They're almost human in that regard."

Ouch. It's a little harder to pretend incomprehension, but they wouldn't understand me if I were to tell them off. Unless one of *them* has a secret implant? If I did it, why couldn't they? It's a giant case of the left hand not knowing what the right is doing, so I make a mental note to prepare my people for this eventuality. We'll guard our tongues unless we're on the ship, or convinced of our privacy in quarters. That includes running a sweep for any potential listening devices. It's incredibly wearing to consider I'll have to be on my guard almost every minute of the day.

"Agreed," Devri says. "The opposition *are* savages, but perhaps we can turn that to our advantage. This female seems cognizant of the niceties." He turns to me then and offers a polite *wa*.

I respond in kind, knowing I'm being tested like an animal that knows one cute trick. Nonetheless, I make sure my bow is a little lower than it needs to be, somewhere between respectful and obsequious. I hold it for a full three seconds before straightening.

"She's almost civilized," Sharis agrees. "If we can make the Grand Administrator see that, perhaps she will set aside her old grievances."

Devri's claws open and close, revealing extreme agitation. "It was a nasty business, the last time we had humans on world."

But before I can hear what would undoubtedly be a juicy piece of gossip, Vel arrives. For the first time, I notice the way the other Ithtorians' eyes skitter away from him, as if they find it unpleasant to gaze upon his unadorned shell. The bounty hunter is the epitome of wasted potential to them,

I suppose. Ithtorians put no stock in happiness or personal pleasure.

"Are we ready to begin?" Vel asks in Ithtorian.

I'm delighted to understand it. He doesn't look at me as he converses with Sharis and Devri. Good of him—I wasn't sure how far his ability to dissemble went, but Ithtorians can be sly, especially when it comes to business negotiations.

"Unfortunately, we are still waiting for Councilor Sartha . . . and the Grand Administrator," Sharis answers.

I realize that while I was eavesdropping, the other council members arrived, so I face each in turn and give a deep, deferential *wa*. They return the courtesy with varying degrees of sincerity. Mako radiates genuine friendliness and sincere curiosity. Karom shows me his claws curled around his forearms in a silent threat he thinks I'm too simple to catch. Somehow I manage to restrain the urge to bare my teeth at him. Vel told me a wide smile would be construed as an aggressive gesture, here.

During this quiet drama, the Grand Administrator makes her big entrance.

Let the games begin.

CHAPTER 10

The Grand Administrator enters with all pomp and ceremony. Her retinue trails her, an honor guard present to attest to her consequence. The low hum of conversation ceases as she takes her place among us. Each council member greets her with a *wa*, lower than any they've offered me or each other, for that matter.

She holds her pose for a few seconds, cognizant of the drama about to unfold. Then she takes her place at the head of the room. The chairs are arranged in a semicircle around the one where she sits. Other than the Grand Administrator, none of us enjoys a position of superiority. She is clearly the leader among us, and her seat reinforces that fact. Red-tipped claws trail idly along her lower limbs, bespeaking faint impatience.

"We all know why we are gathered here," Sharis says. "So I will simply introduce the ambassador and permit her to make the opening remarks."

This is it, time for me to shine. Thank Mary I spent my time on the ship well, and I've prepared a speech for this occasion. Otherwise, I'd be nervous as hell.

Using Vel's body language as a guide, I step to the center of the room. Around me, the council members take their seats, some of them ready to listen and give us a fair shake. Others have already made up their minds. I can tell by Karom's posture that he wants to get this over with and thinks this is a waste of time. I don't imagine we'll sway his vote.

"Esteemed hosts, I thank you for this opportunity . . . and for your hospitality. I come now, ready to articulate the many advantages our people will enjoy, should we join forces on a galactic scale. I have taken the liberty of researching the goods you manufacture, and I can assure you that there is a huge market for the specialized weapons you produce. They would certainly sell well off world, to say nothing of the sophisticated mining equipment. There are a number of automated outposts that would be interested in your droids."

I pause to take stock of my audience's response. Unfortunately most of them are still, and I am not skilled enough to judge a reaction without movement from claws or mandible. Vel looks encouraging, however, as he translates. So I forge onward.

"In addition to commerce, we can offer you a voice in galactic government. If you should choose to join the Conglomerate, Ithiss-Tor will be added to the roster of tier worlds, which are foremost in making policy that applies to all annexed planets. Some are too small in terms of population or annual revenue to qualify for a voting representative, but that is not the case for Ithiss-Tor. You would receive an immediate vote and to qualify for all emergency and protective services at the Conglomerate's disposal.

"In return for these services, we would expect Ithiss-Tor to participate in the senate by electing or nominating your own representative and sending him or her to New Terra. We would also expect your support in the event of any armed conflict and for your people to abide by all Conglomerate laws that do not contradict cultural mores."

This doesn't seem like the time to mention our worry about the Morgut. I thought I covered the topic nicely anyhow by talking about the vague possibility of armed conflicts. I signal that I'm finished speaking by executing a low bow in the Grand Administrator's general direction. Then I wait for Vel's translation to catch up.

A rumble of clicks, chitters, and hisses sweeps over the room. But this time the sounds coalesce into sense for me.

The slim, dainty councilor, Mako, murmurs to Devri, "That was well-spoken."

And he agrees with a twitch of his mandible. "Well enough, but now let us see how she stands up to questioning."

Oh, I'm not looking forward to that.

I have the feeling the Grand Administrator will go last. She'll let her minions wear me down before she goes in for the kill. Not surprisingly, Karom goes first. After being recognized by Sharis, who is moderating the summit, he gets to his feet in a lumbering motion.

"Our economy is solid," he says. "I fail to see the value of gaining more politics for the dubious value of selling our goods off world. Can you defend changing the status quo in such a way, which dishonors the way our ancestors lived, when we gain so little?"

There's a huge advantage in understanding what Karom says as he says it but pretending to wait for Vel's translation. That gives me time to think about how I'm going to answer. And that's a damn good question. How am I supposed to respond? While Vel repeats this dutifully in universal, I ponder.

"With greatest respect, honored Karom, there is a difference between preserving one's heritage and eventual stagnation. There is a precedent that demonstrates how civilizations that failed to evolve eventually fell into a slow decline. Think about that, no new technologies or innovations. Sometimes it takes an outside stimulus to catalyze beneficial change."

Vel translates. I don't like being in the center like this. It makes me think all they need to do is pile up some wood and tie me down. Primitive genetic memory makes me feel hunted. I hope I'm not giving off the stink of fear. I should've asked Vel about that.

Was what I said too much? Did I insult him in some fashion? Surely, Constance would signal me, but she's across the room, out of nudging range. I can feel myself start to sweat, but I don't want to reveal my case of nerves with restless movement. Forcing myself to stand still, I present a composed face as Karom resumes his seat. By the contemptuous click of his claws, he thinks that was a fine piece of specious oratory.

The councilors discuss my answer. A couple of them, Devri and Mako, seem to agree with me. Sartha, who came in just before the Grand Administrator, keeps stealing looks at Vel. She doesn't seem engaged by the summit; the bounty hunter holds most of her attention. Sharis says nothing, but I know he's on our side.

There's a low rumble from the viewing area above, as they register the translation. From what I understand, those observing today's session would all be high-ranking officials, perhaps aspiring council members. Though they don't have a vote on this issue, they do influence the councilors who represent them.

Devri signals Sharis, letting him know that he has a question. The proceedings are very quiet, almost intimidating in their silence. And maybe that's the point because they've managed to intimidate me. Maybe it's a way for them to test my steel.

The tall, coppery councilor stands, offering me a quiet gesture of reassurance by briefly cupping his claws together. For the average Ithtorian, such silent communication offers as much variety in meaning as the sounds they make. It's useful that I remember and identify many of the signs. Otherwise, I might be in a flat panic by now.

"When you say 'all Conglomerate laws that do not contradict cultural mores,' how much latitude is offered when making that judgment?"

Whew, an easy one. I'm so glad I don't have to sweat over this question, especially after the last one. I wait out the translation, pleased to have a ready answer.

"All such determinations are made by the home planet," I say immediately. "The Conglomerate is not interested in forcing people to comply with regulations that would irrevocably alter the way people live. This applies to traditions, customs, and religious ceremonies as well. On Nicuan," I continue, "some Houses still practice ritual sacrifice before a battle—and Nicuan is a Conglomerate world. It is not the galactic government's place to regulate a people's way of life. So as you can see, joining the Conglomerate would not necessarily curtail any of your freedoms, only augment the prosperity you currently enjoy."

"Until you drag us into your wars," Karom mutters. "And spread your filthy diseases by wandering around our planet."

Sharis hisses at him. "You have not been recognized. One more breach of protocol, and you will forfeit your right to remain in attendance at this summit."

With a low sound in his throat, Karom subsides. Devri offers me a *wa* that he holds for more than a count of five, showing very great respect. I return it as he resumes his seat, matching the length of time as precisely as I can manage without looking at a clock. I want the Ithtorians who are watching to take note of how thoroughly I have learned their customs. I am *not* just an ignorant savage.

I can do this. I will do this. I *must* do this.

The carnage from Emry Station flashes into my mind. To the Morgut, we're prey. We don't speak their language. They have no cause not to treat us as cattle and hunt us to extinction. Unless we can show them an alliance with a superior species . . . so failure here doesn't bear consideration.

I brace myself for the next round.

SATELLITE 11.23.044.3340
OPEN-THREAD—THE REAL SYNDICATE
.LIVE-BOUNCING-COMMENTS.

SupremeRula: I think it's ridiculous is what I think. That stupid Jax bint acts like we don't have brains in our heads.

Shaman2: You don't, do ya? It's like she said, they never tell us the whole story, do they? Why did we go running after the Bugs? Didn't we have any other options?

Care-wear: Tired of washing your garments? Our products can help! Our self-cleaning textiles offer a wide variety of patterns and colors. We can even stock your wardrober. If you like Care-wear, you might also consider opening a franchise!

[Moder-AI: Please refrain from advertisements. Further comments of this nature will be deleted.]

NinjaMonkey4000: I had a cousin that borrowed money from the Syndicate. He couldn't pay it back, so they broke his legs and cut off both his ears. I say she's fulla shite.

Dreaminator: Everything's all fragged up. I don't know how we wound up like this, not being able to tell the good guys from bad.

DarkMistress: Ramona shur wuz wearin that dress! She wuz all, BAM and then sum! NEway, I'm bored. NE1 wanna chat? Bounce me@ . . . [removed by admin]

[Moder-AI: Please refrain from sharing personal information on the public satellite channel.]

Deep!Thinker: I have to agree with a lot of what Ramona said. She made good points about cultural relativism, and I had to rethink what I've heard about the Syndicate, based on her remarks. It did make me wonder why we aren't making better use of our own resources.

Sinna: You're a jackass, DT. Ramona used a few ten-credit words, and she looks good on vid, so suddenly the Syndicate isn't the group that kills people who cross them, sells slaves and chem and Mary knows what else?

TheTruthWillSetUfree: If you want the real truth about the Syndicate, never mind what Lili Lightman is peddling, then bounce to [removed by admin]

[Moder-AI: Please refrain from posting outside node information.]

.CONTINUE.
.NEXT-SCREEN.
.LIVE-BOUNCING-COMMENTS.

CHAPTER 11

The day passes in an agony of interrogation.

Karom in particular is relentless. His questions are pointed and nearly impossible to answer without affront. I'm really starting to hate the bastard. But his thinly veiled antagonism seems to make Mako feel more sympathetic toward our cause. I'm less sure about Sartha.

She seems more interested in Vel than any potential alliance—to the point that I suspect they had some connection before he ran away long ago. Karom will definitely vote against us. I can find only one positive in this situation. At least the Grand Administrator can't veto their decision, however much she'd like to. Her languid gestures tell me she'd love to sink those red-tipped claws in my throat to shut me up for good.

The portly councilor tries to trip me up with the riot in the square, but Vel already told me what to say. He anticipated they would try to use this against me, so we worked on our angle last night on the way back to the government center. Somehow, I manage not to spoil the moment by smiling.

"I needed to retrieve equipment from my ship, esteemed Karom, and I did not wish to burden the council, who had already done me so much courtesy. I did not realize danger awaited me anywhere on this world. I had been assured that everything was in readiness for our delegation . . . thus such barbaric hostility astonished me, and I greatly regret that I have caused it, though I am uncertain as to how I have given offense to those good Ithtorians."

Take that, you stupid Bug.

Mary, I'm glad they're not Psi, or this would already be over. I can school my words but not my thoughts.

My tongue feels like I've tied it in knots with all the doublespeak, insults layered carefully within tissue-thin civility. Vel translates, and I'm gratified to see Karom forced to execute a shamefully deep *wa* to me. He falls back into his seat on a wave of lost face. The Grand Administrator herself voices an apology for the behavior of the OP.

"You have my regrets," she says. "Though we pride ourselves on the ability to articulate our views, we would never choose the manner of expression to be so savage."

By the time we break for a late-afternoon meal, I feel as though I've been pulled backward through the engines of a ship. I make sure to observe the courtesies before fleeing for my room. There's a formal function tonight, and I need to rest up for another long session of being on display. Maybe I'll learn something interesting.

Constance and Vel accompany me back to the housing section. He says, "You acquitted yourself well, Sirantha. Devri has been won over completely."

"I noticed his gestures," I answer with a touch of pride.

"I will call for you tonight," he goes on. "And escort you to the hall."

"Thanks. I'm going to rest my brain for a while."

Vel inclines his head. "I have to work."

"You always do," I murmur.

The bounty hunter continues down the hall as Constance and I enter my quarters. A wave of weariness assails me, despite the lavish beauty of my surroundings. The PA studies me for a moment, then offers the following opinion: "It is too bad you cannot simply plug into the terminal to recharge."

She surprises a laugh out of me. "Isn't it? Unfortunately, it's a bit more complicated for humans."

"Do you wish to deconstruct the summit at this time? I recorded the proceedings, as instructed."

I shake my head tiredly, peeling out of the gold ceremonial robe. "Later, please, Constance. I don't want to think right now. Can you check the place for snoopware?"

"Acknowledged," she says.

At the verge of crossing out of the sitting area into my bedroom, I pause as something occurs to me. "Do you remember when I asked you for access to all of Mair's partitioned files?"

"I remember everything you have ever said in my presence, Sirantha Jax."

Dumb question, I guess. She probably keeps logs. Sometimes, she looks so real, with her silky brown hair and wide dark eyes that I expect human behavior from her instead of recalling she's still chips and wiring underneath.

"Then here's the million-credit question. Did Mair leave any notes about March?"

"Searching." Her eyes go strange, scanning side to side as if she has turned her gaze inward. I wait. Then she focuses on me again. "Seventeen days before her last access to my programming, she uploaded a personal journal to the partitioned files. There are numerous voice references to March."

I stand frozen. This had been a shot in the dark, nothing I expected to bear fruit. Now I can't move, afraid to hope there's something in those files that can help me. I make myself continue into the bedroom to grab my civ clothes.

I shimmy into a pair of loose white pants, heart pounding like mad. For a moment, I consider whether I need a sweater. My thin undershirt is enough for hanging around in quarters. The climate control is more than adequate, even if I haven't been able to figure out how to adjust it.

There's also a door in here. If I pass through it, I'll find March on the other side. Before I realized how thoroughly he'd changed, I thought he might want to be close to me. I meant for him to attend the formal dinner with me tonight, but I don't know if he wants to. To my disgust, I'm afraid to open the door that stands between us.

Instead I spin and head back the way I came. Constance is waiting where I left her, ready to resume our conversation. That's the best thing about droids; they don't take your weird behavior personally. Of course, they can also be aggravatingly literal and pedantic, but she isn't as bad as most of her brethren.

I sprawl on one of the sloping seats that's half chair, half settee, making myself comfortable before I make the leap. Am I crazy for thinking Mair can help me from beyond the grave? Maybe. But March is worth it.

"Let's start from the beginning," I say. "Play the first journal entry."

Despite forewarning, it gives me a start to hear Mair's voice coming from Constance, who isn't moving her mouth. The whiskey-low rasp sounds just as I recall from our brief acquaintance . . . before she died to save our lives. Talk about creepy.

"Tanze brought me an unwelcome surprise this afternoon. Instead of Hon, she brought a half-mad Psi along with the ship. She says she didn't have a choice, but I think she just didn't want to end him. That girl has such a soft spot for brown-eyed boys."

I smile at hearing March described as a brown-eyed boy. He'd be boyish only to someone looking at him down a vast age. The old chi-master certainly qualified. I still marvel at the memory of the way she moved that night, running with preternatural speed. I'd never met a real chi-master before, never believed they could really manipulate their physical energy to perform extraordinary feats.

Whatever recording device she used picks up a sigh and a shuffle of movement as if she's pacing. "It took us half a day to get a name out of him. I don't have time to mess with this, if everything is going to come together on the projected timetable. But like Tanze, I can't bear to end him. There's such fire in this man . . . and he might do great things, given half a chance. Certainly he'd be useful, if I can manage to rebuild him."

It's interesting she uses that word. *Rebuild.* Just what the hell did she do to him? I wonder at the mental wreckage that accompanied the process.

Mair goes on, "Dr. Solaith finally returned after a long while training off world. For this project, he needed skills we couldn't teach him. I'm just glad one of our people was willing to learn. Most men would rather fight than think, but Saul has always been different. That commune on Saleris"—she names a high-G world—"really messed up his head when he was a kid. I think someone would've killed him long before now if Rose hadn't been there to stand up for him."

There's a long silence and rustling movement before she seems to remember to say, "That's all for now. End session."

"Prying into my past?" March asks quietly.

I barely manage to restrain a shriek. Somehow I make myself shift slowly on the couch and glance at him over my shoulder. How long has he been standing there? The nape of my neck tingles as I sense him dipping into my thoughts as a fisherman would skim a net across the top of the deep, blue sea.

Red ice washes over me. That's how he feels now, just cold, keen anger. I shiver as he withdraws.

"Long enough," he answers aloud, sitting down beside me. "If you wanted to know, why didn't you ask?"

"Two reasons. The last time we talked, you didn't seem receptive to discussion." That much is true. "You were . . . angry." Now *there's* an understatement. His flat, dark gaze roves my face, but he will *not* unnerve me. "And I don't think you want to change, so you might lie, hoping to misdirect or dissuade me, but you can't stop me from finding out like this."

"I could if I killed you." In a motion so fast I scarcely register it with my eyes, his big hand encircles my neck.

CHAPTER 12

He doesn't seem angry; that's the strange thing. It's an almost casual gesture. That's what scares me most. Possibly without the drugs, he would have done it before I even knew he meant to. I realize I don't know him as well I thought I did.

Frankly, I'm surprised to find this much darkness in March. Somehow I always thought he exaggerated his wickedness out of some misguided need for expiation. But he wasn't kidding. He's a killer, through and through.

I turn my face up, exposing my throat completely.

Constance asks, "Shall I summon assistance, Sirantha Jax?"

If I could, I'd shake my head. Since I can't, I answer, "I don't want negative attention. We spun the riot, but we might not be so lucky a second time."

Especially not if it's tied to March, who escalated the violence.

March watches my face as if he doesn't understand why I haven't panicked. My heart thumps in my chest like a wild thing, but deep down, I can't believe he'll hurt me. Maybe I'm crazy; maybe in a few seconds, he'll tighten his grip and crush my windpipe.

Right now all I can see is him cradling me in his lap and promising he'll always come for me. I see him holding me up in a cold, wet alien jungle, muddy water washing over our boots. I see him kneeling in a primitive hut and sharing my wonder over the baby Mareq. I see him setting off to try to save those weaker on Hon's Station. I see him folding the cheap faux-ruby ring he bought for his sister into my fingers and promising to return to me.

He should be able to feel the golden chain on which I wear that ring. So I hold his gaze and wait for him to notice. Instead of tightening, his fingers splay wide, investigating the fine, woven-metal threads that suspend his token between my breasts. He slides his hand down far enough to lift it, then his dark gaze meets mine, tinged with incredulity.

Cold shivers through me like an ice storm, signaling his presence. I don't know how he stands the emotional chill all the time. These brief touches from him make me want to bundle up, and goose bumps prickle to life, further texturing my scarred arms.

I sense him brushing the memories I've called up. His long fingers curl around the ring, drawing me closer by virtue of tugging on the chain. I don't try to resist, so our brows nearly kiss, just a whisper between us.

"You're still wearing it?"

"You promised to get me something better," I say quietly. "Remember?"

"So if I buy you some expensive jewelry, you'll let me go?" Why does his tone sound so desperate, so haunted?

Is it possible I'm getting through to him in ways I don't understand? I don't know how I feel to him. I don't know how it affects him when he touches his mind to mine. Surely my emotion must spark some kind of reaction.

I make my answer slow and deliberate. "I will *never* let you go. I'll never give up on you. But you can buy me presents if you really want to."

"You're not afraid of me?" An icy brush, as if he seeks to test whether I'll lie.

"A little," I admit. "But I'm more afraid *for* you."

I've never lied to him—and he claims that's why he fell in love with me in the first place. I'm certainly not about to start now, when it would destroy this very nascent accord. The olive branch between us won't bear the weight of a lie. So he can verify the honesty of that for himself. A shudder rocks through him as he does.

"If you can bear it," he whispers finally, "I'd like to come in, stay for a while. Feel how we used to be."

He wants to poke through my memories and feelings, see

if it stimulates an echo. I can live with that, even knowing he doesn't feel what I do. There will be no warm resonance, reinforcing his love for me. He doesn't feel that for me anymore. I should be heartbroken; I *would* be if I believed it was gone forever. Or maybe I'd just square my shoulders and make him fall in love with me all over again.

He's mine.

A deep breath fortifies me for the imminent ordeal. From the last time we did this, I know it'll be painful, but maybe he suffers something like mental hypothermia. Maybe I can warm him up inside by millimeters, even if it chills me to the bone.

"Are you kidding?" I manage a smile. "I want you inside me. I miss you."

Though he doesn't need touch to join with me, I sense it happening as he leans his forehead against mine. Maybe it's a sign of trying to meet me halfway because I know he doesn't like being touched anymore, not even by me. The warmth of his skin belies the blizzard within.

So. Cold.

At first, I can't feel anything but the barren, blasted ice. This is like walking naked across the Teresengi Basin, and it's all I can do not to recoil from the man making me suffer this. I fight to remember why we're doing this. Bracing myself, I wait to gain some equilibrium. It's not all him; I should be in here somewhere, and this isn't *my* emotional climate.

As if from a long distance, I feel my teeth start to chatter. Someone—probably Constance—wraps a blanket around the two of us. I don't know if that will help, but I appreciate the gesture though I lack the wherewithal to respond. Her footsteps trail away. Apparently she's programmed to know when to provide privacy. I appreciate that, too.

Just when I think I can't abide any more ice spiking into my brain to be translated as pain, the atmosphere shifts. The chill tapers off, becoming more bearable. And I feel March touching what I feel for him. He's tentative. He almost seems frightened, like my mind is a jewel box, and he's a child afraid of touching precious things he might break.

But I don't try to stop him.

Warmth suffuses me as he focuses on my memory of the first time we made love. First it's filtered through my perceptions, then it spins. I see myself through his eyes as he comes down to me. I'm smiling up at him, all wild inky hair and eyes pale as moon-silvered ice. March sees me as pure beauty, distilled to its essence, nothing more needed or required. And he wants me in this captured moment—so much he aches with it. He remembers the ache.

I still feel it, even if he doesn't.

I'll always want him. Until every sun goes dark in every sky, until I am nothing more than long-forgotten cosmic dust, I will want him. And even then I suspect my particles will long for his.

Between us, the mood shifts, heating by infinitesimal degrees. Blindly, still lost in the memory, I seek his mouth. Will he permit a kiss?

He does. I sense a shiver rolling through him like distant thunder heralds a violent storm. His stubble scrapes the tender skin of my cheek as his lips take mine. His arms come around me, solid and sure. March pulls me across his lap, and we tangle in the blanket Constance wrapped around us. I fall against his chest, tasting the rough skin beside his mouth. It seems like forever since I've touched him, since he's let me.

I don't open my eyes. I'm afraid if I do, I'll wake alone, my fingers stealing across a narrow bed where I dream alone.

"I want you," he whispers, as if it's miraculous. I tend to agree. "Not the nearest warm body, not a biological urge. *You*."

I don't care if he's just remembering how much he wanted me. I don't care if it's echoed feeling instead of a spontaneous one. Anything is better than complete detachment. Mary, I want him back.

I shift a little on his lap, smiling. "I'd already figured that out." It's progress. I'll take what I can get. "I'm guessing it didn't go this way with Mair."

I startle a laugh out of him, the first since he's been back. "Hardly. She was a little old for me, even when I first met her."

"Good to know I don't need to be jealous of *her*," I joke, thinking of Mair's irritatingly gorgeous granddaughter, Keri.

"You shouldn't be jealous of Keri, either," he answers, just like he used to. I'd forgotten how much I loved having him answer my unspoken thoughts. "She married Lex just before I left Lachion. I gave her away."

"Good for her," I murmur.

Mary, such euphoric relief can't be right. I'm not that insecure, am I? Seems I am. Because I've seldom been happier to hear of a wedding I didn't attend.

We can do this. I'll fight for him. It might not be clean or pretty or by the book, but I can be damn stubborn. I exhale slowly, nuzzling my face against his throat. To my delight, he permits it, arms still fast around my back. Then his hands slowly slide down to my hips, repositioning me on his lap.

"Did you not hear me the first time?" He bites gently on the side of my neck. "I *want* you."

I offer a sweet smile. "And you'll have me. In time."

Good thing the drugs keep him relatively even-tempered, or I'd probably find myself facedown on the floor. I don't kid myself that March is cured. We've just made a little progress, and his first impulse is still to take what he wants.

"What're you talking about, woman?"

"It has occurred to me," I say softly, "that your physical needs may be linked to your emotional ones. Maybe we can use your sex drive to reconnect the two."

I don't kid myself. This plan will run on his endurance, and his patience may not withstand the effort. I may wind up with an infuriated killing machine who doesn't know whether he wants to take me on the floor like an animal or snap my neck. But what the hell, I feel lucky.

"So you're going to tease me until I become the man you fell in love with again?" He fairly growls the question.

I wince. "In essence."

"There are no words for how much I hate this idea."

CHAPTER 13

March leaves shortly thereafter.

Maybe he can only take so much; I don't know for sure that's what it is, but I decide not to press my luck. He actually brushes a kiss against my temple as he goes. That was purely voluntary; he didn't have to. I don't quite dare hope that he wanted to.

Constance glides back into the room when she's sure that he's gone. If she were a real female friend like Dina, she would want to talk about what just happened. Since she's a droid, she's more interested in deconstructing the session from earlier.

So we do.

According to her logs, things went well, but I could've done better. She points out all the weaknesses in my performance, making note of where I need improvement.

"You need to be careful not to antagonize Councilor Karom. By the best of my calculations, he does not like you and will be working actively to entrap you. He will be very pleased if you bring shame upon this delegation as it will prove his point about the general unworthiness of humanity."

"What do you think about humanity?" I ask.

She regards me as if my question is unexpected. "I find it . . . irregular."

I give a half smile. "In what way?"

"In every way. Most of you are very illogical, but I find your loyalty to one another admirable."

"Well, that's good, I guess. Anything else?"

"I also find it curious the way you . . ." She pauses, seeking a word. "Bond."

That requires a little thought, then I realize she has to be talking about what happened between March and me. So she's not *entirely* different from a human friend. She just waited for me to bring it up first.

But I ask for clarification just in case I'm humanizing her in a way that doesn't fit. She could be talking about friendship. "You mean the way I feel about March?"

Constance inclines her head. "It is very strange that you were willing to allow him the opportunity to inflict physical harm. He is stronger than you. I do not understand why you would not simply pick another suitable mate if this one is damaged to the point of being difficult to manage."

I laugh sharply at the description. "He was always difficult to manage. This is just a different manifestation of it."

She looks puzzled as only a droid can. "I see."

Clearly she doesn't. I decide to get things back on track. "What else should I note for tonight's festivities?"

"You are doing very well with body language. Keep it minimal. Avoid excessive hand gesturing. Avoid showing your teeth while you eat."

"So I need to watch my behavior across the board then." I'm sure she thinks she's being helpful, but I already knew that.

She goes on, "You may wish to pay particular attention to Devri. His physiological readings, if I have analyzed them correctly, indicate a certain excitement in your presence. I have insufficient data to determine whether his interest is sexual."

Now *that* surprises the shit out of me. Being attracted to soft-skins would certainly be considered a kink among Ithtorians, if not an outright perversion. I can't imagine such a misalliance being accepted.

"It might just be enthusiasm for the potential alliance," I offer.

"Possible," she acknowledges. "I would need to scan an Ithtorian male who is ready to mate before I could determine the meaning of the elevated heat levels I noted in Councilor Devri's anatomy while you were speaking."

Heh. I don't see us being offered that opportunity, no matter how hospitable the Ithtorians seem. Then something else occurs to me. "Did you notice similar elevations in any other Ithtorians?"

"Searching." She scans her records for me. "Yes. Councilor Sartha also exhibited similar hot points, but you were not the target of her scrutiny."

"Who was?" But I already know.

"Velith Il-Nok."

I shake my head and sigh. It's gonna be a hell of a party.

This trip is way more of a minefield than I expected. Tarn made me think that the Ithtorians were as eager for this alliance as we are, particularly those of us who have seen the carnage that the Morgut leave at isolated outposts. Instead, I'm fighting for their good opinion, swimming against the tide.

Speaking of Tarn, I should check and see if he's replied to the message I bounced to him earlier. I swore after all the trouble we had getting here that I wouldn't play fast and loose, that I'd do this by the book. And that means keeping in touch.

When Constance finishes with her review, I head for the terminal and input my pass codes. The screen flashes a welcome at me, loading my user profile. Because my correspondence has a certain security clearance, I'm asked for a scan, so I lean in and feel a slight tingle as the thin green beam sweeps across my face.

"Sirantha Jax, confirmed," the machine tells me. "Would you like to see your messages?"

"Please." I never can seem to break the habit of saying "please" to machines. If you knew Constance, you might even understand.

Suni Tarn's face comes on-screen immediately. The New Terran Chancellor is a big man with disheveled salt-and-pepper hair, but he offers me a pleased, politician's smile. Behind him is a blue backdrop emblazoned with the Conglomerate's symbol, a stylized sun crowned with a laurel wreath. This is an official communiqué then.

"I'm glad to hear you're taking this task seriously, Ms. Jax. After the road you took getting there, I must admit

I was a bit worried." He gives a nervous laugh and continues, "This message has been scrambled and encrypted so I think it unlikely anyone but you will ever hear this. I have to risk a possible breach in the hope of conveying to you the weight of the responsibility with which you have been entrusted. Perhaps I erred in not doing so before you left."

Shit. I have the feeling I'm not going to like what's coming.

Tarn runs his hand through his already untidy hair, as if trying to think how to frame what he wants to say. "But the fact is, we need this alliance desperately. In the Outskirts, our fleet has been attacked by Farwan loyalists"—I'm surprised to hear that anyone would be loyal to Farwan, after the fascist way the corporation governed, but some people resist change, even when it makes no sense—"independent raiders, Syndicate pirates, and as if that's not bad enough, the Morgut are growing bolder. We've taken more losses since Emry Station, three more outposts annihilated. We seized all assets from Farwan that we could find, including many of their ships, but they have hidden resources, and they're reorganizing."

Double shit. That's the last thing I want to hear. But it makes sense that the highest executives—the ones with all the money and power—wouldn't just tamely roll over and head for prison voluntarily. No, the smart ones would have dug in and shed their outer skins while never changing their natures.

Farwan stepped in after the Axis Wars, quietly offering to negotiate as a new party. They established treaties and trade agreements and took control by millimeters; by the time the devastated Conglomerate realized what had happened, their control had been reduced to that of a toothless diplomatic organization. Farwan won't roll over quietly, and now they're looking for a new way to seize control, changing the names but not the players. The Conglomerate is the best hope to prevent that from happening.

At this point, though, it doesn't look good. They have too many enemies and too little practical experience in doing anything other than talking about problems in an endless committee. My stomach feels queer and tight.

The Chancellor looks exhausted as he leans in, new lines bracketing his mouth. I wonder what the hell has been going on since we've been gone. How many ships have we lost? Are we fighting a quiet war—I start counting enemies—on four fronts?

"If we don't sign the Ithtorians, who have never agreed to *any* treaties, as a symbol of our capability and power, well . . ." His voice grows grave and heavy. "I don't know what will happen." He leaves the rest unspoken; he doesn't need to spell it out for me. "I wanted to be sure you understand the gravity of the situation. Thank you, Ms. Jax. Keep me posted. Tarn out."

Like anybody else, I've seen vids in the aftermath of the Axis Wars. I know how Ambassador Fitzwilliam gravely insulted the Rodeisian empress and how she sent ships to sack every human colony she could find in retaliation. Axis V was the beginning; I saw the piles of burnt bodies and children with flies on their eyes.

Mother Mary of Anabolic Grace. I'm not really the praying kind, but I find my mouth moving in the old, sacred words. Adele, a woman who became like a surrogate mother to me in the time I lived on Gehenna, would be proud. She taught me everything I know about spirituality, which doesn't amount to much.

What I do know is this—I don't want to be the one who brings down the second wave of destruction upon our heads. We're just starting to recover—both humanity and the Rodeisians. We're just starting to relate to each other without prejudice and hatred.

I won't do the same thing here. I won't. My arms wind around me, and I start to rock before the blank terminal screen. Between the stress of securing the alliance, my fear for March, and my subsumed need to jump, I feel like I'm coming apart at the seams.

"Are you well?" Constance inquires.

"No," I tell her shakily. "I'm beginning to think I'm totally fragged."

CHAPTER 14

I have a couple of hours to pull myself together.

By the time I take one last look at myself in the mirror, I decide I'm as ready as I'll ever be. I'm wearing a different gold robe this time. This one has a delicate imprint of leaves embossed on the fabric, but you can only discern the pattern when the light ripples across the luxurious silken folds. The lines are simple, flowing, and leave my arms bare. Constance has tightened up the split-twist on the back of my head.

The final preparation comes when I outline my eyes in gold and paint my lips a cherry red. From taking note of Ithtorian markings, I'm positive that yellow and red denote the highest status in their society. I look good, I think.

I wonder if I need to worry about declining Devri's advances politely. When I decided he was the handsome one, I never expected him to respond in kind.

Constance regards me doubtfully. "Are you sure you wish to wear that lipstick, Sirantha Jax?"

I frown. "Why not?"

"I have been researching the meaning of the Grand Administrator's red claws," she tells me. "And it seems that she is adorned as a symbol of her ability to protect her people. The red claws are symbolic of her rending prey."

I follow that to its logical conclusion. "So by painting my mouth red, I'm boasting of my capacity to take prey down with my teeth?"

"I believe so. I do not know whether such a claim would be considered a bold, admirable move, or a savage, barbaric one."

"Both," Vel answers, as he comes into my quarters unannounced. "You need not wipe it off. It will impress some and for five seconds, offering honor to those studying my movements. The room is a marvel by human standards. On the floor, they've grown that thick, sweet-smelling carpet of foliage, and the walls are hollow honeycomb, covered with the leaves that they use in so many different aspects of their bioarchitecture. Free-climbing vines bloom as they wind around the top of the ceiling, offering flashes of color in red and yellow.

This time, as I descend into the gathering, clicks and chitters resolve into more than noise. It's both welcome and unnerving at the same time. I have to school my expression to blankness when the meanings assigned to sounds flash through my brain.

"Look at her mouth . . . scandalous. Does she think herself a hunter? Pure presumption, she has no claws at all."

Serving-class Bugs circulate among us with crystal salvers full of unidentifiable tidbits. The sauces help further conceal what we might be eating. Ever brave, Dina snags something with a tail off one of the platters and pops it into her mouth.

She makes a face. "It's better if you don't chew."

I pass the cluster of Ithtorians who seem fixated on my mouth, and listen to another snatch of conversation.

"I never thought I would see soft-skins walking among us. Are we going to invite them to our homes next? Disgusting. Sharis has gone mad."

"Well, at least they have some idea how to behave themselves. The last ship that docked here was full of uncouth savages."

The last ship was two hundred turns ago; humanity has made a few strides since then. But I'm not supposed to understand them. So I keep myself from reacting. I reflect that maybe I was better off not knowing—it doesn't look like I'll enjoy this party much.

"And the smell," another agrees. "Wretched."

"Their flesh is constantly rotting off them," one says. "Did you know that? They leave little crumbs of dead skin everywhere they go."

Claws click in shocked agitation. I study their owner, a tall Ithtorian with pale green stripes on his thorax. "That is *revolting*."

Afterward, I realize I've learned to tell the genders apart by the barbs and slits low on their abdomens. They make no attempt to cover their sexual organs, and males are mirrors of the female, everything on opposite sides to allow latching-on for the exchange of genetic material. From what Vel told me, it's not a pleasurable enterprise so much as a practical one. His people don't have sex for fun, not when the female still occasionally loses her mind and tears off her partner's head while in the throes of mating madness.

"This one does not stink," a young-looking female dares to say. "In fact, she smells almost . . . agreeable."

Thanks, Vel. I never thought my personal hygiene would be a subject for discussion at a diplomatic function. My detractors don't have a lot to say to that, so the conversation shifts focus.

"I will concede that they are not as horrible as I recall." Shifting to identify this new speaker, I'm surprised to see Councilor Sartha. "But I do wonder why Velith Il-Nok chooses to spend his life among a lesser species."

Beside me, Vel cannot help but respond to this, as it's a pointed observation within his hearing. "I was not content with the known," he tells her. "I wanted more. That makes me anathema, I am aware."

"Not to me." Her wide, faceted eyes shimmer. "I would never have hurt you, no matter the stimulus. Did you not believe that?"

The arrival of Councilor Sharis forestalls whatever Vel might have said.

CHAPTER 15

"Welcome," Sharis says.

If he could smile, I'm sure he would, just to make me feel more at home, no matter what his people think about the baring of teeth. His *wa* reflects his great desire to do me honor. For whatever reason, he strongly favors the alliance. Unfortunately, most Ithtorians seem to be arrayed against us, and they may sway the vote.

By necessity, Vel translates, though I think we're both tired of the pretense, and it's only the first day since I got the implant.

"Thank you," I answer, returning the courtesy. "This place is marvelous."

Through Vel, we exchange a good five minutes of small talk, paying each other compliments. I find it tiresome in the extreme. If it were up to me, I would ask them to call a vote already and just end this before something terrible happens. I can almost feel it creeping up on me, despite my best intentions. It's the rush of grimspace in my veins—the chaos that ripples through my DNA.

Thanks, Ramona.

But the Ithtorians want ample time to interact with us before they open their homeworld to more human vessels. They want to test and study us before they give us access to their technologies. I can understand their caution, but under the circumstances, it frustrates me.

For all they care, the rest of the galaxy can go frag itself. They don't mind if every other planet in the system implodes, as long as the debris doesn't clog their view of their undoubtedly beautiful cloud-studded sky. I'll have to do some fancy stepping to change their minds.

Hours pass while I do my duty, circulating with Sharis with Vel at my side. March keeps himself leashed. He doesn't even growl, so I think we can conclude that meds are working. Otherwise, we'd probably already have had our first violent confrontation when a Bug deliberately stepped into his path, forcing him to bow and step aside. Whatever the colors on his thorax, the Ithtorian is lucky March didn't twist off his head and shove it down his neck hole.

I don't think anyone is having a great time. My people are busy pretending to be my honor guard. Vel is trapped between his duty to translate for me and the imploring glances that Sartha keeps sending his way. Even with my rudimentary ability to read Bug body language, I can tell she's desperate for a moment alone with him.

I can relate, except I'd settle for being alone, period.

"It's all right," I say. "Go talk to her. I could use a moment anyway."

He studies me briefly, then inclines his head. "I will be right back."

"Vel . . ."

He pauses, glancing back at me. "Yes, Sirantha?"

"What was she to you?"

I'm glad he doesn't pretend not to understand. "We were to be partners," he says. "Her mother and my mother arranged a most beneficial alliance for both our families."

"You didn't want that?"

"I was afraid of that," he answers inexplicably.

Then he sets off to talk to the female who has been eating him with her eyes for the last hour. Maybe that's why he ran; he was afraid she'd do it literally, too. I think there's more to it, though. When I get time, I'll try to coax it out of him.

Before anyone else can move in, I slip off toward a niche I noticed earlier. It has a couple of things I'd call leafy benches, and I intend to make use of one of them. My crew starts to follow me, but I wave them off. "They'll think it's strange if we all disappear. Can you guys hold the fort? I just need a minute."

My bodyguard regards me with icy eyes. "Not a chance. I stick to you like glue."

But for Jael, they let me go without protest. Inexplicably,

Dina has taken a liking to the food, so she and Hit set off in search of some more of those tailed things. In the old days, March wouldn't have ever let me walk away from him. Right now, I'm glad of the space, even as I miss him.

I give a relieved little sigh as we leave the main hall. The nook I discovered earlier seems to be a retiring room. Sinking onto the flat seats, I imagine I feel the leaves shifting to accommodate me, according to the spread of my weight. The warmth feels good, delicately inching up toward my spine.

Jael stands beside me, quietly watchful. I'm glad he doesn't feel the need to talk all the time. For a few moments, I just rest and try to relax. Surely we can leave soon without giving offense. I have to wonder how long it will take, how many of these functions I'll be required to attend before the alliance is put to the council for official approval. The wall behind me is soft with yellow blossoms. When I lean against them, crushing the fragile-veined petals against my gold robe, a delicate perfume surrounds me. It's so soothing I fancy that's what this room is for—rest and rejuvenation, aromatherapy.

Footsteps sound. They seem to be approaching my location. Shit. Someone's found me. I start to get up, and then someone joins the first party just beyond my location. From where I sit tucked in the corner, I can't easily be seen from outside. The sounds of their conversation slowly crystallize into words, thanks to the translation unit.

"Did anyone see you slip away?"

"I do not believe so."

There's a pause. I assume they're scanning the area. My pulse thuds wildly. If they find me here, it doesn't mean anything. They don't know I understand. So I make myself sit still. Maybe I'll learn something. I just wish I could recognize the speakers, based on how they sound, but that's far beyond my primitive skills.

"I do not like the way things are going," the first one says.

"We need to take steps," the other agrees.

"She humiliated you in the summit."

Karom. The second of these Ithtorians is Councilor

Karom. A chill ripples over me. I try not to breathe, afraid something I ate will waft to them on the wind.

"I will take care of her."

What does that mean exactly? Somehow, I doubt Karom intends to make provision for me in his will. I don't know how far I can trust this translation to be accurate, allow for subtleties, nuance, and inflection.

"Sooner rather than later," the other says. "The alliance cannot be permitted to go forward. It dishonors our ancestors."

"Do not fear," Karom replies. "It will be done in two days."

What's "it"? Maybe I make a small sound. To my horror, the two Ithtorians rush into the nook where I sit, back to the flowering wall. *Blank face,* I tell myself. *Blank face.* I try to make myself look stupid as a herd animal, eyes wide and empty.

At seeing them, I offer an abbreviated bow, arms to my chest, but I don't rise. With a languid gesture, I indicate my appreciation for the flowers. They exchange a look. Then the taller one, who I don't recognize, but judging by the colors on his thorax, he's important, says, "She is no threat to us. We do not need to accelerate our plans."

Karom agrees, "Her dog is not here to translate. She only has this worthless soft-skin for protection. But we may wish to take more care in the future. This would have been disastrous if Velith had been with her."

I get the sense that the insult he used is much worse and not analogous to dog, but that was the best approximation my chip could offer. Instinct tells me it's a bad idea to linger here with them, now they know I'm here, so I get to my feet and offer a low, respectful *wa*. I brush past, seeking the crowd I'd fled not too long ago. Jael follows along behind me.

My relief when I spot March is profound. I go to him without hesitation, and to my delight, I feel a little tingle on the nape of my neck. He's skimming my thoughts, just like he used to. Shock stiffens his spine.

You got yourself chipped without telling them?

Ah, shit. Now there's the downside of our relationship.

It's impossible to keep secrets from him. But then he goes a little further, skimming the gist of what just happened. I can tell by the set of his shoulders he'd like to solve this problem with his fists—or maybe a knife in somebody's eye. That, too, is progress. He wants to fight *for* me, not snap my neck with his hands.

I shake my head slowly, wordless. *Not here. Not now. We'll talk later.*

Did he get that?

March exhales slowly and nods. The discussion hasn't been averted, just postponed. I'm grateful the meds keep him from breaking heads the way he wants to.

We need to think and plan, not react impulsively. Too much rests on this alliance for me to do anything rash that might jeopardize it.

I know; it's crazy for me to be the voice of reason, the prudent one, but that's the hat I'm wearing right now, and let me tell you, it's tight across the brim.

Omni News Net: Street Poll

"Hello, I'm Kevin Cavanaugh from Omni News Net. I'm here on Perlas Station, where Sirantha Jax made her escape, thus beginning Farwan's downfall." He turns to a passerby. "Do you have a minute to answer a few questions?"

"Absolutely." The girl smiles at the vid. Behind her, the promenade flashes in garish hues, advertising a wide variety of goods and services, most of them formerly illegal on this station.

"What's your name, miss?"

"Kelindra. With a K."

"What do you think of Sirantha Jax representing your interests on Ithiss-Tor?"

"Well, it's a bit of a joke, isn't it?"

"In what way?"

"What kind of training has she had?" the girl demands. "They may as well have sent me. I saw her for years, showing her tits on the midnight bounce. Table dancing, amateur soft-porn vids, drunk-and-disorderly conduct, barroom brawls . . . how does any of that qualify her to be an ambassador? It's damn near the dumbest thing I've ever heard."

"So you don't think much of her chances then?"

"We'll be lucky if she doesn't start another war."

"Are you worried about your safety here on Perlas?" the reporter asks.

She shakes her head. "Not a bit. This place is more secure than ever, thanks to Jax."

"How so?"

"She got Farwan out of here, so the Syndicate could move in. They now manage and operate more than half the businesses on station. Things are much more efficient these days, and there's very little crime."

From off vid, someone mutters, "That's because everything is legal."

"So you're pro-Syndicate?"

"I work for them, yes. They're fair, unless you owe them money."

"So you advise against taking out loans from Syndicate offices?"

"Well, they're not a bank, are they? It stands to reason they require different terms. But no, I don't recommend borrowing from them. In terms of products and services, however, they offer excellent value. Good manpower solutions as well."

"What do you think of the proposed initiative to outsource Conglomerate military and defensive contracts to the Syndicate?"

"They'd make a good job of it. They know how to teach a lesson so that people don't forget it. One strike from the Syndicate would make our enemies think twice."

"You're not concerned the Syndicate would evolve into another Farwan?"

"Realistically, it's a risk, I suppose, but in this day and age, you almost have to choose between freedom, which can devolve into chaos, and security, which can become a pair of shackles. But at least the Syndicate doesn't attempt to censor the flow of information."

"Thanks for your time, Kelindra. I'm Kevin Cavanaugh and this random street poll bounces live from Perlas Station, where you can already see the winds of change sweeping across the galaxy. Thanks for watching, and keep reaching for the stars."

CHAPTER 16

"It's time to go," March says.

He isn't brooking any argument, so I make my *wa* to Sharis, allowing him to make our excuses. We've been here for hours, so nobody can be offended that we're leaving. Even if I wasn't worried, I'm also exhausted and . . . my feet hurt.

I didn't see Devri or Mako tonight. I'm not sure what to make of that. Sartha and Karom both attended, but the Grand Administrator didn't. I guess she had something better to do. It was, all told, an odd occasion.

With March in captain mode, we round up the rest of our people and head for quarters quickly. In the morning, I have another summit, this time meeting with the captains of industry. The Ithtorians who own controlling interest in the mines are particularly interested in this treaty because of the projected interest in their droids, which are far advanced in comparison to what we use currently.

They want to question me about the conversion of currency and how much a droid, sold for credits, would actually be worth on planet. I'll need to run some numbers in the morning and confer with Constance about the commercial aspects of the alliance. She and Vel are best able to provide me accurate information about the profits the Conglomerate can offer.

I've never been so happy to see the end of a party, which says something, considering my reputation. The gutter press used to stalk me, assured of getting something juicy for the midnight bounce if they just stuck with me. Before falling for Kai, I was known for closing down bars and spending all my creds on a last round for strangers who had become my new best friends. But that was a lifetime ago.

My brain feels a little numb, but I murmur something appropriate as Jael, Hit, Vel, and Dina bid us good night.

Constance surprises me by asking, "Do you mind if I accompany Velith? I would like to inquire about the native flora and fauna."

I hope that's all she asks about. It wouldn't surprise me if she took it into her processor to ask about the elevated heat levels she recorded in Devri, who wasn't in attendance at the party tonight. I try to imagine Vel's reaction.

"No, that's fine if Vel doesn't mind." I glance at the bounty hunter.

He seems willing, if not eager, to put up with Constance, so I give my blessing to their collaboration with a nod. March shoves me into our adjoining quarters without ceremony, then demands, "You got an implant? Do you have any idea what they'll do if they find out? Are you out of your mind?"

"They won't if you keep your voice down," I mutter.

He waves that away. "That's the stupidest, riskiest . . ."

"Sneakiest?" I offer. He gives me a look, and I go on, "Why do you care anyway? I thought you just wanted to get away from me."

"I don't want anything to happen to you. You're mine." The answer slips out from somewhere deep . . . because he looks as astonished as I feel.

Possessiveness isn't love. I'm not even sure it qualifies as an emotion. But if he's feeling territorial, that's progress from nothing at all. I can work with protectiveness. It's a stepping-stone to other things.

"Am I still?" I ask quietly. "Or do you just remember that I used to be?"

His fingers flex at his sides, but I don't feel threatened. It's a restless, searching movement. Belatedly, I notice that he shaved for the party, so his jaw is smooth and strong. I fight the urge to close the distance between us and walk my fingertips across to his mouth. Once, I wouldn't have thought twice about yielding to the impulse, but he's a new animal now, struggling between the man he was and the one I want him to be again.

I hope he wants it, too, at some level. If I believed in

Adele's goddess, I might even pray over it. He means that much to me.

"Mine," he repeats, deep and low. "Sometimes I feel that you're woven into my bones. There's a resonance when I look at you, as if from a part of me that's missing . . . and it won't let me walk away, not even when I want to."

"So you're in this?" I can't hide the tremor in my voice. I don't even try. "You're not going to Nicuan when this is over. To live like a king?"

He shakes his head slowly. "Not unless you'll be my queen."

"Well, I do look better than anticipated in the ceremonial robes."

March smiles. He's not back, not entirely. He's on the cusp, I think, and his recovery will depend on so many factors that it boggles the mind to try to factor them. But for the first time, I feel a glimmer of real hope.

"You want to tell me what had you so twisted up at the party?"

My expression triggered the mental touch, I realize. He saw my face, and he went in instinctively, as he'd always done, when he realized there was something wrong. I touch him on a reflexive level, somewhere beyond conscious thought, and that's how I'll save him, too.

"Do you think you could stand to hold me?" I make the request nakedly, as I would never have done before. But I've made peace with needing him, and right now, I need his heat and strength more than ever before.

I'm not insulted when he has to think about it. "If you don't make any sudden moves, it should be all right."

I tell myself I'm not worried about this at all. He'd never hurt me. After all, he's had ample opportunity. "Then let's go to bed."

With only a slight hesitation, he takes my hand and leads me through to the bed. I'm painfully grateful to have even this much of him back. This is where secrets are shared and empires crumble, not in secret meetings but in darkened bedchambers.

"Jax," he murmurs, and it sounds like an endearment.

"Yeah?"

"Can you find another way? I don't think I can handle the frustration."

He's talking about how I said I intend to tease him to jump-start his emotional responses. I still think it's a good idea, but he knows how he feels better than I do. If he says he can't handle it, I'll find another path.

"Sure."

I don't undress all the way. Earlier, I meant it when I said no sex until he could say he loved me and mean it, but I won't torment him on purpose since he's asked me not to. When we're both in our underclothes, we slide beneath the blankets. He pulls me to him slowly, and I stay still, unsure of how much movement he can tolerate without feeling threatened. Mentally, he may be certain I pose no danger to him, but that won't stop his reflexes from kicking in if I hit the wrong trigger.

His arms feel strong and sure. My breath comes out in a soft sigh as his familiar scent washes over me. I close my eyes and begin a quiet recitation of what I overheard. March listens in silence.

"So," I conclude, "it sounded like they might be planning to kill me. But they never said that outright. All I know for sure? Something bad is going down in two days."

"I wish I could get you the hell out of here," he mutters.

I smile, wistful. "Me, too. But that's not an option." I sum up what Tarn said in his message earlier. God, it feels good to share stuff with him again.

Beside me, he tenses. "Mary. This isn't going to be enough, Jax. Whatever Tarn thinks or hopes, the Ithtorians as allies are not going to warn off regular raiders, let alone the Syndicate or Farwan loyalists. They might give pause to the Morgut, but frankly we don't have any guarantee of that either. We should be out there, marshaling our forces, not wallowing in diplomatic bullshit."

"That's the soldier in you talking."

"Baby, I'm *mostly* soldier, even on my best day. I've spent too many turns mired in mud and blood for it to be otherwise. If you wanted a sweet talker, you should have looked elsewhere." His hands smooth over my head, investigating the pins that keep my hair in place. He pulls them out, one by one, in a gesture that's silently proprietary.

I grin. "As I recall, I tried. You would've killed Hon if I'd gone through with it."

There's no humor in his voice. "Without a doubt."

There's surely something wrong with me because I enjoy a purely atavistic thrill from that certainty. He'd kill for me, no question. And I *like* it.

We drift off with no solutions between us, and that's all right. The warmth feels heavenly, as if I can face anything with him beside me. For the first time since I found him sitting in that dark room, I feel like he might be coming back to me. After tomorrow's merchant summit, I'll play some more of Mair's logs. Using the clues she left behind, almost as if she knew I'd need them, I'll help him find the way back.

In the silence of my head, I say: *I love you, March. Always.*

Though I don't realize I've drifted from waking to sleep, I must have because the world turns to darkness and fire. I can't breathe, lungs burning with oxygen deprivation.

I wake with both his hands wrapped around my throat.

CHAPTER 17

His eyes look weird and wild, too much shine.

I struggle. The fragile flesh at my throat starts to give way, and black spots dot my vision. I buck upward and kick out, but fighting back only seems to make him more determined to kill me. He doesn't realize it's me. In his head, he awoke with an enemy in his bed, but that won't stop my lights from going out for good.

I go limp and, with the last scraps of coherence, try to imagine touching his mind as he does mine. Red washes over me, as if I've done it, but it could be because I'm dying. But no, rage and turmoil accompanies the mental touch. That's not how I feel. I'm scared shitless. I can't speak, clawing at his hands in movements that gradually slow.

March, no. Stop.

His hands loosen. Did he hear me?

Through my spotty vision, I can see when his self-awareness returns. With a sound sharp with self-loathing, he springs away from me, poised like a wild animal unsure how it wound up in human skin. I roll off the bed on the other side onto my knees while pulling air into my tortured throat. My forehead drifts down to the cool mattress, resting while I luxuriate in the ability to breathe. Though he warned me, I feel shell-shocked—and if I'm honest—a little betrayed. I thought there was something between us, something so deep that it would safeguard me from this kind of damage.

My head swims, so I stay down for a little while, waiting for the fuzzy feeling to fade. I'm also waiting for March to say something, but what the hell covers a moment like this? "Sorry" seems a bit slim somehow. The most he could do is say "I told you so," which would only make things worse. I hate admitting he was right.

He *could* kill me in his sleep.

I don't know how to comfort him, or if I *can*. Hell, I could use some reassurance myself. I don't know what I would have said, but when I look up, the door that connects his room to mine is sliding shut. Part of me wants to run after him and demand . . . something—and another part is glad there's now a door between us. *Please don't let this become a precedent.* Him walking away and me letting him.

Once the shock wears off, I stagger to my feet, cursing my own ignorance. I'm flying on instinct here, and it obviously doesn't replace experience. March needs a fully trained Psi adept to help him, and maybe a professional psych, too, but he doesn't like the latter any more than I do, and we don't have much chance of finding the former.

This probably undid any progress we might have made. Now he'll go back to believing he's broken beyond all hope of repair and counting down the minutes until he can walk away for good. He might even be bouncing messages to his merc buddies right now, feeling out the situation on Nicu.

I check the time and find that it's hours before daylight. Unlikely that I'll get back to sleep, so I pad out to the living area, where I find Constance jacked into the terminal. She must have finished with Vel and returned to our suite at some point. Motion sensors kick her out of sleep mode, and her eyes open to regard me with the uncanny alertness that reminds me she's not human.

"Do you require assistance, Sirantha Jax?"

"Maybe." My throat throbs.

I pad back to the bedroom to snag the thin blanket, then return to curl up on the sloping settee thing. Wrapping up helps a little, driving back an internal chill that says I've lost him more surely than when he stayed on Lachion to fight. In the half-light, my gaze fixes on my PA, but I don't really see her.

There's enough left of the old March that he'll want to make sure he never hurts me again, even if that takes putting light-years between us. And I won't chase him. Once he walks away, it'll be for good; I don't give second chances. Kai would have said that once crossed, I'm as forgiving as the wall you hit at two hundred kilometers an hour.

He'd have been smiling when he said it, of course. He knew my faults—and loved me anyway—but there was a thread of steel in him. He put up with a lot from me, but I always knew exactly how far I could push him. A steely glint would come into his green eyes when I passed the point, and he'd say, "Are you no longer happy with me, Siri? Forget the minor stuff. Are you *unhappy*?"

I knew what he meant by that. If I was miserable on a grand scale, then we would have reached our expiration date as a couple. The primary thing I learned from Kai was the importance of free will outweighing hollow promises. I really believe if I had ever said to him, "Yes, I'm unhappy" and meant it as more than a complaint about some small annoyance, he would have opened his hands and set me free, no matter how he felt about the state of our relationship. That was the magic of him . . . and the madness.

It's difficult to live with someone like that. Sometimes he felt like a wisp of light that I had no hope of holding. I could only watch the shine glide along my skin, knowing it was destined to disappear.

Unless I want the same thing to happen with March, I have to find some way to bring him back. I'm *tired* of losing people. It's not normal for a jumper. We're the ones who live hard and die young.

Right now, that sounds pretty damn tempting.

I miss grimspace, but it's a bitch mistress. Each time we jump, navigators are exposed to extreme conditions that fry the brain slowly. Even with those inherent risks, the way I feel right now, a good, hard jump would be the best thing for me.

I've been taking my injections, so my bones have shored up, but when I reach critical mass, there's no telling how the weird repairs will affect my body. It pulls vital components from other systems to rejuvenate grimspace damage to my brain. That's how I wound up with a bone deficiency in the first place. Next time, it could ravage my heart or my lungs, and I'd die too fast for a transplant. Without a regulator to ensure a minor system is tapped, there's no guarantee I can survive even one jump.

I feel that loss every minute of every day. If I compartmentalize it, if I don't let it drive me crazy, well, that's the best I can do. But the longing never goes away. I want it like my next breath. But I have to focus on stupid shit like diplomacy when I want to start screaming.

Constance interrupts the sad loop of my thoughts. "You said you might require my assistance. What service may I render?"

I have hours before I'm expected at the merchant summit. "Would you play the next entry in Mair's journal?"

"Accessing."

Closing my eyes, I wait for the familiar rasp of the dead woman's voice.

"We lost Tanze today." The words come stark and unadorned. I can hear the grief in Mair's voice. Here in the dark, it's more than eerie, as if she's reaching for me from the other side. Adele would probably say there's something of Mary's grace in the technology that allows me to hear Mair's words after her death.

"One of the diggers blew, taking out half the supports . . . and Tanze. It's going to take months to get things running again. Sometimes I wonder if it's worth it. That boy of mine has been useless since his wife died, but I have hopes for the girl. Men." She makes an exasperated sound.

"I don't know why I bother sometimes. Just like that mean, ungrateful bastard. If I didn't know Tanze wanted me to try and save him, I'd have him shot. Never met anybody so difficult and hardheaded." Amusement laces her voice, but then her tone drops lower, as if she's confiding something to her journal that she doesn't ever want anyone to hear. "But I hate how much I'm hurting him. Breaking him down and rebuilding from the ground up is the only way to go, but he doesn't understand why at all. I can see it in his eyes, and he's scared to death."

Breaking him down? She means mentally, right? She didn't hurt him, did she? Then I remember March saying he spent the first three months tied. If I have to treat him as a dangerous criminal, tie him up and torture him in order to reshape his mind, I'm not sure I can. The very idea makes me queasy.

Surely there's another way.

Though it's probably a long shot, I ask, "Do you know anything about the way Mair treated March when he first arrived on Lachion?"

Constance shakes her head without even searching her data banks. "Unfortunately, my knowledge of that time is limited to the information Mair chose to input by various means. I much prefer my current incarnation."

I make myself smile though I'm not sure if she can see me. "Glad to hear it."

"Would you like me to play another entry?"

Pulling my knees to my chest, I nod, grateful for her company. "Play as many as you can before daylight. Maybe Mair left something that will help us."

The voice of the dead woman fills the darkness.

CHAPTER 18

[Timestamp: 23:04, 114.55.980]

It's been a month since Tanze died. I'm going to ramble a bit here because I can't grieve in front of anyone without showing weakness, and I'm not allowed to be weak. But here in my room, surely I can be permitted a few moments to remember my best friend. I can be a scattered old woman whose best turns are behind her.

Tanze. I didn't realize how much I'd come to count on her. In the past few months, she was more help than Jor. I wonder if people would have accepted her as my successor if she'd lived. They might have challenged her, but I'd have put any number of credits on her fighting.

When that ship stranded her here, it was the best thing that ever happened to us. Jor found her sitting at one of the automated hangars and brought her home like she was a stray. It was rough on her at first. We aren't always friendly to outsiders, especially not with people muttering how her people came at us during the Axis Wars. I just wish I'd told her how much I came to appreciate her over the turns. Maybe I did that when I adopted her formally as my own, I don't know. I'd like to think she knew at some level. It's just not right for an old woman to outlive the people she loves.

I'm trying not to show how much I miss her. The clan expects me to be the tough-as-nails old bird, so I deliver, but it's wearing me out. In the mornings, my joints hurt more than they used to, and meditation only goes so far. I can't turn the pain off anymore, not even by directing my chi. I can only dull the ache.

Saul tells me there's nothing he can do either. This old body is just wearing out, and we don't use Rejuvenex, for obvious reasons. Besides, I don't want to see 150. I'm plenty old enough.

Keri is coming along nicely, though. I'm glad to see she's inherited some of my steel. I know she misses her mother—and Tanze, who was like a surrogate to her—but she's bearing up well. Her lessons are coming along, but I have to keep shooing the little rat away from where we keep our resident madman.

She seems to think she can save him, but I'm not letting March near her. He's dangerous, and I don't know if he'd hesitate over killing a kid. I haven't made nearly enough progress with him to risk letting him loose among the rest of the clan. Frankly, if it wasn't for the fact that I promised Tanze, I'd have given up on him.

He's got a strong mind, which just makes it harder to break him down. The barriers he has in place are all but impossible to get through—and it hurts me as much as him when I manage it. People sure steer clear when the screaming starts.

The irony? It's enhancing my rep. Word has gotten out that I've taken a hostage, and I'm torturing him for fun during my free time. The other clans are starting to contact me, putting out feelers to try and discover who we're holding. By the time I'm finished, they'll think I'm ruthless enough to do almost anything.

That can only shore up our position here. It's been a constant struggle since we lost production in the mine. The Gunnars are snapping at our heels and the McCulloughs are right behind them. Just thinking about it all makes me so tired, I'm tempted to head for the caves, slit my wrists, and wait for something to eat me.

I won't do that to Keri until I'm sure she's strong enough to take over, though. Mama didn't raise any quitters, or I wouldn't still be here, fighting on. Especially not when my only child seems to have given up. I'm worried about Jor, no lie. Sometimes I think he's aiming to follow Janel into the grave.

Sometimes I ask myself if the freedom is worth it. There are so many dangers. We could pull up stakes and move, join an easier colony. But then we'd have people telling us what we can and can't do, making us follow their rules. I never did well with that, which is why I wound up here in the first place.

I guess I feel like I'd be insulting the memory of everybody who died, fertilizing this place with our blood and bone, while we tried to eke out a living. Now we've sunk our roots deep, and maybe we're not altogether safe, but who can say they are? Even beneath the titian skies of Gehenna, there are rapists and robbers within the dome, monsters in human skin. At least ours come clearly marked with fangs and claws.

Ah, frag me, I'm tired. I need to sleep. I have to tackle March first thing. More in the morning.

[end session]

[Timestamp: 12:47, 115.55.980]

Brutal. That's the only word I can find to describe what just happened. My head feels like somebody hit me with a hammer, but honest to Mary, I'm lucky that son of a bitch didn't kill me. He surely tried.

[Rustling sounds, dictation pauses]

I never knew anybody who could do that, but . . . untrained Psi are rare. And he's the strongest I've ever met, maybe even a level ten. It wouldn't surprise me a bit if he's killed with a pure rush of power straight through the brain. Started a fatal aneurysm. The first thing I need to do is check that.

I don't want to neuter him entirely, but I can't leave him with *that* ability. It's too easy, too tempting. If he wants to kill, he should be forced to use a weapon.

It felt *damn* good to turn the tables on him. When he

went for me, it opened him up, and I went in hard. I hope that taught him once and for all that if he hurts me, I'll give it back a hundred times over. He was still screaming when I left.

At the same time, I feel like I just kicked a dog that doesn't know anything more than being kicked. Once you push an animal past a certain point, it can't be saved. All it knows is pain and rage. It doesn't know any other way to respond; it's been burned into its brain. I'm just not sure if that's the case with March.

Maybe I can teach him something else. Maybe I can rewire him from the ground up. But I won't succeed through hurting him, I know that much.

This morning, when I checked the bounce, I found a copy of his file from a merc outfit on Nicu Tertius. I asked for that weeks ago, but the satellite relays are none too good out here. Most times I don't mind the isolation . . . that's exactly why we're here.

March apparently served two tours with them before starting his own company. He's known to be a ruthless bastard who takes the jobs nobody else wants. His men don't have a high survival rate, but those who do walk get paid like conquering kings, so there's no shortage of men looking to sign on with him.

Why am I working so hard on this? Apart from that promise to Tanze, frag me if I know. Just . . . the more he fights me, the more I want to win. I guess I'm as stubborn as he is. He's a challenge I won't walk away from unless I have no other choice.

I'll say this, though. If I can't win, then he'll have to be put down. Power like his, unchecked by care or compassion, just can't run free. I hate to agree with the Corp, as Farwan tends to be full of self-important tight-asses, but at least their Psi program prevents the creation of monsters like this.

When I went to him, I caught Keri on the verge of going inside. If she wasn't such a huge pain in my ass, I'd be proud of her determination to get what she wants. The little rat must've been spying because she had my security codes. I changed those and shooed her off to run some drills. Intuition tells me the future lies with her, not her father, so I can't let some lunatic merc cut her off at the knees before she's barely begun.

Mary, I love that girl, but I'm too old to have the raising of her. I try not to resent Jor for the way he's abdicated all his responsibilities. I know he's grieving, but I want to kick his ass. The only thing stopping me? He'd just let me with a hangdog look, then go back to staring at old vids, while chewing on his cigar. There are quiet ways to die where the body just doesn't notice that the heart is gone, I guess.

Well, whether I like it or not, I have work to do. If I don't keep this clan going, nobody will.

[end session]

[Timestamp: 22:55, 125.55.980]

Connections are everything. Without them, the system stops working. When too many connections break, the center cannot hold.

I've never been this tired in all my life.

I broke a man today.

It's a terrible thing, and I won't know for months yet whether there's any putting him back together. I've never done the like to any living thing, and I wish there had been some other way, but if there was, I couldn't find it. I couldn't fix what was broken without smashing him into pieces and starting from the ground up.

My master would've been able to find another way, but so much of what he knew was lost. I wasn't his best student, just the most determined. If any of the others survived, I haven't heard.

Maybe with its demons, Lachion is the only thing that kept me safe all these years, out of Farwan's reach. If they don't understand it, they want to study it, and once they figure it out, they sell it. I'd rather face a caveful of Teras than a squad of gray men. At least with the monsters, I understand what drives them.

I wish I could say the same of my son. There's no helping him, I think. I have to accept that and keep moving toward the goal.

Today, March wept like a baby in my arms, and that was the worst of it. A man like him would hate this worse than dying if he could see it through my eyes. I have to hope that pushing through the darkness will bring us both into light, or I'll never be able to live with what I've done.

There's so much darkness in him to navigate. Never saw any Psi who survived to maturity without learning to shield. For so many years, he's been in other people's heads, their dirt and dishonesty clinging to him so that he can't get clean of it.

But now that there's nothing left of him, I can pass through and repair that which is broken. I can help him become the man he should have been. It won't be easy, but I won't give up either; it's too late for that. I've seen too much of what drove him on.

What my old master said is true: love can make us do dreadful things.

[end session]

[Timestamp: 2:17, 154.56.980]

I fixed him. I wasn't sure until I was put through an awful crucible. May Mary never test me so again.

Yesterday, I let him move around. We spoke instead of battled. There was no anger in him. He seemed calm, almost gentle. When I tested him mentally, I found his Psi abilities intact, but he appeared free of the taint.

The mind is like a world unto itself, built from oscillations of memory and shards of self. When someone is damaged, they need to be fixed. My old master would call it Psi-surgery. He'd also have beat me within an inch of my life for doing it free hand. But I managed it. I excised the darkness and reconnected the emotional links that make him human.

And it's a damn good thing.

You see, Keri succeeded in seeing the prisoner today. She said she was working on her forms; but before her trainer realized she was gone, the little rat had slipped into March's cell.

Changing the codes didn't do me any good. The kid can't stand secrets, and she has a way of ferreting out whatever she wants to know. The alarm sounded on my comm when she went in. I've never been so scared in all my life as when I ran to save her. The idea he had a hostage, an innocent who could be made to pay for what I'd done to him, made me sick. I couldn't have run any faster from death itself.

By the time I got there, she'd undone his restraints. I froze in the doorway, watching. I knew I couldn't let him suspect she was important to me. I raised my mental shields, vowing quietly to give him nothing.

"Who are you?"

The stupid girl smiled at him, all big eyes and elbows. "Keri. Who're you?"

"Your grandmother's prisoner."

Well, I thought she'd shoot me herself.

Keri never did respect my authority. I expect she never will. She demanded to know what he'd done to deserve it, and I found it impossible to explain.

I looked him straight in the eye. "If I let you leave this room, will you swear yourself to me and mine?"

"I will." There was no shadow in him. He actually smiled. Maybe he doesn't remember the worst of it anymore. Mary knows, I tried to blur that part.

I don't know what the future holds, but I think I did what was needful. He's one of mine now.

[end session]

CHAPTER 19

At dawn, I stand before the window, looking out over the capital city. Constance sits quietly behind me; she's a restful companion. We've come to the end of the references to March in Mair's journals. I feel oddly as if I've passed straight through her soul and emerged on the other side, still *me*, but inexplicably altered as well.

Ithiss-Tor is a study in contrasts. Cities are built aboveground, but research facilities burrow deep into the ground, presumably to hide technological advances from prying eyes. Commerce and politics are the chief interests here, so I suppose it's fitting that we're about to combine the two.

I turn from the window and head for the bedroom, trying not to think about what I learned about March. Trying not to think about how much hell he's already been through. What was it like for him after he left last night? Is he punishing himself, or is he just angry that I didn't listen to his warnings? Right now I'm not sure if he has the capacity for remorse. His mind feels alien to me, full of rage and choked aggression.

Mentally, I try to shift gears. I need to think about the next meeting. Every day we move a little closer to signing the deal. Astonishingly enough, I'm doing well, impressing them with my regard for their customs. Ramona will be *so* pissed when I succeed. I won't let myself think about the consequences of failure.

After a quick san-shower, I examine my reflection in the glass. The scars offer nothing new, but I'm going to have to do something about the marks forming on my neck. Basic cosmetics won't be sufficient to cover them, and I don't dare alter my costume at this juncture. The Ithtorians are accustomed to seeing me in the gold robe, and I'll admit to a certain superstitious attachment. Things have gone so well thus far that I don't want to jinx the success by switching my wardrobe. But that leaves me needing to do something with my neck.

Before I can rethink it, I pick up the comm and beep Vel. He answers on the third chime, and I say, "Did I wake you?"

"No, Sirantha. I have been awake for some hours. What can I do for you?"

Points to him for knowing I didn't call him just to chat. "Could you come see me, please? We'll talk about it then."

"With pleasure." He disconnects without further conversation.

Maybe I'm paranoid, but I don't think this issue needs to be broadcast on the wireless. The Ithtorians could easily intercept and have it translated. I don't want this getting out. Good or bad, what happens in my bedroom stays there.

Except for the time that private vid wound up on the midnight bounce, but I had *nothing* to do with the distribution. If I'd been sober, I wouldn't even have let the guy record us. That was turns—and scars—ago, however.

Regular scans assure me my quarters are clean, at least, so I wait for Vel. It's light enough now that we don't need the artificial lamps. He'll know how to handle this.

He arrives quickly, thank Mary, and I rise to greet him. I've internalized this movement; the *wa* has become second nature, but it gives him pause. Before speaking, he responds in kind.

I wish I could better read the precise angle of his head, the length he holds the pose. Thousands of meanings can be concealed in that gesture, but I'm a novice. It will take me turns to gain more than rudimentary proficiency. I can detect insults more easily than the layered meanings. After all, I focused my training there, so I'll know if someone was offering sincere courtesy or false respect.

As he straightens, his mandible moves in some subtle meaning. "Your manners have become . . . exquisite, Sirantha. The shading you gave that *wa* . . . it was poetic."

Surprise washes over me as I register the compliment. "Really? What did I say?"

"In the time after the broken sunrise, brown bird looks to white wave. The sky does not touch, all songs have ceased. It is far and lorn."

"I said all that with my *wa*?" I ask, astonished.

He confirms with an inclination of his head. "Very . . . nuanced."

"Ithtorian must be . . . such a beautiful language." For the first time, I wish I had a mind capable of interpreting the sounds without a chip, matching them to images and symbols on my own.

"It can be. I gather this is a matter of some urgency?" he says quietly.

"Yes." I show him my throat. "I need you to figure out a way to make this into a show of strength. I can't show up with bruises forming on my neck. If I understand your people correctly, it will mark me as fragile, which weakens my bargaining position."

Vel approaches me, tilting my head with one claw. "March did this?" His neutral tone reveals nothing.

"He didn't mean to." How disgusting. I sound like a woman defending the man who beats her. "He wasn't in his right mind."

"Nonetheless, all the face you have built up since arriving would be completely eradicated, if it were known that you allowed a male to damage your person. Here, it is the *males* who have their heads torn off by their mates. Occasionally, anyway."

Did he just make a joke? It's hard for me to tell. His humor tends to be so subtle and dry that if I blink, I miss it.

"So what do we do?"

He turns my face this way and that, examining the injury. "No structural damage, merely superficial discoloration." I smile at the way he makes me sound like an old corrugated shed, discolored by exposure to the elements. "If we summon Doc to treat you, someone will report it. Likewise, if you go to the ship."

I shrug. "He doesn't have anything to make bruises

magically disappear anyway. That hasn't been high on our list of ailments to address . . . for obvious reasons."

Vel drops his hand from me. "In this situation, there is only one thing we can do."

"And that is?"

"Paint you."

Refusing to explain, he leaves to gather supplies presumably related to his odd pronouncement. After his return, he begins by mixing the ink. The color turns a deep forest green, rich and dark. It even smells a bit like a wood after dark, pungent but fresh, and clean. I freeze when he produces the device with needles jutting from it.

"Are you sure this is a good idea? Are you sure this is even *safe*?"

"It will not harm you," he assures me. "This process will merely produce a personal adornment I believe you call a tattoo. You can have it removed later if you prefer, but it is imperative that we cover this injury before the summit, and this is the only means that my people will find comprehensible."

As he cleans the needles, I back up a step. "I could . . . wear a scarf."

"Something wrapped about your throat would imply you felt threatened and saw the need to protect your vulnerable points. No, this is best. It will conceal your injury, and choosing green—the color of commerce—will be taken as a statement regarding your capacity to create prosperity. At the merchant summit, they will respect such a show of strength and confidence."

Well, when you put it that way, it *does* sound impressive. I just wish it didn't involve needles in my throat. But I said whatever it took, I'd make this happen, so I can't back down now.

I have one final, perfunctory objection, even though I've made up my mind to accept the inevitable. "You don't have to do the acid wash on my skin, do you?" I really don't want that damaged any more than it already is.

Vel glances at me, his faceted eyes glittering in the morning light. "No, Sirantha. Unlike our chitin, your skin will take the color without that step."

"What will the design look like?"

In answer, he sets down the equipment he's prepping and moves to the terminal. Constance watches us wordlessly. Vel reaches around her and taps away, eventually pulling up a hauntingly lovely pattern with green as its primary color. It looks like the coppery patina of aged metal, interspersed with the delicate strength of growing things.

"That's lovely. Who first designed it?" Random question, born of admiration.

But his answer surprises me. "I did." He pauses, studying the screen with an intensity I cannot interpret. "I was not always a bounty hunter. Over the years, I have lived many lives. Most beings do."

There's a strange profundity in that. I remember Mair's journal entries and wonder where she came from, what she was like as a young woman. What drove her from the only home she ever knew to settle on Lachion? What made her stay when she realized it wouldn't be as easy as they might have hoped when the first ships arrived? Nothing ever turns out entirely as we expect.

Melancholy brushes me with its dove gray wings. I touch my throat, imagining Vel's pattern on my skin. Oddly, I'm not even reluctant anymore; the rightness of it is undeniable. We'll turn this setback into an asset, and I will come away better for facing my fear.

"Let's do it," I say softly. "Before the light leaves us behind."

After I've said that, I realize it was a strange way to express my concern for the passage of time. What the hell is that chip doing in my brain? Rearranging the way I use language, among other things. I can only hope it doesn't do anything worse. I trusted Vel blindly with the installation, just as I'm doing now.

"Lie back then. I added a mild topical anesthetic to the mix," he adds as he fills a cartridge with the dark green ink. "You won't feel a thing."

Closing my eyes, I turn myself over to him completely.

CHAPTER 20

At the merchant summit, I feel like a queen.

True, I wear the crown around my throat instead of atop my head, but I think the Ithtorians take the point. When I first enter the chamber, they murmur at the sight of me. I wish I was better at reading their body language, but I take comfort in the fact that there's no human more schooled in it than me. So in this sense at least, I *am* the best humanity has to offer.

"It is a bold move," I hear someone saying.

"She is a cunning strategist," another agrees.

"And she understands our ways better than I would have imagined. Perhaps they are not all tree-dwelling savages."

"Do you think she understands what it means?"

"I can only presume Il-Nok explained before he made the offer."

Well, I *think* he did. But now that I cast back, I can only remember discussing that it would be taken as a show of strength. If it has any other significance, we didn't discuss it. Nonetheless, I would have agreed to cover up the damage. As he said, it was the best solution.

"Who knows what that dog will do?" another replies. "His choice of partner indicates that he is no better than the lunatics we send to the mines."

I'd love to get a look at the mines, which serve both as a source of revenue and a penal colony. There are deposits so deep and difficult to reach that the owners are reluctant to risk their costly droids in the hope of tapping them. That's where the mad labor force comes in.

If an Ithtorian refuses to conform to behavioral expectations, that's where he or she ends up. Talk about peer pressure. That's a system I can't get behind; I think people can be trusted to know what makes them unhappy. Maybe we don't always know what we want exactly, but we can usually say what we don't with a fair amount of specificity. No wonder Vel left.

He was right about something else, too. I didn't feel more than pressure while he worked on me, and the resultant tattoo is beautiful and delicate, covering the mark of March's hands with the green chain. My skin itches a little, but I can resist the urge to scratch, which would inflame the area and take away from my aura of confidence. Shoulders squared, I survey the room.

Another snippet of conversation comes to me. "From what she said in the earlier summit, we can expect a one-to-one exchange rate. That is, we will receive a full credit for every karel we invest outworld, and receive a full karel for every credit we convert back."

"That is more than fair. I am especially interested in hearing about the opportunities for droid export. I just bought 40 percent into a research consortium."

"Is that the one they started under Mount Eyetooth?"

Mount Eyetooth? I remind myself that the chip does pretty well, conveying approximate meanings from a dissimilar language. I don't recognize these merchants, but many of them have been watching my performance from a distance for several days. Now they will have a chance to inquire about the new markets I've promised them. This may actually turn out to be more difficult than Karom's interrogation, given my lack of background in business.

From my left, Constance slides a thin datapad into my hand. "I have been working on this all night. It contains projected figures related to Ithtorian exports that should be accurate to the tenth decimal place. I believe it will enhance your presentation."

I skim the numbers, then commit them to memory, before handing it back. "To say the least. You're the best."

As always, she says modestly, "I am here to help."

Sharis hastens over to greet us. He seems surprised by the necklace imprinted on my skin, but he covers it by executing a respectful *wa*. I return the courtesy before we attempt to communicate aloud, wondering what the minutiae of my movement said to him. Vel could tell me, but I don't even want Sharis, who seems to be on our side, to realize how much I know. It's better if they underestimate me.

"It is my great pleasure to greet you this morning," Sharis says. I pretend not to understand, allowing Vel to translate. Then the councilor goes on, "You have greatly impressed the council, and I am cautiously optimistic about our chances when this matter is put to a vote."

Once more, I pause before making my response. I'll have to be careful not to answer before Vel is done speaking. It's slightly disconcerting to hear everything twice before I can answer, but I need to get used to it.

"When is the vote?" I ask.

"The day after tomorrow."

Something about that date niggles at me, but before I can put the pieces together, Devri joins us. He makes his *wa* to me with a grace that seems oddly suggestive. I don't know why I think that, except for the arch of his spine and the proximity at which he chooses to make it. When Devri straightens, his head very nearly brushes my chin.

My gaze flicks to Vel, and, by his tension as he returns Devri's bow, I have the impression he agrees. I won't be able to confirm until later, but I make a mental note to do so. We can watch the logs if we need to. Constance is recording this session with her ocular cam. Maybe I need to ask Vel about the meaning of the hot spots on Devri's anatomy, too. I hadn't wanted to bring it up, but it might be a factor we need to plan for.

In lieu of a more formal verbal greeting, Devri says, "I like your neck paint."

At least, that's the best translation my chip can offer. Vel puts it slightly differently. "Our color looks lovely on your skin."

Is that a mere compliment? Looking to Vel for guidance will lessen my personal strength, so I simply reply, "I appreciate your kindness."

Should be safe enough.

"I am hosting a private dinner party this evening," Devri continues. "I would be honored if you would attend as my special guest. I have a number of associates who wish to make your acquaintance."

I watch Vel as he translates, hoping he'll give me some sign of whether he thinks I should accept the invitation. Unfortunately, any indication I could detect would certainly alert Sharis and Devri as well. They are more sensitive to subtle movements.

Sharis agrees, "I would be honored to see you there."

"May I bring Vel and Constance?" If it's not a formal state occasion, then I don't need the honor guard that escorted me down here. "And my bodyguard?" I add reluctantly. Jael will most likely insist.

Earlier, March didn't look at me, not even once. He didn't ask how I was. He didn't even seem to see me.

And as soon as they walked me into the hall, Hit, Dina, and Jael all departed. They hate the uniform they have to wear for the sake of appearances, and none of them enjoys being surrounded by Bugs. Sometimes I feel like I'm going to lose all my friends over this alliance. I can't explain the feeling, but since we arrived, I feel cut off from the old, easy camaraderie, like I'm not one of them anymore.

Maybe they feel like *I've* changed. The old Jax wouldn't have had the patience for this posturing. She'd have told the Ithtorians, *Here I am. Vote now. If you don't want to ally with us, go frag yourselves.* But the old Jax never saw anything as more important than herself either—except possibly Kai. However, the old Jax was also honest to a fault. So maybe they think diplomacy is making less of me, as it's teaching me to dissemble.

"Certainly," Devri says.

Fantastic. More time on display. More time watching my every move and focusing on not showing my teeth. I hear myself answering on automatic. "Then we would be delighted."

We must have gotten here a touch early because the rest of the council is just arriving. Sartha comes in behind Mako and Karom. I don't know what Vel said to her last night, but she doesn't even look at him. Something in her body language tells me she's sad. I don't know why that would be the case, though. Vel told me his people don't form emotional bonds as we know them, so whatever was supposed to happen between them—and didn't when he left—she could only have been disappointed that one of her schemes didn't come to fruition. Doubtless I'm projecting a human response to her based on what I know of their history.

Vel touches my bare arm, a gentle reminder that we need to move. Before the Grand Administrator arrives, which signifies her readiness to begin, we array ourselves in a semicircle around her empty seat. Otlili never lets her people forget, even in her absence, that she possesses all the power. I admire that even if I can sense her antipathy.

Ten minutes later, she deigns to join us. Her honor guard is larger than usual today, a full score of low-ranking Ithtorians who walk at her back. On closer inspection, I notice they're all males.

Otlili does not bow to anyone in this room. Instead, she surveys us all with cold, glittering eyes. Her gazes linger on me, taking my measure. She has noticed the mark I bear at my throat. It feels like an empty boast now, not strength but effrontery. I feel the ice of her regard all the way down in my bones, and despair tries to follow.

In that moment, I feel sure there is no way I can prevail against her. I should confess my silent transgression before she discovers the chip on her own. My muscles quiver with the effort to remain silent.

After what seems an interminable silence, she says at last, "Let us begin."

.OPEN-TRANSMISSION.
.THE REAL SYNDICATE IS A LIE.
.HIDE-MESSAGE-ORIGIN.
.AUTO-FORWARD-ALL-NODES.

I'm nobody you've ever heard of, and if you knew me, it wouldn't matter. My face wouldn't convince you if my words don't. Nonetheless, I'm going to tell my story, and it doesn't matter if the Syndicate kills me for it. After all, they've already taken everything else.

I ran a small shipping company out of Gehenna, where it's easy to get black-market goods off world. The docking officers there expect to be bribed to look the other way, whether it's slaves, weapons, chem, or contraband tech like code breakers. I never dealt in any of that. My company specialized in textiles: nonsynth luxury items handwoven on Gehenna. It's nearly a dead art, so I could command ridiculous prices from those who liked the cache. We didn't sell in bulk, but the cost made up for low quantity.

In my father's day, Gehenna wasn't quite the smugglers' paradise it is today, but since I'd learned the business from him, I did my best to keep away from all that. I didn't interfere with other people's choices, and I hoped they'd leave me alone, too.

They didn't.

It began about ten turns back, with an ominous visit from a man in a suit. He asked why I didn't belong to the local guild and implied that I'd be sorry if I didn't pay my dues. Well, I know a protection racket when I see one, but I figured it would be smart of me to pony up a few credits in order to be left in peace.

But six months after I joined the guild, I was approached a second time. One of my fellow members needed my help. After having run afoul of the docking agents one too many times for failing to pay his bribes, he wanted to use my textile to conceal a shipment. When I asked what the cargo would be, a man visited my house in the middle of the night and left a dead rat underneath my pillow.

I got the message. The Syndicate likes good sheep who follow orders. They don't want you asking questions.

They never told me what I was to ship, so I didn't agree to it, and when the time came round again to pay dues, I refused. I wanted no part of an organization that would kill animals. I'm amused now at my naiveté.

Of course, things escalated. The Syndicate doesn't allow people to walk away, whatever propaganda they're selling now. By this time, I was married and had a daughter. She was four turns old. I didn't know then what lengths they would go to, or I would have conceded defeat. Hindsight offers such bitter clarity.

They began by trying to intimidate people not to do business with me. In some cases, it worked, and I lost revenue. The company suffered, but my weavers were loyal. Nobody else could fill the niche, so we soldiered on.

Thus, the Syndicate pulverized one of the weavers' hands. She didn't die of her wounds; but she lost her vocation, which was both an art and her greatest joy. I paid her compensation, and the company suffered more. Around this time, my spouse begged me to yield, but I was inflamed with a sense of persecution, injustice, and righteous indignation. That day, I went to the authorities with my complaints. I named names. I offered to stand witness in a trial against my tormentors. That night, my place of business burned to the ground, with my spouse and daughter inside.

If you take nothing else from my words, know that these are not the people to whom we should trust our children and our defense. They have no honor, and they worship the credit as supreme. There is no crime too heinous if there is profit in it. Monsters that wear human faces run the Syndicate. How is that better than the Ithtorians? And at least I can say the Ithtorians have done me no harm.

When my world burned, I fled Gehenna. I am now in hiding. If they wanted to, they could find me. Their resources are infinite, and I am but one voice, crying out in the dark. I believe now they let me live as an example. They think me broken. But there is no enemy so dangerous as the one with nothing left to lose.

.END-TRANSMISSION.
.THE REAL SYNDICATE IS A LIE.
.HIDE-MESSAGE-ORIGIN.
.AUTO-FORWARD-ALL-NODES.

CHAPTER 21

Thanks to Constance's figures, I don't make an ass of myself.

Her work allows me to field all their questions and sound like I know what I'm talking about. Maybe this is common for people in my position, but I feel like an enormous fraud. I don't have this information by virtue of my own efforts or intellect. I just happen to know some really brilliant people—if she can be classed as such. I'm including Vel in that assessment, of course.

But maybe that's all politicians do. Take other people's work and make it sound pretty. By the time the summit is over, I feel weary and dispirited. No surprise, given how little I slept the night before.

The chatter of excited merchants washes over me as they file past, each offering me a *wa*. I return them one by one, being careful with my movements. Soon only our party and the council remain in the hall.

To my surprise, the Grand Administrator dismisses them. "I will take the afternoon meal with the ambassador. Your translator alone may remain."

I hope I make a convincing show of puzzlement as the rest of the council files out. My acting skills aren't really that impressive, but maybe they'll suffice for a species that isn't too conversant with normal human responses. Unlike me with Vel, they didn't have a human friend they could use to enrich their understanding.

After he translates, I tell Constance, "Head for our quarters and wait there. If you can do some more work on the alliance advantages, I'd appreciate that very much."

"Acknowledged." She excuses herself with an impressive *wa* to Otlili.

I'm a little disappointed that we won't get this meal on vid so we can deconstruct it later. I'll just have to rely on Vel's memory since Otlili would never approve use of his ocular cam. Remembering the intensity of her regard when she first arrived, I try not to be nervous about this unexpected honor. I tell myself she can't know about the chip.

"We will dine in my quarters," the Grand Administrator says.

It astonishes me how she treats her escorts as if they aren't there. Despite the way their presence asserts her importance, her gaze never touches on them. It's as if they exist solely to bolster her consequence. They step aside in a rigidly choreographed maneuver that allows Vel and me to fall in behind Otlili.

I'm relieved to realize she doesn't expect to converse while we're on the move, so I can luxuriate in the rich scent of growing things. We pass through the heart of the complex, which is among the loveliest gardens I've ever seen. Exotic flowers, capped with delicate white petals, framing a pale yellow center, stand nearly two meters tall. More startling, they turn their faces toward us as we pass by.

"The Kiss of Teeth," Otlili says.

I assume she's naming the plant for me, having rightly discerned my interest. She leads us to a lift, but I'm still watching the flowers over my shoulder. They seem to be tracking us somehow. I don't know if I find their blank, blind faces lovely or creepy.

"They stand guard," Vel tells me softly. "If anyone attempted unauthorized access to the Grand Administrator's quarters, the Kiss of Teeth"—he uses her words, but I have the sense they aren't precise, much as many Ithtorian words and concepts lack a corresponding equivalent in universal—"would sound the alarm and attack the intruders."

We step into an oblong tube that seems to give slightly beneath our feet. There isn't room for her escorts, so they pause, making their *wa* to her in unison. As the lacy lift doors glide shut, I notice that the guardian plants have strange spines all down their trunks—or would that be stems? I wonder if they're strong enough to pierce a chitin shell. If they are, they'd certainly be able to eviscerate a human. I make a mental note to stay out of this part of the complex if I'm not escorted by Otlili herself.

There are no windows, giving me the sense there's not quite enough air for the three of us. I'm pressed arm to shoulder against Vel, registering his hard carapace more than I usually do. The silence grows heavy, laden with unspoken things. It seems as though we ascend for at least five minutes, but I'm willing to concede that impression might be claustrophobia talking.

Somehow I manage not to gasp as the doors open at last, revealing the palatial penthouse apartment the Grand Administrator calls home. Her idea of décor differs from mine slightly, but I admire the complex lattices and backless stools that offer the closest thing to furniture I can recognize. Otherwise, the place is full of marvels, more living chairs that have been painstakingly woven and cultivated until they take the shape their crafter desires. It bespeaks a vast patience that humanity generally does not possess.

The use of glastique—or some equivalent substance—transfixes me. Unlike my quarters, which are well swathed, light streams into this room, almost shocking in its brightness. She can see the city spread below her at all times, a 360-degree panorama. Her space hasn't been divided by doors or arches, either. Apparently, she eats, works, and rests all in one location.

"Magnificent, is it not?" She moves to the front of the apartment and gazes down at the capital as Vel translates.

I get the feeling she isn't talking about her quarters so much as the municipality sprawled beneath her feet, both figuratively and literally. Since she isn't looking at me, I risk a glance at Vel, who urges me forward by virtue of a quiet tilt of his head. So I join Otliti at the window, hoping she won't push me out of it. I don't see an operating mechanism, but that doesn't mean the pane isn't keyed to her touch.

"I am particularly impressed with the architecture." Since I'm not sure how she'll take my observation about outward steel hiding such soft, lush beauty, I decide to leave that unspoken.

According to the chip, Vel phrases my words as: "You are powerful builders."

After a moment, the difference in nuance becomes clear. In my original comment, I complimented an inanimate object. Vel switched the focus slightly, addressing its makers. With him on my side, no wonder we're doing so well. He's been making the most of everything I say, giving my words the best possible spin.

We turn from the wall of windows in unison, inspecting each other. It's most likely an inappropriate observation at this moment, but I notice that the barbs on her lower abdomen point downward, whereas the male hooks curl upward, giving me a clue regarding Ithtorian sexual positions. *Femme dominant, male on his back.* I could have done without that mental image at this moment. *Stupid unruly brain.*

For the first time, Otlili meets my gaze straight on as if daring me to make a mistake. Her eyes glimmer like polished obsidian, hard as if they have been hewn out of some ancient volcano. There is nothing of kindness or compassion in those eyes, nothing of empathy, just the weight of an immense, alien intellect. Only the fact that she must find me equally inscrutable offers any consolation.

"I do not like your kind," she says baldly. "No good has ever come when humanity lands on Ithiss-Tor." Her gaze goes to Vel. "First when he left with them, destroying so many hopes and dreams, then . . . when he returned. We come from a long, proud tradition of hunters who take what we want. I do not like parlaying with a species so weak, they lack all natural defense mechanisms. No fangs, no claws, no armor. Just hideous pink flesh." She shudders delicately. "And the way you must augment yourselves by artificial means? It disgusts me."

Now that's quite an opening salvo. I'd like to tell her to fuck off, but I count to five, manage not to show my teeth, and come up with a diplomatic reply while Vel buys me time with his unnecessary restatement. To inspire me, I remember Karl Fitzwilliam, the worst ambassador in the history of the universe.

"I understand we must seem very different to you," I offer

with what I think is admirable aplomb. "That's why this is such a valuable opportunity for both our peoples. I hope we may come from this alliance with a greater measure of understanding and appreciation." I cap the shit with a deep *wa.*

There, take that. Though it feels hideously unnatural, I don't lose my cool. Don't blow my top, or show her my teeth. Mary, but I want to get out of here. It's only been a day, and I'm dying for grimspace. With attitudes like hers, I think what I said is about as likely to happen as me discovering a cure for Jenner's Retrovirus over my morning meal, but I can only do so much. Permanent change takes time.

"Which brings me to my next point," the Grand Administrator continues. "Though I do not like your people as a whole, I admire your tactics. Your strategies have proven sound and effective, winning support where I would have imagined it impossible. Since I enjoy seeing a female in a position of power, even among lesser species, I invited you to dine. I believe we have something to discuss."

I must be careful not to show comprehension too soon, so I merely watch as she raises her arms and wings spread from her back, tissue thin and somehow sensuous, shining with ruby red and glowing gold. In the center, on each side, shines an enormous eye. I've seen similar displays before in nature, generally designed for threatening off intruders. For pure and lovely exoticism, I don't think I've ever seen anything that surpasses Otlili. I pay only half attention as Vel murmurs her words over again.

"Do we?" I ask.

Slowly the Grand Administrator brings her arms down without collapsing her wings. She crosses them over her thorax, showing me her red-tipped claws. I don't need Vel to point out her rudeness. In fact, from what I recall, her posture borders on aggressive. I find myself gazing at the eye jutting from her wings.

"Yes," she confirms. "If you do not take your ship and depart within twenty-four hours, I cannot guarantee your safety."

CHAPTER 22

As conversational gambits go, that's a hell of a way to start a meal.

I'm not sure whether I'm being warned or threatened, and she doesn't give me an opportunity to inquire. Instead, she summons an automated attendant the likes of which I've never seen. It prepares the food inside what I'd call its chest cavity, then folds outward to accommodate us as a makeshift table. We eat standing up with a minimum of conversation.

No wonder Tarn said there would be great interest in their droid technology. This could make the kitchen-mate obsolete. Of course, for humans to warm to the brand of tech, we'll need to throw in a couple of chairs, but I can see the appeal overall. Call the bot to make you dinner on the terrace while you lounge, enjoying the sunset. There will be a lot of money in this.

While musing on the commercial applications, I taste bits of this and that. I can't recognize most of the dishes served in heavy sauce. The food tastes strange and pungent, with a coppery cloy that reminds me of blood. Flesh slips down my throat, slick and rubbery. I don't like it at all, and the silence isn't helping.

I suspect she remains quiet to keep me off-balance, knowing I must be thinking about what she's said. Her tactic works like a charm; I find myself feverishly turning over the possibilities while trying not to watch how the food she devours appears to still be squirming. The Ithtorians think humans are disgusting because, among many other offensive habits, we're also carrion eaters. In our past, we've feasted on dead flesh, even if now we prefer synthetic proteins. Vel's people find that repugnant, as even now, they like their food fresh to the point of wiggling.

Finally, the interminable luncheon ends, and Otlili seems ready to elaborate on her words. But first I must thank her for the hospitality.

"You have done us great honor, and we feel privileged to be in your company."

After Vel relays my words, she acknowledges this graciously, but that's not why I'm here. She can find someone to flatter her, probably much better than me, at any hour of the day. She's the most powerful person on Ithiss-Tor, after all.

"You are to be commended for your patience," she says then. "And though I have been favorably impressed with you, ambassador, I cannot say my overall opinion of humanity has changed. My people would be irrevocably altered—lessened—should we come into regular contact with your kind. I do not particularly wish any harm would befall you, but . . ." She pauses delicately, the force of a thousand rivers powering words unspoken. "This alliance will never come to pass. I strongly recommend that you take your team and depart before the matter is put to a vote."

A threat then.

"I regret that I am unable to comply with your recommendation."

I wish now that I hadn't eaten at her table, but surely she wouldn't poison me here and now. For all she knew, I might have heeded her warning. A murder attempt in daylight seems a bit precipitous, and the Grand Administrator is not known for her impulsive nature.

She regards me for a moment from eyes that give nothing back, a dark infernal sea teeming with her clever conspiracies. "Not yet," she answers with the air of one making a final judgment. "But you will."

That sounds like a promise, but if she has her way, I won't live to regret my choice too long. I feel strange and dizzy, sick with too much unfamiliar food. Vel guides me through the courtesies in departure. I'm vaguely aware that my *wa* is not good, but if I bend too low, I might sick up on her rug. What the hell did she serve me?

I want to ask if she slipped me something, but it's not like anyone would believe me. She could deny ever having me up here. The room blurs, two of everything swimming in a bizarre array of inexplicable colors.

Once we step into the lift, Vel takes my arm, supporting me. "At least you walked out on your own two feet."

My tongue feels weird and thick. "Most people don't?"

Vel sounds grim. "Most are not invited at all. And the ones who are have a history of disappearing."

I should have known that. Why didn't I know that? I mumble something incomprehensible. The world flickers in and out like a corrupt vid file. Belatedly I realize this coincides with my blinking. So I do it three or four times just to test the theory.

His mandible works, but there's a delay, and the chip is feeding me what I think is native Rodeisian, except I don't know that language, so I can't understand anything from the weird racket in my brain. I find myself wondering if he's ever lain down like a good submissive male for Sartha. Maybe she misses the sex. Maybe that's why she's still sad he left turns ago . . . and why not, I'd miss him too if he left. But for her, it's been longer than that, actually—

Holy shit, is that a giant crab? No, that's my foot.

We're at the bottom somehow now. I don't remember riding down, and we're facing those bizarre plant soldiers again. Do they attack people for leaving without the Grand Administrator? I press my spine against the back of the lift. I'm not going past them. There's something *wrong* with those things. Their blank faces seem inexpressibly evil, like a white cloth pressed against a madman's leer.

"Come, Sirantha. Take a step for me."

I'm appalled to hear how young and scared my voice sounds. "No, please don't make me."

"This is what she wants," Vel says firmly. "She wants to undo all your work. When people see you acting like a terrified, truculent child, it makes Karom's case. Humanity is impulsive and irrational, reckless and unpredictable. You cannot gauge their future behavior based on past precedent. So I need you to walk for me. Take a step. Say nothing. I will take you to your room and look after you. This will not kill you, but you might wish you were dead before nightfall."

I rein in my irrational terror of the plants long enough to fix on something he's said. "She *did* give me something."

"A spice in that blue sauce reacts on human physiology as a powerful hallucinogen. I did not realize until after you had eaten it. I am sorry, Sirantha. I fear I have failed you. But if your mission is to succeed, I need you to take a step. Just one. Come."

"You didn't fail me." Even brain-fuggled, I know that much. I can't make myself walk past those plants. I can't. So I close my eyes and pretend they're not there. "Can you lead me?"

I might have been able to say that to March, once. Not anymore. That means Vel's the only person left I trust completely. In answer, he takes my arm. As he asked, I take a step. Then another. In comparison with the world zooming in and out of focus, the darkness feels comforting.

We're stopped only once, and Vel tells some importunate well-wisher, "The ambassador is meditating. She will converse with you later."

Glee zings through me. They won't know that humans don't generally amble around with their eyes closed as part of any spiritual regime. Still, I'm relieved when the door to my quarters glides shut behind us.

Vel guides me to the sloping settee where I listened to Mair's journals last night instead of sleeping, but I can't lie down in my ceremonial robes. I'm afraid I'm going to hurl all over them. I try to explain that, but the words come out all jumbled. After taking stock of the situation, Constance escorts me to the bedroom, where she helps me into what passes for my pajamas.

With the best of intentions, she tucks me in, but I don't want to go to bed because that'll mean being alone. So I stumble back into the living room. I try to ask how long before this wears off but the question comes out, "Jump weasel wants a dark shooter."

Well, shit. I haven't been this fragged up in turns. Hard to believe I used to do this for fun. I don't like the way the world keeps reinventing itself for my amusement, and I'm starting to feel really queasy. By fighting it instead of enjoying the show, I'm no doubt making it worse.

Vel leads me to the settee again, then kneels beside me, looking into my face. "It is going to get a *lot* worse," he tells me. "Do you understand that, Sirantha?"

I understand that his right eye is slowly sliding to the side of his head. Then it zips down to his neck and keeps going, a sly, saucy little thing that winks at me as it goes. It's hard for me to keep track of what he's saying when his face is doing that. I squeeze my eyes shut, and the pressure on my lids gives the darkness a red tinge. I feel his claws rake through my hair, unpinning the mass with Constance's help.

"I will stay with you. Do not worry," Vel says, but he sounds like someone else now, as if his voice has shifted, and if I open my eyes I would see another in his place.

Then I'm lost to fever dreams.

CHAPTER 23

I have the odd impression I've been here before.

What do they call that? *Déjà vu.*

Kai snaps his fingers to reclaim my attention. "I asked if you're ready twice now. Are you all right?"

I rub my head, which pounds like a class P drum. "I think so."

"Are you sure?" His gaze searches my face. "I know this is a long haul. Do you have a couple more jumps in you before we hit station for some R&R?"

I flash him a grin. "Absolutely. Where are we headed again?"

His fair brows go up, indicating we've been over this once. "That's it, I'm bouncing a message to command. You're not—"

"Sure I am." I catch his hand before he can call. "We're scouting for new beacons to the Csom Run, then we're checking one with a weak signal on the way back."

That sends a little shiver of pride through me. We're one of only ten teams experienced enough to repair the beacons. It's not a physical repair so much as a mental adjustment, and we've only been doing it for six months. Without an influx of our energies, linked through the nav com and filtered through me, the beacons would die. Other races help, of course—humanity doesn't do it alone.

Kai levels a long look on me. "You're acting weird, Siri."

"I'm good to go, I swear. We're in the hot zone?"

In answer, he powers up the phase drive. We've chosen a sexy two-seater this time, no messing around with medic or engineer. Our CO doesn't like it when we go off on our own, but payroll approves because they don't have to cover the extra personnel, so nobody objects formally.

I'll be spending a long time in grimspace this run. Mentally, I prepare myself for it as I jack in. Kai's already there and waiting. He welcomes me with a chaotic burst of warmth. I could swim in him like this forever. Bits of memory brush me, revealing what he treasures most. There's such sweetness in him, a candor and simplicity.

The ship shudders as we make the leap, passing into grimspace. Pleasure spikes through me, as if I'm taking a hit of my favorite chem. It sings through my veins, echoing the mad whorl of colors outside the view screen. If I had to describe it, I'd say it's like entering the heart of a dying star.

I close my eyes to the pull and listen to the beacons pulsing. They offer me their locations, and with them, the keys to the universe. From here, I can go anywhere, as long as I know what the echoes mean. Over drinks I once gave the analogy that it's like interpreting sonar for the deaf, and that's near enough.

Kai holds the ship steady, waiting for me to parse the pulses and translate them to distance in straight space. I'm looking for an echo of the Csom Run, the farthest we've ever gone. It's past the Outskirts, well beyond the borders of civilized space. Beyond the Csom Run lies the Empty Cascade. And nobody knows *what's* out there.

Got it?

We won't know for sure until we get there.

But yes, I'm all but positive I've found which beacons mark the Csom Run. We'll know when we come out the other side. Kai guides us smoothly to where we need to be. Colors burn outside the ship, immolating us in the glory of the cosmos. I luxuriate in the feeling, as I never feel more at home than when I'm right here. Leaving is always terrible, as if I've lost a part of myself that I can never get back.

At least not until the next jump.

The phase drive hums as we make the leap back. It was a smooth run, no surprises, and I'm purring with satisfaction. I unplug and check our location on the star charts, then punch the air. *The Csom Run.*

Kai's green eyes glow with the joy of our shared achievement. "We did it, Siri. Nobody's ever been out here before."

And here we sit, taking it in. Beyond the view screen, threads of red light swirl, kindling the darkness. For a moment I just watch in awed silence. We're not close enough to be imperiled, thank Mary.

"Twin planets?" I ask.

"It looks like it, but I've never seen two so close to a red giant before."

"We should log this, take some images, and get out of here."

He nods. "Agreed. Once we check out that last beacon, we can go home."

Kai handles the vid footage. The Science Corp will have a field day with this. They're studying the age at which a sun becomes a red giant, and methods to prevent the transformation. Personally, I think the credits could better be spent elsewhere, but you never know when a dying world will be willing to pay through the collective nose.

I feel sure and strong as we jump again, as if I could do this forever. Though I know that's not true—I've seen the damage grimspace has done to my colleagues—it doesn't feel like it can touch me. Without false modesty, I know I'm the greatest navigator of my time, and I love my life.

Grimspace reels me in like a lover. I soak in the delight without losing myself to it. Beacon 1476-1 needs a look, so we make our way to a spot where I can reach it. There is no distance in grimspace as we conceive of it in straight space, more points of contact from which one world leads to another. I've entertained the idea that we could access other dimensions from here, but it's not time to test my theories. Not that Kai would let me.

I wouldn't, he tells me. Humor permeates me. *We have a job to do.*

This beacon is faint and thready, on the verge of going out. Since it's one we use often, that can't happen. I reach out to it and find it's drenched in darkness. The beacon fills my head with alien images, as it always does when we touch them. Kai and the nav com keep me anchored while I work, letting the necessary power flow through me. I don't like being a conduit, but sometimes there's no choice. It doesn't hurt precisely, but I can't imagine it's helping me either.

By the time we're done, the beacon pulses strongly, back in tune with the others. To my mind, the beacons are almost like living musical instruments, full of tones and resonance that take us where we need to go. I'm tired now, so I locate the one nearest to the station. Kai responds, sensing my failing stamina.

We push through, and I'm shaking. Repair work takes a lot out of me.

The gutter press greets us like conquering heroes. Since we filed our report on the way in, they already know about the Csom Run. We pose for a few minutes, answer some questions, then it's off to the bar to celebrate. The night blurs into random faces, loud music, and too much liquor.

My head pounds as I open my eyes. The décor gives me no clue as to where I am. Bunk, wardrober, plain gray walls: it looks like any number of generic stations where I've been quartered over the turns.

A slender hand with long, artistic fingers pushes the hair away from my face. I melt a little, tracing my gaze from his palm to the crook of his elbow, up over his shoulder and onto his dear, beloved face. He wears a tender, amused smile.

"You really tied one on last night, didn't you?" Kai asks. "I didn't think you were going to wake up before nightfall."

Happiness sparkles through me. I never get tired of seeing him here when I wake up. But my head really does hurt. I struggle upright, moaning. "I . . . did I really—"

Shit. That's not good.

He confirms, "Twice."

"Did it make the midnight bounce?"

"Doesn't it always? Don't worry, love, you have a great pair."

That's only marginal comfort, given the way I feel. I'm going to hear about having my tits on the news again from my CO. Not looking forward to *that* conversation. But maybe the Csom Run will win me some slack.

The man doesn't seem to have a perceptible sense of

humor, so he'll lecture me on how I have a responsibility to maintain a certain image, uphold the good name of the Corp. It didn't work when my dad used that line on me, so it sure won't now.

"How long did we slam? Are we due to jump soon?" I can't believe it, but I've totally lost track of time.

"Not until tomorrow. We have one more day of R&R before we go back on."

"Any more 'rest,' and I'll die," I mumble, falling back onto my pillow.

He brushes the hair away from my face, whispering, "Don't even think about it, lovely. There's no way I could live without you."

A sweet little spear runs me through. He says it gently, easily, as if there's no shame in his need. Despite my aching head, he can do the craziest things to my heart. After Simon, I swore I'd never let another man matter to me like this. I promised myself I'd live hard, a different warm body in every port, and refuse to give of myself in any way that mattered. And for the longest time, I did.

"You're such a sweet talker."

He shakes his head, fingers threading through my tangled curls. "Nothing's sweeter than the truth, Siri."

Ah. He's the only one who ever calls me that. At first he did it to irritate me because it's such a soft little name, and I didn't think it fit me. But slowly, he tamed me to it. I may not be a gentle woman by most standards, but I melt for him.

Right now, I do it literally as he finds pressure points just beneath the base of my skull. The headache from excess drinking starts to fade. I can actually open my eyes all the way without feeling like daggers of light are slicing through my brain.

"Mmm, thanks. You're the best. What did I ever do to deserve you?"

"Nothing," he says, straight-faced. "You're a very bad woman. I just took pity on you and decided to save you from yourself."

That's not too far from the truth. After I split with Simon, he watched me run wild for months, going through more men than whose names I could remember, before he asked, "Why not me? You've tried everyone else in the known galaxy."

If it hadn't been so accurate, I might have taken offense and asked why he'd even be interested in such a slut. In my mind, he'd always been off-limits. I mean, we had to work together. And if I screwed things up between us, as I seem to have a knack for, then it would make our job downright awkward. I can't even remember why I said I'd think about it, but I know we wound up drunk that night. Maybe he did that on purpose because Mary knows, after I've downed a few, I'm a sure thing.

I smile, as he means me to. "Shower?"

Kai agrees, swinging me up in his arms with a whipcord strength that used to surprise me. He's not tall, slim rather than muscular, but it would be a mistake for anyone to judge him weak. We fit like interlocking puzzle pieces, and I love him so much it hurts. Our relationship didn't start like fireworks, but more of a gradual spark building to a high and steady flame.

I never think about losing him. Lucky for me, jumpers don't have to worry about that. We don't live long enough to grieve, except for each other—and that's why I stopped making friends among my fellow navigators. After I spoke at the fourth funeral in as many turns, I just didn't have the heart for it anymore.

Like in all station quarters, the san-shower is small and cramped when you wedge two people into it, but we manage. He's the only person who ever dares tickle me. It's a little-known secret that I go mad when you go for my ribs. Kai carries me out, clean and squealing, when we're through.

"Feeling better?" he asks, brushing his lips across my temple.

"Much. What do you want to do today?"

If he's correct—and he generally is—this is our last rec day before we go back on rotation. We should make the most of it.

He pretends to consider. "We could spend the day naked."

I raise a brow. "Aren't you tired of me yet?"

"Never. We still haven't done it upside down or sideways. I could requisition a pair of antigrav boots."

Kai is the only one who ever makes me giggle. "I'm not sure this room is big enough to accommodate such ideas."

"Damn. And imagine the looks we'd get if we tried to use the sports deck."

"Well, there *is* a certain athletic quality to what you've proposed."

He shakes his head with mock-sadness. "But I'm afraid I never thought of sex as a spectator sport."

"So no antigrav boots on the sports deck. Where does that leave us?"

"Together," he murmurs.

I love the way he wraps me close, chin to shins, and tucks his face into the curve of my throat. He breathes me in as if I'm as essential to his well-being as oxygen. The day passes in a sweet blur of lovemaking and playful teasing.

Later, we take a walk on station, hand in hand, and I don't even care that people mutter jokes as we walk by. Yes, we're a big cliché—pilot and navigator, madly in love. We're another statistic, another couple who couldn't resist the enforced intimacy of jacking in together.

I like to think it might have happened anyway, even if we weren't a pilot-jumper pair, but at base, I don't really care *how* it happened. I'm just glad it did. He makes me happy, happier than I can ever remember being.

With Kai I have a sense of security and equilibrium. His gentle patience keeps me from flying to one extreme or the other. He checks some of my destructive impulses, helps me think before I act; but I never feel like he's trying to control me. Kai makes a joke, and I laugh, but then I realize he has a point. I stop and think, something I wouldn't do on my own.

We have dinner at the Starburst, a restaurant on station whose walls are patterned with the constellations outside. The food is good, the company, exquisite. To my mind, this has been a perfect day.

In the morning, we go back to work. We're supposed to explore a slice of stars in the Outskirts, jump from a little-used beacon, and see if we can find anything new out there. This is my favorite part of the job.

"So who do you want from the pool?" I ask. "We need a medic and a gearhead."

"Not Watkins. The guy drives me nuts."

Kai draws me close, and I snuggle up, closing my eyes. The insistent beep of his comm annoys me. A bleak feeling comes over me, and I desperately don't want him to answer it. I even grab his hand to stop him.

He frees himself with a puzzled look. "I have to take it, Siri. It's the CO."

I feel like I've been hit in the chest with an iron fist. *Oh, no. No.*

"Mauro Kai here." He pauses, listening.

I'd almost forgotten his first name was Mauro. I never call him that, though he prefers calling me by my given name. To me, he'll always be Kai. I move, restless. Foreboding builds like static in the air before a storm.

"Yes, sir. No, it's no problem at all. We'd appreciate the extra time off afterward. We'll be glad to help you out."

Somehow I know what he's going to say. We're not going exploratory tomorrow. Someone has fallen sick, so we're taking a passenger vessel, the *Sargasso*, to Matins IV instead. A shudder rocks through me.

"We can't go." I push upright and clutch his shoulders, trying to think of a way to warn him, some way he'll believe me. "I had a terrible nightmare about this. I . . . dreamed you died, Kai. So . . . please, humor me. Let them find somebody else. When the ship lands safely, you can laugh at me if you want."

In the half-light, his smile is excruciatingly tender and sad. "But I *did* die, Siri. I can't stay with you here, much as I want to, because you have work to do out there. It's time for you to wake up, love."

CHAPTER 24

I awaken, weeping as if my heart will break.

It's like losing him all over again. With her hallucinogenic spice, the Grand Administrator has done an unspeakably cruel thing. In a long history of being wounded, I don't think I've ever hurt so badly when the loss wasn't fresh.

He didn't just die yesterday. I wasn't just in bed with him. He didn't just tickle me in the shower and tell me he can't possibly live without me. Outside the dream world, his face has started to grow blurry. I can't remember his features without looking at them. I can only remember the way he suffered before he died.

They built a monument to the *Sargasso* on New Terra, for Mary's sake, and it has his name on it. He's one of the lost now. Tears pour down my cheeks unchecked. Through the blur of new grief, I see Vel and Constance hovering. They don't know what the hell to do with me, it seems. The room smells vaguely of sickness, and mortification joins the awful broil in my stomach. I hope I didn't make too much of a mess.

Then Vel proves he's learning. He hugs me, claws cradling my shoulders. It's less awkward than the way he embraced me on Lachion. His chitin feels cool and smooth against my overheated skin. Before now, it's not a brand of comfort I would have acknowledged as effective; but even through his chitin, the contact helps. It's not an aggressive act. I'm not his hostage; I'm his friend.

Whatever happens, I don't doubt that Vel cares about me. He must be experiencing scorn and discrimination on levels I can't even fathom, but he's *here*. I don't know what to do with my arms, whether I should hug him back or sit quiet.

He answers the question by helping me up. "The worst is over. You may experience a little dizziness, but the bulk has burned through your system."

Calamity averted. Nobody important saw me melt down, so I guess that means it never happened. I smile, but the movement hurts, and it's a parody of what a smile is supposed to signify. "No, the worst is just beginning. See, I lost him . . . *again.*"

They both pause. My PA is probably searching her files for references to this mysterious "him." Then Constance touches my hair tentatively, as if testing the idea of contact as an instrument of reassurance. "I have nothing of value to contribute. My parameters do not expand to encompass loss."

I'm sure for her, one human is much like another. Mair stopped accessing her files, then I showed up. Out with the old, in with the new. Right now I half wish she could rewrite my brain to make me more like her.

"Forget anything you dreamed while under the influence," Vel says quietly. "Or it will drive you mad."

Easy for him to say. I'm utterly humiliated. Did I writhe and moan, dreaming of how we made love on our last day together? My thighs feel sticky, proof of how real the delusion seemed. Did Constance log my dream-orgasm for later deconstruction?

"You have one hour before Councilor Devri's social event," the PA adds. "I can ready you for the occasion if you permit it."

Ah, what the hell does it matter? Despair washes over me. Kai is lost to me, and after last night, I'm starting to think March might be, too. My fingers brush my throat. All I have left is work, so I need to do my duty; but the only way I can manage is to turn everything off. Compartmentalize.

None of this matters. This didn't happen to me. It was some other Jax they broke.

I stagger toward the san-shower—copied from our design and installed to make us feel more at home—undress, then rinse off the sour stink of fever sweat. Since neither Vel nor Constance cares about nudity, I emerge naked and ready for them to pick out my clothes. He's supposed to escort me anyway. He may as well take a proprietary interest in garbing me appropriately.

I already wear his pattern on my skin. For all I know, that means I'm now his chattel, and he could sell me to the mines if he wants to. Mary, when will this ache go away? I feel like I did back on Perlas Station, trapped and helpless, with no way to assuage the ache.

Like a passive doll, I stand quiescent while they do the work. If I hadn't promised to attend, I would send excuses—but Devri and Sharis might take offense—and I cannot afford to alienate my few allies. In the glass, I see a remote stranger, pale but well-groomed. The gold robe strikes the only familiar note, but I'm indifferent.

I feel hollow.

"You are now suitable for a diplomatic function," Constance pronounces.

"Good. Would you show Vel the readings you took at the first summit? The ones of Councilor Devri."

Maybe this numbness is a good thing. Otherwise, I would have felt embarrassed about grilling Vel over sexual matters. Now I just wait for him to view the footage Constance feeds into the terminal.

Devri comes up via thermal imaging, and I can see the hot spots right away. Vel studies them for a moment, then turns to me. "He was stimulated by your display of confidence and expertise during the session," he confirms. "If you were . . . interested, he would present for you."

"Really? Why?" I don't even ask what that entails. "I thought your people found humans disgusting."

"In most cases," he agrees. "But a powerful, dominant female lays the most eggs, thus providing the most offspring—and the best chance of dynastic immortality. Thus, we are conditioned to be attracted to such displays. In your case, the attraction is more psychological than biological, and for Devri, it is apparently strong enough to override your lack of physical beauty."

"Good to know. I might be able to use that. Turn off the feed, Constance."

The PA complies. "It is good to have my suppositions confirmed."

I should feel something, knowing one of the Bugs wouldn't mind doing things with me that I can't even imagine. Shock, revulsion, naughty interest? But there's nothing. Maybe if I close my eyes, if I go back to sleep, I'll find Kai again. It felt so real. I couldn't remember anything of my life as it is now. I went back to *before* any of this happened. Before I lost him. Maybe I can get back there. Mary knows I want to.

But not right now.

"Is it time to go?" I ask.

"Yes. Are you ready, Sirantha?" Vel gazes at me as if in assessment.

Maybe he wonders if I'll hold together long enough to show off my *wa* for Sharis and Devri. Well, I'll do my best. I want to succeed here. I want to leave something behind that matters when I join Kai, so in a hundred turns, people will look at the solid friendship between humanity and the Ithtorians and say: *Ambassador Jax did that.*

Seems like a worthy legacy.

"Let's do this."

My balance feels a trifle unsteady as we walk but nothing disastrous. The jungle wonders of the government complex leave me unmoved for the first time. It seems like a lifetime since we came from the Grand Administrator's apartment.

We pass through a tunnel that leads to the councilors' annex. I have the sense of being entombed, but not even my latent claustrophobia can penetrate this thick, lovely veil of numbness. Nothing can reach me in here. Nothing can hurt me.

Just before we reach Devri's place, Vel stops walking and performs the lowest *wa* I've ever seen from him. In a human being, I would take his body language for misery and regret. I'm not sure I can trust my instincts where he's concerned, though. Being surrounded by his people, I understand better now how alien he is.

"I am sorry," he says then. "I would not have had you suffer like this for worlds. Had I known she meant to do this, I would have advised you to reject her invitation regardless of the offense it caused. It is not . . ." He pauses, the vocalizer seeking a word. "Fair. You have been injured enough."

"Damn few things are fair," I answer. "Life has never been one of them. But I appreciate the thought." The ice around me gives a little crack, and I don't want it to. Because then I'll have to feel what's underneath.

Jael turns the corner then. He comes toward us at a run, sleek and clad in black. I note that the damage to his face has healed fully. "Trying to leave me behind?"

I smile. "I keep trying, but it never works."

Before he can reply, I step forward and let the door scan me. This is one of their technologies I like very much. Instead of a door-bot, they simply have a holo-cam that registers the image of anyone who comes within one meter of the door. If you stay still, the door projects your image on the other side, and if your presence is expected or desired, the homeowner lets you in. It's very quiet and civilized.

A few seconds later, we're admitted to the apartment. Devri's dwelling is different from the Grand Administrator's. It's a full jungle in here, with trailing vines growing from the walls. Beneath our feet, the ground gives with each step, a soft loam. The room is heavy and damp, a little warm for my tastes, and redolent with the perfume of blooming flowers that taste syrup sweet on my tongue when I inhale.

Looks like the party is in full swing. I recognize a number of Ithtorians from the merchant summit. Devri immediately breaks away from a female to come greet us.

"So glad to see you." He executes a lovely *wa*, and I remember the hot spots on his lower abdomen. I wish I could interpret body language as Vel does. Maybe it would tell me whether Devri has wicked intentions.

Still, this should be interesting.

CHAPTER 25

Devri exerts himself to be charming.

Through Vel, he shares amusing anecdotes about the way the tide can turn in any business deal, no matter how secure the investment seems. I must admit, he's good company. I acquit myself fairly well for someone who didn't know what day it was three hours ago. Jael stands quietly by my side; but since I know what to look for, I can tell he's on guard.

After half an hour or so, Devri asks, "I need to talk to Velith for a moment. Do you mind?"

I gather he needs a private moment. He can't be asking for that because he's worried about *me* overhearing, so it must be the others he's concerned about. It's probably related to the conspiracy I overheard yesterday, or maybe Devri knows about the Grand Administrator's threat. Vel should give me a full report when he returns. So I give my blessing, and they leave the living area.

The world has a strange distance, as if I am in it but not part of it. Ithtorians give me a wide berth as if my soft skin might be contagious. If I stay here long enough, I might internalize their opinion that my unarmored flesh is monstrous. I already feel raw and vulnerable, as if I'm revealing parts of myself that ought to be covered. I fight the urge to cover my bare arms, taking comfort in the scars that thicken my fragile skin.

What kind of creatures are humans anyway? We lack claws or fangs; we have no natural defense mechanisms. When I consider, it *does* seem wrong, like we went awry somewhere on the evolutionary ladder. I'm used to the sounds of Ithtorian language: the clicks and chitters don't strike me as strange or alien now that I'm able to understand them.

Jael sets his hand on my arm. "Are you all right?"

"Other than being drugged, forced to experience painful hallucinations, and threatened with death? Yeah, I'm great."

His whole body goes taut. "Who threatened you?"

"The Grand Administrator. What're you going to do about it?"

His icy gaze searches mine, verifying that I'm serious. Then he says, very softly, "I could kill her."

He means it. Being Bred means he's not subject to the same limitations as other men. For a moment, I'm sickly tempted. If she's removed, and they don't trace it back to us, maybe someone more amenable to our cause would be appointed. But no, it's too big a risk, and I can't unleash Jael here. He's like a double-edged sword.

I shake my head. "No. That's not the way to go. But . . . I appreciate the offer."

"I'll do whatever it takes to keep you safe. I'll alert the others to the danger as well." By his expression, he's preparing to lecture me about March some more.

Holding up a hand, I forestall that gambit. "Not right now, please. I'm still feeling a little fragile."

It's a painful admission, and I hope to Mary he doesn't ask why. His frost blue eyes search my face, then his face softens. "You look like I felt, the time they told me what I was."

My heart skips a beat. This is the first time he's referred to being Bred in more than a flippant sense. There's real emotion here, and I don't know what to do with it. "How old were you?"

"In biological terms? Twelve. But they accelerated our development, so I don't know exactly how old I am."

"There were more of you?" I try to keep my tone gentle.

He nods. "I came from a pod of ten. I thought they were my brothers and sisters until that moment. They raised us crèche-style, and let us believe we were orphans. They wanted to reduce the risk of madness and other disorders.

Even so, it didn't entirely work. Seven of us died before reaching maturity."

"I'm sorry."

"Don't be. It was the experiments that came afterward, not the revelation. Some of them didn't have a very high tolerance for pain."

"I'm surprised they let you go."

A cold little smile twists his mouth. "They didn't."

There are so many questions I could ask, but Sharis comes up to us, offers a *wa* that inexplicably reminds me of the ocean, then chatters as if he's been drinking, forgetting I'm not supposed to understand a word he says.

"What has happened to Velith? It is most impolite of him to leave you with only this worthless soft-skin for escort."

I regard him with a polite, blank expression, trying not to reveal comprehension or amusement at his assessment of Jael.

"My apologies." He bows again, talking more to himself this time. "I occasionally forget you belong to one of the subspecies. Sometimes you almost seem smarter than a cave beast, but that must be Il-Nok's influence. He remains well-spoken even after so many turns away. Just think of what he might have achieved."

Never have I resented this chip so much. I can't show interest, can't indicate that I want him to keep talking. The noises he makes with jaw, mandible, and throat are supposed to be a meaningless cacophony to me.

He falls silent, standing with me out of a desire to be courteous, I suspect. His presence keeps anyone else from approaching, so they content themselves with staring. Sharis seems to be watching the door, waiting for someone. When the door projects an image of Mako, he perks visibly. His departing *wa* says he can't wait to talk to her.

Jael doesn't pursue the other conversation. Quietly brooding, he keeps an eye on things, alert to movement all around me.

A low hum emanates from the walls. I think it might be music. Their claws twitch as if in time to some beat I can't quite hear. It's like they're all playing the same instrument, eerily in cadence.

No sign of Sartha. Definitely no sign of Karom. This isn't his kind of party, not with the filthy soft-skins wandering around like they own the place. The guests seem to be on the young, radical side. They're all for progress.

Two merchants I recognize from this morning watch me from across the room. One is tall and tawny; his companion is smaller with a parti-colored thorax. Neither wears the marks of notable achievement, but I think it's a measure of their youth rather than failure. Their talk washes over me, bits of speculation.

"Do you think she has accepted him as a full partner?" one asks.

"Unlikely," the other answers. "Even if he chose exile over life in the mines, the son of Nok would never sink so low. He might be mad, but he is not depraved."

Vel? Mad? Could this relate to his lack of conformity to expected societal roles? For the first time since awakening, I feel a flicker of interest, but I can't move closer. It would look odd if I sought out a particular conversation without my handler's guidance.

"Can you imagine?" the first marvels. "Being so alone, no house to which I might bring glory, no mate to share my success. I think I would prefer death."

"You are not known for your bravery, Kalid."

"It would not require bravery to have you killed."

"So you have claimed, more than once. And yet here I am."

"One day, Arqut, you will push me too far."

"Unlikely. You need me too much."

Now I remember what role they played in the meeting. Arqut and Kalid have partnered in a new consortium devoted to starship technology. They're interested in improving the phase drive, something nobody has attempted in hundreds of turns.

Every spacefaring race uses this technology for long hauls. In fact, the plans were waiting for us in ancient ruins we unearthed on our moon. Interestingly enough, the same thing has happened to all species in some form or another. If not their moon, then they found the data sealed in some forgotten subterranean city, in a grand, dusty ziggurat or a jungle-covered pyramid.

It is as if the information has been seeded for us, hidden until we were advanced enough to know what to do with it. No species has succeeded in updating the original schematic, however. Without fail, alterations to the core design have resulted in dreadful accidents and excruciating death. After a while, we gave up trying to make it better; we just accepted what we'd been given.

So it'll be interesting to see what these two can accomplish, assuming the alliance goes forward. Before now, there's been no reason to focus on star-tech since the Ithtorians are so xenophobic. They've been content with what happens on their own world up until this point, but Kalid and Arqut hope to make a fortune on the cutting edge.

With so much powerful opposition, I don't give good odds on their success. That's too bad because they have invested their personal fortunes in this endeavor. They're bright-eyed and idealistic, convinced they can improve the ancient technology. An idea begins to germinate as I listen to them bicker. By the time Vel comes back, it's a full-blown plan.

"I have much to tell you," he says. "For obvious reasons, it should wait until we are alone, but . . . suffice to say, I learned much of interest from our friend Devri. He has been briefly detained. He asks that you enjoy the party in his absence."

The concept of friendship is a human one, not natural to the Ithtorians, so this will be a most intriguing conversation. Apparently I can still be engaged intellectually, even though my emotions seem to be shrouded in layers of ice. I agree with a nod that the discussion will keep, fixing my gaze on the merchants opposite us.

"Let's renew our acquaintance." I nod at Kalid and Arqut. "Can you come up with something suitably flattering?"

Vel answers, "I believe my skills are adequate for the task." He leads the way across the room. Their mandibles move in what I take to be astonishment at being singled out like this. "The ambassador wishes me to convey her admiration for your incisive questions this morning. She recalls the two of you as being particularly astute."

That works.

Filtered through Vel, the conversation is stilted at first, but that's all right. I'm just laying the foundation right now. Curious, a few other merchants gather around us. Within minutes, I identify them as potential investors who want to hear the human ambassador opine regarding the consortium's chances of financial success.

"With such fine minds like Kalid and Arqut at the helm," I say in measured tones, "I would ordinarily expect a *brilliant* future." The pause is deliberate, and my audience isn't immune to the implied "but."

"What causes your qualms?" an obliging Bug asks.

I glance at Vel, feigning a conspiratorial exchange. He doesn't know what I'm doing, but he plays along, inclining his head. *Good man . . . er, Bug. Whatever.*

My hands twist together before me as I try to project an anxious quality. "I do not know whether they will have the opportunity to pursue this venture," I whisper at last. "If it comes to a vote, I have no doubt the alliance will pass, but I fear it may not reach the council to be decided officially. I have been given to understand that those items proposed, which the Grand Administrator does not personally support, have a way of being tabled. She gave me this information at a private luncheon."

Jael flashes me an approving grin. "Well played."

Shock rocks through Vel as he realizes what I'm doing. Nonetheless, he restates my words in even more cagey terms. By informing the merchants of her threat against my person, I alert them to the potential loss of revenue. Money is power, especially here, and more than one ruler has been deposed because she mucked with the profit margins of those who put her on the throne.

They can decide what, if anything, they want to do about this. I'm not at all surprised when Arqut and Kalid make their excuses, execute a grateful *wa*, and depart early. I suspect they're going to be talking to colleagues, alerting them to the possibility that the human ambassador won't survive long enough to see the job done.

Jael excuses himself before the party's done. I think even my bodyguard can't stomach too much of this despite what Tarn is paying him. "You'll be safe enough with Vel," he whispers. "But comm me if you need anything?"

I nod.

Intrigue is exhausting. By the time we leave the party, I decide I could sleep for a week. I have the funny feeling, though, that if Vel could smile, he would be doing so now.

"That was inspired," he says as we walk back to my quarters. "A masterful strategy, I might even dare say . . . Ithtorian."

I smile. "So I'm becoming more like you, even as you become more like me?"

His steps still. "No, Sirantha. I am no true Ithtorian, as anyone would tell you."

"I don't want anyone to tell me. I'd rather you did."

Vel hesitates so long that I think he's going to refuse. And then: "Very well. Perhaps it is time I told *someone*."

ACCESSING ARCHIVE FOOTAGE . . .

Omni News Net: Special Bulletin—Outpost 8

You are about to receive an update intended for adults: children under the age of fifteen should not view the following images. It is not our intention to glorify violence, merely update our viewers. If you have any serious medical conditions, you may wish to have your AI screen this story. Omni News Net is not responsible for any psychic, emotional, or spiritual damage incurred by the following bounce broadcast.

EXT. OUTPOST 8—TWILIGHT

Smoke rises from the settlement, indicating heavy-weapons discharge. Corpses litter the ground, savagely devoured and dismembered. There are no signs of life except for the man facing the vid. KEVIN stands outside the outpost, head bowed in mournful silence. At last he raises his eyes, his expression reflecting absolute horror.

KEVIN

I'm here in the aftermath of the attack. This is one of the oldest human settlements in the Outskirts, named for the order in which the colonies were founded. These settlements speak to our determination and our refusal to accept limitations. Where other locales took on names, Outpost 8 kept its numerical designation as a sign of pride. Longevity doesn't come easy when you live out on the frontier, but these people were an example to all of humankind. Now, the laughter is silenced, and their machines work no more. More than a thousand people lost their lives here.

Two days past, their call for aid went unheeded. Right now you're seeing what happens when the establishment fails. The Morgut took this outpost, but they do not possess any capacity for mercy. Outpost 8 was a haven for traders and spacers; they were peaceful and offered no defense.

KEVIN moves through the carnage. He pauses beside the remains of a small child. Her flesh is torn and bloody, great chunks of meat missing from her corpse. She lies apart from the other bodies that litter this hopeless, hellish landscape.

KEVIN

Her face will live forever as part of this atrocity. I ask you, what can we do? What hope can we offer in the face of such incomprehensible barbarism?

.END-ARCHIVE-FOOTAGE.

CHAPTER 26

My quarters are dim and silent when we return. Somehow it fits the somber mood that has fallen between us. If somebody had told me I would come to care so much about the Bug that hunted me nearly to my death, I would have said they were crazy. But friendship comes in many sizes and shapes, sometimes in weird wrapping.

Constance normally sits at the terminal in sleep mode, locked in an eerie facsimile of sleep. I've told her she can shut down when she's satisfied with her day's work; if I need her, I will activate her manually. That eliminates the need to explain that she's not always a welcome eavesdropper. I have strange guilty twinges over this.

Tonight, she's nowhere to be found. I don't worry overmuch over that, however, as I want to hear what Vel has to say. Her company, artificial as it is, could only inhibit his unexpected decision to share. By tacit agreement we pass from the living space, beyond the glastique glitter of the cityscape.

I curl up on the bed without changing from my ambassadorial gear and wait for him to begin. Vel stands half in shadow, staring out. I wonder if he sees anything at all, or if the view has become superimposed with something else, if he sees ghosts in the glass as I do.

"As you know," he says at last, "I am the offspring of a politician named Nok. What I did not tell you—though you may have already learned this via gossip by now—is that at the time of my birth, she served as Grand Administrator. She expected great things from her progeny, and she ruled her brood with an iron claw."

He pauses, as if remembering and sorting his memories to best relate them. I feel as though I'm being granted a secret, sacred glimpse at the core of him. I haven't been this near to the real Vel since we huddled together in an icy cave, half-convinced that day would be our last.

"Do you mean she didn't care what you wanted?" I draw my knees up to my chest, studying him in the half-light.

Vel is a bizarre amalgam of the alien and the familiar, soaked with shadow. His eyes glitter strangely, taking the light as a human's never would. I consider inviting him to sit down; there's a chair by the window, but he's surely comfortable enough in my presence that he doesn't need to be set at ease. His posture radiates a tension that runs through him like a poison, which can only be purged through confession.

"She cared only what was expected," he says, after consideration.

I notice he refers to her in the past tense. "Is she—"

"Deceased?" he supplies. "Yes. Many turns ago now."

"I'm sorry. Go on." I remember how my questions made him tighten up before, so I resolve not to interrupt him anymore.

"My youth was like any other," he continues. "I was educated in an upper-class crèche with a focus on diplomacy and politics. From an early age, I knew they expected me to follow in my mater's footsteps, though as a male I had one strike against my chances of taking up her mantle as Grand Administrator.

"But I was never interested in what they wanted me to learn. The process by which we added honor to our chitin intrigued me from the moment I saw one of Nok's assistants return with xanthic stripes for some accomplishment. At first, they encouraged my interest because they took it as a sign I wanted to learn how to accrue my own face for personal achievement. They thought me . . . ambitious." His pause suggests a subtle melancholy, a desert of the spirit full of remembered sand and bone.

"Instead, you were interested in the art of it," I guess aloud quietly. "In the colors and patterns, lines and shapes."

He inclines his head. "Nok was appalled when she realized what fascinated me so. Such endeavors bring no honor to a house. The work of hands remain the dominion of the lowborn, those who have no training in the use of higher intellect. If I pursued such a path, I would shame my family as surely as an admission of infirmity or impairment. After all, we do not adorn ourselves for pleasure."

I scowl. "Humans do. On Gehenna, there are entire studios devoted to the beautification of the body via graphic art."

"That is merely another argument against the practice," Vel tells me gently. "You are primitive beasts, only a few short millennia removed from drawing on cave walls."

That doesn't seem like a fair criticism. Ithtorians *live* a lot longer than we do. But I know he doesn't share his people's bias, or he wouldn't be here with me in the first place.

"So what happened?"

"I studied secretly for a time. Learned how to mix the acid wash from the house artisan, how to structure the rank signs, and how to apply the ink. He knew my interest was inappropriate, but those of low caste do not argue with their superiors, even if the instructions are wrong."

That makes me perk up. "And do you believe yourself superior, based on who laid the egg that hatched you?"

Vel answers seriously. "I am the product of one of the oldest, finest houses . . . and yet I am also proof that lines do not always breed true. Some offspring are fundamentally flawed, askew from the standard." I have the feeling he doesn't mean "standard" exactly, that the chip has failed to translate for me precisely.

"You say that like it's a bad thing."

"They do not prize individuality," he says then. "That is a human trait. They prize achievement that enriches the collective within our birth-given strata."

I get that. "You defied your heritage to be an artist, just like I did in becoming a jumper. My parents expected other things from me, too."

"It was, perhaps, a little more complex." At last he moves from the window, seating himself in a movement that seems more hinged and alien than when he wears faux-human skin. I still marvel at that ability; his people can excrete a substance they shape into the ultimate camouflage, giving them any appearance they wish.

He goes on, "When I was betrayed—as is inevitable—my behavior so shamed Nok that her existing rank was stripped from her. By my transgressions, I stole two turns of work from her."

I wince. "And they removed her colors?"

"Yes." The stark response illuminates how much the impact of that still resonates with him across the turns.

"Oh, Vel." I can only imagine the shame.

"Nok told me then—I could go into politics as befitted my station—or she would have me killed. She made sure I understood that she had plenty of other males to carry on her genetic legacy, which is *officially* propagated through her female offspring." The chip can't begin to encompass the intensity of what he's relating, so the toneless translation that echoes in my head underscores the somber moment.

"Is that when they arranged a match for you with Sartha?"

"Partnership," he corrects. "But yes. It was decided I needed a female to guide me, as my judgment was so clearly debased. I went into politics, as they wanted. I climbed the ranks, but I was forbidden to have my carapace imprinted with my achievements for twenty turns." He considers this for a moment. "It was a light penalty, all things considered. They could have judged me a lunatic and sent me to the mines. Without Nok, they doubtless would have. If I had disappointed her again, she would have disposed of me quietly."

Ah, Mary. I want to hug him, but I'm not sure if he would take comfort in it. *To hell with it,* I tell myself. Customs and proscriptions don't apply between friends. He can push me away if he doesn't like it.

I leave my seat silently and wrap an arm around him. There's room for me to sit beside him, so I perch there. If he wants to put some distance between us, I won't resist. The problem is, I'm just not sure what he needs.

"I'm so sorry, Vel." Maybe words can make a difference, this once.

"So you see," he goes on, as if I haven't spoken, haven't

moved. "I am not a model of my species. I am the worst they have to offer, and I was so . . . other among my own kind that when the first human delegation landed—when I was on the cusp of being named Grand Administrator—I ran rather than face a lifetime of quiet desperation."

I think about how to respond for a moment. "Maybe you're not what Nok wanted or expected in her offspring. Maybe you're different from other males, but that doesn't mean you lack value. I'd be dead many times over if I wasn't lucky enough to know you."

Is that enough? This kind of stuff doesn't come easily to me. I don't like talking about my feelings, and it's hard for me to tell people they're important to me, sometimes until it's too late. Then I can only whisper into the great beyond, hoping they can somehow hear me through aching dark, saying:

I miss you.

I cared about you.

You mattered.

I hope March knows that, if nothing else.

"The stench of failure will cling to me always." There is a bleak finality to those words, as if he can never forgive himself for what he is not, no matter what the grace or beauty or strength of what he has become.

The dark binds us and hides our sins. I do not ask him to go away when I curl up on my lonely bed. Tonight Vel is a celestial body whose light yields no warmth. As I stare, sleepless, into silence, I see us trapped together across the turns in tents and caves and starships, two together . . . alone. He sits vigil beside me, distant as a glimmering star.

CHAPTER 27

The dark breaks wide in fragile rays. Dawn on Ithiss-Tor is more subtle than other sunrises. I have lost count of the worlds where I have stood and watched the light rise, peeling away the sky, sometimes in quiet colors, and sometimes in raw, violent slashes, as if the goddess I don't believe in has cut her veins. And sometimes, as on Gehenna, the sky changes not at all, just endless night, or endless brilliance—and after a time, the constant uniformity makes you feel as if you are the thing that must give way.

I feel like that now.

I sense a breaking point fast approaching, and then things will be different ever after.

Vel left at some point. I must have slept, although I have no recollection of doing so. I wish I knew how to comfort him for the failure he wears writ in invisible ink on his bare chitin. His lack of color shames him as scars from prison manacles might a human. Yet he seems so sure and confident in most regards, so maybe it's just the strain of being here. There's an argument for wrapping up quickly. The last thing I want to do is cause Vel more pain.

In a few hours, I will have obligations. I'll be expected to answer questions, allay doubt, and make myself amiable to our supporters. Right now it's time for me to do something for myself.

So I cross to the door that connects my quarters to March. I haven't passed through since our arrival on planet, too afraid of the worst, but really, the worst has already happened. There is nothing left to fear.

He can't remember how it feels to love me. And each

time, that awareness hits me in a deep, raw place, too bleak for tears. It's an ache for which I have no name because I have never lost a love like this before.

Jumpers aren't equipped to deal with loss. We're wired for the thrill of exploration; we're not known to be steadfast. And yet I find my palms pressed against the smooth veneer of the door, longing for my lover with a ferocity that does not ebb.

I want him back. If I have to tame him like a savage beast, I will find the patience. And if I have to teach myself to perform some mysterious mental surgery, then I will do that, too. So I gather my courage; it hangs in tatters after our last encounter, not because he hurt me but because I know deep down it damaged him more. He is a creature gone feral, having forgotten the scent and direction of home.

The door between us slides open when I touch the pad. It gives me hope that he hasn't keyed it against me yet. Maybe he hasn't altogether accepted the notion he's broken beyond repair.

Like me, he cannot sleep. He does not turn when I step through, but I sense his awareness in a subtle shift of his posture.

"How bad is it?"

That much has not changed at least. I can still taste his meaning from a sparse handful of words, based on my knowledge of how his mind works.

I shrug. "No permanent harm."

"Not this time. That's why we need to stay away from each other, Jax." He pauses, fingertips tapping some quiet pattern against his thighs. The low tone of his voice hides a wealth of despair, like dark water over jagged rock. "There's no coming down from the ledge this time. And I don't want you caught in the blast radius when I blow."

My smile feels taut and uneasy. "You talk like you're packed full of timed explosives."

"That's not a bad analogy."

"No? I happen to disagree. In my opinion, it's terrible."

He looks so weary that it breaks my heart. I can tell he's not sleeping any better than I am, though for different reasons.

"What do you want, Jax?"

You. I don't say it aloud, but this is March, which means I don't need to. An icy prickle tells me he's brushed my thoughts with a helpless compulsion he cannot control any more than I can stop longing for him. We're like magnets with an opposite charge. No matter how we fight it—and I did in the beginning because I wasn't nearly ready for him—we can't resist the pull.

I remember our first time, the impassioned tension of his face as I rode him. If I close my eyes, I could find all his scars with my fingertips. I remember my fierce euphoria at finding him whole in the Gunnar-Dahlgren underground. We took each other with teeth and tongues and ravenous relief.

A shudder rocks through him. "I swear you're trying to drive me crazy . . . and it's a short haul. Remind me how great the sex was, then tell me we can't have any unless I can say 'I love you' and mean it."

Put that way, it does sound cruel.

"I used to have no problem with meaningless sex," I say quietly. "But then I fell in love with Kai, and he taught me there could *be* more. Then . . . too soon after I lost him, I met you. I didn't want to want you. I didn't want you to fit me."

He stares at me silent as a stone.

"I just wanted to grieve, but you kept pushing until I realized that I'd never stop aching unless I opened up to you all the way. So here I am, begging—" My voice breaks, so I try again. "Begging you not to give up. Begging you to keep trying. Because I don't think I'm strong enough to survive losing you. I'm at the wall over this, and I don't have anything left."

There it is, my soul laid bare. It's a raw, ugly thing, covered in half-healed wounds, and I've placed it at his feet. Now he can stomp me into nothingness, get his own back for the way I nearly broke his heart once before. But if he does that, we've lost everything, and I will have no choice but to admit it.

March says nothing.

I'd rather crawl over broken glass than admit this stuff to him, particularly when his face in profile offers as much softness as a titanium pylon. I struggle onward, drowning in his silence.

"Go on and read me. I know you said I'm the strongest person you've ever known, but even durable metal has a breaking point. There's too much riding on this mission, too much weight, and I need you—"

"Shut up, Jax." Does his tone sound tender or impatient? I've lost all ability to judge. He sits forward then, elbows on knees. "Can you say you're not afraid of me?"

"I'm not," I answer promptly. "You didn't mean to hurt me. No matter what nightmare had you trapped, you weren't fighting *me* in it."

His teeth glint like bone in a smile that holds no sweetness or joy. "Is that a hint? Would you like to take a walk through my nightmares and plant flowers along the way?"

"You don't know me very well if you can say that with a straight face," I bite out. "No, baby. I'd like to wade in there with my steel-toed boots on and kick the shit out of anyone or anything that hurts you."

"That's my girl." The words slide out of him with a sound so faint I might have imagined them.

But I didn't. Unbelievable joy rockets through me. He said it, and now he's looking at me dead on with a question in his eyes. The answer will always, always be yes.

"Damn right."

"Mother Mary," he breathes. "How you shine."

I shake my head. "The light is yours. Right now you can't see it because you sit in shadow, but all I do is reflect you."

That doesn't sound like anything I'd say or even think, but it's true. On my best day, I'm not a thinker. I'm a boiling pot of impulses and snap judgments. Now that I know about my unique genetic heritage, I tell myself grimspace blazes in my DNA, inciting me to extremes. Unlike other jumpers, I was conceived in grimspace, a happy quirk of my mother's quest for greater thrills. Doc thinks that exposure rewrote my DNA, resulting in a mutation that allows me to heal the grimspace damage that destroys other navigators.

But not me. I endure, and I flail, and I inflict collateral damage with my dangerous impulses. So maybe this chip has made me more able to articulate my private convictions. Or maybe the shift has been a long time coming. Nothing stays the same, not even me; all metals can be melted and refined.

His eyes close, his lush lashes making extravagant fans against the blades of his cheekbones. I can sense he's thinking hard, on the edge of something big. I just hope it doesn't break my heart. At last, breath slips out of him in a little sigh.

March stands then, as if he's made a difficult decision. "You *really* want to know what I dream about? I'll show you."

Dread sluices down my spine. I can't imagine how bad this will get, but I fix a smile on my face.

"Come then," I whisper, beckoning.

He takes me. A wall of ice rears up inside my head. Two separate things struggle in one space. Then he and I merge into . . . we.

And it begins.

CHAPTER 28

The stench of rotten meat pervades everything.

There's a cloying, coppery tinge to the air that tells me I've stepped into a charnel house. The dead are everywhere, piled so high now I can scarcely pass through the tunnel. My boots squelch in dead flesh that's devolved into organic sludge as it rots away from the bone. My first impulse is to turn and run, but I'm not alone in this, and the other half of me—the March half—knows that he has to finish the job. There are more to kill.

Shit, I recognize this place. While it shares certain infernal, subterranean traits associated with the mythic depiction of hell, I've *been* here before—and not just emotionally. When we walked out of the Gunnar-Dahlgren underground base, I'd thought myself lucky to be alive. I had no idea what I was leaving March to face alone, or I wouldn't have gone. I'd have fought harder, begged him not to stay. I think I'd have done *anything* to prevent him from going through this.

His grim determination overwhelms my nausea, and we move forward. Footsteps behind tell me we're not alone. I ride his memory, unable to impact the events. We trek through the dark stone passages, rooting out pockets of resistance. Most of the McCulloughs that have gotten trapped down here are wounded and starving.

That doesn't alter March's resolve. They are the enemy, and they must die. He kneels beside a young soldier, whose enormous eyes glitter in the torch-tube someone shines down on him. His face is all sharp angles, a geometric study in atrocity.

He tries to form a word through parched lips. "Please."

Though I don't want to see what's coming, I can't look away, tied to March as I am. He won't give the order to someone else. The blood will be on his hands. He draws a knife from its sheath on his thigh. The soldier sees what's coming, I think, because he tries to crawl away. His limbs won't hold him, and he collapses.

March rolls him over, his motions economical and precise. With a monstrous mix of resignation and expertise, he holds the head steady and jams his knife up through the man's chin. The jawbones guide the blade into his brain, and death is nearly instantaneous. Someone weeps nearby, a low and broken sound.

Men should never sound like that. Even as I register the thought, we move forward—and with a smooth motion, March silences the sobbing. Again and again he uses the knife to put down these men with no more hesitation than I would show in shooting a rabid animal. With each execution, I feel his detachment growing until he's like a small boat bobbing in the middle of a vast and trackless sea.

We push forward. Find two more makeshift encampments full of desperate men. They're too weak to fight, and some of them beg for their lives. They promise to move off world, severing all ties to kith and kin. March is implacable. One by one, they die.

I understand the idea in theory. He's making an example of Clan McCullough, teaching the others what will befall them if they come after Gunnar-Dahlgren. That sounds smart in the abstract, but when a human being kneels before you, begging for mercy—and finds none, well. You can imagine what it's like.

Behind us, his company moves in silence, just booted feet against the rock. Are they glad to see their enemies crushed or tired and heartsick as I am, just from the relatively brief time I've spent in March's memories? I don't know how he's not entirely a monster. Doubtless he'd argue that he *is*.

In the distance, I hear the eerie sonic shrieks of feeding Teras—and the resultant howls of the men they're devouring. It feels like an eternity before the death cries go quiet . . . but that's worse. I want to turn and look at the clansmen at our backs, wondering how this is affecting them.

But March doesn't turn. Finally, his comm unit trembles against his thigh. He takes it in hand and says in an undertone, "Go."

"No more life signs," a male voice reports. "We've scoured them clean."

"Then it's time to end this," March replies. "I want all units assembled at the south entrance in ninety minutes."

"Roger that. I'll spread the word. Dirge One out."

I vaguely remember that a dirge is a song they sing for the dead. Cold washes over me. I'd like to be able to question what comes next, but I'm a passive observer; I can't impact or change events. Maybe I'll ask March a few things once we're done.

The beauty of memory is that he can choose what parts to leave out. We flash forward in time—I only know that because he's aware of all the minutiae he doesn't share, such as getting back to base camp when each step feels like a kilometer—and then we wait for the rest of the troops. Filthy, exhausted, and blood-spattered, they trickle in.

Ten men make up a patrol, as the tunnels don't lend themselves to larger groups. Five pairs is a substantial number when the fighting takes place in such confined space. I can tell they've taken losses, but it's not as bad as it would have been if they didn't have a fallback. That showcases Mair's uncommon ability to guess at what's coming and anticipate what will be required.

They form up before March, and, by their regard, I see he's one of them, their general if not their chief. I didn't understand that until this moment. His relationship with Gunnar-Dahlgren is knotty and complex, something from which he'll never walk away. Thanks to Mair's intervention, his life will never entirely be his own.

To be precise, he can't imagine not answering if Keri calls on him for help. Despite my petty jealousy, there's no romantic component to his affection. The fact that she was a child when they met precludes him from seeing her in that light. In some ways, she's akin to the sister he lost. Mair told him to take care of Keri, and he's doing his best to hold up his end, no matter what it costs him.

He waits for them to fall quiet before speaking. "It's time for us to go on the offensive. We have a cache nearby, so we'll go out through the rubble and head for the gear. There, we'll find two pearl-class rovers waiting to take us to the McCullough compound. Intel tells me they don't have a fall-back. We've decimated their numbers and left them nowhere to go. Most of their women and children have already fled off world, and, if we finish this properly, they won't be coming back."

A rousing cheer goes up, echoing weirdly. The rest of the encampment shouts back, catching fire at the idea they'll soon be delivered from exile. March lets them scream their fill, then holds up a hand for attention. "I'm sending coordinates to each patrol leader. You'll be responsible for getting your team to the cache at the appointed time. Once we reach the McCullough compound, what's our strategy?"

A tall, scarred soldier replies, "No quarter."

His men echo the cry. "No quarter!"

I've seen enough war vids to understand what that means. I don't want to see the rest, but I can't pull from his true-life nightmare. I asked to see what he dreams about, so he's serving it up. It feels like I'm crying, but I can't touch my cheeks to be sure.

From here, we flash to what must be the McCullough war room, bodies everywhere. March was kind enough not to show me all the killing, but the carnage can't be avoided entirely. I know that it was barely even a fight. The McCulloughs were broken when they lost in the tunnels. I know the man I love used his knife again and again on enemies too young to die, thrusting the blade cleanly up through the chin.

We stride toward a surprisingly young man. He can't be more than twenty turns, full of invincibility and dreams of grandeur. Like the rest, he's thin and wild-eyed, hair standing in a crazy tangle. By the way he's dressed, I realize this is the McCullough. Everyone else is dead.

He tries to run, but the floor is slick with entrails. The

reek of voided bowels doesn't affect March, but I want to scream. It's beyond anything I could have imagined. The McCullough slips in the spilled blood, falling hard.

"I have a wife," he begs, as he scrambles backward on feet and hands. "Children. I was only trying to secure their future. Let me go to them, please. They're on Arcturus." He names a small colony in the Outskirts. "Don't do this, please. I'll accept exile—"

This time, there's no clean thrust through the chin. March rams his knife upward through the rib cage, knowing precisely how to find the heart. I imagine the way it pierces lung first, then slices clean through. The McCullough lets out a horribly childish whimper and crumples. March leaves the blade in the body.

His voice is toneless as he says, "Hostile takeover complete. Begin an inventory of property and assets; we take possession immediately." He grabs a man I recognize, but whose name I cannot recall. "Top priority is finding out what they did with the Teras."

The soldier acknowledges with a sharp salute. While his men get to work, March stands staring at the river of blood running beneath his feet.

CHAPTER 29

I come to myself huddled in a shivering heap on the floor, my face wet with tears.

March sits a few meters away, still sprawled in a pose that somehow suggests tension instead of ease. His long fingers tap out a message against his thighs that would break my heart if I could translate the mournful tempo into words.

"So now you know what I dream about," he says at last. "And there's more. You want to see it all, Jax?"

For once, I have no quick comeback. Hell no, I don't want to see more. Honestly, I wish I hadn't seen that much. The worst thing? He has to live with those memories. No wonder he took the meds from Doc without complaining. If I'd lived through what he has, I'd want to forget my own name.

I start to wonder if fixing him is beyond my ability, no matter how much I love him. Right now, I feel weird and frozen. They say wild animals belong in their natural habitat, not among people they could savage while simply following their nature. So does that mean he should return to Nicu Tertius?

Finally, I answer, "I think that's enough for now."

"Aren't you going to tell me how much you love me?" His voice is mocking, acid-etched. "How much you're dying to be with me like we used to be?"

He expects things to have changed, and right now I feel too shaken to offer convincing reassurance. But I'm too stubborn to do what he expects. So I come up on my knees and gaze up at him.

"You can love somebody without loving what they do. I wish that hadn't been necessary, and I wish you weren't so fucked up over it, but seeing what happened on Lachion didn't change anything for me. Not really." As I say the words, I'm surprised to find they're accurate.

I haven't touched him since I came in the room, but I still want to. I wish I felt like I could crawl into his arms and let him lose his pain in my body. At this point, I'm afraid of the route something like that would take. My love isn't blind or foolish, and I don't have a death wish.

But it's not like March went on a killing spree for fun. He waged war to save the lives of people he cares about, after the McCulloughs started the conflict. Now he has to deal with the aftermath, but he won't do it alone. He keeps trying to drive me off, but I'll be damned if I'll go.

He shakes his head. "Are you that desperate not to be alone?"

That hurts, but I shrug it away. "No. What we have is that good." Not until the awareness flashes in his eyes do I realize I've spoken in present tense. His face softens almost imperceptibly as I go on, "I want to help. I just don't know what to do."

"I never had anyone love me like you do," he whispers, almost despite himself.

I smile. "Kai taught me. The one you don't like me thinking about? I didn't know how to love somebody before he showed me."

He struggles for words, his voice rough and low. "Then I think maybe I'm grateful to him instead of jealous."

"Why would you be jealous of him?" The question slips out. "He's *gone*."

March shrugs. "He seemed to hold a part of you I could never touch."

"Kai was a warm sunny day, and he trickled into every fiber of me. You're more like a strong rain, but you've gotten inside me just the same."

His mouth twitches. "Not lately."

I grin, grateful he can joke at all. "Not what I meant. What were you dreaming about last night, March?"

Yeah, the night he choked me. I hope he doesn't show me. I want him to *tell* me. He dragged me into his nightmares to try to change my mind about him, so show-and-tell versus voluntary sharing represent different things.

A silence follows the question, but March seems pensive and uncertain, not full of impotent anger. Finally he says, "Our patrol couldn't get back to base one night after you left. We had to camp in the tunnels, so we split the watches. The kid on fourth shift was young, and he must've nodded off. I woke up with a McCullough on top of me, just barely rolled away from his knife."

He won't look at me as he goes on, "I choked him to death with my bare hands. When I bumped up against you in my sleep, I must've thought—"

"You were back there," I finish. "In the tunnels. Because you're not used to sleeping with me."

"Don't make excuses, Jax. There's something wrong with me. I'm sure they have a name for it, something with initials, that requires me to be further medicated than I already am or . . . confined. I just don't *care* anymore."

I arch a brow. "Then why did hurting me bother you?"

That stumps him. Finally, he comes up with, "I don't target women or children."

But it's more personal than that between us, and March knows it. He's not broken beyond repair, just badly damaged and caught between memories of how we are together and the seductive pull of a life without fear, pain, or regret. I can understand the draw, but it's not right, and I won't yield him to it.

If only I could dive into him, the way he pulled me into his memories. Something from Mair's logs nags at me—she stressed the importance of connections, but she could slip inside him and look around. If only I could—

"I have an idea," I say softly. "Are you willing to try something?"

Once he would have said yes, no questions asked. Now he says, "That depends."

"We don't need to touch."

"Then it won't be much fun," he decides aloud. "But why not?"

He seems surprised when I say, "Put your boots on. I'll be right back."

I'm gone before he tries to read me. I've been listening to Mair's journal, hoping I'd find something to help, but everything she did is geared toward the Psi-gifted. Now I think I know how I can approximate that. I remember how she said the mind is like another world. Well, I'm an expert at exploring new worlds. In fact, at one point, I was the very best.

In my quarters, I find a long coat with a hood. I tug that up immediately. No point in drawing attention, making the Bugs wonder what the ambassador is up to so early in the morning. They'd certainly assume the worst. Most of the Ithtorians would recognize me on sight, but the other humans in our delegation don't get so much coverage. In the hood, I might be any one of them.

By the time I return, March stands by the door, ready to go and wearing a mystified expression. Too bad. I'm not going to explain my intentions. He might balk. I'm grateful that he doesn't pry; there's no icy prickle that signifies he's reading me.

We speak little on the way to the underground tram. Thankfully, the chip includes both written and spoken meanings. So I can understand the symbols now, and we make it to the spaceport without incident.

The guards on duty have been instructed to permit humans free passage within the docking area, so we board as the day lengthens into full brightness. Excitement overpowers my general weariness.

This is a much bigger vessel than I'm used to, so I have to ask directions to the cockpit twice. The skeleton crew on duty at this hour reveals little interest in our progress. From his expression, March has some inkling what I intend; but he doesn't protest, just follows me in silence.

When we finally arrive, I find things in order, well-maintained equipment if not top-of-the-line. The controls shine as if they've been recently polished. Whoever jumps here takes great pride in it. That's a good omen. With a little shiver of pleasure, I settle into the nav chair and invite him with a gesture to take his place beside me.

"I don't think running away is the answer," he says with amusement. "Plus, I think we still have people on world."

Maybe he doesn't know after all. It's nice to know I can still surprise him.

"Wrong. We're not running away."

"Kinky jacked-in sex?" Now *he* raises a brow. Somehow he manages to sound both hopeful and dubious. Whether he realizes it or not, he's been thawing slowly, joking with me the way he used to.

I shake my head as I power up the nav system. "Nope. Just jack in for me, okay?"

It's a leap of faith. I can't explain why, but I think it'll be less likely to work if he knows what I intend to do. The human mind has natural shields, he told me once. So if he figures out what I'm planning, his will come up. He won't be able to help it.

In response, he plugs in.

CHAPTER 30

I jack in as well, and the world goes dark.

Ordinarily, March would be gearing up for a jump, checking equipment. His connection doesn't rob him of external perception as mine does. If this were a real jump, I would sit like a blind woman waiting to feel him join me.

But this isn't a regular session.

Thanks to wetware, the nav computer hosts our combined consciousness, and I intend to use that in a way the designer never intended. Knowing Farwan, there's probably a warning written up in a navigation manual against trying something like this. To hell with it, I never read those anyway. I spare a curse for my ex-husband, who was in charge of safety when we met. I hope Simon's been shanked in Whitefish by now, or at least been made somebody's bitch. He certainly tried to make me his.

I'm reassured to find March receptive, if a touch wary. If he brings mental walls up, then I'm doomed to fail. Tentative, I reach out, seeking a union like we had when Vel chased us through grimspace. Though he doesn't actively try to push me away, he doesn't draw me in either. I'm going to have to work for this.

March feels remote, as if his memories don't entirely belong to him. Most times, that's probably a good thing. Maybe this damage is a defense mechanism, preventing him from feeling the pain. I'm sure the drugs don't hurt either.

For a while, I let myself drift, offering quiet mental touches now and then to get him used to me again. It's different from having him in my head; I don't suffer the same icy burn because we share a neutral space. He relaxes by degrees, and I register the slow shift reflected in his thoughts.

I'm not there to poke around or learn his secrets. Instead, I do as Mair suggested and treat his mind like a world to explore. To aid in that, I visualize the inside of his head as if it's part of grimspace. Now I consider what I do when I make a jump and find that the beacons are weak and don't connect properly. His emotions, now locked away, become beacons, and I listen to their pulse. They're faint and thready, slowly starving from lack of nourishment.

Eventually, I find them, charting his mind as if it's a new jump. I've always been good at spatial relationships, translating abstract ideas into real points that can be located, and this is just another application of that ability. Soon I've mapped out the various control points.

Here lies motor function; over there is higher thought. Just as all beacons are linked, so should his mind be, but he has dark spots that interfere with connections being made. If I continue the analogy of looking at his damaged psyche as if it were a broken beacon, it will require energy to effect a repair. Ordinarily, that energy comes from the pilot-jumper bond and filters through me into the beacon.

Unfortunately, there's only me. March can't fix himself, or he'd have done it. That means I need to give twice as much. I don't know if I can survive that. I keep my fear locked down behind small partitions he won't notice if I'm careful.

What are you up to, Jax?

Trust me a little longer.

I remember the way he brought me nearly to climax with his mind alone. Though certain mental manipulations can be very powerful, he's had turns to practice them. Misgivings strike. Maybe I shouldn't be rummaging around in here; I might do untold harm. So to test myself, I find his pleasure center and envision a soft touch.

His reaction is immediate, a quick intake of breath and a shuddering exhalation. Dopamine floods his system, relaxing him further. That's good. I don't want him tense when I make my move.

Time. We have plenty of time. I let him relax and soak in the sweetness while trying to cover my uncertainty. Though I didn't do the work very long, I know how to fix a beacon.

I can't overthink this. That's not my strong suit, so I do what I do best.

Leap.

I frame myself as liquid light, able to pass cleanly through any part of him. I'll be the connective force, renewing links that have lapsed. I surge from dark spot to dark spot, illuminating with a warm shimmer. I will the synapses to fire in my wake and remember their prior functions.

Come on, you're not dead space in there. Come back online.

My whole being focuses on this working. He's a broken beacon, and I *can* fix him. I circle endlessly, jumping through the cold places, infusing each one with everything I feel for him. It's like running naked through walls of ice, but I don't stop. Love pours through me. If he's an empty vessel now, then I'll fill him up again.

Once, I'd never have thought I could open up like this for anyone, but apparently there's no limit to what I'll do for him. At the end of each circuit, I brush up against his pleasure center, making him gasp. I'll make damn sure this is good for him—he won't want me to stop until something shifts.

I feel myself weakening. Pain pierces me, just like when I linger in grimspace too long. The human body creates a finite amount of energy, and I'm feeding it to him, just like the beacons. How much of me will it take to make him whole? Steeling myself, I continue my work, and, thank Mary he's too distracted by the pleasure of it to notice what it's doing to me.

Maybe this can't work. Maybe I need someone else here to help me, as when we repair the beacons, but surely one man won't require as much power. And there's no one else. I wouldn't even ask it, not knowing what the consequences could be.

What will I give to heal him?

The answer is everything. I push harder, and feel something tear free inside of me, and it hurts as if I've jabbed a knife into my skull. My teeth tear at my lower lip to swallow the instinctive cry.

Thus powered, my internal movement sparks a chain reaction; heat rises in my wake. When I shift my perceptions, a golden trail shimmers between the dark places, infusing them. Primitive satisfaction surges through me. Yeah, I *want* to imprint myself on him. I want to be so deeply inside him that he'll never shake me loose.

Slowly, I watch the connections renew themselves, fueled by my borrowed energy. Light flows smoothly from point to point, no more breakage. There's still weakness, but with the flow returned to its normal course, natural healing should complete the process I've jump-started. Maybe I'm not Psi, but I'm fragging stubborn.

The pain gradually spirals down to bearable levels. I try to check myself as I did him, but I can't see if I did any permanent harm. Time will tell. Since joy spreads through me, whatever I broke, it wasn't my emotions.

"Mother Mary," he breathes. "You . . . *navigated* me, Jax."

The fact that he's speaking aloud is a measure of his awe. I don't even know what to call what I just did. A highly unorthodox form of mental surgery, I suspect, and nothing I'd ever try on anyone but March. We're woven together in ways that even the tightest pilot-jumper bond doesn't begin to touch.

In answer, I give another soft stroke to his pleasure center, doing to him what he once did to me. Who says I'm incapable of learning from example? I don't have the ability to go into his head as he comes into mine when we're not jacked in, but here inside the nav computer, we're equals.

He groans, and there's something incredibly rousing about knowing I can make him feel like this without a single physical touch. His breath sounds ragged, as if he's run a great distance—I delight in that, too. Raw lust pours out of him, suffusing me in need. But there's more, too. Thank Mary, there's more.

I don't want to have sex while we're jacked in—that's just too porn vid—but if you don't unplug this minute, I can't be responsible for what happens next.

So I take the warning and pull out. "You all right?"

"No," he says deliberately. Before I can ask, he yanks me up out of the nav chair. "Lock the cockpit until further notice," he tells the computer. "No manual overrides."

"Acknowledged," the ship AI responds.

"Jax," he whispers.

And then his hands are on me, pushing me up against the smooth metal door that protects us against prying eyes.

His lips find my throat, and he kisses upward over my jaw to my mouth. I kiss him back with all the pent-up longing. My arms go around his neck, but it's not enough.

We strain together, reveling in the renewed heat between us. His body feels lean and hard against me, and he trembles with the ferocity of our mutual need. I don't need foreplay; I just need him.

He comes into me mentally as he lifts me physically. There's no cold now, only heat. *You like it here? And here?* I gasp and groan. March stimulates three separate places—at the same time—which leaves me feeling like I might go over just from rubbing myself against him.

Mary, I need you.

Is that him or me? At this point, I'm not sure, but the thought applies to both of us. A few tugs at our clothing and the necessary parts are bare. The door feels cold against my naked skin. March boosts me higher, taking me, and my ankles lock at his back. His mouth is ravenous on mine, a hurried nuzzle of panting kisses.

No tenderness this time, just raw, scorching power. I run my fingers over his shoulders, then drag downward with short, blunt nails. In answer, he pushes me tighter against the door, pinning me completely except for the wicked movement of his hips. I reply with tight little rolls, inciting him to frantic excess.

"March." My head falls back, hands tangling in his hair.

Orgasm crashes through me. I tense in his arms, riding the furious sensations, only dimly aware of the way he pushes closer in short, staccato strokes, losing himself in me. His breath gusts against the side of my throat, soft little nonsense words that I can't translate into meanings.

There's no playful fight for supremacy this time, just the two of us, raw and candid. We've been apart too long for this act to have any implication of power or dominance. At base, this is an affirmation of what we are together—and how much we need one another to be whole.

He exhales against the top of my head. I feel shudders still rocking through him. His arms tighten around me as he breathes, "Jax. Ah, Jax. Sweet Mary, how I love you."

And I go boneless with delight.

.CLASSIFIED-TRANSMISSION.
.REQUESTED STATUS REPORT.
.FROM-EDUN_LEVITER.
.TO-SUNI_TARN.
.ENCRYPT-DESTRUCT-ENABLED.

Chancellor Tarn,

As you asked, I have prepared a dossier regarding the greatest areas of concern.

1. Escalating Morgut attacks, including the destruction of Outpost 8
2. Increased instance of Syndicate strikes, unless the shipping company has a contract for protection
3. Complete disregard for interstellar legislation
4. Failure to meet certain standards in public safety
5. Inability to efficiently utilize seized Farwan assets
6. Lack of faith in Conglomerate leadership

1. Escalating Morgut attacks

The Morgut have grown bolder in recent months. They no longer fear reprisal and treat human beings as prey. As the Conglomerate has heretofore not offered any significant deterrent, we can expect this pattern to continue.

Of the past seventeen attacks, there have been only four survivors. This includes ships, outposts, mining colonies, and deep-space stations. My sources advise me that there is a panic stirring, and that people are beginning to say it's not safe anywhere.

2. Increased instance of Syndicate strikes

Using Gehenna as an example, eight out of every ten ships that leaves port will experience a hijacking attempt sometime between departure and destination. The merchantmen report these pirates are professional, organized, swift, and merciless. If the freighter attempts to fight back, the crew is slaughtered, but for one man, who is put adrift in an escape capsule and left behind as a warning.

A recent ad campaign has aired, offering security and peace of mind for a reasonable fee. It depicts a middle-aged male, smiling in relief as he settles down for the night; the scene then shifts to his property, being protected by armed guards. According to recent polls, the Syndicate has gained ten points in public regard, thus reflected in the purchase of private contracts. Their market share continues to climb. As under Farwan, people have responded well to the iron fist in a velvet glove, as proffered by the Syndicate.

3. Complete disregard for interstellar legislation

In the past four months, twenty ships have been intercepted attempting to bring contraband onto New Terra itself. Freighter captains argue that since they must now pay more for protection to ensure their cargo arrives safely, they can no longer afford to ship regular goods and must resort to the higher profit of black-market trading.

Additionally, the independent raiders have grown bolder and will attack cargo vessels right in the hot zones. They lie in wait along heavily traveled jump routes and attack the merchantman as he comes out of grimspace.

4. Failure to meet certain standards in public safety

When Farwan policed the star lanes, they deterred such crimes, not via prevention, but through relentless pursuit of their adversaries. They spent countless credits on jurisdiction and punishment, earning their reputation for brutal justice. Their focus was not preservation of human life but minimizing lost profit. Regardless of focus, however, they did offer a certain measure of safety in interstellar travel. To date, the Conglomerate has failed to establish any like service.

When the average person thinks of the Conglomerate, he sees an ineffectual organization that has no might or military force with which to enforce its will.

5. Inability to efficiently utilize seized Farwan assets

Conglomerate constituents feel that current expenditures are shortsighted and work solely to preserve the interests of humankind when the organization purports to offer true and democratic representation to all species. Recent construction on New Terra reinforces this perception. The new senate facilities, while providing a sense of pomp and tradition, do little to reassure the common man that he will be protected if he leaves New Terra.

6. Lack of faith in Conglomerate leadership

Confidence in the Conglomerate has reached an all-time low. Ten out of every fifteen individuals surveyed state they believe some alternate form of government would prove more effective. Constituents also desire a return to the days of empire, including standing armada and trained soldiers ready to go to war on their behalf.

Ten companies that had requested Conglomerate aid in protecting their cargo have since withdrawn their petitions. Four planets have seceded from the proposed Summit and ask they no longer be considered tier worlds, hoping for neutrality in the coming conflict. The crisis has reached critical levels, and if this alliance does not come to pass—or offers less-than-anticipated results—our situation will become untenable.

My proposal—including financial plans, budgets, resource allocation, and personnel recommendations for newly created positions—is attached.

.ATTACHMENT-PROPOSED_SOLUTIONS-FOLLOWS.
.END-TRANSMISSION.

CHAPTER 31

The AI interrupts us to proffer a mild warning. "A number of individuals are approaching the cockpit. Their vitals indicate agitation."

I never know if AIs are programmed to sound like that, or if it's some developer's quirk slipped into a prototype ages ago. Someone tries to open the door, then bangs with both fists. Through the metal, I hear Dina swearing.

"There's a group of angry Ithtorians screaming for blood outside the ship," she shouts. "What the frag have you done now?"

Shit. I have no earthly idea. Whatever's wrong, we didn't do it; nonetheless, a cold feeling rises up in me. It's probably good they roused Dina. She has an impressively royal demeanor when it suits her. I thank my lucky stars that she and Hit prefer to sleep on the ship whenever possible, when they aren't needed for some diplomatic display.

"Stall them," I call back, frantic. "Is Hit out there? Ask her to use the wardrober in my quarters to get me something decent to wear. You know the parameters?"

"Roger that," the tall pilot answers.

I need a san-shower, but we probably don't have time. March lets me slide down his body as he steps back. His expression is rueful as he shakes his head.

"Our timing has always been rotten," he mutters. "But I think this might be just be the worst."

I agree wholeheartedly. Instead of getting to enjoy the rosy glow of endorphins inspired by heel-banging sex, I have to scramble to figure out what's gone wrong. *Dammit.* And

I thought things were going as well as could be expected. For Mary's sake, I thought we were on the verge of signing a treaty, even bearing in mind the Grand Administrator's objections.

March unlocks the door, and I go at a dead run toward my quarters. I hear his footsteps behind me. He's dressed at least. Good thing he was sitting in trousers and a shirt when I pulled him out of his room.

"Fasten your pants," I whisper.

His hands get busy. Since it was so early when we went out, I just put the hooded coat over my thin ki pants and sleep cami. I should know by now that things never go as I expect. The reason why I don't expect trouble probably reflects some innate lack.

Mary, could this get worse?

We pass Dina en route. "Make it quick," she calls. "I don't know what exactly has happened, but they think you're trying to make a run for it."

Shit. That's really not good. Okay, so maybe on the surface it looks bad, finding the ambassador on board the ship in the wee hours, coincidentally after something's gone wrong; but we can straighten this out. I take a deep breath and dodge into my room, where I find Hit waiting with a suitable gold, sleeveless robe.

Bless her attention to detail.

It will be cold outside the docking area, but I can live with that. More than ever, I need to show strength and authority. No time for modesty, so I shuck my clothes, exposing my scars fully. Hit averts her eyes, but March has never looked away from me, not even from the first day we met.

As best I can, I assemble myself into the image of the ambassador the Ithtorians have come to expect. Then it's time to head for the doors. The Bugs won't board us, as that would be construed as an aggressive act and terminate the nascent accords between our peoples, but as we approach the exit ramp, I can hear the commotion just outside.

For the first time, the clicks and chitters sound enraged and dangerous. Thankfully Dina has managed to keep them contained, and I meet Vel coming up as I step out onto the ramp. Thank Mary. He can help me smooth things over, if it can be done at all.

I pause to ask in an undertone, "What's going on?"

Anyone else would chide me for not being where I'm supposed to be at this hour, but Vel doesn't waste time with recriminations. He deals with situations as they are instead of as they should be. His side-set eyes glitter in the overhead lights as he buys us a little time by greeting me with a particularly poetic *wa*.

The chip surprises me by offering visual signals shifted to word meanings: *When the dark breaks, white wave looks to brown bird. There will be no tears born of new light.* I realize that's what I called myself in the *wa* he translated for me. He must be white wave. I don't know how I know that, but he's acknowledged it by referring to himself that way.

"Sharis has been admitted to the medical facility. At this time, he is critically ill, and the physicians do not know whether he will survive the night."

Aw, shit. He's one of our strongest supporters, which might be why he wound up in the hospital. That doesn't explain why I have the Bug Gestapo clamoring just a few meters away. They look like they want my entrails on a stick.

Then it dawns on me. "No. Surely they don't think . . . what possible reason could *I* have for jeopardizing my mission?"

Not when so much rests on my success here. I grind my teeth against the urge to start swearing in every language I know. But I can't fly off the handle. I've been cool and calm so far. This isn't the time to break precedent.

"Not you, necessarily," he replies. "But they believe it was someone from our delegation. Preliminary toxin screenings have indicated he was slipped a quantity of citric acid, which is nutritious to humans and—"

"Poison to Ithtorians," I finish grimly.

Vel inclines his head. "That is the current conjecture."

It goes without saying that an Ithtorian could still have done it, intending to make it look like we did. Is that something those extremists in the park who nearly killed me would do? Well, I don't have time to cycle through all the potential suspects right now.

I have to talk these Bug soldiers down before they send all of us to the mines. Sentencing without a trial wouldn't be constitutional for a native, but as foreigners, we lack the same rights. My fingers tremble as I step forward, so I lace them together.

"I am deeply saddened to hear of Sharis's illness," I begin. "I have come to respect him greatly during my time here. I will, of course, cooperate fully with the authorities to try to bring his attacker to justice."

Vel translates for me, putting a more polished spin on my words. Thank Mary for his political background. The soldiers rumble and hiss.

"More lies," one of them says.

"We should slay the lot of them," his commander adds. "And let the Iglogth sort them out. I knew nothing good would come of allowing humans back on world. There were reasons we banished the scum in the first place."

A deadly chill radiates from Vel, standing beside me. "May I remind you that our party possesses a personal warrant of safe passage from the Grand Administrator herself? I understand you perfectly, and any hostile action taken toward me or my companions will result in your immediate death. The Grand Administrator does not take kindly to having her pledges foresworn by a filthy lot of untaught foot soldiers."

Go, Vel.

I can almost see them deflate, duty supplanting aggression. The captain steps forward and executes a lovely, apologetic *wa*. "I beg your pardon, ambassador. We allowed our grief and outrage to overwhelm our better judgment. We beg that you will not report our transgression to the Grand Administrator."

"I share your grief and outrage," I answer smoothly. "Thus, I understand it. Only let me know what I may do to facilitate your investigation. I, too, want the culprit brought to justice with all haste." In conclusion, I offer an acknowledging *wa*, fluid motion that shows I have the capacity to forgive his transgression.

To my surprise, Vel relays my message word for word.

Maybe I'm finally getting good at this. I'm not sure it's a skill I really want, however. March fell in love with me because I had no doublespeak at all. Whatever I thought, I never hesitated to say it. How will he feel about a woman grown expert in prevarication?

Warmth surges through me, the likes of which I haven't felt in so long, I almost cry out. March fills me like he used to, easily, softly, and it takes all my will to school my features. *Don't worry,* he tells me tenderly. *It doesn't matter who you've been, who you are, or who you become. I'm with you every step of the way.*

Mary, how I needed to hear that.

"At this time, all diplomatic processes will be placed on hold," the captain continues. "The vote will be delayed until after Councilman Sharis has recovered from his illness and the guilty party apprehended."

I acknowledge that with a nod. Doubtless that's just what the Opposition Party wanted. The Bugs have learned to interpret the inclination of the head as a positive response, so Vel doesn't need to translate.

"Then, if it pleases the ambassador, we will escort you to the center for jurisprudence."

At any other time, the commander's formality would amuse me. Not now. We stand at the edge of a terrible precipice, and I'm the only thing that can keep us upright.

Hope my balance is up to the task.

CHAPTER 32

Jael trots along beside me like an annoying pet. The apparent threat to his generous salary, paid by the Conglomerate, has roused him to near agitation. He doesn't seem to care about Sharis's health, but he has all kinds of advice for *me*.

"Don't go with them, Jax. This is nothing but a trumped-up excuse to take you into custody. They're not going to let you help with their investigation. They're just going to hold you so you can't get in their way."

"I realize that," I tell him darkly. "But it's in our best interests to cooperate fully, whatever that entails. The alliance he proposed stands on shaky ground, and I have to do whatever it takes to steady it. Do you have *any* idea what's going on out there?" I gesture vaguely above my head, encompassing the universe entire in the motion.

"Yes." His voice is grim. "But you can't do any good out there if you let them send you to the mines down here."

"For Mary's sake," I say in exasperation. "I'm not going to the mines, just to an interview room. I don't have anything to hide. I didn't do this to Sharis." I keep walking, and add over my shoulder, "And I highly doubt any of us did. If I had to bet, I'd lay money that it was someone in the OP or one of the Grand Administrator's minions. But just to be thorough: Where were *you* tonight after you left the party, bodyguard?"

Shame colors his reply. "Playing Charm with Dina and Hit. I'm sorry I left you, but that shindig was bloody boring. I stayed as long as I could take it."

"Some help you are. Your paranoia is *not* an asset."

Now there's some irony—me accusing someone else of paranoia. Maybe it's a sign I'm recovering from the havoc the psychs wreaked upon my psyche. Dina always said I just needed time, and it seems like she's right, as usual.

A question occurs to me. "Have you seen Constance tonight? She's usually working in my quarters, but I haven't seen her since this afternoon."

He nods. "She was in comms on deck two, looking through the archives. She said you asked her to research something."

I said anything that could help the alliance go forward, as I recall. Well, that's one worry off my mind. "Good to know."

Hit and Dina had scrambled into their honor-guard uniforms while I was changing, and they're marching along behind us. I haven't had a chance to savor the fact that March is back, but he's part of me in a way he hasn't been for months. Telltale warmth results whenever he brushes close with a mental touch.

His solid presence at my back gives me more comfort than I like to think about. It would be exponentially worse if he weren't here. That also applies to Vel, who's taken a position directly behind me next to March.

We have Bugs on either side of our six-person crew. Maybe they haven't said so in as many words, but this is an armed escort. I know what would've happened if I had protested or tried to return to the ship. Best if I keep things civil.

In the pit of my stomach, I register the worry that we're fucked, and there's no fixing this. The chief proponent of the alliance has been poisoned . . . with a uniquely human compound. We can eat citrus fruit all day long and lick the juice from our fingers without suffering any harm.

That's assuredly not true of Ithtorians. Sharis may have suffered irreparable damage, and I'm heartless because I can only think about how it's going to impact humanity. I took Chancellor Tarn's message to heart, and I feel quietly frantic at the idea of things falling to pieces here. Mary curse it,

I wanted to succeed, and I was doing so fraggin' well, better than anyone could have predicted.

I let none of this inner turmoil show on my face as we pass from the spaceport down the tunnel that leads to the underground. Without a jacket, it's cold as hell, but I manage not to shiver, showing I'm impervious to discomfort. But it's only the tight clench of my jaw that prevents my teeth from chattering.

Thankfully, the tram isn't far, and the Bugs herd us toward the proper station. Silence becomes the order of the day, so I listen to the quiet hum of machinery until the commander says, as the tram slows, "We disembark here."

It's become second nature for me to let Vel tell me what I already know before I make a move. So after he does so, we head for the "center for jurisprudence." Since we enter via a lift inside the tram station, I don't get a look at the building's exterior.

Inside, it's typical of other Ithtorian spaces, full of lush color and blooming plants. The flooring gives way softly underfoot, rich and loamy in a way that seems strange to me, even after spending time here. I'm used to rugs or tile, so I find their bioengineered furnishings a little disturbing, but then . . . they find it disturbing that humans surround themselves with the deceased and inanimate. No wonder they call us carrion eaters.

With some disconnected portion of my brain, I wonder what weapon sculpted their world in permafrost. Their physiology is better suited to a tropical environment, akin to Venice Minor, yet they dwell on Ithiss-Tor, which is more akin to Ielos. They strive to create their sultry paradises indoors.

To my distress, they show us into separate rooms. I sit down nonetheless and arrange myself as if I am perfectly at ease. I've come to learn that face is everything, so if I comport myself well here, perhaps something can be salvaged.

"We wish to speak with you first, ambassador," the commander tells me. "Thus, your translator will remain here for now."

This time, I almost incline my head *before* Vel translates. Catching myself, I sit like an uncomprehending stump while the bounty hunter rephrases what I already know. Then I indicate my understanding, so the captain goes on:

"Velith Il-Nok will then be required in the other interview chambers. You will be detained only long enough for us to ascertain the whereabouts of your core party. Eventually, we will probably wish to speak with everyone aboard your ship."

"Will you be interviewing *everyone* who had access to Sharis's quarters?" I ask.

They know as well as I do; that encompasses a lot of Bugs, including the Grand Administrator's personal assistants and countless underlings who are always scurrying to do someone's bidding. Vel puts the question to the commander with a touch more tact.

"Of course." I don't imagine the guard leader's distaste at having to placate me. He executes a perfunctory *wa*, then says, "The interrogator will be with you shortly."

Once they've gone, I take stock of my surroundings. There's only one door, no windows. In some ways, it's like we've been left in a small garden to relax. The petal-soft leaves that furl into the chairs we now sit upon are very soothing, and the sweet scent I've noticed pervading most public spaces is present here as well.

In other ways, I feel totally confined, as if all these other living things are sucking up the air. With some effort, I make myself calm down. This isn't the time to think about the walls closing in or the stench of burning flesh.

"How bad is it?" I ask Vel, sotto voce.

"That depends on a number of factors." How like him not to want to commit to a prediction, like I'll blame him if he's wrong.

"Analysis?"

"If one of us did this," he says deliberately—and I'm momentarily distracted to hear him identify himself as one of *us*, "then our chances of getting off world are slim. We landed under the flower of peace. If one of us attacked Sharis, then they will want to punish all of us for the transgression, however unfair that may seem. And human beings have no rights on Ithiss-Tor." He spreads his claws. "I will do my best to argue that only the guilty party should be penalized, but I cannot guarantee results."

Well, that's bleak as hell, but I can't believe one of my people would do this. Everyone knows how important our mission is. Even if they haven't seen the private reports I receive from Chancellor Tarn, they've certainly heard about the escalating Morgut attacks on the vids.

Emry was just the beginning.

To make matters worse, we've also got the Syndicate, independent raiders, and Farwan loyalists going head to head. But I can't think about the way the galaxy is going to hell right now. I was doing my best to patch things up, help the Conglomerate show its power and competence by bringing the Ithtorians aboard. Until this very substantial hitch.

I'm not the praying kind, but I can't help asking for a little help. *Mary, please don't let Sharis die. We need him.* There's no sense I've been heard, but I derive a bit of comfort from the ritual. Maybe that's the magic after all.

"I can't say you pull your punches," I murmur. "If one of them did it, the OP perhaps, would they ever admit it? Or would they try to cover it up?"

Vel considers and eventually has to spread his claws in puzzlement. "I cannot say. It would be a dishonorable act, to say the least; but, as you have already discerned, face is not comprised of always doing the right thing, here. Sometimes prestige is earned by doing the wrong thing . . . and not getting caught."

Huh. Wonder why I'm not reassured.

CHAPTER 33

The Ithtorian who joins us after what seems like hours— and doubtless we're intended to be sweating by now—is unknown to me.

A quick glance tells me this is a male. He stands taller than most of his fellows, and his thorax seems elongated, as if he has an extra segment, though I can't say for certain from my quick visual scan. The interrogator also gleams sickly yellow, which fills me with foreboding.

Then I realize *why* it bothers me. The odd, artificial color of his chitin will never show the high honor of xanthic stripes. That means he must operate outside the system; nothing he does can earn him face . . . or result in its loss. That doesn't bode well for us.

"I am Ehon Il-Chath." His *wa* of greeting sets my teeth on edge.

I don't like the angle of his bow, or the way he nearly shows me his claws. He doesn't lower his head either; instead his side-set eyes bore into mine in oblique accusation. Obligingly, the chip provides references that expand upon my unease: *In the time after all-sorrow, gray adder devours the vanquished.*

Like hell.

How I wish I could attempt to infuse a rebuttal in my answering *wa*, but whatever I say, I can't look like it was on purpose. So I keep my face blank as I reply via body language. I think something of my natural feeling slips through because the interrogator takes a step back before catching himself.

"This is merely a formality, but I must ask a few pertinent questions," he says, taking the seat opposite. "I will not keep you long."

Just long enough to search our rooms for traces of citric acid, right, Ehon?

I sit impassive while Vel relays the meaning, then I incline my head. "I'm happy to help. We're all shocked and saddened to hear what happened to Sharis."

Mary, but I'm tired of hearing myself spouting platitudes. No matter how sincere you are, if you repeat the same sentiment often enough, it starts to sound fake, even to your own ears. Pretty soon, I won't mean anything I say; I'll just say it because I know I'm supposed to. And that was most of the reason I ran away from the future my parents had planned out for me. If I don't find some other line of work soon, I'll turn into a politician, and there will be no saving me.

Ehon consults a datapad, leaving me a little time to think. I manage to ignore the growing ache inside me. Being in the cockpit wasn't necessarily a good idea, for all it helped March. It roused a nearly ungovernable desire to say "fuck it" and just head off into the stars. Let mankind worry about itself for a while. That's the old Jax talking, and I have to admit, there's something seductive about her thought processes.

The interrogator gets right down to business, once he's acquainted himself with the facts of the case. "Can you tell me your whereabouts between the hours of midnight and five in the morning?"

They don't tell time like we do, but the chip couches the question in terms that make sense to me. I slant a glance at Vel as he translates. What will it mean for him when word gets out that he spent the night in my room? I have no idea what interpretation his people will put on that. Just based on the way they've treated him to date, they'll probably assume he's an utter deviant, but since he's attached as my cultural liaison, they can't pass judgment and send him to join the other mental defectives doing hard labor.

"What time did we leave the party?" I ask Vel.

"An hour past the new day?" He's come to count time as we do, no surprise, given how long he's lived among us.

I nod. "Let's go with that."

The interrogator watches us with an unhappy cant of his head. He doesn't like that we can discuss things without him understanding us, but unless there's another translator on world—and there isn't—he has no choice but to trust Vel. He breaks in to demand, "What is she saying?"

Vel replies smoothly, "She is merely asking what time we departed Councilor Devri's flat in order to answer your question accurately."

Ehon leans forward, seemingly titillated. "The two of you were together last evening?"

"I accompany the ambassador to all social events," Vel responds, in what I imagine to be a quelling fashion. "How could she communicate, if I did not?"

With a click of his claws, Ehon dismisses the issue, borderline rudeness there. "So you attended a party hosted by Councilor Devri last night, and neither of you departed until quite late. Were you together the entire time?"

I have to admit that we were not. I wait until it's safe to answer, once Vel has repeated everything, then I say, "Vel spoke privately with Devri for a time, and Sharis himself kept me company. He only left my side when Mako arrived. I stood in full view of a roomful of Ithtorians during that time."

Which is all to the good. Ehon seems to be trying to establish opportunity, so I'm glad I never wandered off on my own. Vel tells him what I've said, and the interrogator taps his claws thoughtfully, processing the information. Then he enters it via a series of taps on the datapad.

"Very good," the interrogator says. "Once you left the party, what then?"

From my peripheral vision, I glimpse Vel nodding ever so slightly as his vocalizer restates Ehon's question. Giving me the go-ahead? Okay then, I'll spill.

"Vel and I went back to my quarters then," I say quietly. "He remained there with me until dawn."

I assume he'll correct me if that's wrong. It might even have been his early departure that woke me this morning. For some reason, I'm not at all surprised to hear him repeat my words, nearly verbatim.

Ehon recoils visibly at hearing this, so I don't need to be told what interpretation he has put on the information. He clicks his mandible in fastidious dismay, but to his credit, he does not pursue the matter further. The interrogator simply enters the facts into his datapad. Discretion aside, I have no doubt he'll be drinking on this for days.

"Are you both willing to speak oaths that neither of you left each other's company during the early-morning hours?"

Vel doesn't wait for my response. "Yes."

The interrogator levels a hard look on Vel. "You would not *lie* for the ambassador, would you, Il-Nok?"

A hiss escapes Vel. He curls his claws in deliberate insult. "If you were not an interrogator, I would demand satisfaction."

"And Councilor Devri will vouch for your whereabouts prior?" Ehon asks, ignoring Vel's outrage.

When I'm given the opportunity to answer, I say, "He will . . . and a hundred other prominent Ithtorians, as well. As I recall, we had a lovely conversation with two merchants named Arqut and Kalid."

Ehon makes further notes on his datapad, then he unfolds to his feet. "I believe I need nothing further at this time. But if I do need another moment of your time, I will know where to find you. I will permit you to escort the ambassador back to her quarters, but I require you to return to assist with the other sessions within an hour." His *wa* in parting sends a cold chill down my spine.

Gray adder hunts soft, sleepy prey. Quiet kill.

I cloak my visceral reaction, stilling my shiver. *Thanks for the warning, asshole, but I'm not as sleepy as you think.* After I reply with a controlled *wa*, I step out of the interview room, grateful to leave the sticky heat and the cloying smell of hothouse blossoms. Vel follows a few steps behind, one claw on my shoulder, not for guidance or protection, but in accordance with some tradition that escapes me at the moment.

"This looks bad for you," I say, once we exit the building. A cold wind sweeps over me as we make for the tram.

"The further degradation of my reputation is scarcely a matter of concern to me," he returns. "It already hangs in tatters, and there is no altering that we provide each other with an alibi, so it is fortuitous I felt moved to indulge in a confessional last night."

My teeth chatter in response. Vel hurries us into the station, but I tell myself he is fondly amused by my long-standing tradition of never having a coat when I need one. This time, however, he doesn't have his bounty-hunter pack to amend the lack.

Once I've warmed up a bit, I protest, "They're going to think you're a deviant."

It doesn't seem fair that they always think the worst of him. He regards me for a moment, only the distant rush of the tram to break the silence. Here, near the jurisprudence center, it is oddly deserted.

"And that would make me perverse, if it were true?" The vocalizer renders the question conversational. "If I enjoyed human lovers?"

My eyes widen. "I don't . . ."

Hell. I didn't see this coming. Of all possible outcomes, I certainly don't want to wound him. After all, it's not my repugnance speaking; it's the way his people seem so uniformly revolted by human beings.

"Let me simplify matters, Sirantha. Living in exile made me rethink many taboos I took for truth. All beings experience loneliness in some form or other, and over my long exile, I did take human lovers, but they generally did not know my true form. In fact, you *met* one of them."

Before I can frame a response to that, our train arrives.

CHAPTER 34

As we board, questions bubble on the tip of my tongue, such as *Who? When?* and *What happened between you and her?* Or *him*, I suppose. Though it's a tough call, I decide circumstances don't lend themselves to prying into Vel's private life. We have more pressing concerns.

So I simply say, "No, that doesn't make you perverse. I should have realized you'd adapt to life off Ithiss-Tor."

And as he said, no being wants to spend all its time alone. His relationships might not even be primarily sexual in nature, and even if they are, it's none of my business. I can't entirely quash my curiosity, however. We've met a lot of people in our travels, so which one was it? And did he or she realize who Vel was?

Ithtorians are uncommonly long-lived, so he might stay with a human lover for a great span of time by our standards. At regular intervals, he could even age himself appropriately, but he would need substantial privacy to do so. I consider watching someone you care about grow old and die while you remain perpetually the same. It doesn't sound desirable; in fact, it sounds like a particularly hellish punishment.

Even if he can't love as humans do, even if the bonds he forms are not the same, it stands to reason that loss hurts him. I cannot imagine it being otherwise for any sentient creature, which is why I am haunted by the image of a frog-mother on Marakeq keening her sorrow to the indifferent stars.

"I applaud your restraint," Vel says eventually, as we disembark.

Suspicion blooms, distracting me from the unquestionably fascinating subject matter. It seems odd they would simply let us walk away, given the severity of the crime. Before we've gone too far, Bugs emerge to tail us discreetly. If we inquired, doubtless they would say it's for our own protection, but I realize our days of free passage are over. We won't be able to make a move now without it being documented in triplicate and reported to five separate factions.

I pretend to ignore them as we head for my quarters to wait for the others. They'll start by interrogating my inner circle, but eventually they'll want to talk to the whole crew. Instinct tells me I can't sit by powerless while that happens; I need to find some way to get them to make me part of this investigation, or I'm going to lose all the face I've built up over my time on planet. But maybe I'm not the best arbiter of what should come next. My instincts aren't infallible, as I've learned to my cost.

Once we're safely inside, Vel checks the place for newly implanted listening devices. To nobody's surprise, he finds one. They must plan to teach someone to interpret, or maybe they'll lay hands on a chip somehow. If they bounce an order off world, they can purchase plans for one and have it built. That will take days, but until then, they'll have a log of everything we say.

While I consider the problem, Vel excuses himself with a silent gesture. When he returns, he has his bounty-hunter backpack. At first I'm surprised the Bugs didn't confiscate it; but then, if I know Vel, he secured it well before leaving his quarters.

He works quietly for a moment, then he says, "I've programmed it to report a random and banal variety of small talk in a fair approximation of our voices. They'll notice the pattern eventually, once they have some way to understand what's being said, but this should buy us some time."

"Thanks."

My rooms have been searched. Though I don't have much in the way of possessions, I can tell things have been moved and replaced. I check the sleeping area next. At least Constance is still on the ship, where she's safe.

"Will they want to question Constance, too?"

"They think she is human," he points out. "It is natural she would be taken for interrogation when they realize she has been omitted from their lists."

Ah, shit. "How bad will it be if they discover her true nature?"

"Bad. Prestige is earned by *not* being caught."

I suspect he's understating the problem. Can Constance keep up the charade under duress? She's not programmed to dissemble. I feel myself start to sweat. It feels like everything is crumbling to pieces, and there's not a damn thing I can do about it. The worst part is—if they catch me in one deceit, they'll start looking for other offenses.

They might scan me and find the chip.

How I wish I could just jump and get the hell out of here. I'm so hungry for grimspace and the distant throb of the beacons, the colors streaming through my mind. A shudder rolls over me, nearly bending me double. When things were going well, it was much easier to block this craving.

Now all my instincts are telling me to cut and run—that it's not going to get better. It's only going to get worse, and I don't want to be around when it does. That's definitely consistent with my instincts. In the past, I haven't been the most reliable individual; I think of my own well-being first, and to hell with everyone else.

If my mother knew, she'd be laughing her ass off. What did she say? That my mere presence would be enough to create havoc, despite my best intentions. Mary curse it, I don't want to prove her right.

Focus, Jax. What allies do you have on world?

"Would we be able to see Devri?"

"We cannot keep the visit secret from security, but yes, we should be able to access him. If we cannot, then things are worse than I had imagined."

I consider that. If we draw attention to him right now, we might lose an ally. On the other hand, if we do nothing, we've already lost, but I'm not the best at judging what differentiates a strategic retreat from a virtual surrender here. Maybe lying low for a while would be the smart thing. All diplomatic functions have been suspended while they figure out who poisoned Sharis.

"I need to know what you talked about when you had that private chat."

Vel answers with no hesitation. "Devri alerted me to the existence of extremist factions that would stop at nothing to prevent this alliance from coming to pass."

"So they wouldn't balk at attempted murder."

"Hardly. Neither of us imagined they would move so quickly, however."

"Can he help us?" It's a bald question.

He hesitates, then finally offers, "I do not know."

I don't like that answer. When Vel finds himself stumped, we must be in a world of trouble. I know I can't sort this out on my own, though.

"I'd better bounce a message to Chancellor Tarn," I decide aloud. "No more playing fast and loose, guessing at what's best. I'll do as I'm told."

"I wish I had recorded that for posterity."

As I fire up the terminal, I laugh ruefully. "I hear you." The bounty hunter helps me with double-layered encryption, then I summarize our current circumstances to the best of my ability, concluding with, "Jax, standing by. Please advise."

It'll be tomorrow at the earliest before I hear, however. We need to get through the day without making things worse. Given the situation, that's a lot like saying we just need to balance the boiling pot of water on our heads for the next eighteen hours without spilling a drop.

Easier said than done.

After that, Vel takes off. He has to help with the interrogations. Under the circumstances, he must feel really trapped.

If you didn't already know, waiting sucks. I don't want to go wandering around the government center and encounter possible hostility, which would further weaken my position. But I don't enjoy hunkering down and hiding either.

Then it occurs to me. March might have a problem in custody. He hasn't taken his meds yet today, and it hasn't been very long since I worked on him in the cockpit. *Please, don't let all that progress be lost. Please don't let him go nuts.*

I don't want to have suffered like that for nothing. I can't imagine how he'll respond to questioning, let alone how he'll react to being locked up by hostile Bugs.

I start to feel sick.

Dina and Hit are the first ones released. They come to my quarters right away, as if we'd planned it. I'm so relieved to see them that I greet both women with a hard embrace, which turns into a three-way hug. Dina rests her golden head against mine for a moment, and, as always, she smells of springtime.

Hit laughs softly, giving us both a squeeze with her long arms "If Jael were here, he'd have a helluva spike right now."

I smirk as I step back; the levity helps. "You two okay?"

"More or less," Dina mutters. "Ehon asked us the same questions 140 times each."

"It helped that we were together last night," Hit adds.

I nod, taking a seat. At least I have company for the vigil. Clearly it's going to be a long night.

CHAPTER 35

I haven't slept.

Jael joins Dina, me, and Hit shortly before dawn. It goes without saying that we won't retire until we're all reunited. March still hasn't been released, and I'm worried about him. He's not secure enough yet to take this kind of stress. If he relapses, I don't know what I'll do. I didn't even get to enjoy having him back.

In late morning, Tarn's image comes up on the terminal, stern and uncompromising. I've played his message once, and I still can't believe his recommendation. The last part is the corker.

"I repeat, don't do *anything.* Allow the Ithtorians to do their jobs. Show them that we, as human beings, respect their methods. I have no doubt they will soon apprehend those responsible for the attack on Councilor Sharis, and they will respect your patience."

Gah, patience. Not my strong suit.

If he wanted passivity, Tarn sent the wrong woman to Ithiss-Tor. Dammit, now I wish I hadn't asked for his orders. This way, if I act otherwise, I'm disobeying his directive. Though it goes against every impulse, I tell myself I'm going to be good this time. No more going off half-cocked, doing what I think best.

I'm playing this crisis by the book, so if Tarn says stay, I stay. That's not easy, however, because I can't stop fretting. I wish Vel was here. Deep down, I know what he'll say. Humans have almost no rights on Ithiss-Tor, so they can do damn well what they please, as far as we're concerned. That's what scares me.

It's nearly nightfall, and I've lost two games of Charm by the time March appears. Tossing my cards aside, I go for him at a run. He has to be exhausted, but March catches me up in his arms and holds me to him, burying his face in my coarse curls. His heat is the best thing I've ever felt in my life, but it gets better. March *reached* for me. We stand there like that for uncounted minutes, and nobody says a word.

"They like me for it," March says, low. "Thank Mary, they have no proof."

I step back, eyes wide. "What? That's ridiculous."

He shrugs, coming into my quarters. "Not so much. I'm a trained soldier with a history of violence. I've also killed for pay. To an outsider, I'm their guy. Now they just need to make the facts fit my profile."

Jael scowls. "What you're saying applies to me as well, mate. Why'd they cut me loose so fast?"

Despite myself, I smile at him. "You just don't look like a criminal mastermind, pretty boy."

The merc growls something at me, but Dina glares him to silence. We don't have time to pander to Jael's ego. Before it can become an issue, the door chimes again, and I answer it to find Vel standing there.

Excellent, we're almost all present and accounted for now.

Except Constance. I'm afraid to contact the ship to see if she's there. The Ithtorians may be able to translate the inquiry, then they'll realize they're missing a member of my team. That's assuming they don't have her now. I wish I knew if inaction was the best course, here. I know Tarn doesn't give a rat's ass about my PA, but I do.

In a reflex that's become second nature, I greet Vel with a warm, affectionate *wa*, layered from the angle of my head to the fold of my fingers behind the slant of my forearm. This time I know exactly what I'm saying:

Brown bird welcomes white wave. Wander no more, dear traveler.

Vel pauses so long that I think I got it wrong. Then he returns the greeting with heartbreaking sincerity. *Brown bird honors white wave. The sea ever seeks the shore.* Something tells me the chip is incapable of processing the nuances, but

I can read between the lines. I'm pretty sure he's telling me he feels at home with me, and I could never seek a higher compliment.

"You're all done translating for them?" Hit makes it sound like he's an enemy collaborator, so I affix a cool look on her.

I might like her for how happy she seems to make Dina, but that doesn't mean I'm going to let her turn that tongue on Vel. "It would be worse if he refused to aid the Ithtorians. We have orders to cooperate as they request and otherwise stay put."

Dina snorts. "Since when do you follow orders?"

Don't let her rile you, dammit.

"Since I got us into so much trouble on the way here," I say quietly. "What we're doing is important, and I've got to trust that Tarn knows what he's doing. It means disaster if we fail."

Surprise registers in the mechanic's jade eyes. "You really mean that."

I nod. That seems to sober everyone in the room. Responsible Jax, who gives a damn? Call the gutter press; many of them were hoping to retire on my bad judgment. But there will be no more glimpses of my tits on the midnight bounce, no more private vids leaked, no more drunken table dancing. Over the past ten years, the universe has seen me do many amazing and scandalous things, but this just might be the most shocking.

"They have dossiers on all of us," Vel adds. "Ehon did his best to coerce a confession out of March then and there. I have never seen anything quite like it."

"There has to be some reason they've zeroed in on him," Hit says.

Dina agrees. "It doesn't make sense otherwise."

"Sitting around wondering about it won't solve anything." March strides toward the terminal, and I'm happy to see his take-charge attitude emerging. "I'll call Doc aboard the ship, see if he can figure out some treatment their physicians may have missed. If we can save Sharis, it'll look a helluva lot better for us."

"Fantastic idea." No wonder I love this man.

He loses himself in the conversation with Doc, which—if translated—will do much to exonerate us. I don't think the Ithtorians will think us clever or devious enough to come up with such a convoluted plan to poison Sharis, then save him, establishing ourselves as heroes via our own misdeeds.

Jael and Hit share a significant look, and he asks, "Do you think they'll let us go back to the ship? I'd like to get some gear just in case we have to defend you."

I glance at Vel, who answers, "It is unlikely."

The merc pushes to his feet. "Then I'll do some scouting. I need to know every possible route they can take to come after you. Maybe I can also scrounge up some tech from here that can be useful."

"We'll come with you." Hit stands also. "It's not smart to wander around alone right now."

Dina throws down her cards. "Agreed. Let's see what we can do."

Once they've gone, Vel catches my eye. I interpret his gesture as wanting privacy, even though March is the only one here, so I sidle toward the sleeping area.

"We must locate Constance," he tells me, once we're alone, relatively speaking.

It doesn't strike me as strange that he and I should handle this extra crisis quietly. No reason to give everyone else more to fret about it—and he knows this world best.

"I completely agree. Jael told me she was working on the ship last night. Did the Ithtorians scoop her up from there?"

He spreads his claws in a human expression of puzzlement. "She was not among those taken for questioning."

"The Ithtorians know about her," I mutter. "Given time, they'll realize she's unaccounted for. That won't look good . . . she's my personal assistant. What's she doing, I wonder? This kind of autonomy isn't like her."

Vel considers. "What was your last instruction to her?"

In a moment, the exact verbiage comes to me: *If you can do some more work on the alliance advantages, I'd appreciate that very much.* I groan aloud. *Ah, Mary, no. She didn't. She wouldn't.*

"What?" Vel asks.

Yes, she would, a little voice says. She's a helpful administrator PA, housed in an ambulatory casing. She'd do whatever it took to complete her assignment.

"I told her to research the advantages of the alliance further."

Vel tracks my thought process like a, well, bounty hunter. "She may have determined she needed more data on my people before she could offer concrete value."

"So she's doing field research," I conclude. "Can we look for her?"

If I get her back intact, I'm going to be more careful how I phrase things. Though she seems so human and capable, she's more like a small child in terms of the literal way she looks at the world. She wouldn't have considered the ramifications of what she was doing, only the most efficient method of carrying out my instructions.

Vel shakes his head. "Not easily. If she has managed to pass undetected this long, perhaps we underestimate her abilities. I hope she has not come to harm, but it will certainly arouse suspicion if we go in search of her now. We cannot be caught attempting to leave our housing complex, so for now, we must maintain a holding pattern, as Tarn instructed."

I hate hearing that.

Three days pass, the Bugs pursuing their painstaking investigation. They won't tell me anything when I inquire. We're confined to our wing of the annex as best as I can tell "for your own safety." Apparently it's getting ugly out there, and I suspect it won't improve as long as we remain in hiding. To my mind, doing so reeks of cowardice and guilt.

Sharis clings to life stubbornly, and that's my sole comfort. If he dies, events escalate from nasty to irreparable. Doc hasn't come to any conclusions, nothing the Bugs don't already know, but he has a lead on a regenerative nanoprotein string that might be able to do something about the internal burns Sharis suffered when he ingested the food laced with citric acid.

We live in hope that Doc will be able to reverse some of the damage. A very chilly Councilor Karom calls on the morning of the fourth day. He doesn't bother with a *wa* over the vid.

"Please inform your pet," he addresses Vel, "that Sharis will never again enjoy full health, even if he survives. I am not alone in blaming your delegation. It is only a matter of time before one of you is arrested. You might find it wise to flee before we discover which of you vermin did this."

Yeah, running away would solve all our problems. I disconnect the call without bothering with any of the outward trappings of diplomacy either. Maybe we *should* leave. I don't think the alliance is going to happen now. Nothing I do hereafter will make a difference. Despair weighs on me, knowing how bad it is in the star lanes already.

Raiders, Farwan loyalists, Syndicate skyjackers, and the Morgut rampaging unchecked—Ramona will love this. People will queue up to pay her protection money. The thought of her satisfaction absolutely galls me.

And we still haven't heard from Constance. She's not just my PA; she's also my friend. Didn't she try to comfort me after the Grand Administrator drugged me, and I dreamed about Kai? When I woke, it felt like I had lost him all over again. Constance was kind, and she touched my hair that night. I haven't seen her since.

Jael told me she was fine, so I didn't worry until the next day. And then I listened when Vel said it wouldn't be prudent to search for her. But if she were human, I wouldn't have listened. I'd have searched before now. Guilt becomes my constant companion, and not even March's arms around me can dispel the gloom that's fallen.

On day five of our polite incarceration, things go from bad to worse.

HARD Times Hit Dobrinya Asteroid

[ONN: byline Lili Lightman] Fighting broke out today on a mining colony hard hit by the food shortage. Gaunt-faced men wrestled for the last packet of paste while starving children wept. The riots continued until volunteers put themselves in peril to pacify the situation. There were ten serious injuries and one fatality by the time the dust settled.

Dobrinya asteroid is harsh on its settlers, one of the most extreme environments that allows for human habitation, for it is impossible to step outside without a pressure suit. This small outpost makes its living from the uranium mines. There's big profit for those willing to put up with living so far from civilization, but their survival relies on regular trade vessels to make the difference between credit-rich and provision-poor. These people cannot farm outdoors. They have a finite amount of space upon which to subsist, and as miners marry and have children, the population is increasing.

"Supply ships don't run as regular as they used to," mine manager Olen Brown said. "It doesn't matter how many credits you have in your account. If the merchantmen can't make it through, then we don't get organic for the kitchen-mate. By the time the last ship got here, we were down to almost nothing and trying to jury-rig the recyclers to purify our waste."

Pirates have plagued this particular trade route, preying on both freighters carrying supplies and those loaded with ore slated for processing. The more daring raiders sell the stolen goods to the Dobrinya miners at a ridiculously inflated price. Colonies everywhere are feeling the pinch of a disordered galactic economy.

"Sometimes you don't have a choice," longtime resident Basil Knapp said. "Recently, we bought from the pirates, which only encourages them. But it was that or starve. Dobrinya has been good to me, but if things don't take a turn for the better, I may need to move somewhere safer. Problem is, I don't know where that would be."

There are a few alternatives they can explore. Jere Bowen, local physician, proposed the following: "Since we can't rely on regular shipments anymore, we need to work on becoming self-sufficient. Laying in a hydroponics garden would be the most practical solution. Unfortunately, we didn't foresee this, and we don't have all the components. That means we need to order supplies . . . and, well, you see the problem there."

It's definitely a volatile situation. Supply store clerk Sadie Reid asked, "Why is it that nobody is doing anything about this? I feel like we've been totally abandoned out here. Doesn't anyone care whether we live or die? After they murdered Miriam Jocasta, I never thought I'd say this, but . . . I miss Farwan. They were bastards, but at least they kept us safe."

Bolstered by overpriced supplies, things have calmed on Dobrinya, but the population is sadder and more subdued in the aftermath. During this hardship, they can only cling to one another in the face of a government that seems to have forsaken them.

CHAPTER 36

A full complement of Bug soldiers shows up at my lodgings.

No conversation, they simply come in, according to the commander's directive. They make for a particular section of wall, and, while I watch, not understanding what I'm seeing at first, they dismantle one of the sections.

There's a secret cache inside.

A technician seizes the item and logs it on a datapad. My heart sinks. I don't need to be told what they've found. *Shit.* Someone really went to a lot of trouble to make it look like we were behind Sharis's poisoning.

"Ambassador—or should I call you spy? We will be taking you and your translator into custody for further questioning." The captain seems pleased with this development, as well he might.

"Custody" is probably a euphemism for holding us indefinitely. I don't *understand* this time. How can things have gone so drastically wrong? I did everything by the book; I took Tarn's suggestions seriously and did my best to comply.

Think, Jax. If I let them take Vel and me, there's no coming back from that. The alliance will never happen, even if we're eventually exonerated. I have to find some way to spin this, but I'm coming up blank. There's just no good reason why I'd have citric acid hidden in a tiny vial inside one of my walls.

"I had no opportunity the night Sharis fell ill," I point out. "And no motive."

The commander doesn't care. Once Vel translates, he replies, "Il-Nok may be lying for you, or perhaps you poisoned the food at some earlier time, knowing Sharis would not eat it until later."

There are more holes in this theory than in a piece of green Gehenna cheese, but I don't think they're looking for logic. They want a scapegoat, someone they can hold up to the general populace and say, *This is the culprit. Enjoy her punishment! See, now you can sleep safely again. We've taken care of the problem as we always do.*

They must've analyzed all the scans they took the first time they searched my quarters. Bugs are slow but methodical when they work, and they would have left no centimeter unexamined. That's when it occurs to me.

"I knew you had checked this place thoroughly," I say then. "If that's mine, why wouldn't I have moved it before your return? That makes no sense at all. The person who planted it either didn't know you'd taken readings or didn't care. Neither applies to me."

"Perhaps you were unfamiliar with the way our technology works." The captain is out of patience with me. "Will you come quietly, or must I use force?"

Every muscle bristles with the urge to fight. My stance says, *Bring it.*

"It's mine," March says into the silence. "They knew nothing about my personal agenda." He stands tall and strong, arms behind his back. There's a certain resolve about him, as if he knew this was inevitable.

Oh, Mary, no. I remember him saying, *They like me for it.* In awakening his emotions, I've also aroused his monstrous sense of accountability. Coupled with impossible altruism, I know *exactly* why he's doing this.

No, no, no. I don't want him to *save* me. I want him to *stay* with me. Tears prickle at the corners of my eyes. He didn't do this. He wouldn't. But he seems so firm; maybe it comes from the knowledge he's delivering us from an ugly situation. Something tells me March would rather die a hero than as an old man in my bed. We share that in common.

The crew freezes, as if they don't dare breathe. Everything holds a queer, polished sheen from the glimmer running along Dina's golden hair to the glamour of Hit's dusky skin. The light refracts to the chitin of the Bugs standing by with weapons. At any moment, this could turn into a bloodbath to make Fitzwilliam's colossal blunder look like a minor glitch.

"And I *didn't* realize your scans would show spatial anomalies," March continues, seemingly oblivious to the tension. "I never meant to cause any trouble for you personally, Jax. But I'm a purist . . . it offends me to think of allying with these monsters. However bad it gets out there, we can handle it on our own, as we always have. Nobody bailed us out in the Axis Wars."

The conviction in his voice alarms me. While Vel relays March's words, a look of stunned heartbreak shines in Dina's clear green eyes. Hit takes her hand, probably trying to comfort, but Dina shakes her off.

"No," the mechanic says. "He's lying, he has to be. Don't let him do this, Jax."

I don't know how she thinks I can stop it. The wheels are already in motion, and they're not going to listen to anything I have to say. They wanted a scapegoat, and now they have one. I could kill him for this, but I'm terrified the Bugs will do that *for* me. March will wind up in the mines, and he won't even have his emotional detachment as a defense mechanism.

Still, I try. "Scan him to make sure he's telling the truth."

I know the Bugs have the technology, but the commander reacts as if I have suggested something vaguely obscene. "Do you call your own lover a liar, ambassador? One wonders at *your* judgment then, as I can smell him all over you."

Vel repeats the insult, and, by the way his claws unfurl, he would like to teach the captain some manners. Under any other circumstances, I'd let him. With untold effort, I manage to keep my cool when all my instincts are telling me to wade in and wreck this room, then run for it.

Too much rides on this for me to yield to my impulses, but using my head instead doesn't come easy. I'm afraid I don't think fast or clear enough to save March from himself. He's determined to die a martyr, the son of a bitch. Now I know what it's like for him when I obsess over when I'll die in grimspace. I don't like the taste of my own medicine at all.

"He would do anything to protect me," I say then.

And I know it's true. Vel relays my statement.

"A protective deception?" The commander taps his claws against his carapace, thoughtful. "It is an intriguing concept, ambassador, but you might consider this: Only a full confession can trump what has already been said here. Does that mean you wish to make a full confession?"

I should. *If we both confess, they can't convict either of us, can they?* A little voice answers, *They can call us collaborators, and send us both to the mines. But at least we'd be together . . .*

I think while Vel repeats the commander's words. If it was just me, I would speak without question, but so many people are counting on me. I don't know if there's anything that can salvage the situation here, but I can't give up. Not even to save my lover. The matter has to be put to a vote.

"I wish to make a full confession," March says.

His dark gaze touches mine. Warmth surges through me, telling me he's come inside me. *It's all right.* Even now, he reassures me. *Your mission is bigger than both of us, and we both know this is the only way. Do the right thing, Jax. Live for me.*

A sob tries to fight its way out of my throat. Before I can process what's happened, the soldiers take him. Their captain lingers only long enough to advise us not to go anywhere, but I'm the only human who understands him. Vel hurries after them to assist with translation.

"Well, here's a bright side," Jael says. "This shouldn't stick to the rest of us. If your boy Doc can rig a treatment, and you lot patch Sharis up, that'll look mighty good for your alliance. Daft of March to go out like that, though, and that's all I'll say on it."

"You have no idea what kind of man he is. So *don't* talk

about him," Dina snarls. "Or I will knock your teeth so far down your throat you'll be picking them out of your shit for a week."

Jael smiles, but it's not pretty, doesn't match his face. "You'd be welcome to try."

I have no stake in this argument. I don't much care if they kill each other. Hit can rein them in—or not. Right now it's a matter of supreme indifference to me.

With a pained sound, I sink to the floor. The tears I've been strangling sluice down my cheeks unchecked. *Oh, Mary, I'm so lost.*

"Both of you shut the hell up." The pilot sounds almost casual as she kneels beside me.

To my surprise, she wraps her arms around me like Adele might have done. Hit doesn't offer platitudes. She can't guarantee it'll all be fine, but I'm grateful for her warmth. For a killer, she has good people skills; no wonder Dina digs her.

This is not who I am. I don't do well playing by other people's rules. This job is killing me. Worse, it's killing March.

Something's got to give.

CHAPTER 37

"Right," Hit says eventually. "I let you grieve, but now it's time for action. What're we doing about this, Jax? Clearly this can't stand."

Maybe I just needed to hear it. Whatever the case, her positive manner catalyzes me away from looming despair. With an appreciative nod, I sit away from her and push to my feet. Movement always helps me think.

"He'll buy us some time in custody," I say slowly. "But we have to make it count. If we take too long, they'll send him to the mines, and—"

"Then it will be all but impossible to retrieve him," Vel supplies, returning. "March refuses to accept my advice or assistance."

"Either he's ready to die," I mutter, "or he trusts us to get him out of this."

Dina scowls. "Let's assume the latter."

"Vel?" I turn to the bounty hunter with a question in my eyes. "I need to know the best course here. Is there any way we can secure both the alliance *and* March's release at this point?"

He considers. "Unlikely. You will have to choose, Jax. It is possible that the vote would still come in your favor, as you have cooperated fully and made a highly civilized impression by turning over the guilty party."

I didn't want to hear that. "So it's March or failing here, like Fitzwilliam did on Rodeisia. That's what you're telling me."

"I am afraid so."

March knew that when he confessed. The bastard knew. *Ah, damn. Why?* Sorrow flashes through me. This Jax is broken and unable to function, so I push her to the back of my brain. It's time for a new one, canny and ruthless.

Dina brightens when I say, "Then there's no question of what we'll do."

No, there isn't.

The mechanic rubs her hands together. "So what's the plan?"

"Call Doc to see if he's made any progress on a treatment. Vel, get Devri on the comm. Ask him how it looks for the vote."

Vel complies without question. I don't know what I did to deserve his loyalty, but I can trust him more than anyone else in my life. The mechanic might well turn on me when she finds out what I intend. The clicks and chitters of his conversation come through in words via the chip, but I can't tell what Devri is saying, based on Vel's end of the conversation. It sounds like he's doing a lot of listening.

"Shouldn't we be getting our gear?" Dina looks puzzled. She really doesn't realize that I've made the hard choice. "A few days ago, we managed to scavenge some good stuff and hide it nearby. We need to find out their patrol schedules, then work out a battle plan. It won't be easy getting off world, but—" When she sees me shaking my head, she slams a fist into my mouth.

My head rocks back, and I can taste blood from my split lips, but I don't take a swing at her. Inside, I feel those layers of ice gaining power. Hit grabs Dina's arms and holds her while she struggles.

Dina curses me in at least four languages. "How could you? Heartless bitch!"

"If we save him, it won't be with guns and bloodshed," I counter.

Her words burn me with their scorn—and their truth. "You don't even want to try! Just like you almost left him on Hon's Kingdom. Somebody gets to be too big a burden, you walk away."

Sickness spirals through me. She's right. I considered leaving March behind when I thought he was too injured to move. Just for a few seconds, and Loras—the comm officer we lost—served as my conscience. March always said it doesn't matter what you *almost* do. He understood then, and he will now, too.

I steel myself with the surety that I'm not the same person I was then. "Right now, the alliance has to be our first priority. We'll take care of him after we complete our primary objective. But March is a soldier," I tell her quietly. "He understands the risks. Soldiers die in wartime. You know that. And you know *him*. Tell me he'd be okay with condemning thousands of innocent civilians so he could walk free. Tell me he wouldn't hate that more than dying with honor." I step forward, holding her green gaze with mine. "Go on. If you can say it, I'll change course right now."

But she can't. Her lashes sweep down, shielding her damp eyes. "Not like this," she whispers. "It wasn't supposed to be like this."

My heart should be breaking, too, but there comes a point when you're so inured to loss that you no longer feel the lash. Hit wraps her arms around Dina from behind, and I hug her straight on, letting her head drop to my shoulder. Her tears drip against my neck. I feel immovable like a stone.

In the background, I can hear Jael talking to someone. I'd have to turn around to see what's up, and that can wait. If I lose Dina here, too, I don't know what I'll do. I stroke her hair, marveling at her intensity.

"You have my word," I murmur. "I will continue my own investigation, now that the Ithtorians are placated. And if I find out one of our own is responsible, I will peel his skin from his living body and feed it to him."

"I want to be there." Dina gets herself under control and steps back. I stifle a smile at how Hit knows exactly when to let go. They're really good together.

"That's a promise. If it's one of the Ithtorians, though, we may never see justice. You understand that?"

She nods. "Good of the many outweighs the good of the few. I have a diplomatic background, Jax. I understand strategic sacrifice. Just . . . not March. He's given enough. You know?"

Yeah, I get that. He's earned a lifetime of peace and happiness, but some people never get what they deserve. That's why there are saints in gutters and sadists in palaces.

"I have a bit of good news," Jael puts in. "While you ladies were being emotional, I checked in with Doc. He's sorted something out. He wants us to swing by the ship. We're not still under house arrest, are we?"

"Let's find out." I head for the door.

No sensors go off; no alarms ring. There doesn't even seem to be a guard nearby. That means they believe in March's guilt. Now that they have him in custody, there's no reason to watch the lot of us.

En masse, we head for the underground. First stop is the spaceport. Doc will need our help getting to the hospital. Of us all, only Vel is supposed to understand the mass transit system.

Thankfully, when we arrive, Doc is too distracted to ask about March. I don't think I could face telling him right now. Instead, he's all enthused about testing his treatment. Sometimes I forget how much of a mad scientist he is—in the best possible way.

"Great work," I greet him. "I can't stress how important this is. Are you sure it will work?"

Doc frowns. "As sure as I can be from running simulations."

Rose pins me with a hard look as we go. "Don't let anything happen to him."

Or you'll hunt me down and kill me. Got it. The implied threat doesn't faze me; to do me bodily harm, she'll need to join the queue.

She's been his lover for many years. From Mair's journals, I know Rose fought for him when he first arrived from the commune on Saleris, answering the advert for someone willing to train as a geneticist to aid the clans. The other men found him weak and laughable because he wouldn't fight back. They aren't married, but she loves him fiercely. The woman clearly doesn't like him disembarking, but we need him to explain what effect the regimen will have. Likely their physicians will want to test it to prevent further harm, but I have high hopes.

If one of ours can help him recover, it will help the alliance immeasurably. And after March's sacrifice, I *can't* fail here. I have to make it worthwhile.

"Don't worry," I tell her politely. "We'll have him back before you know it."

Then we're off to the hospital.

Not surprisingly, Sharis is well guarded. Vel has to explain our mission to four different commanders, going up the food chain each time, before one of them thinks to fetch the doctor in charge of the councilman's case. After fifteen minutes of milling around, he escorts us to a lounge to wait.

Activity prevents me from thinking about what I've lost. Somewhere deep inside, I'm dying, but there will be time for that later. A navigator always makes one big jump before the end anyway. Mine has to be spectacular to live up to my reputation.

Eventually, a Bug physician deigns to come see what we want. Doc launches into a long, technical explanation, which Vel translates. At first the Ithtorian doctor doesn't seem to believe what we're saying. He thinks it's a trick, although why we'd be dim enough to tell them we're trying to finish Sharis off—well, it really illuminates for me just how stupid they think humans are.

The light dawns, gradually. How it must sting that the idiot soft-skins came up with a cure.

"We will need to test this extensively," the doctor says, taking the datapad with Doc's results on them. "And verify your results. But if your findings are accurate, we will be beyond grateful. We are unable to do more than keep him stable, unfortunately. Citric acid is an alien toxin, and thus, we have never had a case like this before. Trying to figure out how to treat internal burns has stumped us."

"We just want him to get better," I say sincerely.

The others echo my concern. That seems like our cue to let the good Bugs get down to business. We can't be too pushy about this, or they'll become suspicious that there's something hidden in the data. Scary how well I've come to know their thought processes since we've been here. They'll waste crucial time trying to deconstruct what Doc has found instead of verifying his treatment.

I execute a respectful *wa* in parting as if the best of me isn't sitting in a cell, awaiting judgment.

CHAPTER 38

My first sign things have changed for the better comes when a courier intercepts us on the way back to the government center where we're lodged. A quick check tells me he's male. That's common; males often hold low-ranking, fetch-and-carry positions here. He's also lacking any stripes on his carapace, so he's either young or incompetent. I don't remember seeing this particular Bug before.

"Councilor Devri would like a word with you," he says with an obsequious but somehow insincere *wa*.

I return his polite discourtesy, layering my bow with meanings I'm not supposed to understand. Maybe it's petty, but I enjoy puzzling them and making them wonder if it's a fluke, like a dog that can howl in tune. The messenger regards me for a moment with his head canted at an insulting angle.

Behind him, water trickles down the textured walls, making a soft sound that offers the illusion of privacy anywhere in the complex. The pallor of the organic building material contrasts sharply with the lush, extravagant colors that grow in a riot all around us. On the far wall, there's a climbing plant with large, spiky leaves in a green so bright it almost looks artificial, and the blooms look like blood.

There are not nearly enough doors in any of their buildings. Everything stands wide open, full of scrolling arches that make me think of hives. Mary, but I would love to snap my fingers three times at the lot of them and go get March. Instead, I make my expression welcoming without showing my teeth. Vel translates unnecessarily—and I'm tired of that, too. The air is too thick and sweet, a little too warm.

Ithtorians prefer to keep the indoors like the tropics they no longer enjoy outside, but I'm no hothouse flower.

"We'd be honored to see Devri," I answer at length.

"Only you and your translator," he cautions me.

Well, that's a familiar theme. Does that mean Devri doesn't think the authorities arrested the right guy, or does he really not trust us now? If that's the case, it's a fierce blow. Besides Sharis, he was the strongest ally we had. If he thinks we'll take hostile action against him if he sees us all, then we're fragged.

The others shrug to show they don't mind being excluded.

"I think we'll head back to the ship, actually." Dina doesn't look to Hit for agreement, taking her acquiescence for granted.

Doc agrees. "Rose will worry if I tarry too long."

He still hasn't asked about March, likely figuring he's off brooding somewhere. Maybe it's better if he believes that for as long as possible. I sure as hell don't want to be the one who breaks the bad news; Doc will be devastated. Something tells me March is like a son to him. They've known each other for turns. I realize now I'm not even sure how long it's been. Long enough for him to be saved and lost and saved again. Long enough for him to fight a war to repay a dead woman's kindness.

I can't continue with that train of thought. It'll break me.

So the other four return to the spaceport, leaving Vel and me to be escorted to Devri's apartment. Though we know the way, the messenger dogs our every step. I'm not sure if it's meant to be flattering, or if he's been charged with retrieving us like a couple of lost parcels. Thankfully, he doesn't say much along the way.

My heart isn't in this anymore. I'm doing the right thing, but I don't *want* to. With all my heart, I wish I could scrub out my moral conscience and say to hell with the rest of the universe. I want March, and I honestly don't care how many obscure outposts the Morgut ransack as long as we can find a quiet corner to hunker down somewhere.

I also know March would never forgive me for making that decision. He'd find it unforgivable, and I'd still lose him. At least this way he *respects* me.

Fucking cold comfort.

I want to hit somebody. It's getting harder to restrain my impulses. It's not easy for a navigator to stop jumping, and the stress of my current situation exacerbates the problem. One day soon, I'm just going to blow, and it will be *spectacular.* I hope our business is done by then because nothing Vel does will hide the fact that the ambassador has gone barking mad.

I need to jump. I need to get away.

I *don't* need to be following some stupid lackey up the lift to Devri's flat. Of course, I'm doing just that, which should tell you just how wrong things are. Once we arrive, the messenger makes himself scarce.

Unlike the last time we were here, the place is empty. I pretend to admire the garden atmosphere, but in truth, I want to go home. I miss furniture made of synth, and solid floors, not stuff that squishes underfoot.

Devri doesn't keep us waiting long. "If Sharis recovers, I am going to call the vote," he says without preamble. "Otherwise, you have no hope."

A blunt answer. Well, I respect that.

After the obligatory pause for Vel to do his thing, I answer, "I guess you know that we've been to the clinic?"

"Indeed. I applaud the notion of putting your personal physician on the problem. It shows your willingness to aid us in times of need, very astute."

Huh. Even Devri doesn't think I might truly care if Sharis lives or whether he's crippled for the rest of his life. I frigging hate politics.

"He is a scientist foremost," Vel corrects. "But you are essentially correct. How long do you estimate it will take for your people to validate his data?"

"No more than a day. If this treatment can help, then time is of the essence."

"It's early yet," I muse, once Vel has given me the opening

by summarizing their exchange. "So the vote could take place as soon as two more days?"

That's longer than we expected before this mess began.

I'm tired of hearing everything twice. We might be able to let Devri in on the secret, but I'd rather not chance it. He might surprise us in a bad way by switching sides and running to the Grand Administrator for the prestige of betraying me. I'm not entirely clear on whether loyalty is a virtue here; initial impressions indicate it's situational, impacted by what decision results in the greatest personal achievement.

So explain Vel, a little voice demands. And I can't. It bothers me that he sees himself as defective when he so clearly embodies so many virtues, as humans judge such things. If I were a religious sort, I might think that Mary and his Iglogth had done some sort of drunken swap one night, and he wound up with a human soul in a Bug body.

Maybe that comes from living among us, though. It's a question of nurture versus nature, I suppose. But he said he was different from the beginning—

"—factors would need to align."

Shit. I missed what Devri said. This time, it comes in handy for Vel to repeat:

"If Sharis shows improvement as projected by your doctor's treatment plan, then he could be well enough to vote by the day after tomorrow. Of course, a great number of factors would need to align."

Got it. So we have two days. In that time, I might be able to find the bastard who's responsible for this mess. I'd like to kill him myself, but maybe, just maybe, I can save March if I present them with this other person along with some compelling evidence. Now that we're no longer confined to quarters I can begin my own investigation. Vel can surely help with that.

March doesn't expect me to save him. I know that. He gave himself up for the greater good, knowing there had to be a whipping boy. But I can't let that stand if there's anything I can do about it. I waffle between grief and despair, not knowing whether his death is inevitable, or if I'll make this worse. Regardless, I won't give up on him until they actually put him on the tram to the mines. Hell, maybe not even then. I've acquired something of a reputation for achieving the impossible; that's why I'm here.

I incline my head. "I suspect you didn't call us in to talk about Sharis."

Devri seems pleased by my acuity. "Clever female. As a matter of fact, I did not. I wanted to warn you."

Oh, this doesn't sound good. I sit quiet, waiting for the rest.

"My sources tell me that the Grand Administrator does not intend to let you leave the planet. She is highly incensed that one of your party dared to attack a council member. At this point, nothing will appease her but a series of executions. She feels a strong precedent must be set."

My stomach heaves. "Even if the alliance passes, she *still* wants to kill us all?"

"In a word? Yes."

CHAPTER 39

Vel and I have been left to our own devices. Over the past few days, he's become the best friend I have. I don't know if he'd be happy to hear that or entirely alarmed. I doubt I'll ever field-test it. Some things are best left unspoken.

This late, the halls are clear and quiet. Our first stop is the bank of cameras, where Vel installs a gizmo that should scramble them long enough for us to get past unnoticed. And if they ever ask us about the suspicious glitch, well, we'll alibi each other again.

Let them keep suspecting what they will about that. It's bloody convenient.

"Are you positive this thing will work?" I ask.

There's a certain irony as Vel answers, "No."

Fair enough. He's been in exile a long time, and technology may have outpaced him. Regardless, we have to try.

"Do you feel like laying odds?"

"If you would be silent for a moment, Sirantha, I might be able to finish." That's the closest he's come to losing his temper in a long time.

I respond by falling quiet, as he requests. My breath seems overly loud, so I try to restrain myself. Finally, the lights on the side of the surveillance units go yellow. Excellent. We scuttle past and pause long enough for him to unlock the door. Once inside, I take stock of the security station, little bigger than a san-closet.

During the day, this is manned by a bored guard, who dozes over the displays. These cameras are tuned to a little-used tube station, but Vel can patch into other units from this location. That's why we're here.

He produces another small device and sets to work. Though it's superstitious at best, I cross my fingers that he can get a jammer running. That will give us an opening for him to hack into another security terminal. Theoretically, the jammer will prevent their equipment from detecting the breach. Otherwise, they'll dispatch a team to the site of unauthorized access before we can discover anything useful.

We shouldn't even be here, but it's such a welcome relief from sitting around that I can't worry about it. Headlong action is my natural state, not prudent patience. A few seconds later, Vel nods—the device is operational.

I know my role in this mission. Stand guard and keep a good watch on the hallway. If it looks like anyone is coming in here, sound the alarm. As I understand it, he knows a secret way out of here . . . unless they've changed the layout of the security station since he was here, always a possibility.

While he works, I peer out the slats in the thin, strange door. It's made of a matte substance that in some fashions resembles metal, but in other ways, not so much. After three minutes, he detaches the jammer from the terminal and pushes to his feet.

"I jacked their surveillance on Sharis's quarters. We will examine everyone who came to see him up to twenty-four hours before he was poisoned. Let us go."

I'm on board with that. Cautiously, we slip out into the hall, and I'm relieved to find nobody coming around the blind bend where I couldn't see from inside the room. The late hour and this station's remote location both contributed to our decision to stage our break-in here.

A san-bot zips down the hall toward us. The thing seems quite agitated, and it bangs into my foot repeatedly. I glance down in puzzlement, then step over it. On the way back to my quarters, tension roils inside me. I know the magnitude of what I've done. If they find out, the alliance is finished. Hell, maybe it is now. Maybe I'm kidding myself I can still make it happen. I won't know for sure until Sharis wakes up—or not.

Once we arrive, Vel snaps a manual lock onto my door. We don't want their people coming in while we look at these holo-files. Since we have a long time to cover, we'll be watching these for a while. If someone calls while we're occupied, they'll doubtless put the worst possible spin on it. Another Bug will assume Vel is busy being deviant with his pet soft-skin.

"This will take a while," the bounty hunter says as he dumps the data from his pad into a portable player, no surprise that he doesn't want any trace of this info in their terminals. "You may as well make yourself comfortable."

The feed flickers to life, showing a 3-D representation of the hallway outside Sharis's flat. These are the results of public security cams at work, recording routinely those who come and go. Apparently, it functions as a wondrous preventive because nothing deters crime so much here as the fear of getting caught. Incompetence is the bogey that haunts all Bug dreams.

In theory, investigation sounds exciting. It sounds like there would be lots of sneaking around, lots of thrills and danger. Turns out, not so much. Oh, we did sneak into that remote security station, but afterward? This investigation turns into a game of "whose eyes will glaze over first?"

To keep myself attentive I make notes. By the end of the day before Sharis was poisoned, we have a list of five Bugs and one cloaked figure. They must assume that one is human because Bugs don't wear clothing as a general rule.

Unless he's trying to make someone think *he's human.* In that case, Vel could craft himself into anyone he wanted, but his countrymen consider it debased and dishonorable, used in any fashion other than to stalk prey. Most Ithtorians wouldn't even have the necessary skill to mold the excreted material, generally used for insulation against the cold, to look like a credible human being, let alone a specific person.

This is the last caller, someone who showed up after Mako left in the middle of the night. Since we departed from Devri's early, I didn't see them leave together, but Sharis and Mako have become partners since our arrival on world. The timing seems interesting.

"Can you freeze this?"

Vel does so, and we examine the small, grainy figure from all angles, but the camera is fixed. We can't add data that isn't present. Unfortunately, there's no way to get a look at the face.

"How tall is he?" I ask aloud.

"It is hard to say for certain with only blank walls for comparison, but I would estimate . . . at least two meters."

"Not me then." I flash him a smile. "Or Doc, Rose, or Dina. What's the short list of people who are tall enough to throw that silhouette?"

Vel considers in his measured way, so I start ticking them off, answering my own question. Though I hate to name them, I have to be comprehensive. "March. Jael. Hit. Any number of clansmen, serving aboard the ship . . . they tend to be tall. Can you pull up personnel files and run a scan based on height parameters?" When he nods, I add, "Good. Get me that list soonest. I have some people to talk to."

It's not impossible we could have wound up with a purist in our crew, I suppose. From what I gather, Doc put things together in a hurry, doing March a personal favor when they caught my transmission. In addition to their recent wedding, Keri and Lex are still cleaning up the mess on Lachion. It's a wonder she let March go at all.

"Of my people, only Devri and Ehon come to mind as being tall enough," Vel says eventually. "Unless the individual wore a prosthetic device of some kind."

"Like heels?"

"Or headgear. We have no way to determine what is beneath that cloak based on the image here."

I offer, "The Grand Administrator is tall."

He shakes his head. "Not her style. She would never do such a thing herself."

"But her lackeys might if she wants us off world bad enough."

"Unquestionably. She might even consider it fitting punishment for Sharis, who defied her in persisting with this notion over her objections."

Something else occurs to me. "Is there a way for you to

get into their private files on the OP? We need to know which of their people are tall enough to fit this as well."

The sheer amount of work we need to do in the next forty-eight hours boggles the mind. So many people to check out, so many leads to chase. We don't have nearly enough manpower to handle this internally—and to make matters worse, we have to use the utmost discretion. If the Bugs find out we're poking around when the matter is officially closed, it won't be good.

"I can do it," he says quietly. "But time runs against us. You do realize that, Sirantha? It will take time to run down each person and interview them. Since all we have is a suspicion—and we may be incorrect about this dark figure—please do not pin all your hopes on this."

My weary response lays my soul bare, showing him more than I ever meant. "I don't know what else to do."

CHAPTER 40

I commandeer the aft lounge to do the crew interviews.

Vel spends a couple hours working on various bits of tech that mean nothing to me. It's a good thing he's so gifted at this, which strikes me as curious, considering he once wanted to be an artist. So I ask.

"How come you became a bounty hunter? I know you told me about meeting Trapper, but didn't you want to paint or something once you got away?"

Vel spares me a brief glance. "I had already learned a hard lesson about that, Sirantha. It . . . hurts when I create. This is just another marketable skill."

Interesting. It's also a lesson in how sometimes people's dreams shatter, but the pieces don't come out clean. Instead, the shards linger beneath the skin, even after the wound seems to have healed. I let it go, sensing Vel doesn't want to talk about his failed artistic aspirations. I can't help touching the tattoo around my throat, however. In some ways, I'm like his living canvas, a memento of the life he'll never live.

That makes me sad.

Turns out, there's only one person we need to talk to straightaway. While Vel's scan came up with a ton of crew members who fit the height parameters, only one of them has left the ship. Sure, someone might have compromised the logs, but they'd need both training and opportunity to erase all trace of their passage. If we get nothing from talking to this guy, then we'll take a look at the people who would know how to do that.

I'm dressed in a severe black jacket and matching trousers, giving me the vague look of authority without affiliating me with any particular group. It feels good to change out of that stupid gold robe. I've taken an unreasonable loathing to that color over the last few days.

Curiously, my hair has begun to grow out even more since we arrived, now past my shoulders. I suspect there's something to inspire growth in the air here, something that keeps the plants blooming. Human personal designers would love to know the secret of that, I'm sure. To prevent it from softening my face, I've slicked my hair back and bound it in a band. With Vel at my back, I imagine I look harsh and intimidating. It's a start.

Though it's standard security protocol, it really helps in this situation that they keep a log of everyone who boards and disembarks. I take another look at the ID that's been bounced to my datapad. There's not much about this crewman here, just his blood type and next of kin. Still, we need to have words, so we send for him.

When he arrives, the clansman stands to attention, arms stiff at his sides. He's tall, or he wouldn't even be here, but this kid can't be more than eighteen. What's his story, I wonder? Couldn't wait to get off the Lachion rock, gravity holding him back? Maybe he's a colonist who's always been secretly yearning for the stars.

He doesn't make eye contact, as if it would be disrespectful. Or maybe he has something to hide. It's also possible he finds Vel unsettling in his native form. I wish Constance were here to read the boy's vitals. I haven't thought to ask Vel whether his ocular cam has thermal settings, but we'll capture a visual log at least.

"Argus Dahlgren?" I put down the datapad.

"Yes, ma'am." He does not relax one iota.

"Why don't you take a seat?" I indicate the spot opposite me.

It took Vel a couple of hours, but he's rigged the chair as a lie detector, using contact points. I was all for doing it openly, but he pointed out that a skilled adversary can beat such devices pretty regularly, *if* they know it's been hooked up. So we're running beneath the radar on this one.

He looks very young and worried as he sits down. I don't know if Argus even left the spaceport. He was under strict orders to stay on the ship, so maybe that's what he's nervous about. That's what we're trying to find out. It may have been nothing more than a dare or a bet, something that would give him bragging rights back home.

His pale eyes flicker to mine at last. Surprise rocks through me. His irises are like mercury, sparked through with silver ice. Contrasted to his shock of black hair, it marks him as a jumper. Well, no *wonder* he left the ship. As a whole, navigators tend to be governed by their impulses, so this ambassadorial gig has been pretty close to hell for me.

"Would you like something to drink?" I ask, now wanting to set him at ease.

I'm pretty sure this isn't our guy. He's not caught up in some purist movement that doesn't want humanity associating with filthy alien scum. He's just a kid hungry to see everything in a way he probably doesn't even *understand* yet.

Before Argus can respond, Vel says, looming behind me, "You can attend the niceties later, ambassador. He has some questions to answer first."

Ah, now I get it. Well, it makes sense for Vel to play bad cop. Argus seems half-terrified of him as it is, and he hasn't even *done* anything yet. *Yep, welcome to the weird, wide world, kid. Untold wonders await.*

"Very well." I sit forward, inviting confidence. "You want to tell me what you were doing dirtside?"

To his credit, he doesn't try to play it off. "I was curious," he says with a touch of defiance. "And bored with hanging around here."

A bored jumper is never a good thing. We need to get him into training and focus his need to explore, but *where*? Right now, everything is in flux, and they've closed the academy on New Terra. Shit. Maybe I'll wind up a teacher someday after all.

But first things first.

"What did you do while you were there?"

"Nothing," he mutters. "But not for lack of trying. I couldn't figure out how to get out of the docking area."

I'm inclined to believe him, but I slant a glance at Vel to confirm. He inclines his head ever so slightly. Okay, him, too. We're in accord then. I'll switch tacks before we cut him loose.

"Do you know of anybody who doesn't approve of us being here?" I ask casually. "Any complainers on the ship?"

Argus shakes his head. "No, ma'am. Doc recruited us because we've all talked about seeing the stars at some point or another. There aren't a lot of ships going out from Lachion. March handles most of our off-world runs, and he keeps a small crew."

"So as far as you know, there aren't any dissident factions among your mates?"

He looks genuinely bewildered. "Any who?"

Despite the severity of my task, I bite back a smile. "Never mind." I turn to Vel with an inquiring look. "Further questions?"

"Nothing at this time, but . . . we know where to find him." That sounds positively ominous. Shame on Vel for trying to rattle this kid's cage—then again, maybe he needs a lesson. Something irreparable could happen to him if the Bugs catch him.

"So can I go?" Argus sounds eager to get away from us.

"Almost. Just one more question—would you like to be a navigator someday?" I assume he knows he *has* the J-gene.

"More than anything," he breathes.

I try not to wince. Mary, was I ever that young or that eager? I suppose I must have been. Running off to the Academy against my parents' wishes indicates I was.

"I'll see what I can do for you." When his face brightens to near nova, I caution, "I'm not promising anything, mind, but we may as well put you to work doing something you'll be good at. You realize things are in a bit of disarray just now?"

There's no point in telling him about the dark side: the compulsion to jump once you've tasted grimspace, the addiction to something that kills you slowly, and the way you won't, in fact, know just before your last jump. Let him enjoy the thrill of the idea for a while first. I certainly did.

He nods. "Yes, ma'am. It's been that way ever since you took down Farwan. Is it true you discovered the existence of the Marakeq ten turns ago? The chieftain said she saw you pick a fight with six armed Gunnars with her own eyes. So did you really pull Hon's heart out of his chest with your bare hands? The stories they tell about you—" Argus freezes, probably realizing he's said too much. He looks as if he's scared I'll tear the tongue right out of his head.

That's when I realize—he's afraid of me every bit as much as he is Vel. We're like the wicked witch and her demon familiar or something. Together, to this kid, we must seem like the stuff from nightmares and legends.

How the hell did *that* happen?

Omni News Net: Opinion of the Week

Dear Ms. Lightman:

I think you did your viewers a serious disservice in not offering a counterargument to the comments made on your program by Ramona Jax. Don't let the Syndicate's slick PR department fool you into thinking they smell rosy. How can I be so sure? Well, I used to be the Assistant Director of Public Relations for Farwan Corporation, New Terra headquarters, and I recognize a spin job when I see one.

The Syndicate is a parvenu compared to us; nonetheless, their latest crop of advertisements is tailor-made to reassure the average consumer. If you compare the two, you'll realize that their new slogan "Protecting your world" is a direct theft from our campaign ten turns ago. I wrote the ad copy myself, including the phrase "Protecting your world." They've also lifted our image in terms of showing average people going about their lives while the Syndicate works for them in the background. You'll see lots of happy, smiling citizens in these ads, and it's a good, solid strategy.

If the common folk see Syndicate guards as helpful often enough, they'll eventually integrate that view as part of their personal belief system. That kind of thing can be broken down into ad exposures and simple mathematics. For example, if a person encounters this depiction of a softer, gentler Syndicate three times within twenty-four hours, that image will soak in on some level. Repeated exposure over time kept me earning big credits for many, many years. This experience impacts brand loyalty and decision-making. There will come a point when people just won't care about the truth, and all the exposés in the world won't matter.

It was my job to make sure Farwan came out of any situation, however grim and catastrophic, looking like white hats. Based on what I'm seeing on the bounce now, it wouldn't surprise me if some of my former colleagues have gone to work for the Syndicate, because that's some truly excellent PR, and I know that of which I speak.

If the Conglomerate doesn't get its act together, it will be too late.

Ordinarily, I'd be amused to see them fail—history suggests it's their specialty—but this is no laughing matter. Take it from a reformed company man. If these thugs establish themselves as the galactic governing body, we'll wish we lived in some other universe.

Sincerely,
Alfredd E. Pruitt

CHAPTER 41

"Here's where it gets tricky," I say with a sigh.

I don't want to interview Dina, Hit, or Jael, but we can't leave any stone unturned. They need to sit in the rigged chair without knowing they're being tested. They won't be on their guard as much, so I need it to seem casual.

It can't seem like an interrogation. I also don't want them ever to know I felt like I *had* to ask. That kind of thing can end a friendship, but when it comes to March's life, I can't trust any of them.

I don't think Dina would ever do anything to hurt him, but maybe she didn't realize he'd feel obligated to confess to get me out of trouble. Once, I thought she hated me enough to hide the poison in my room on purpose, but that's not true anymore. She doesn't fit the height profile, but that doesn't clear her as a conspirator. Even if my gut says she'd rather die than do this, I must validate intuition with investigation.

Hit and Jael, I don't know nearly as well, but I've come to think of them as friends. I'm afraid of how they'll take it if they figure out what I'm doing. I don't have so many friends that I can afford to offend them. But if they want me to find out who poisoned Sharis and get March out of the hot seat, they won't mind my crossing them off the list of suspects with a few pointed questions, so maybe they'll just be mad at me for a while over the subterfuge.

"Ideas?" I ask Vel.

He understands the way my mind works nearly as well as March. "Order food," he suggests. "It will make the occasion seem more social, as if you want commiseration with the frustration of your task."

Before I can send for anything or anyone, Vel's personal communicator beeps. The person speaks too faintly for my ears, but when he terminates the conversation, he looks stunned. "Sharis is awake. And he's asking for us."

A weight lifts. "Let's go see him."

"We will have an armed escort," he warns, as we head for the door. "They are taking no chances this time, even on us."

Vel wasn't kidding. There's a complement of six Bugs in full military regalia, which means they have the same color stripes and are carrying weapons. From what Vel said, those little units have enough electricity to turn us into heaps of smoking coal. I'll watch my step.

In the hall, a san-bot emerges from the honeycombed wall, driving itself around me in circles. Something is seriously wrong with these things. Whoever's in charge of maintenance is doing a shitty job.

The guards don't say much as they take us to see Sharis. At his door, the commander searches us thoroughly and takes even our personal electronics. We're permitted to see him only if we're willing to go with just the clothes on our backs. Fair enough—I don't want anything else to happen to him either, but part of me wonders if they're being this cautious about other Bugs.

Even though they're almost sure we had nothing to do with the attack on Councilor Sharis, they also make us step into a decon chamber to make sure we haven't rubbed any toxins on our skin. This paranoia, however, speaks volumes about how the general Ithtorian populace feels about human beings. They believe we're all capable of horrific things, and since I've killed with a disruptor and watched a man's chest turn itself inside out, I can't really argue.

When we finally get in to see him, Sharis is reclining on a bed that most closely resembles a divan, if said divan were made of some organic material that constantly rippled beneath his weight. I'm told there's some symbiosis between the average Bug and this bioengineered furniture. He appears to be in possession of all his faculties.

"Forgive me if I do not get up." His sense of humor seems to be intact as well.

Vel steps into his role as translator while I greet Sharis with a particularly deep *wa*, layering it with my regret. *Brown bird wishes your pain away to the land of ghosts and sorrow.* That gives Sharis pause. By now, he must be wondering how I understand so much, nuances that simply cannot be conveyed via human language.

I'm starting to think the chip Vel implanted in me must be a prototype or a mod to existing technology, something he's been working on privately. It governs a lot more than just language translation; it's as if it has cultural information implanted as well. Maybe I should be worried that it will melt my brain at some point, but I trust him. I make a mental note to ask him about it and turn my attention back to Sharis.

"Certainly," I reply. "You do us too much honor by permitting us to attend you in your time of infirmity."

Vel repeats my words nearly verbatim.

Sharis's claws still their restless movements against his carapace. "It is more that I fear I will not have the opportunity to speak with you again."

Alarm sparks through me. "Why, what's wrong?"

"Karom has put a motion before the Council to have me judged unfit to continue to serve. He has proposed that I be sent into the country for the sake of my health. My seat will be filled immediately by their nomination."

I glance at Vel, quietly horrified. "Is that *legal*?"

With every appearance of regret, he inclines his head. "If a councilor is determined to be unable to carry out his duties, he can be replaced."

"Just by the other council members voting on it?" That seems like too much power, but the Grand Administrator can veto any of their choices, if I recall correctly.

"Yes," Vel answers.

"Thanks to the ingenious treatment devised by your ship's doctor, I *will* recover. They have forgiven other councilors longer and more debilitating illnesses," Sharis continues bitterly. "But they want to be rid of me because I am the voice of change. Once I am gone, there will be nothing to stop them from steamrolling over Devri, and the alliance will be put down for good."

"That . . . will be devastating," I answer quietly. The diplomatic ship has sailed. It's now time for some plain talk. "We need the support of your people in the coming war against the Morgut, not because we need cannon fodder, but because they fear and respect you. If they see your people as willing to side with us in an armed conflict, it will make them less likely to attack us."

Vel translates, using some sound I haven't heard before to denote the Morgut. The chip tells me he's called them "Eaters-of-the-Dead." That name sends a cold shiver straight through me. I try not to remember all the blood on Emry Station, the webs, and the cocoons stuffed with human corpses that nourish their young.

"We taught them to respect us, long ago," Sharis acknowledges. "But we have not touched the stars in hundreds of turns. Our ancestors explored, fought, and conquered, but the wayfarers brought back a hideous plague from their travels that nearly decimated our population. At that time, we closed our planetary borders, and we have only permitted outsiders twice since."

The first time was when Trapper Farley landed with the first human delegation, who were too ignorant to realize they'd "discovered" a closed planet and a people who wanted nothing to do with the wider world. Now that I know more about the history involved, they were lucky they weren't summarily executed.

And now, there's us.

"I'm very sorry." There doesn't seem to be anything else left to say.

The councilor spreads his claws, then turns them down as a sign of his helplessness. "I cannot get them to change their minds or shift away from old manners of thought, but the truth is, we are stagnating. No new technologies have been invented in more turns than I can recall, and our ships are now utterly antique. Humans have fast, versatile minds, a side effect of being so short-lived, no doubt. We need to recapture that spark, or we will die. Not quickly, but slowly."

"There may be a way," Vel says, as if he's been thinking. "When were they going to vote on your replacement?"

"One hour."

"Can you walk?" Vel demands.

Sharis seems startled, but then he pushes himself from the divan. He sways for a moment, still weak from the aftereffects of the poison. "I . . . believe so."

"If you can make it to the council chambers, it will show your strength. Accept no aid, and do not rest along the way. They will find it hard to prove your infirmity if you are there to confront them over it. If you are strong enough to do this, you can call for an immediate vote on the alliance, preempting their agenda. At least this way, if you lose, you gave it all you had."

I can get on board with that.

"I can do this," Sharis says, determined. "I truly believe this is best for our people, and I will not yield meekly."

It's an effort for him to project strength and confidence, but he does so as he strides from his sickroom. Somehow, I manage not to cheer him as we go. Ambassadors have to think of their dignity.

As we walk, a small san-bot scuttles out of the wall and nudges my foot. I sigh and step over it, having more important things to worry about.

Time to put this to a vote.

CHAPTER 42

Bravery isn't just facing down a bunch of guys who want to kill you.

It's also leaving your hospital bed in order to fight for what you believe in. It would've been easy for Sharis to let them roll over him, much easier for him to call it quits and accept his forced retirement. Instead, he sweeps into the council chambers like he owns the place. I can only imagine what it's costing him in terms of stamina, but you'd never even know he'd been ill to look at him.

Our arrival finds everyone arrayed in place, probably discussing his removal. This room is cool and quiet, devoid of the hothouse trappings that characterize the rest of the complex. Since we surprise him in the middle of the room, Karom has been apparently pacing while the others occupy their assigned places. I can't read Devri at all, which surprises me. You'd think he could permit himself some trace of satisfaction after he stuck his neck out to warn us. But perhaps that would be dangerous.

As if against her will, Mako rises and takes a step toward Sharis, which seems to denote gladness. Maybe the Bugs don't form bonds as we do, but she wasn't happy about having her lover's guts burned up with citric acid. Then she checks herself, resuming her place. Protocol trumps personal business here every time.

Karom recovers first, asking, "What are you doing here? You should be resting."

Sharis takes that opening and spins it like a pro. "I am perfectly well, thanks to the treatment the human doctor devised. Such innovation is just *one* of the benefits we will enjoy when the alliance goes through." He tosses down the figurative gauntlet.

The stout councilor recoils, casting a worried glance at the Grand Administrator. Her red claws trace an intricate pattern against her carapace, but unless we're too late, she can't eject him from the room if he's well enough to attend the session under his own power. Vel knows the ins and outs here; it may be the advantage that saves us.

Sartha responds sharply, "You would not have been sick at *all* if not for the humans. They are little better than animals."

I wince. She's coming down hard on the other side. If I had to speculate, I'd say her history with Vel has made her bitter and inclined to punish us because Vel prefers the company of vermin like us. I'd like to tell her not to take it personally—he ran away from everything, not just her—but I doubt it would do any good.

Given March's confession, it's going to be hard to spin her accusation, but Sharis manages. "Animals know no higher reason. If your accusation applied to the humans, they would not have cooperated with our investigation, or permitted the culprit to be taken into our custody, subject to a penalty of our choosing. That shows great respect and desire for accord between our people, does it not?"

"It does," Devri agrees.

Whew, he's still on our side.

"Furthermore," Sharis adds, "we cannot judge all of humanity by the actions of one. Are there not Ithtorians who are sent to the mines for their weak minds or deviant natures? Would we send them forth for all the universe to judge *us* on their merits?"

A general click and chitter follows, councilmen talking among themselves, but even those who loathe us and want us gone cannot argue the point.

Devri takes up the thread so smoothly, I could almost swear they practiced this. And maybe they did, just not under these exact circumstances. "Since we are all gathered here, I put forth that we should put this proposed alliance to a vote. We have enjoyed ample time to make assessments and decide the matter."

"Seconded," Sharis says promptly.

Now it's on the table before anyone can filibuster or suggest more delays, wherein more stuff could go wrong. *Good going, guys.* Vel and I stand poised. He doesn't translate for me this time; I'm sure they imagine he'll summarize afterward.

Karom makes an angry sound as he resumes his position. Each councilor has a touch pad. The orange one means no; the blue one means yes. Once a vote has been called, it's as simple as that, and I almost can't breathe for the tension. This is the defining moment, a validation or repudiation of everything we've worked for.

They begin in ascending order—in other words, the least senior member casts first. In this case, that's Sartha. I'm not surprised when an orange glow encompasses her chair. She's made it clear she wants to see the back of us . . . and maybe Vel freezing to death in a ditch somewhere in the bargain. Her sorrow has hardened into something sharp and hard since the last time I saw her.

Devri follows. His seat flashes blue, so we're tied at one and one. I can't remember who's next, but Mako's light rings blue, too. Sharis must have done some smooth talking to get her to go up against the Grand Administrator, who doesn't vote in such council matters but can make her displeasure known in more subtle ways, such as with prestige appointments, and say, assassins arriving in the middle of the night.

Two to one.

With sudden relief, I realize I know how this is going to go. And sure enough, Karom votes no, so that an orange halo encircles him. It gives him a faintly infernal air.

Then it's down to Sharis, who presses blue.

Final score: *three to two.* There are five council members, so there can never be a tie, only a swing vote, which means Mako's support was key. I feel dizzy with relief. Despite the attempt on Sharis's life, we did it. I can't wait to bounce a message to Chancellor Tarn. I can almost hear Dina's excited whoops—

Except she's not happy with the decision I made to let them take March. So there won't be any celebration there, and I still only have a couple of days to prove he didn't do it. They'll be sentencing him soon, then it'll be too late.

Somehow, I manage to school my features into some facsimile of gladness and appreciation as Vel explains to me what just happened. I offer a fine, restrained *wa* to each council member as they pass by and murmur something banal, knowing Vel will make it sound nice regardless.

"At your earliest convenience, we would like you to carry our acceptance to the Conglomerate," Sharis tells me. Something in this tone tells me this is a warning as well as a request. "Please tell them to arrange a summit, wherein we will meet and discuss the shared goals of our people. We look forward to meeting all of the representatives."

Leave? That's my first frantic thought. *They want me to* leave*? Oh no. No.* But from their perspective, my work here is done. I'm not a diplomat permanently attached to the human embassy on Ithiss-Tor. Such a thing doesn't even exist yet. I'm a goodwill ambassador who has done her job, and now it's time for me to skedaddle.

But I *can't*.

While Vel translates, I try to come up with an alternative, but thinking isn't my strong suit at the best of times, and my pent emotions are threatening to swamp me. "I can bounce him a message," I offer. "Then when he replies, I can brief you on the location selected for the summit."

Devri has paused beside us, giving me a strange look. "We can access information via satellite relays, just like anyone else, ambassador. It is highly preferable that you deliver the message in person. We anticipate there will be retaliation for this victory, and you . . . are the softest target."

I understand the danger, but my stomach hurts at the thought of leaving March behind. I didn't want the sacrifice to be real and permanent. I didn't want that. I always thought I'd have time to turn things around, but things have happened so fast—

I can't give in without one last try. "Sharis, you said your ships were antique. How will your representative get to the summit if we don't give you a lift? It's been hundreds of turns, right? Do you still have trained jumpers standing by?"

Brilliant, I silently congratulate myself. I'm betting they don't. They haven't planned this far ahead. Deep down, they didn't really think they'd get the support they needed. Still, I wait, every muscle tensed for their reply.

Devri shares a look with his coconspirator, and then responds tiredly, "You make a valid point."

Thank Mary.

Then I realize what I've done—volunteered to transport an important Ithtorian dignitary. If anything goes wrong, it'll be just like the *Sargasso* all over again, and I barely scraped out of that with my sanity intact. And some days, I wonder. I shove the terror and nausea down.

The important thing is, I've bought a little time. I just hope it's enough.

CHAPTER 43

I'm at my wits' end.

Dina still isn't speaking to me. The investigation is going nowhere, and time is running out. I've just heard from Sharis that March will be sentenced in the morning. This is just a formality, of course. Everyone knows he's going to the mines for the assault on a councilman. If Sharis had died, he would have been executed.

We still haven't found Constance. Though we first thought her disappearance had something to do with research and that she'd show up in time to help us make the alliance happen, I'm starting to think she knows something she shouldn't. It worries me, but I've been unable to focus on her when I need to find a way to free March.

Jael has moved into the quarters that connect to mine. He was furious when he heard about the anticipated threat. It's a wise precaution, and I don't have the energy to argue, though not from any illness of the body. I've been taking my injections daily, so I'm pretty close to a hundred percent; the bone loss caused by repair of grimspace damage is nearly restored. Instead, it's more a sickness of the soul.

In some ways, this mission has been the worst failure ever while simultaneously being my greatest success. Now I'm starting to wonder if I can live with myself. In the bleak, silent hours of the night, I'm sickened by the way I let March sacrifice himself. I should have at least tried to protest. Instead, I put too much faith in my ability to land on my feet.

Thing is, that doesn't apply to anyone else.

Ironically, the fact that I'm lying awake at this hour, fretting, saves my life.

One minute, I'm staring at the ceiling, which offers no answers to my problems, and the next I'm rolling over the side to avoid the blade that comes whistling down at me. I hit the floor with a thump and yell for help. Even if I wasn't in my sleep cami and ki pants, unarmed, I'd still stand no chance against a determined Bug assassin. It pursues me with merciless intent while I scramble backward on the heels of my hands.

The connecting door flies open and Jael launches himself through the air. He lands on top of my attacker, taking him to the ground with his weight, but the Bug is agile and quick. He flips Jael, who counters with a wrench of his arm. The merc is having a hard time with this opponent because of the natural body armor.

Their lightning-fast moves are hard to track with the eyes, but instead of watching in stupefaction, I do the smart thing. I shove to my feet and sprint for the terminal in the next room. I tap it to life and bring the AI up. From the noises, the fight seems to be slowing, but I can't tell who's winning. The communications suite connects to their security, and using color codes, my AI can alert their system of any emergency situation.

"Security needed in my quarters. Assassination attempt in progress."

"Acknowledged," the machine tells me. "Have you sustained injuries that result in a significant loss of arterial blood?"

I stare at it in disbelief. "Yes."

Maybe that will get them here sooner. There's a small pause while the machine alerts certain linked systems. It's marvelous how machines can communicate on a level that surpasses language, but it's also a little terrifying.

"Dispatch notified. A team should arrive at your location in two minutes. Thank you and have a nice day."

From the muffled thuds and thumps coming from the next room, I should really get out of here because Jael might wind up incapacitated. Since his enemy doesn't know how quick he heals, he won't realize he should sever his head or cut out some vital organ. He'll come after me, maybe with a knife stuck somewhere unpleasant for his trouble, but that won't save me from the same fate while Jael regenerates.

Thanks to genetic engineering, his body can take insane amounts of damage, so there's an obvious advantage in a Bred bodyguard, but Jael's not invincible. On Emry Station, I saw him fall. In fact, I thought he was dead until he made me pull the spiked Morgut limb out of his guts.

I hesitate, eyes on the door. Two minutes until security arrives. Should I head out into the hall to wait for them? If this Bug had backup, surely he or she would have already come in, as the "simple" job has taken way too long already.

With a sigh, I make up my mind. I'm not leaving. Unfortunately, I don't have so much as a shockstick, so I start looking around the room for anything I could use as a weapon. There's a heavy pot full of greenery in the corner of the room. That might do some damage, provided I'm strong enough to lift it.

Determination makes me so. Jael cries out as I reach the doorway. The Bug has jammed the serrated blade into his side, twisting. He has a fair notion of human anatomy, so on anyone else, that would be a kill shot. As luck would have it, his back is to me, so I stagger toward him and cosh him in the back of the head with all my might. It's not enough to do real harm, but he seems dazed, staggering forward like a drunken sailor.

That dropping of his guard gives Jael the opening he needs. He strikes, using brute force to push through the Bug's natural body armor. My would-be assailant shrieks at the upper edge of my register as it dies.

With a grunt of effort, Jael retrieves his weapon from the corpse, one hand holding the blade in his side. When it comes out, it will make a hell of a mess. I don't dare touch it without Doc here.

"Thanks for the assist." He gives me a searching look. "You all right?"

What a question . . . I should be asking him that. "I am now. Security is on the way to clean this mess up. I'll buzz Doc now." I make the call quickly, not liking his pallor. "Are you in a lot of pain?"

He manages a smile. "Best not to talk about it. Or breathe, much."

He staggers, so I help him to the wall for support. I'm guessing sitting would hurt worse, so I put my hand over his,

his blood seeping through my fingers. His breath comes in jagged rasps. I let him lean on me while I buzz Vel on the emergency channel. I'm willing to bet he beats security here.

"Anything more I can do?" It sinks in then. He saved my life.

"Talk to me," he grits through clenched teeth.

So I do, rambling about the significance of the attack. "Sharis and Devri warned me. The Grand Administrator told me her intentions up front. So I can't claim I'm surprised. If I die on world, they'll express condolences to the Conglomerate, claiming it was an unfortunate side effect of progress . . . and they can't be held responsible for the actions of disgruntled fringe groups. In fact, they can even say, truthfully, that they advised me to depart. Now that the alliance has passed, my importance has dropped to nil. The fact is, I'm no longer irreplaceable."

"Not to me," he says softly. "You think I'd let just anyone see me like this? I'm so weak right now that I could be killed pretty easily, if you wanted to do it. I never thought I'd say this, but . . . I trust you, Jax."

"That means a lot to me."

I'd like to touch his cheek or offer a tangible gesture to show I appreciate his faith, but I'd just smear him with blood. His feelings don't change reality, either. Every moment I linger on world, I increase the risk to myself and my crew. At what point do I cut my losses and roll out?

My heart says never. I've learned enough about being a soldier from March, however, to realize that's not a practical answer, and he wouldn't want me to kill myself for his sake. But I don't want to live *without* him even if it's for the greater good.

"This is bad," Jael tells me. "There's only one of me, and I can't stay sharp forever."

I sound tired and snappish when I answer, "Sorry it's been such a hard job keeping me on my feet, but if you want your payday from Tarn, you'll stay with it because we're not done here. I'm not leaving anyone behind."

"Oh, Jax." His expression gentles in a way I can't tolerate.

"Shut it."

"Look, darling, nobody blames you."

"*I* blame me." The response slips out before I can stop it. "So does Dina."

"She shouldn't," he says softly. "This wasn't a military operation, and you're not our commanding officer. And even if you were . . . well, all leaders know that conflict comes with a certain level of acceptable loss. You said it yourself."

Yeah, but I didn't *mean* it. That was just something I said to keep the others from panicking. Mary, I hate when my own words come back to bite me. I thought I'd have March out of this mess by now.

He goes on, "You've given this your best. Nobody expects you to do the impossible . . . save the day every time. Hell, you've already accomplished more here than anybody ever has. And you've already sacrificed so much . . . how much is enough? Do you have to give your life, too?"

Mary, his words make so much sense. It's like hearing what my subconscious has been whispering for days; the selfish part of me nods in vehement agreement. When do I get a break? When do I get a rest? The only person who ever gave me a quiet place to call my own without asking anything in return lives in a tenement on Gehenna.

"Please, don't."

I hate him for saying what I've been thinking over the past few days of banging my head against a wall so high I can't see the top of it. I don't know if I'm strong enough to withstand the temptation to ease back into my old skin. The old Jax would love to go back to living for herself; she's tired of sorrow and sacrifice. She says it's been a damn long time since we lived for the thrill of it.

He leans toward me, taking my hands in his. "No, I have to speak my mind. Just from what I've seen during the short time I've been with you, people seem to think it's fine to force you to do things you don't want, over and over again. I've been there. I know how it is when people use you. They offer you a Hobson's choice that's no choice at all. It's time to walk away, Jax."

CHAPTER 44

Is he right? Maybe I'm just too stubborn to know when I'm licked. I don't want to undo all the good I've done here for selfish reasons. I waver, thinking of how easy it'd be.

But . . . *no.* I can't leave him. To this day, it haunts me that I considered leaving March on Hon's Kingdom and that it took someone else to make me do the right thing. His injury made him a liability; I thought he'd slow me down and lessen my chance of survival. Back then, that was all that mattered to me.

Kai's loss haunts me. And it haunts me that I couldn't save Loras. I can still see his face as the door closed on him, trapping him on the wrong side. I'll carry that until I die; I just don't have the fortitude to bear any more weight on my soul.

"No." I say it aloud for emphasis. "I'm in this until the end, and if you don't like it, take one of the shuttles up, turn on the emergency beacon, and hope for the best."

"Fine. Your funeral." His hand goes to the knife in his side, covering where I'm putting pressure on the wound. "I'd say it's mine, too, but I've always found it difficult to die." Beneath the levity of his tone, I glimpse the stark solitude of a man who has always been alone and always will be.

Vel arrives before I can reply. He takes stock of the situation with a glance, then he checks out Jael's injury. "Did you notify Dr. Solaith?"

"He's on the way," I confirm.

Though he has to come from the ship, Doc turns up before the security team, which makes a joke out of their emergency-response system. But maybe they give better service to citizens. They could hardly do worse.

Saul takes a look and regards him incredulously. "How aren't you dead? Never mind, don't tell me now. Let's get you taken care of."

The Doc I know and love doesn't insist on answers before helping someone who's in pain. That can wait. While he's working on Jael, the Bug squadron finally deigns to put in an appearance.

There's no question this corpse shouldn't be on my floor; it signifies criminal trespass and my bedding is shredded where the knife went in, so that validates my claim of a murder attempt. At least we're spared a situation where they try to make this my fault. I was in my bed, exactly where I ought to be. Still, I can't help but notice that the security personnel don't care much.

None of them ask any questions. They just remove the body and cleanse the stain on the ground. The team leader adds, "We will be checking all possible leads. We apologize for the inconvenience."

Inconvenience . . . ? It's all I can do not to go upside his head with another decorative pot. Vel restrains me with a claw on my shoulder. His body language says a confrontation would be pointless. I agree, but I'm spoiling for a fight. Every spark of jumper in me wants to make somebody sorry. I rein in that Jax with great effort, and, instead, offer an insincere *wa* of thanks.

Afterward, I take a look at how the patient is faring. While I look on, Doc finishes closing the top of the wound. "Ordinarily, I would never do it this way," he says with a disapproving frown. "There's too much internal damage just to seal it up and hope for the best, but Jael says he'll be fine."

"He will be," I agree.

Maybe it's callous, but I'm not that worried about him. After all, I've seen him heal worse. On Emry, I didn't have any niceties like liquid skin, antibiotic preventives, or a sonic cleanser either.

"I didn't want the blood all over the floor," Jael says in a self-deprecating tone. "Gut wounds bleed like a son of a bitch. It was better to have a professional at hand."

"Try to limit your movement," Doc says. "And take it easy for the next couple of days."

Jael mutters, "Unlikely. Jax is determined to stay, despite the danger."

"Such attacks will escalate," Vel predicts. "Until you are dead or . . . gone."

I joke, "I thought they were one and the same." Nobody seems to think that's too funny, but it's the middle of the night, dammit. I sigh and run my fingers through my hair. Finally, I offer, "I'll be careful, okay?"

"Do that," Doc admonishes. "I think I'll head back."

"Thanks for coming out," I murmur.

Jael seconds that, rubbing his side. Doc's obviously distracted, or he would have asked about March by now. I'm hoping that distraction will hold, but I guess my wishes carry no weight. Saul draws up short of the door and turns back slowly.

Of course, it's the million credit question. "Why isn't March with you? And where is Constance?"

I wish I could answer the second, and I wish I *didn't* know the answer to the first. Before replying, I take a seat because this could take a while. I gesture at the place across from me. Vel and Jael join us, more from expedience, I think, than any desire to participate. Being the bearer of bad news is clearly my job.

"He's been arrested," I say starkly. "And he's due to be sentenced tomorrow, today actually, and sent to the mines within a few days. It's only because their justice system works so slowly that he's not already there."

The saving grace in the situation? Doc's temperament. His eyes go dark, but he doesn't lose his cool. He merely asks for all the details, and we spend a good hour filling him in on what he's missed by staying on the ship so much. Certainly, I don't blame him for that. If I didn't have to be here, I'd be on the ship, too. Unless there's a medical emergency, he has research and Rose, not necessarily in that order, to occupy his time.

When he says, "Let's look at the facts objectively," I stifle a smile.

We should have brought him in long before now. Outside of Constance and Vel, Saul is the most logical thinker among us. Once he's sure he has the big picture, I pause to consider if I've left anything out.

Oh yeah . . .

"I also think Constance knows who orchestrated the attack on Sharis," I add. "Since the Bugs don't have her, that's the only explanation that makes sense."

"She could tell us if she's still functional," Doc offers.

Vel says, "Functionality is no barrier. I can still salvage the data unless the damage is all-encompassing."

For the first time in longer than I care to consider, I feel a flicker of hope. Maybe I couldn't do this by myself, but that's fine. I should've called a crew meeting over this two days ago instead of working secretly with Vel. I can see now, by trying to take it all on myself, I've done everyone a disservice. They don't need me to shield them from reality. Good intentions can cause a wide variety of terrible results.

"So instead of trying to find out who this hooded guy is, we should be looking for Constance?" I gaze around at my team to make sure we're on the same page.

Jael asks, "What hooded guy?"

"We've got an image on one of the static security cams, showing someone sneaking into Sharis's quarters. Around your height, too." I smile at him. "But you were playing Charm with Dina and Hit that night after you left the party, right?"

"Lost more than my shirt," he grumbles in confirmation.

I go on, "We think it was an Ithtorian, who donned clothing to make himself seem human to the casual observer. Most wouldn't know how to do what Vel does . . . that technique takes time and practice to master."

"And they consider using our ability in such a way a greater shame than resorting to cloth," Vel adds.

"Yes, it's only to be used as insulation for the honorable stalking of prey on the great tundra." I smile to show I mean no insult with the cavalier summation.

Saul stirs, restive. If he has to be up in the middle of the night, he wants all of us focused. "We've gotten slightly off task. Does Constance possess any feature that could be used to track her? I know the PA-245 is an expensive model. It stands to reason its owners would want to be able to retrieve it if lost or stolen."

Genius. Though I don't know off the top of my head, I glance at Vel. He's already at the terminal, working, as he answers, "There should be. If she has any power left to her at all, I should be able to devise something that will pick up her signal."

"We should have thought of this sooner." Regret pierces me.

"You should have brought this to me sooner," Saul says with some asperity.

Jael makes a product of yawning. "I can see you lot have it all under control, so I'm going to catch a few winks before the next assassination attempt. Thanks, Doc."

Lost in schematics, none of us pays him any mind as he slips out.

CHAPTER 45

Tarn's response to the message I bounced days ago, regarding the successful alliance, finally arrives the next morning. There's no telling whether the satellites were acting up or whether he played my message for a hundred different people before answering.

To say he seems surprised doesn't quite encompass it. During the course of his reply, he says, "I can't believe it," more than once. I should probably be insulted by that. He closes with, "Just sit tight. Once we've had a chance to make arrangements, I will notify you of where to take the Ithtorian representative."

So he actually approves of the way I've been handling the situation? That's a relief. More than anything, I don't want to mess things up, but I'm walking a tightrope that gets thinner with every step.

After sending Tarn the equivalent of "you got it, boss" via bounce, I go see how Vel is coming with the gizmo that will detect Constance's frequency. We all agree she knows something important, or she wouldn't be missing, so it's become top priority to find her. He's gifted with electronics, but he has to modify some of his existing equipment, as there isn't a bounty-hunter outlet store anywhere on world.

From somewhere deep inside me, I can feel the grief and fear banging like a drum. I'm able to ignore it for now, keep it under wraps and pretend I'm sure everything will be fine. It will serve no purpose if I break down.

Hit stops by shortly thereafter, checking in on me. She's been protective since I displayed such weakness. "Everything all right?"

"Yeah. We're looking for Constance. How's Dina holding up?"

She shrugs. "She thinks a lot of March . . . and she's mad at you. I don't think it's because she really believes you're to blame, but sometimes you just need to be angry at somebody, y'know? It can't be March because he's gone, being all heroic and shit. I don't know how you put up with it. I'd rather serve my own time in the mines than have somebody do me that way. The guilt would be worse than the punishment."

"It does get old," I admit. "Sometimes I wish he was more . . . ordinary, but he wouldn't be the man I love if he was."

"The bitter with the sweet," she agrees.

"So what do you guys do to keep from going nuts with boredom anyway?" It's a casual question more than anything. I don't want to talk about March anymore because that sharp, stabbing pain in my chest is back.

Hit makes a face. "We play a lot of Charm."

"That's right," I murmur. "Jael mentioned he played with you the night Sharis was poisoned."

Her whole body freezes. "He was with us for one hand, Jax. No more. So if he's using us as an alibi—"

"He's lying."

So we have one merc, whereabouts unaccounted for, who fits the height profile. If he did this, I'll kill him. Rage crashes over me, and my hands curl into fists. Yeah, I know he's had a rough life and never found a place he belongs. It's no wonder, if this is the way he treats people who take him in.

"You want me to keep this quiet?" Hit asks.

"Please. Right now, it's just a suspicion, nothing that will get March off the hook. For all we know, he hooked up with some Ithtorian babe." We both shudder over that. "I need evidence, and the last thing I want is for Jael to bolt before we find it. If he did this, I'm handing him to the Bugs in chains."

Vel glances up as I step into my bedroom, which he's turned into an inventor's lab. Metal bits, wires, and tiny glittering chips litter the table. The guts of some device are showing beneath the casing, but I don't know enough about this sort of thing to judge how the project is coming.

"Nearly there." He answers my unspoken question. "But please take a seat, Sirantha. Your presence will slow me down if you hover."

No hovering, gotcha. Within half an hour, he closes the thing up, then programs it via remote. Lights spring up on the exterior, which is surely a good sign. As I look on, he tinkers with it further, and the color shifts to green. Vel gets out his handheld and taps away at it for a moment. If I had to speculate, I'd say he's linking them somehow, so he can better interpret what the tiny transponder detects.

"Anything?" Though I know questions annoy him when he's trying to work, I can't resist.

His answer floors me. "She is nearby."

"What are we waiting for? Let's go!"

"Because apparently, she is also here, here, here . . . and here." Vel turns his handheld toward me so I can see the different signals.

They seem to be of varying strength. "What does that mean? Is she in pieces?"

"That is one possibility, but I have drawn no conclusions at this time."

I stand up, relieved to have something to do. It's also good I don't need to wear my ornate gold robe anymore. "No point in sitting around speculating. Let's just go check out each location."

Vel leads the way, and we swing out of my quarters toward the first point on the map. All of them are within the government center somewhere, so this shouldn't take too long. As we approach the first site, the signal grows stronger, flashing with great urgency. Unfortunately, it also lies behind a door marked PRIVATE: AUTHORIZED PERSONNEL ONLY.

Dammit. I should have known it wouldn't be that easy. I glance both ways and see no patrols, but that won't be the only security. Vel is already making his own assessment, checking out what we'll need to get inside without getting caught.

"I need you to take this over to the access panel on the far wall," he tells me.

There's no time to ask why, or what I'll be doing. I'm capable of following directions blindly if I trust the person issuing the commands. "Then what?"

"Keep an eye on the camera angle. When it pans away, you will have thirty seconds to open the access panel and align this"—he holds up a small, flat silver device—"with the bottom edges of the controls. That will take care of the cameras, giving us a three-minute window to get through the door. If it takes us any longer to get out of there, they will eventually see us breaking and entering."

He doesn't need to tell me that's an outcome best avoided. I don't want us all sent to the mines. Hell, I'm trying to save March from that fate.

"Camera pans away, thirty seconds, three minutes inside. Got it. I'm ready."

I amble down to the end of the hall and pretend to check out the rampant greenery. It seems like asking Vel the name of the plants would be carrying the pretense too far, so I simply bend to examine the waxy green foliage. The moment the camera's off me, though, I go to work on the panel. I'm conscious of the seconds ticking away as I seek a catch that will spring the panel.

There, found it. My heart thuds in my ears as I fit the gadget into place. At first nothing happens, then it purrs to life. Since it's thin, I'm able to close the panel on top of it, giving no sign of what we've done. If we have time, it would be smart to remove it, unless it dissolves on use, like the best black-market ware.

"Good job, Sirantha. Five seconds to spare."

Time for Vel to do his part. First he attaches a code breaker to handle the lock. That's serious contraband, available only on Gehenna. I'm a little amazed and impressed that he managed to sneak it on world with all the scans and tests they put us through before allowing us to leave the docking area. Then again, he may have returned for it. After that first time, security slacked way off, as though they didn't consider we could simply make a second trip to the ship.

Using the tech, he pops the lock easily and we're through. This isn't a simple maintenance closet, which I already suspected. In the first room, the walls are plain and pale, the floors bare. I would guess they're designed to feel institutional, although that could be me imposing human values on Ithtorian culture. We come to another door, complete with security pads. It doesn't take Vel long to crack those either. Whatever happens in this suite, they don't want a record of it because there are no cameras anywhere to be found.

"Interrogation chambers," Vel explains briefly. "For criminals more dangerous than they considered us to be . . . or we would have been in here ourselves."

From the stains on the floor, I suspect it's used for more than just interrogation. There's nothing in the first two rooms. We come to another door, also locked, and the signal seems to be coming from beyond it.

"How much time do we have left?"

"A minute, forty-five seconds," he answers, going to work on the security pad.

I tick off the time as the door snaps open. To my vast disappointment, there's only a tiny cleaning droid in there, attending to some hideous spillage on the floor. It's some bodily fluid I don't want to identify, the remnants of somebody being tortured.

The little machine gets very agitated when it registers our presences. It woos and hisses at us, skittering in circles. *Shit.* Does this thing count as a witness?

He's thinking along the same lines. "I was so sure my calculations were specific enough to target only Constance." He makes a sound that the chip can't translate, but I know intuitively it's a curse. "We will have to take it with us. We cannot chance that it is aware enough to realize we do not belong here and report our presence."

I agree, so I snatch it up. Though it's small and looks like a spidery crab, the thing is heavier than it looks, solid metal. Vel reaches over to power it down before it can beam any information about its circumstances. The central computer may wonder what's happened to it, but surely units break from time to time. It won't be flagged as urgent, I hope. Then we head for the door.

Once we're safely outside again, thirty seconds to spare, I offer, "Maybe it will help you refine the program so you don't pick up any more cleaning droids?"

We have five more spots to check out yet, but I don't feel too hopeful anymore. In any case, I hope we don't encounter anyone on the way back to my quarters. I can't think of a single compelling reason why we'd be appropriating a cleaning droid.

ACCESSING TRANSCRIPT . . .

Omni News Net: Profile of an Unsung Hero

TAMIKA NAVARRO, AGE 27

[Lili Lightman faces the vid wearing a serious look. The set is empty but for her and a wall of screens that offers shifting images in tribute to a courageous young woman. They start with pictures of her childhood, progress through her teen years, and end with her graduation photo, where she's proudly clutching her credentials.]

Lili: Three days ago, Tamika Navarro died protecting the people she served.

Ms. Navarro was raised in a spacer family, and she was traveling the star lanes as soon as she was old enough to jump. She worked on freighters, saving enough money to put herself through medical school. Once she completed her training, she went to work for Phas Shipping as one of their company physicians.

Her crewmates remember her as kind and calm in a crisis. She always had a moment to help out, even if the problem wasn't medical in nature. Her dedication often caused her to work long hours without submitting a chit for extra pay, knowing the shipping company could little afford it. Dr. Navarro might have made better credits elsewhere, but she grew to care deeply for her crew and considered herself responsible for keeping them healthy and whole.

Three days past, she faced her greatest and final challenge. When the Morgut attacked their vessel, intending to devour the crew and steal the cargo—ore out of Dobrinya mining colony—Dr. Navarro kept cool. The officers attempted to drive off the other ship, but their weapons were insufficient for the task.

At 03.45, the Morgut ship docked with the freighter *Good Hope* and began their feast. Amid screams of horror and anguish, Dr. Navarro laid an irresistible lure. Using spare transfusion packs, she put down a blood trail and led the Morgut to the jettison chamber. This quick thinking saved the rest of her crew.

She had no time to get into a suit, so when she hit that button, she chose her death knowing it meant survival for everyone else. A few monsters evaded her trap, but the crew, thus bolstered by her sacrifice, managed to slay them. The cost was high, and Dr. Navarro paid the ultimate price, but the end result is this:

I have the first survivors of a Morgut attack with me on the program today. You can look on their faces and know they are here because of Tamika Navarro. [Lili glances off vid, beckoning, and a group files into view, nearly twenty men and women in all.]

Captain Chegal, would you like to say a few words?

Captain Chegal: I would, Ms. Lightman. Thank you. [He is a man of middle years, silver-haired and weathered.] We have no words for how grateful we are, but we've petitioned Phas Shipping to rechristen our ship. [He pauses, obviously overcome by emotion.] From this day forward, she'll be known as the *Tamika Navarro*. If she ever becomes less than starworthy, she'll be retired and find a good home in the interstellar history museum on New Terra.

Lili: Thank you, Captain. That's a fitting tribute. [She faces the vid once more.] This is the way we win over our enemies, not with bigger weapons, or faster ships, but with human courage, ingenuity, and sacrifice. Don't lose hope. We've faced the darkness before—it has nothing new to teach us. As we go about our lives, let us remember the example Dr. Navarro set for us. At the right time, anyone can be a hero. Thanks for watching, and keep reaching for the stars.

CHAPTER 46

Vel tinkers with his tech for a good hour. When he fires it back up, the signals don't change. If time weren't ticking away, I would be amused by his frustration. He's not used to failure or incompetence.

I suspect it's been a long time since he didn't simply do whatever he set out to. When you're alone like he is, you can't rely on other people. Maybe that's starting to change a little, though. I seem to spend more time with Vel than with anyone else.

That means I know better than to interrupt him, but it's hard for me to sit still when I need to be *doing* something. I'd love to go see March, but they probably wouldn't let me in. And it will be impossible to leave him there, so when I go to him, I need to be able to take him with me when I go.

"I just do not know what is wrong." He sits forward, laying down his gadgets with what seems like a weary, hopeless air.

Hesitantly, I slip from my seat and kneel beside him. I think this is the first time I've tried to reciprocate the quiet support he's given me. A quick mental run-through of Ithtorian customs gives me precious little to work with; they're not big on reassuring gestures, but I can think of four ways to let him know he's an incompetent buffoon.

So I go the human route and cover his claw with my hand. "I don't think it's your fault. There has to be something else going on, some factor we can't plan for because we don't know about it."

Vel tilts his head, gazing down at the contrast between his green scale and my tan skin. I'm surprised when he curls our hands together briefly before letting go. Such gestures don't come easy for him, so my heart gives a little tug.

"You can be very kind, Sirantha."

I smile, straightening away from him. "Don't tell anyone. Maybe we should check out the other sites, just in case?"

He agrees, so we go looking.

We find five more cleaning droids, though none so carefully concealed as the first. No sign of Constance, however. So now we're sitting in my quarters with all six of them, and I'm overwhelmed with a what-the-hell feeling. I've *never* known Vel to go wrong with technology.

He keeps poking at his handheld, checking and rechecking the device he built, based on Constance's schematics, but it keeps telling us the same thing. According to it, she's here in the room with us in the form of six agitated san-bots. Well, they were agitated when we first *found* them, but right now they're deactivated.

A ridiculous idea occurs to me, but that's sort of my specialty at this point. "Let's say you're right. So maybe they weren't disturbed because we were in no-access areas. Maybe they were trying to tell us we were on the right track?"

Vel puts down the gadgets to regard me, canting his head in puzzlement. "What are you suggesting, Sirantha?"

"Well . . . have you ever known a san-bot to care who came and went in its assigned sector? They're generally not that sophisticated. But their behavior was atypical, so we took them with us because we were worried they might report us. That's not normal for a cleaning droid. Well . . . in most places, it's not. What about here?"

He considers. "No. Unless things have changed since I left, these units do not function according to the usual parameters."

I continue, "And Sharis said things don't change here, right? No new tech. If that's the case, nobody would be thinking about making san-bots more autonomous."

At last he gets what I'm driving at. "Shall we power them up simultaneously, since we have gone to the trouble of collecting them?"

"I think we better. If something goes wrong . . ." I shrug.

"We can make a colossal mess, then when security arrives, we'll claim we needed all these bots to mop up after our orgy. That'll be in keeping with what they think of us."

Vel makes a sound I've come to recognize as signifying amusement. "Fair enough. These three are mine."

I cross the room to activate the others. They come online at more or less the same time, but it's only when the last one powers up that things get interesting. A thin beam of blue light bounces from each to each, then sparks the console. For a moment, nothing else happens, and then an image of Constance projects outward from our terminal.

"Can you hear me?"

"We can," I say in delight. "What happened? Where are you?"

"It was Jael," she answers at once. "He tampered with one of your walls, and when I questioned his actions, he tried to disable me permanently."

Gotcha, you bastard.

I wish I didn't feel so sick and betrayed, but there it is, a huge lump in my stomach. I suspected earlier after talking to Hit, but I didn't want to believe it. I wanted there to be some other explanation, but he's the one who told me Constance was on the ship the night she disappeared. He lied to me, every step of the way.

That bastard. He was so kind when we left March on Lachion. For Mary's sake, I let him hold me while I cried. And now I want to kill him slowly. His ability will certainly make *that* easier.

But I have the advantage. I know he can't be taken in a straight fight, so I'll come at him sideways. A drug slipped into his food seems like fair recompense for what he's done. I imagine his shock and horror when he wakes to find himself bound. I'll need to ask Doc for an extrapotent narcotic. There's no telling how fast his body may burn through the substance. It's a serious break for us that Doc will have Jael's records on file because he treated him right here in this room.

"How did you wind up in this . . . state?" Vel gestures at the six san-bots.

They've returned to their standard protocols as they whir around the living area, looking for something to clean. I have no doubt we could turn them loose in the hallway without any untoward consequences. It occurs to me that we don't want callers while Constance is talking to us. For the time being, it's better if nobody realizes she's back . . . and telling us everything she knows. So I secure the door.

"To avoid permanent decommission, I bounced my consciousness and all relevant data to the nearest unit."

I nod. "Which happened to be a san-bot."

"But this unit did not have the processing capacity to host me, and I would have burned it out in a relatively short time."

"So you spread yourself out among six units," Vel guesses. "Remarkably clever."

"I am pleased you found me."

Me, too. I'd hug her if she wasn't an ethereal stream of data at the moment. "So what happened to your casing?" I can't bring myself to say "body." That sounds like she's dead, and we're talking to her ghost.

"He has hidden it. I will beam the location to your handheld," she tells Vel, "but I am unsure whether it can be salvaged. Jael seemed intent on damaging it beyond repair."

"How do you know where he went with it?" That seems remarkable.

"Simple," the Constance holo answers. "I followed him in my new casing. Nobody pays any attention to san-bots. I tried on more than one occasion to attract *your* attention, Sirantha Jax, but you ignored me as well."

I wince. "Sorry about that. Look, we need to go find your old casing and see if it can be fixed." I glance at the bounty hunter. "Will you be able to run a diagnostic to see if the Lila unit is totaled?"

"That much I can do. Dina will need to handle any actual repairs."

"At any rate, it's proof, so we need to retrieve it. There should be traces of Jael's genetic material left, proving he was the one who dumped the casing."

"It offers corroboration," Vel says. "We should go without delay."

I nod. "Constance, can you stay out of sight for a little while? Don't show yourself to anyone but us, not even if you think you can trust them."

"Acknowledged." Her image flickers and disappears.

"Don't shut yourself off. I want you logging everything that happens within sight and hearing of this console."

She gives the response that never fails to make me smile. "I am here to help."

In parting, I ask, "Are you comfortable there in the terminal?"

Not that there's anything I can do about it right this minute. We need to move. Still, it seems polite to ask.

Constance considers for a moment. "It is better than being split in six fragments."

"Glad to hear it. Can you conceal yourself from anybody who might be snooping around?" That's probably a dumb question, but I'll err on the side of caution for once in my life. I know; it's one for the record books.

"I can," Constance replies.

"We're out then. Be careful." I pause at the door, uncertain if this is appropriate. *Ah, to hell with it.* "I'm really glad you're back."

After he verifies the location, Vel and I head for the spot where Jael dumped her casing. As we walk, a thought strikes me. "Shit. Last night, when we were talking about looking for Constance, he left. You think he went to do something with the evidence? Maybe he was worried the unit would still broadcast somehow."

"That is a legitimate concern, but there is no way to alter events that have already occurred. All we can do is move faster, Sirantha."

So we do.

CHAPTER 47

Vel and I follow the directions from the handheld. We range into a little-used part of the government center; I hope we're not trespassing. Instead of the lush, tropical environs in the public areas, this is all bare and plain, some matte metal that could use a good cleaning. From the dirty treads on the floor, heavy equipment is often brought through this way.

We pass a few low-ranking Bugs as we go, but nobody seems overly curious. Then again, I'm not dressed as the ambassador, and I doubt they'd recognize me without the gold robe. The only common theme between my public persona and the real Jax is the green tattoo around my throat.

Still, at any moment, I expect someone to stop us and ask what the hell we're doing. Tension settles in my shoulders. This part of the complex isn't for public passage. What are the penalties for being here?

The device beeps faster as we get closer, distracting me. Finally, we make the last turn and wind up outside a maintenance closet. Once we step inside, it becomes clear the spot we're trying to reach is somehow behind the wall. Vel fiddles with it, and the access panel pops open.

We both stand for a moment, cursing. Now it's just an empty space through which maintenance droids can pass to make repairs. In other words, Jael has indeed moved the Lila unit. No wonder he wanted me to get off world as soon as possible. He must've known his fiction wouldn't hold forever.

"Our next move has to be finding that damned interrogator and telling him the truth," I say decisively.

Vel agrees, tapping his handheld for a few seconds. "He is currently at the center for jurisprudence."

I make a face. "Where else?"

On the way, we don't say much. Vel guides us smoothly from the tram to the lift that adjoins the building. Most complexes connect via underground, and it's rare for Ithtorians to need to go outdoors, which is just as well, given the nuclear winter out there. There are no hitches in our mission until we hit the outer office.

A low-ranking male objects, "You may not interrupt the interrogator. If you care to make an appointment, he will see you at his earliest convenience."

After Vel translates, I draw myself up, trying to look intimidating. "I am the ambassador from New Terra, and I have information he'll wish to possess immediately. I wouldn't want to be in your shoes when he finds out you delayed me."

Fear of his boss's wrath seems effective. The Bug leaps to his feet and retreats into the inner office, presumably to relay the information. A few minutes later, Ehon himself comes out.

"I trust this is important, ambassador?" The interrogator waves us back to his sanctum sanctorum.

"You have the wrong man in custody. March only confessed because the poison was found in my quarters. He was trying to shield me. Through a private internal investigation, we've discovered the real culprit."

I quickly outline the circumstances . . . and how he tried to do away with one of my staff members. I don't dare tell the whole story because they don't know Constance is a droid. I'm not sure how they'll take that revelation. We don't dare do anything that will screw things up now that the alliance has passed. Vel confirms my caution with a slight inclination of his head.

By the time Vel has rephrased what I said into the best possible form, Ehon has started tapping his claws against the chitin of his chest. That's not a good sign. "But this person somehow survived the attack and being held for days against her will?"

After Vel relays the question, I nod.

"Will this person testify in front of the tribunal that she saw this mercenary hide the vial in your quarters?"

Ouch. Therein lies the rub.

"She . . . can't."

Ehon is out of patience with me. "So you bring me this story with no physical evidence and no witness? Just what do you expect me to do with this information?" He sits forward, glittering gaze fixed on me. "I will tell you what I think, ambassador. Now that the alliance has passed, you are trying to save your lover without regard for our justice system or the truth."

Pretending I don't understand keeps me from doing something stupid. I wait for Vel to speak before I protest, "That's not true. I just want the real guilty party to pay."

The interrogator checks something on his terminal. "He *is*. This is a moot point, ambassador. Even if you had evidence, the offender was sentenced this morning, and we do not try the same crime twice. The prison convoy left for the mines two hours ago."

Oh, Mary, no. Anguish crashes through me, smashing barriers I've put in place. I'm drowning in it. March thinks I didn't even care enough to come see him, not once, not even to say good-bye. He probably thinks I've written him off. That's what the world would expect of the old Jax.

Easy come, easy go.

I can't imagine how alone he must feel right now.

From somewhere far away, Vel and Ehon seem to be talking, but I can't hear them through the roaring in my head. *Too little, too late.* Through the sheen of tears, I offer a clumsy *wa* in parting as Vel drags me out of the interrogator's office. He keeps me upright, but I can't seem to make my legs cooperate.

Vel gives me a little shake. "Sirantha, pull yourself together. It is beneath you to stand and weep like a woman. You can do better than this."

Well, I am *a woman.* But his brusque treatment helps

more than a soothing pat. With great effort, I battle it back and try to think. "Where are the mines from here?"

He regards me for a moment, incredulous. "You cannot be thinking of a rescue?"

"You bet your ass I am."

"They are eight hours by underground," Vel replies. "And I do not know of any way to get inside from the surface."

"So we might need to stow away." I make a mental note. "Well, we're going to get in there somehow, leave Jael in March's cell, and get the hell off world."

I know my orders are to wait for the summit to be decided and transport the Ithtorian representative, whoever that turns out to be, but Tarn can send another ship. My presence here isn't vital. The delegate will still arrive on time for the peace conference—such things take time to arrange. If we play this well, they'll never know they have the wrong human. I suspect we all look alike to them anyway.

If things go badly, it will destroy the alliance and any hope for Ithtorian assistance in the coming war. I know that. For March, it's a risk I'm willing to take.

Despite his obvious misgivings, Vel tells me, "I am with you until the end."

That declaration makes my heart twist inside my chest. I don't deserve that kind of loyalty from anyone, let alone someone like Vel. You could search the galaxy thrice over and not find his equal.

Having a plan helps, however impossible. I head for the underground, already planning our next move. "We need to get Doc, Dina, and Hit together quietly. We can't let Jael know what we're planning, or he'll bail. I wouldn't put it past him to steal our ship and leave us stranded here."

"We should stay off comm channels," Vel says. "I do not know what he can do, but it is best to assume he has the ability to listen in."

"You don't think he has some kind of tap on my terminal, do you? Would he know that Constance has taken up residence there?"

We take the lift down to the station while he thinks about that.

"I do not know," he says eventually. "Before yesterday, I would have said it was impossible for a PA to split into segments and hide within the processors of six separate cleaning droids. I no longer feel able to predict what might happen next."

"You and me both," I mutter.

When we reach the ship, we find Dina and Hit together, no surprise there.

"Emergency meeting in my quarters," I say, ignoring Dina's fierce scowl.

I don't have time to fight with her if we're going to make this happen.

Next we go looking for Doc. He's working on something in his lab. When I step closer, I realize he's tinkering with samples of my DNA and that of Baby-Z. Remembering the little lost one gives me a pang. I guess he's back to his original assignment, which was to try to come up with a species that could jump without the aggravated risk of burnout.

"What do you need, Jax?" he asks.

"Your help. Come to my quarters as soon as you wrap up here."

CHAPTER 48

Once everyone is assembled, the door is secured, and Vel has set up his signal jammer to make sure we're not being bugged, I fill them in. It doesn't take long to explain what happened to Constance and Jael's role in it. By the time I'm done, they look livid—with the exception of Doc. He just seems puzzled.

"That son of a bitch," Dina growls. "I'm going to pull out his spleen and make him eat it."

"Do we know why he did this?" Doc asks.

I shrug. "With all due respect . . . I don't give a rat's ass. It's what, not why. Here's what I need from you, Saul—a sedative powerful enough to make a Rodeisian sleep for a week." Jael has lost my loyalty, so I don't hesitate to explain. "See, he's Bred, and he heals crazy fast. Pain doesn't faze him either. It's unlikely we could take him in a fight."

"I could," Vel says quietly. "But it would be messy, and I would sustain grievous physical damage in the process."

"That's best avoided," Hit says. "And it would slow us down. As I understand it, time is critical."

My thoughts exactly.

I go on, "So here's my idea. At this point, he's afraid we're going to find out what he did, but he doesn't realize we already have. He did something with the Lila unit when he found Vel was building something to try and track Constance. To his mind, he's covered his tracks completely, and he won't be expecting us to make a move on him. It's imperative we all pretend nothing's changed if we run across him." I glance at Dina. "Can you do that?"

For a moment she struggles with the idea of not moving on the man she wants to kill, then she says, "Yeah. I can. I will. Don't worry, Jax. I'll hold up my end."

"Great. Then this is what I need from you and Hit . . . he's been hanging out with you guys, right? So invite him to your room tonight to play Charm. Don't insist. Just mention casually that you'll be playing, and he's welcome to stop by."

Hit murmurs, "I can do that."

I glance at Doc. "Can you use the med data you took when you worked on the wound in his side? To make the sedative."

He nods. "I can . . . but I don't like it, Jax. Are you *sure* he did this? Have you talked to him? He took a knife in the gut for you. It makes no sense that he'd save your life but poison Councilor Sharis for no apparent reason."

"Doc," I say dangerously, "don't even think about talking to him about this. If he's alerted, then our whole plan goes to hell. I don't care if it doesn't make sense. I know what Constance said."

"Somebody could have reprogrammed her," Saul points out.

Vel shakes his head. "A PA of her caliber has protocols in place that will initiate a self-destruct if unauthorized personnel attempt such a maneuver."

I try to keep my cool when I have about a thousand conflicting impulses roiling in my head. Screaming sounds good. So does punching something. Beneath it all, the need to jump ravages my nervous system. I can feel myself starting to unravel, so I direct my attention elsewhere while Doc thinks.

"That reminds me," I say. "Dina, I need you to head for my quarters with a memory spike big enough to hold an entire PA, including all programming and files."

"Mother Mary," she mutters. "You don't ask much, do you?"

"Can you do it?"

After a little bitching, she admits, "Yeah, I can. I'll take care of it as soon as we're done here. Where is she?"

"In the terminal in my quarters. I'll signal her that you've been cleared. I told her not to show herself to anyone."

Hit nods. "Smart. We might've lost her if she hadn't been so damn resourceful."

Yeah, that surprises me a little, to be honest. She's definitely gone beyond the parameters of her helpful administrator chip. Dina or Vel might want to compare notes later on and see what makes Constance tick.

I glance at Doc, figuring he's had long enough to weigh all the angles. "Look, I know you don't like passing judgment, but Jael's guilty, and I want March back. Are you in or out?" He hesitates, and I add, "If you say out, I'm confining you to the lab with no comm until we're done. Nothing personal."

"I'm in," he says heavily. "I can't leave March to rot in an Ithtorian prison. I'll get started on the drug dosage right away."

"Excellent. I'm afraid I need to ask one more thing of you, Doc."

He looks apprehensive, rubbing thumb and forefinger over his gray goatee. "What is it?"

"Vel and I will join the game at Dina's place. Jael will think that with everyone where he can see them, he has nothing to worry about. You'll catch him off guard."

Saul's expression shifts to abject horror. "I won't hurt anyone, Jax. I *don't* cause harm." His face goes grim. "There are enough people who do so gleefully without my adding to it."

"That's why you're perfect for this job. You come up behind him and fill him full of sedative. It won't technically hurt him."

"A semantic difference," he tells me coldly.

I hate to play this card, but I'll do anything, *say* anything, to see March safe. "So you're ready to risk letting Jael get away then? He's smart, or we'd have been onto him long before now. If anything goes wrong tonight at Dina's place one of us could be seriously hurt, maybe even killed. Then who's going to rescue March?"

I stretch my legs out, leveling on Doc—one person who's been unfailingly kind to me—my coldest look. "But I guess you'll be fine with that because you'll have your principles intact. I hope they're enough to sustain you when you have to tell Keri what happened to March."

Dina's swift intake of breath tells she can't believe I said that. For a long moment, nobody speaks in this frozen tableau. I can hear Hit breathing next to me.

Then Doc says softly, as if his heart is breaking, "What time?"

"Yeah," Jael echoes. "What time?"

Ah, shit. I turn slowly to find him standing in the doorway. He cracked Vel's security and slid in without anyone noticing. That speaks volumes for his skill level. I wish that didn't also mean we're royally fragged.

The merc saunters in wearing a cocky smile. "Seems strange that you'd be having a private party, and I'm not invited, y'know?" He nudges me with his foot. "What's up with that, Jax? I did save your life. What happened? Am I not your best mate anymore?"

"That depends," I say slowly.

"On what, darling?" He stands between me and the door.

I don't have a weapon to hand, and he does. Jael spins it elegantly in the palm of his hand, but his reflexes are lightning fast. I don't know how much he heard, so it might be worth our time to bluff. No, forget that. Now I'll take Doc's advice since *my* plan has gone to hell.

"On whether you tried to kill Sharis and destroy everything I've been working toward. Saving my life just isn't that major in comparison. I'm not that important."

"Your man seems to think so," Jael says, still smiling. "I heard he's already on his way to suffer for you. Touching, that, if a little foolish for my tastes."

"Answer the question," Dina demands.

Jael shakes his head. "You seem to have all the answers. What could I add?"

"The truth," Saul says. "You could tell us why. Help us understand you."

"Oh, I'm dead simple, Doc. I like credits, lots of them. Your mother pays very well, by the way, Jax, a grand way to make a little extra on the side. Tarn hasn't been shelling out as fast as I like, and let's face it . . . I'm made for more interesting jobs." I wonder if anyone else notices the faint, bitter stress on the word "made."

He thinks of himself as something less than human, though he's technically more. Mary curse it, I don't want to pity him when I loathe him so much, but I know what it's like to be despised and hunted. I've never been more miserable than when everyone thought I was responsible for the crash of the *Sargasso*. So maybe I understand the reason he's like this, but it doesn't change anything.

At least I understand his abortive apology on the skiff now.

"So it was just another job to you." I'd thought I was over the sting, but hurt bubbles up anew. "I cared about you, you know. I thought we were friends."

His cocky smile flickers. "Men like me don't have friends, love." Some of his flippancy fades, as he regards me. "But I never meant anything to happen to you. I don't have anything against you, quite the contrary. You've been good to me. I thought they'd never search your quarters. I figured you'd have immunity by virtue of your post."

"Forgive me if I don't swoon over your good intentions." My tone could cut glass. "What the hell do you want from us?"

"Right now? Passage. We've stayed long enough. Wouldn't want to wear out our welcome." He gestures with his weapon. "I'll send you and Hit to do your thing in the cockpit. I'll be keeping Dina, Doc, and the Bug to ensure your good behavior. If we don't wind up on Gehenna within twenty-four hours, I'll start killing them one by one."

"Okay," I say, placating him. "You're in charge. We won't do anything dumb."

I glance at Hit, who gives me an infinitesimal nod. Trusting that she has a plan, I suck in a fortifying breath and climb slowly to my feet. Jael tracks my progress with his gun, and I'm careful not to make any sudden moves.

Hit does that for me. Almost before I can track the movement, she dives across the room and stabs him with the hypo from her pinky nail. His weapon discharges as he goes down, but luckily, it hits the furniture. One of the chairs now sports a smart smoldering spot.

"You may be Bred," she bites out, lips pulled back from her lips in a feral snarl, "but you don't threaten the woman I love and get away with it." She gives his inert body a kick for emphasis. "It's a lethal poison for anyone else, but I think *he* should survive it."

I take cover. Jael thrashes for a while, but as his nervous system shorts out, his convulsions slow so that the weapon tumbles from his hand. Dina steps out from behind her chair and falls into Hit's arms. They kiss with a tenderness I've seldom seen between two people. I make myself look away, not knowing if I'll ever see March again.

That hinges on Jael.

So let's hope his metabolism won't permit him to die from this either. Otherwise, it puts a serious crimp in my plan. We need to leave a living human in the cell to work in the mines. That's the only way this goes undiscovered. The Bugs will forgive us for scarpering off; I'll ask Sharis to tell everyone I heeded his warning about the danger.

"Well," I say, "that didn't go as planned, but in some ways, it's better and more efficient. Dina's off to fetch Constance, and *we* need to steal a tram. Shall we talk about phase two?"

CHAPTER 49

I'm nervous.

The plan has so many prongs that I have trouble keeping track of them. Right now, if all has gone well, the ship is telling the docking authority that they have orders to quit the planet immediately, based on the threat to the ambassador, and that another ship will arrive to take the representative to the Summit, once a location has been agreed upon. They will then pause just outside sensor range, so Dina and Hit can sneak back into the atmosphere and land a shuttle near the mines to wait for us. We're going on the assumption we'll be able to find an exit once we're inside.

As for Vel and me, well, we didn't need to steal a train. Instead, we're traveling openly on one. This has to be the first time that humans have ever passed for Bugs, and this getup is hot, heavy, and restrictive. It took Vel hours of shaping the material to make it look convincing. Good thing he has an artistic background and practice making himself look like someone else. I suspect he's never reverse engineered the process in this way before. To make matters worse, I can barely see out of the side-set eyes, and I can't make a sound before we reach the mines.

Jael lies at our feet in unbreakable restraints, muzzled like an animal. He regained consciousness about an hour ago and has been glaring at us with implacable hatred ever since. I feel the weight even if I can't see his eyes. That's too bad. He's going to pay for what he's done, even if I can't interest the Ithtorians in carrying out the sentence. I don't imagine he's any happier in his disguise than I am, but I don't care about that either.

The underground seems to cover the entire surface of the planet, zooming through darkness as if the world is honeycombed with such passages. Our ride is so swift and smooth that we cannot be touching the ground. For a moment, I marvel at that and speculate about the nature of the magnetic field that powers the technology.

Once we're inside, Vel will need to hack their system quickly and find out where they're keeping March. Pretty much everything hinges on that. Then he'll need to snag the codes that authorize us to place a prisoner in his area. But I don't have doubts. I can't afford to entertain them.

Still, Dina and Hit have orders to wait for us no more than twenty-four hours. If we don't turn up by this time tomorrow, they know they're supposed to rendezvous with the big ship and get the hell out of here, and they'd better follow orders. I don't want anybody else getting caught in the cross fire.

If I didn't need Vel to make this work, he wouldn't be here. I wish I could do this on my own, but I can't. The chip only lets me *understand* Ithtorian; I don't have a vocalizer to simulate language. I can't cut through systems like he does either, so he's critical to our success.

The underground has no windows, and the interior lights flicker from time to time. Like the other guards, we stand motionless. The rest of them don't have any prisoners they're transporting. I can only assume they're reporting for an extended shift at the mines. *Wonder who they pissed off to get this assignment.*

It seems like an eternity before we arrive, but the tram eventually slows. A red symbol lights up, and I know even before Vel cues me that this is our stop. Vel tosses Jael over his shoulder with casual strength. No doubt the merc would struggle, but the manacles he's wearing subject him to subtle electric shocks that, instead of hurting him, turn his muscles to pudding. I just love Vel's bounty-hunter pack. As Hit predicted, Jael shrugged off the poison in record time, but it was long enough for our purposes.

Vel waits for the other guards, learning from their example, and I stand quiet, doing the same. When they disembark, they head for a tall, solid metal door at the top of a sloping ramp. There's a reader everyone is supposed to use, but once the first guy does it, the rest of them just catch the door and pass through. That's a break for us since we don't have credentials, and I suspect they wouldn't be easy to forge on the fly.

We fall in at the end of the line, following the other guards up a spiral walkway that leads to a platform. From there, they all go their separate ways, and I can see we've reached the staging area for the mine complex. Before we left, Vel did all the research he could on this place, based on limited available information, but he couldn't hack their system from outside.

I follow him down a corridor where the flooring is made of some dark, dull metal. The rough obsidian walls glitter with starry luster, probably whatever they mine here. Vel doesn't appear to be paying any attention to our surroundings, but I'm positive he knows where we're going.

The mining area is vast and sprawling, but the security is less on this side. Going the opposite way on the platform would take us into the prison complex, where they break the prisoners until they're docile enough to work in the mines. At that time, they're also fit with an ankle bracelet that detonates if they roam outside their assigned area.

I know why we're going this way first, but it doesn't stop my heart from pounding like a class P drum. Any minute I expect someone to stop us, but guards are few and far between on this side. The miners we pass don't even stop their work as we go by. Most of them look thin, weary, and utterly beyond hope. I've never seen such dull eyes in a Bug; it's like they don't even see us anymore.

Vel makes a swift right turn, carrying Jael over one shoulder as if he could bear his weight forever. Thankfully, the plans he found for this site are relatively up-to-date. We stand outside an abandoned guard outpost. At one time, this site was manned and used to keep tabs on the prisoners close-up. They've since found better ways to break the prisoners and make them docile, so they don't need the same number of guards. Given the trouble, they haven't removed the equipment, which is downright antiquated.

Let's hope it's still functional.

Vel crosses behind the work area, dumping Jael none too gently on the ground. Once more, my job is to look out for anybody who might question what we're doing. So far, it's just miners as far as the eye can see, mechanically operating the machinery. In fact, the constant roar of equipment makes it hard to hear myself think.

"It is functional," Vel says, as if he heard my unspoken worry.

Though I don't stop my paranoid sweep of the corridor to either side of us, I know what he's doing. First he'll use his jammer so they can't pinpoint the site of unauthorized access, if they even notice it. Then he'll find out where March is being kept.

I just hope they haven't hurt him too much. After all he's been through, it'll take more than a day to break him. He won't be docile enough to work yet, not by a long shot. At least, we're counting on that.

If he's accepted his fate, and they've put him to work out in the mines, we won't be able to find him until after his shift is over . . . and here, they work twenty-four hours. But maybe Vel could find out what hours March works on his system profile. I don't know how much information the Bugs keep in a central location.

That will complicate matters considerably. Our plan counts on mobility and speed. If we have to hang around down here for an extended period of time, it increases our risk of being discovered—and having our ride take off without us. There's no point in borrowing trouble, however.

Once he's found March's cell location, he'll look for the codes they use to assign prisoners to that area. And then we'll head that way with Jael. In theory, it all sounds pretty simple. In practice, I'm so scared I could die.

Thank Mary, Vel is always so cool and calm. I don't think I could've done this with anyone else. This is probably the stupidest and most dangerous thing I've ever done . . . in a long history of same.

March is worth it.

"Found him," Vel says at length.

Not fast enough. There are a couple of guards on the way. Only one positive, they haven't seen me yet.

"We've got company," I whisper, darting around behind the workstation.

It's not a big area, but if we crouch, we might be able to hide. Of course, there will be no explaining that away. I glance at Vel, hoping he'll know what to do. If we clock these two guards, we risk them waking up before we're ready and sounding the alarm. I don't feel good about killing two Bugs if we don't absolutely have to. Maybe we should try talking to them.

He answers by hunkering down, making himself as small as possible. I take his example and hope for the best.

CHAPTER 50

They pass by without even looking in our direction, though not because of Jael's cooperation. The bastard thrashes—or tries to—in hopes of attracting their attention, but he only succeeds in relaxing his muscles to the point that he can scarcely move. I love that he can be immobilized with the equivalent of deep-tissue massage. He can't even claim we're hurting him.

When I'm sure the guards have had time to get out of sight, I return to my post. Vel gets back to work as if nothing has happened. He still has more data to locate.

"Transfer codes," he says with satisfaction.

Only then do I realize he's been speaking Ithtorian the whole time. That surprises me. I've gotten so used to the sound of the language that it doesn't even register anymore, as long as I understand his meaning.

"Ready to move?"

In answer, he shoulders an increasingly limp Jael, and we retrace our steps back to the platform. It's deserted now as we're slightly off shift. I hope that doesn't cause trouble, but we couldn't have gone straight into the prison area.

Our first test comes when we reach the initial checkpoint. There's a bored and slightly bloated Bug sitting at a terminal. I can't see its sex organs, but I assume it's male. Females rarely get sent to work here.

"State your business," the guard demands.

Vel bluffs. "We have a prisoner for placement in sector 1167-A."

"Why is he unconscious?" That sounds like a careless question.

"He resisted at his sentencing."

The guard clicks his claws in disgust. "So many of them do, as if it changes anything. Crazy savages. Codes?"

As Vel supplies them, I hold my breath. The guard inputs them and a light comes on. What does that mean? I feel myself start to tremble, fear sweat slipping down my spine. My idea of hell would be eternity down here.

Already the walls feel like they're closing in on me. I can do this if it means saving March. I push the terror into a hard little knot and swallow it.

After what seems like forever, the guard says, "Clear," and buzzes us through. The security door just past him clicks open.

Vel leads the way since he's memorized the layout of the place. We repeat that process at two more checkpoints, but the codes are good and current, so nobody questions us. They've never had any trouble out here, so they're not expecting any. That works in our favor. Besides, who the hell, besides us, would try to sneak a prisoner *into* the mines?

I concentrate on keeping my movements Bug-like. I don't want to attract untoward attention. Down here, though, nobody looks too hard at anyone else. Even the guards have a hopeless air. I guess they know there's no recovering from whatever disgrace landed them here in the first place. The only thing worse? Being confined here instead of assigned here.

We travel for a good long while. Apparently March has been put in a remote area. The last checkpoint lets us into the prison proper. This area has been carved from solid rock, and the cells are primarily caves fitted with metal grates. I've never seen anything like it. These prisoners are devoid of the most basic necessities. They're forced to sleep in their own filth, no bath or toilet facilities. It's beyond horrifying.

The prisoners don't call out as we pass. Most of them simply lie curled on their sides, waiting for the next cruelty. No wonder they're so docile once they move to a better area. They'd probably do anything to avoid being returned to this place.

And I let them send March here. I let this happen. My heart breaks.

Vel says then, "Unless they have moved him and not recorded the switch, March is just up ahead, Sirantha. Do you want a moment with him before I bring Jael in?"

I almost forget and answer in universal. Just in time, I simply incline my head.

"Then you will need this. Simply press it up against the lock and wait."

He's pressed a code breaker into my hand. Though I've never used one, I've seen March and Vel do it. It requires no special skill, just this piece of hardware. I nod my thanks, and Vel pulls back into a niche in the rock wall. I shouldn't linger long before we move, but I appreciate him giving me this time.

March's cell is no different than anyone else's, just a dark hole in the rock. Since he hasn't been here long, it doesn't stink like some. In this uncertain half-light, I can't even make out if he's in there, but it doesn't stop me from putting the code breaker to work. Slender filaments snake out into the lock.

A moment later, the door swings open, and the item trickles away into chemical dust. That must have been the last charge. Trembling all over, I step into the cell. As my eyes adjust, I see March slumped against the far wall.

"I didn't think I was due for another beating for hours yet." But his voice sounds tired, not defiant.

Shit. He thinks I'm a Bug.

My hands are shaking so bad, I can hardly get the headpiece off. Finally, I manage, and he leans forward to get a better look at me, as if he thinks his sight might be playing tricks. He comes up on his knees, knuckling his eyes for good measure.

"I must be dreaming."

I shake my head. "You're not."

I think this is the first time I've ever seen him totally overcome. March struggles visibly for words, and finally comes up with: "What're you doing here, Jax?"

"I tried to get them to let you go, but your confession was all they wanted. They don't care about the truth. They don't even care which human suffers, as long as one of us does, but it must give them special satisfaction to know they've taken someone important to me. It's an indirect way of punishing me, too."

"That doesn't answer the question." He hasn't moved, hasn't tried to take me in his arms.

I continue my story doggedly. "So I made up my mind to fix this. Jael belongs in here, not you. As far as I'm concerned, he can rot here forever in your place. I don't care after what he let them do to you."

"It was Jael?" Now he's surprised. "What the hell—"

"My mother," I answer bitterly. "She bought him on Venice Minor. I should have wondered why he drew the line at slitting her throat, but I didn't know him well enough to realize he'd kill *anybody* if the price was right. Credits are the only god he acknowledges. The bastard was still doing his job as my bodyguard while working to undermine the alliance. He figured he could collect both payouts as long as the alliance failed, and I didn't die here."

"Tarn would have to pay," March agrees. "But they won't listen to you . . . so you sneaked in . . . to say good-bye?" He looks older somehow, thin, battered, and inexpressibly weary, possibly even of life itself.

His lip is split, and even in this light, I can tell he has a black eye. There's crusted blood all down his neck. I can't imagine what the rest of him looks like. Rage flashes though me. Right now I would like to blow this whole planet to pieces.

I try not to consider that this is the ending he wants, dying like a hero. So I take a breath, mustering the courage to go on. "You proved once you'd kill the world for me. I may be doing the same thing . . . I don't know if the alliance will hold, if they notice the switch. They might see it as treachery and call everything off. I don't know, and I don't care either. See, the world isn't worth saving without you in it."

"Jax—"

"Vel is waiting in the hall with Jael. Dina and Hit have a shuttle hidden nearby, and the ship's in orbit, waiting for us. We need to get you out." I manage a smile then. "You have three minutes to decide, Mr. March, and the clock is ticking." There's a flicker of recognition as he remembers his words in my cell that day.

I have the feeling he really thought he'd been abandoned. That hurts as much as anything he could have said. Or not said. I can't believe he doesn't know I'd walk through hell for him. I can't believe he doesn't realize there are no circumstances under which I'd give up on him. I'm not that Jax anymore.

"Well . . . I'd be an idiot to say no after you went to all this trouble, wouldn't I?" He pushes to his feet though he can't stand upright in here.

I slip out the open cell door and signal Vel, who brings our replacement. From here, the plan is simple. March dons the Bug disguise Jael had on, and we walk him out, leaving Jael in his cell.

Now we just need to find an exit.

THE CONGLOMERATE NEEDS YOU!

The Armada motto:

"We make war that we may live in peace."

The time has come for us to return to the days of empire. We will build a strong tomorrow, and you can be a part of it. We will fear nothing but injustice. Join now! Fight for liberty, truth, and right! There can be no greater good than to give yourself for your people.

Don't miss this opportunity to see the stars

Full training provided

Includes special, credentialed career paths

500-credit signing bonus

Enlistment term, three turns

Recruitment offices on all tier worlds

Bounce inquiries to 12.45.900.78.0987

CHAPTER 51

"*This isn't over,*" *Jael says, as Vel takes off his muzzle.*

Next, the bounty hunter removes his restraints. We can't leave any sign this isn't the same human they had before. I'm counting on the fact that we all look alike to them . . . and even if some guard notices, he won't want to get in trouble by being the one to point it out. How do you explain winding up with the wrong prisoner in a completely secure facility? In such a case, the person who reports the discrepancy is almost certainly going to be blamed, harking back to a long, proud tradition of shooting the messenger.

Jael fixes on us a look sparkling with hatred. "They won't be able to hold me. And I *will* find you."

I smile from the other side of the grate. "Good luck with that."

"Word to the wise," March says. "Yelling just pisses them off."

"From here, you cannot speak," Vel tells us.

I know that, but March needs the reminder. Jael's suit is a tight squeeze for him in the shoulders, but he wedges into it. Vel takes a moment to paint some stripes on it, differentiating him from the Bug we carried in. Clever. It wouldn't pass muster close up in good light since the colors are clearly painted, not etched in the usual way, but down here, it should do.

We pass through the checkpoints easily, just three Bugs returning from a patrol. We're only stopped at the last one. The guard eyes us. "Everything quiet in there?"

"There is one troublemaker making noise," Vel says. "Otherwise, yes."

"Good. Going off duty?"

"Food break."

The guard accepts this without question. "Enjoy. See you later."

Like hell.

To my surprise, Vel takes us straight back to the staging area. "One glitch," he says in an undertone. "I did not mention it earlier, Sirantha, because you were worried enough. But when I was using the workstation, I could not find an exit not linked to the underground. This place is completely secure."

Well, shit.

Our ride off world is already in orbit. We have to get to the shuttle within twenty-four hours. If we take the underground back to the city, that's eight hours gone. Then how do we get back out here? We have no ground transport, and the Ithtorians don't travel on the surface, because of the hazardous conditions.

"They have to get fresh air in here somehow," March says. It's a little disconcerting to hear his voice coming out of a Bug head. No wonder he thought he was dreaming when I opened his cell.

"That was my first thought as well," Vel answers. "But according to the schematics, they use fissures too small for humans—or Ithtorians to pass through."

"So what do we do?"

Vel seems none too certain, hesitating before he speaks. "My scans are not entirely accurate with so much rock around us, you must understand . . . but they indicate there is an abandoned area in the mines. There may be holes once used for structural supports, which have since been relocated. I cannot determine whether these shafts go all the way to the surface, but they offer the only outlets not connected to the underground."

I shrug. "So let's go."

He's not telling us everything, but standing around here will just get us caught. Without further conversation, he leads across the platform and into the mines. The metal sheeting bangs underfoot. As during our last foray, the workers don't pay us any attention. Some of them operate heavy machinery in the large caverns. Others use hand units to take samples. Starry ore glitters in wheeled tubs.

We pass a few other guards, but they don't speak. They

also roam the place in twos and threes, so our number doesn't attract any attention. Eventually, we come to a rusty old locked door. March and I stand watch while Vel gets it open.

On the other side, Vel says, "From here, it does not matter if we speak. There are no miners and no guards over here."

"Do we know what lies ahead?" I ask.

"There was no data regarding this area in the archives, but I note a number of large life signs ahead of us. They may be hostile."

"Then I'm taking this off." March pulls off his Bug head. "I can't fight this way."

I agree with that, so we take a moment to pull off our suits. Mary, I smell rank. Vel sprinkles them with dry acid chem-burner and in short order, they're reduced to dust. He's amazing at leaving no trace of where he's been or what he's done there. I love that gift now, since he's no longer using it to hunt me.

"You got a shockstick in there for me?" I ask Vel.

In answer, he hands me one, and I power it up. We haven't come this far to be stopped by a few cave beasts. March accepts a shockstick and a knife. He can probably use both at the same time—stun and stab.

"This way to the first shaft." The bounty hunter leads.

March falls in behind him, and I bring up the rear. It occurs to me we finally have the time for me to ask some questions. "Vel . . . I've been meaning to ask you. This chip you implanted in me, it's experimental, isn't it?"

The bounty hunter casts a glance over one shoulder. "How did you know?"

"Because it governs more than just speech." I explain how it helped me understand body language as well.

"Wait a minute." March stops walking, his hands curling into fists. "You put something inside her that hasn't been fully tested?"

"Not by any formal authority," Vel admits. "But my own research indicated I have perfected the prototype."

For a long moment, March stares at him. "If it was anyone else, I'd end you. Don't screw around with her safety, you understand me?" He touches my throat with care and delicacy. "It's bad enough you put your mark on her to cover something I did."

"So you realize you hurt her. Then perhaps it is *you* who should not 'screw around' with her safety." Vel starts walking without waiting for a response.

March lunges as if he's going to start something, and I snag his arm. "We can't fight down here. You know that, right?" In the distance, I hear something rumbling. It sounds big and angry. "That's our obstacle. Not each other."

He follows in furious strides, but he's not angry with Vel or me. The connections I restored also include their share of guilt. The bitter with the sweet, as Hit said.

In the darkness, I can hear the monsters gathering. Grunts and muted roars echo through the empty mine shafts. Are they talking about us, trying to figure out what we are? I assume they've smelled Ithtorians before. I wonder what they eat down here, if there's a complex ecosystem underground, driven off the surface by nuclear winter.

It stands to reason that there would be. So maybe all the creatures aren't dangerous. Bearing out this possibility, something flutters past my face, but it doesn't bite or sting. I shudder, my breath sticking in my throat. The little thing comes back. Flutter, flutter, flutter. I'm afraid to ask Vel to shine the light on me.

"Are you feeling this?" I ask, low.

Not webs. I know the sticky horror of that all too well. More like . . . wings?

The bounty hunter swings around. "A deraphid, though I have never seen one of such size before, and the wingspan is extraordinary." He extends a claw, and the insect leaves its inspection of my cheek to light on his fingertips. "Remarkable."

Once I control my instinctive terror, even I can see the thing is harmless. It has no weapons, no stingers, nothing that could pierce the skin. With its smooth, sleek body and translucent wings shining green-gold, it's almost beautiful.

"How does it survive down here?"

"It must eat parasites from other creatures and perhaps mold and fungus."

Mmm, tasty.

Vel flicks his fingers gently, and the deraphid goes about its business. Reassured that everything down here doesn't want to eat us, we head toward the shaft. That reassurance doesn't last long with the growling in the distance. I can hear movement nearby.

I try to focus on March and Vel. My heartbeat thunders in my ears. It seems I always face my private devils underground, fighting not to relive the *Sargasso* crash. Instead of charred metal and meat, I have solid stone.

The black walls sparkle with untapped ore. With Vel in the lead, I can only follow, and hope that the beasts I hear all around us aren't as close as they sound. Maybe the dark and the echoes have disoriented me.

Unfortunately, they *are* as close as they sound.

The thing lurches out of a side passage, a monstrosity of white fur and slavering fangs. It stands twice as tall as me, and probably five times my weight. The roar echoes off the rock walls, paralyzing me. I stare up at its hideous, eyeless face, and shudder. This creature could unhinge its jaw and swallow me whole.

Thankfully, Vel doesn't have the same response. He goes for the thing's hamstring, assuming it has one. March dives low on the other side, and they slice in unison as the monster makes a grab for me. I hit the ground, diving between its legs.

The creature screams in pain. Shit, it's going to fall on me. I scramble back as it goes down and wind up half-wedged beneath its massive shoulder. It's not dead, just wounded and furious. It turns its head and snaps at me. The fangs graze my shoulder, sending pain ripping down my arm. Blood trickles from the wound.

The horror of being trapped beneath a dying thing nearly shorts out my brain. It's all I can do not to lose my mind and scream until my voice is gone, but before they kill it or get it off me, I take the easy way and pass out.

I come to myself later—how much later, I don't know. March cradles me against his chest. The stink of monstrous blood is all over me, but apparently that's a good thing because the other cave creatures leave us alone. In fact, they whimper as we pass by.

"Most intriguing," Vel remarks. "They have acknowledged us as superior predators, and they mourn the passing of one of their own."

March looks thoughtful in the light thrown from the torch-tube. "That suggests a certain level of sentience."

Call me crazy. I'm not that interested in the thinking skills of the things. I just want out of here before I give in to the panic clamoring through me.

"I'm okay," I manage. "You can put me down now."

March smiles. "I know I *can*. I just don't want to. I like holding you." His voice drops. "I didn't think I ever would again."

Huh. Well, I could argue with that, but . . . why? I nestle close to him. Later, we're going to have a serious talk about his opinion of me.

We walk for a long while. In the dark, I have no way to measure the time. Finally, we reach the first shaft.

"This is it," Vel says, gazing up.

It's a reverse pit, no hint of light to give us hope it might go all the way up.

March sets me on my feet. "Somebody needs to scope it out, make sure it doesn't shrink suddenly so that all three of us will get stuck up there."

"It is narrow," Vel agrees.

I try to make myself sound braver than I feel. "That's my cue. I'm the smallest."

This is no different than rock climbing, I tell myself. Except that it's small, pitch black, and I don't know what the hell is up there. "If you have a rope, I'll take it up with me and secure it so you guys can follow when I find a good place."

They won't be able to climb as I do, using hands and feet to scramble up. They're just too big. Their shoulders will just barely clear the shaft.

"I don't want you doing this," March says. "We'll keep walking."

"Like hell. I want out of here." Without waiting for more protests, I take the cord from Vel and loop it around my waist. "Wish me luck."

Instead, March snatches me close, despite my stench, and kisses me hard on the mouth. "Be careful. I love you, Jax, and we have a lot of lost time to make up for."

Tears prickle at my eyes. "Damn right. I won't be long."

I hope.

CHAPTER 52

Going up that shaft is hell.

It's a good thing I've been taking my injections because I need every flicker of strength to keep scrambling upward. Dark looms above and below me. I have a torch-tube in my pocket, but I don't dare get it out. The yellow-green glimmer might draw attention I don't want. I'm pretty sure I've climbed high enough to hurt myself severely if I fall. I don't think about that.

My hands are raw, and it feels like the soles of my shoes have given way as well. I don't know how far I've climbed, but I can no longer hear March beneath me. In the beginning, I could hear his soft words of reassurance. Now it's me and the rock and the dark. The weight of it feels like my tomb.

To my vast relief, the shaft hasn't narrowed. I think it must have been drilled because it seems to be a uniform width all the way up. I just don't know where it ends.

I keep climbing. It seems like an eternity. The last time I was alone in the dark like this, I yielded to blind panic. Doc had to talk me through it, but that can't happen now. March and Vel, the two people I care about most in the world, are down there, counting on me. They can't come up this way. If I don't reach the top, we die in darkness.

Scrapes dot my palms from the constant abrasion against the rock, and though they sprayed liquid skin on the punctures at my shoulder, I can feel the bond slipping. My wound will be bleeding soon. Mary grant the smell doesn't lure something to me.

This is easier if I close my eyes and just focus on heaving myself upward. I can pretend it's not dark, that I'm not weary and losing faith. My arms and legs are tired, trembling in my muscles.

I can do this. I must do this.

Desperation drives me on. I stop and rest twice in as many minutes. You can't imagine what it's like to try to catch your breath, bent double, with only the strength of your thighs keeping you from falling to a hideous death. At this point, it's more stubbornness than strength driving me on.

I promised myself I'd get him out of here. So I keep climbing.

My muscles strain with exertion, and my mouth is dry. I can feel my lips cracking, but I don't have anything to soothe them. The dust feels like it's ingrained in my skin.

At last I feel a cooler breeze on my face, which means I have to be getting close. I redouble my efforts, inching my way upward. My hands scrabble at the stone above me until I feel what seems like a ledge.

With the last burst of my energy I push upward and out onto a stone lip. The shaft has joined a cavern, I think, which I confirm by cracking a torch-tube, the only one I have. For obvious reasons, I didn't want to carry extra weight when I went up.

Finally, a break. There's an outcropping of stalagmites nearby, which tells me this is a natural cave. I tie the rope around one of them, three sturdy knots, and tug until I'm sure it will bear their weight. Then I drop it down the shaft and hope it's long enough.

I don't think they'll hear me if I shout, and even so, I'm not sure I want to risk attracting anything else to my position. I have no idea what lives here. I could drop my light to get their attention if the rope doesn't do it, but I don't want to wait in the dark.

Relief crashes through me when someone tugs twice on the cord. They've got it. In the sickly, citrine light, I watch the rope go taut. That means somebody's climbing.

I sit there, weak and trembling, until I glimpse March, about ten meters down. Though I'd like to help him, I don't have the strength to pull him up, so I just stay out of his way. I marvel that he's able to do this after twenty-four hours of abuse and privation. He's so damn strong it amazes me.

"Thank Mary," he breathes when he sees me sitting there. "That was the longest hour of my life."

Is that all? The time seemed much longer to me, somehow. March comes to me on his hands and knees, shaky with relief. And, despite his filth and my smell, we curl together like interlocking puzzle pieces. Listening to his heart there in the greasy light thrown by the torch-tube is the closest to heaven I'll ever be.

Vel comes up faster. He's in better shape than me, and he hasn't been beaten like March. I'm almost ready to move by the time he unties the rope.

"Good work, Sirantha. Let me scan the area and see where we are." The bounty hunter goes to work. I don't know how long it is—I'm content where I am—until he says, "This way. These caverns parallel the surface."

"Did you find an exit?"

"More or less." Vel starts walking, just as eager to be gone from here as we are. "I found a fissure I can widen with a laser."

Then we walk. I'm so exhausted now that I can hardly think. I just follow Vel and March, one foot in front of the other. I've lost track of how deep into our twenty-four hours we are. Mary, I hope nothing has happened to Dina and Hit. They *have* to be waiting for us.

After an interminable hike, we come to the end of the natural caverns. Beyond lies the mountain wall, but Vel simply walks over to a tiny crack, pours some kind of reagent on it, then whips out a cutting laser.

The area fills with smoke and dust, making it hard to breathe. I cover my mouth and nose, but it doesn't help a lot. March digs through the infamous bounty-hunter pack to find us some water, if nothing else. We can't eat with so many foreign particles in the air. I sip through the cloth mask, grateful for small comforts. The bounty hunter works tirelessly, crawling deeper and deeper into the fissure to work.

Just when I think I can't stand it anymore, Vel beckons us. "We must crawl out. I am afraid to risk a wider cut, lest I destabilize the mountain and cause an avalanche."

Yeah, we certainly don't want to wind up buried in rock and snow. That's not how my story ends.

"Thanks, Vel." I'd kiss him, but I'm too tired. "You did great, all the way."

March agrees. "I'd have said it was impossible to get out of here. I guess that means you two did the impossible."

I go first. It's a tiny crevice that sparks my claustrophobia. At first I have a hard time making myself go deeper. In here, I can hardly breathe. The rock scrapes my sides, so I can't imagine how it is for March and Vel. They might have to squirm through on their sides or bellies. Thinking about them distracts me, but as it gets colder, I realize I'm almost there, so I crawl faster.

We emerge on an icy mountainside in the middle of a blizzard. The shock of the cold steals my breath, and my lashes immediately freeze over, going spiky with ice. As quickly as possible, we don some thermal gear and set up our signal for Dina and Hit. It would have been smart to put it on before we came out, but the channel Vel cut simply wasn't wide enough to permit extra centimeters. In fact, the bounty hunter had to shove his pack before him.

Despite the all-weather gear, my teeth start to chatter. I've been pushed to my physical limits, and I don't know how much more I can take. I've gone somewhere beyond exhaustion. Everything seems strange and distant.

As we wait, March wraps his arms around me. "We're going to be fine," he whispers. "You did it. We made it out in time."

I can only guess whether we did. For all I know, we might be abandoned, marooned on this icy mountainside. Despair plucks at me with icy fingers. Countless minutes pass while we huddle together for warmth. There's no shelter to be had, unless we go back inside. If we do that, we admit failure—that they're not coming.

At last, just as I'm about to lose hope, lights appear in the snowstorm, just down the slope from us. I start to run.

We did it. They're here. March is safe.

Dina and Hit hug us tight as they pull us into the shuttle, but they don't waste time with questions, though the mechanic levels a look on March that promises she'll kick his ass for him later. There will be a time for talking, affectionate ass-kickings, and joyful reunions. It's *not* while we remain on Ithiss-Tor.

Hit immediately starts the systems check that will take us out of the atmosphere. "Hold on," she says softly. "There are gonna be some bumps as we go."

"Let me trick out the readings." Dina taps away at the panel. "Okay, we're good. Strap in, you three."

We comply, Vel and March on either side of me. As the thrusters burn, I can hear the hiss of melting snow. The shuttle slides hard starboard as Hit takes it up, the wind buffeting us all the way. I've never been more conscious of how thin a skiff can be. Then the sky opens up to us, a white tornado bleeding gray at the edges. We pierce the heart of it, the dreamy landscape receding beneath us.

"You know they may never let you come back," I tell Vel quietly.

He lifts his shoulders. *Yes, I know,* he says without a word. *I accept exile if it comes to that.*

But maybe it won't come. After today, I believe in miracles.

I take March's hand in mine, glorying in the fact that I can. My euphoria lasts only until we've reached the ship out in orbit. There's talk of a party, but I don't have the energy. Instead, I stagger to my quarters, wanting a shower, but I find a message from Chancellor Tarn waiting for me instead. With a sigh, I play it.

"You did well, Sirantha, better than anyone could have asked, but I am afraid it was not enough."

I sink into a chair, shaking with dread. March curls his hands over my shoulders, watching with me in silence. I remember how he said we needed to be out there, marshaling our forces, not wallowing in diplomatic bullshit. Mary, I don't want him to fight another war.

Tarn continues, "Our worst fear has come to pass. Though I do not know *who* supplied the intelligence, the Morgut know the Ithtorians no longer have a powerful fleet. To prove their strength, they have attacked an installation shockingly close to New Terra. We need all hands—" The satellites give up at this point, leaving me wondering what's next. One thing's sure, though.

The war has begun.

Read on for an exciting excerpt
from the next book in the
Corine Solomon urban fantasy series

HELL FIRE

by Ann Aguirre

Coming April 2010 from Roc

I'm still a redhead.

Before we left Texas, I touched up the roots with Garnier Nutrisse 64-R, and then I had some tawny apricot highlights put in. I guessed that meant I intended to keep this color for a while. Symbolic—I'd made a commitment, at least to my hair.

Too bad I couldn't do the same with Chance. I didn't trust him entirely, and what was more, he didn't trust me either. He secretly thought I'd leave, which I had done; die, which I'd *nearly* done; or break his heart. I just hoped I wouldn't combine the three.

Until we resolved the conflict between us—such as his gift, which might kill me like it had his former lover—I couldn't be more than a friend to him. He knew it, too. I think he'd known as much even when he pressed the point on Chuch's couch, back in Laredo.

Chuch is a friend who helped us out of a dangerous situation where we managed to piss off a warlock *and* the head of a cartel who had a score to settle with Chance's mom. Two days ago, Min took the bus to Tampa; she's safe at her homeopathy store. There's nothing to link her new life to her old, and if she hadn't gone back to Texas, Montoya would've never found her. But we'll call her daily, just to make sure.

If Montoya managed to replace his pet practitioner, then it might be possible for him to track Min. I didn't know how much talent she had in the Art, so I could only hope she knew how to cook a charm to block scrying from her store. Me? I had no aptitude at all. That was ironic, considering my mother was a witch.

I was a little worried about reprisals. Chance's mother made the Montoyas agree to a pact preventing them from striking at her son, but I had no such guarantees. But it would take a little while for Montoya to find someone to replace the warlock we had killed. So I banished the dark thoughts and focused on the road. We were almost there.

The Mustang purred along, underlining Chance's silence. He wasn't happy about this trip to Kilmer, Georgia, but he'd promised, and I wanted answers. He owed me.

When he showed up at my pawnshop in Mexico, asking for my help after our breakup eighteen months before, I agreed because he swore to turn his luck toward helping me find out what happened the night my mother died. This point was nonnegotiable. I had to understand why it happened, and who was responsible. I wanted justice for her death.

We passed the wood that encircled the town. Sometimes, as a kid, it'd seemed to me that someone had simply burned a patch out of the forbidding forest, and there, Kilmer had been built. The trees had grown back in around it, overhanging the rutted road.

With the windows open, I could smell dank vegetation heavy in the air, and pallid sunlight filtering through the canopy overhead threw a sickly green glow over the car as Chance drove. McIntosh County didn't get snow, didn't get earthquakes, and the median temperature was sixty-six degrees. It was also deeply historical, containing forty-two markers. I knew all about local history: how old King George Fort was built nearby in 1721, how Highlanders voted against slavery in 1739—not that it did them any good in the long run—and how the War of Jenkins' Ear motivated early settlers to attack Spanish forts. There were still ruins on Sapelo Island.

Just a piece up the road, there lived the only known band of Shouters, a Gullah music group. I'd seen them perform the shout-ring once at Mount Calvary Baptist Church. I couldn't remember which foster parent had taken me; there had been so many, and most of them had thought I could benefit from religion in some form or another. On paper, this seemed like the perfect place to live, steeped in cultural heritage and tradition.

On paper.

The rules of the Deep South lasted here long after laws and social expectations changed in the wider world. White men did as they pleased, and everyone else kept their mouths shut. I couldn't rightly say I'd missed it.

"This place has a weird feel," Chance said, breaking the silence at last.

"You're getting it, too?" I'd always thought it was the trees, but we'd passed beyond them. Now only scrubby grass lay between the weathered buildings of town and us. Overhead, the sky glowed blue and white, a pretty, partly sunny day that should've warmed me a lot more than it did.

"Yeah." Before he could say more, a dark shape darted in front of the cherry red car. Chance slammed on the brakes, and only the seat belt kept my head from kissing the dash. The car fishtailed to a stop.

Butch whined and popped his head out of my handbag. He was a little blond Chihuahua we'd picked up along the way; I'd sort of resigned myself to keeping him, but I hoped we hadn't scared the shit out of him. I had important stuff in my purse. I soothed him with an absent touch on his head, my heart still going like a jackhammer.

"What the—"

Chance motioned me to silence as he got out of the car. Hands shaking, it took me two tries to do the same. I checked the back, staring into the dead air beneath the tunnel of trees. Black skid marks smeared the pavement behind us.

He knelt and peered under the Mustang. Despite my better judgment, I joined him. Butch hopped down and backed up three steps, yapping ferociously. A low animal growl answered him.

Near the tires, a big black dog lay dying, a Doberman. We hadn't hit him, but all the blood oozing out of his ragged wounds told me he wasn't long for this world. He'd come from the tall grass that lined the road, or maybe from the trees beyond the field. A hard shudder rocked through me, and the air turned as cold as a northern winter night.

"Something got at him," Chance said finally. "Are there bears here? Wolves?"

I had no idea. It sounded unlikely, but possible. I wasn't a wildlife expert under any circumstances, and I hadn't been to Kilmer in nine years. Things changed; habitats evolved. But times must be tough if wild animals had been forced to resort to hunting dogs.

I couldn't seem to look away from the shadow-dark flesh. The animal gave one final whine, as if it understood we couldn't help, and then it died. I saw the moment its eyes went liquid still, living tissue reverting to dead meat.

Never one to miss an opportunity, Butch scampered into the weeds and did his business. I exhaled in a long, unsteady sound and then pulled myself to my feet using the Mustang's hood. If I believed in omens, I'd say we were off to a hell of a start.

Chance went to the trunk and wrapped his hands in rags he used to check the oil. Yeah, Chuch had taught him how, threatening to kill him if he didn't look after this car better than others had fared under his ownership. So far he was doing okay.

Wordlessly, he reached under the chassis and towed the carcass to the side of the road. That was really all we could do without a shovel, but I appreciated the kindness. Otherwise, that poor animal would be splattered all over the road when the next car came, and I thought it had suffered enough.

Even if we'd had digging tools in the car for some unlikely reason, I wouldn't have been interested in hanging around here. My intestines coiled into knots over the idea of losing the light out here within a stone's throw of those dark trees. The whorls on the bark looked like nothing so much as demonic sigils in the wicked half-light, and the long, skeletal limbs stirred in the breeze in a way I simply couldn't like.

There was a reason I hated these trees. I'd hid among them while my mother died.

While Chance took care of the dead dog, I gave Butch a drink and tried to reassure him that he wasn't doomed to suffer the same fate. His bulging brown eyes glistened with what I'd call a skeptical light as I hopped back in the